"In spite of the cold, it's a lovely evening to go caroling, isn't it?"

The thick snow obscured the horizon and made it feel as if they were riding inside a glass snow globe. The twins tried to catch snowflakes on their tongues between giggles.

Their first destination was only a mile from John's house. As Lucy and Megan scrambled down from the sleigh, John offered Willa his hand to help her out. When she took it, he gave her an affectionate squeeze. She graced him with a shy smile in return.

"Was this what you imagined Christmas would be like when you decided to return to your Amish family?"

She shook her head. "I never imagined anything like this. Do you do it every year?"

"We do."

"You aren't going to actually sing, are you, John?"

He threw back his head and laughed. "*Nee*, but I will hum along."

"Softly, dear, softly," she suggested.

He wondered if she realized that she had called him *dear*. It was turning out to be an even more wonderful night than he had hoped for.

After thirty-five years as a nurse, **Patricia Davids** hung up her stethoscope to become a full-time writer. She enjoys spending her free time visiting her grandchildren, doing some long-overdue yard work and traveling to research her story locations. She resides in Wichita, Kansas. Pat always enjoys hearing from her readers. You can visit her online at patriciadavids.com.

Leigh Bale is a *Publishers Weekly* bestselling author. She is the winner of the prestigious Golden Heart® Award and was a finalist for the Gayle Wilson Award of Excellence and the Booksellers' Best Award. The daughter of a retired US forest ranger, she holds a BA in history. Married in 1981 to the love of her life, Leigh and her professor husband have two children and two grandkids. You can reach her at leighbale.com.

USA TODAY Bestselling Author

PATRICIA DAVIDS

Amish Christmas Twins

&

LEIGH BALE

Her Amish Christmas Choice

LOVE INSPIRED
INSPIRATIONAL ROMANCE

LOVE INSPIRED®
INSPIRATIONAL ROMANCE

Recycling programs for this product may not exist in your area.

ISBN-13: 978-1-335-21899-5

Amish Christmas Twins and Her Amish Christmas Choice

Copyright © 2020 by Harlequin Books S.A.

Amish Christmas Twins
First published in 2017. This edition published in 2020.
Copyright © 2017 by Patricia MacDonald

Her Amish Christmas Choice
First published in 2019. This edition published in 2020.
Copyright © 2019 by Lora Lee Bale

This edition published by arrangement with Harlequin Books S.A.

For questions and comments about the quality of this book, please contact us at CustomerService@Harlequin.com.

Harlequin Enterprises ULC
22 Adelaide St. West, 40th Floor
Toronto, Ontario M5H 4E3, Canada
www.Harlequin.com

Printed in U.S.A.

CONTENTS

AMISH CHRISTMAS TWINS

Patricia Davids

This book is happily dedicated to Tony Hill, a wonderful, helpful son-in-law and a loving stepfather to my two precious grandchildren.

Thanks, Tony, for all you do. Love you to pieces. Oh, and don't forget to mow my lawn.

Mama Pat

And all thy children shall be taught of the Lord;
and great shall be the peace of thy children.
—*Isaiah* 54:13

Chapter One

John Miller squeezed his eyes shut and braced for the impact of the bus hurtling toward the back of his wagon.

God have mercy on my soul.

A powerful draft knocked his hat from his head as the bus flew around him, missing his wagon by inches. The reckless driver laid on the horn as he swerved back into the proper lane. John's frightened team of horses shied off the edge of the highway, jolting the wagon and nearly unseating him.

He quickly brought his animals under control and maneuvered his wagon back onto the roadway. It took longer to get his heart out of his throat. When his erratic pulse settled, he picked up his black Amish hat from where it had fallen onto the floorboards and dusted it against his thigh. *God must still have a use for me here on earth. I'm sorry, Katie May. One day I will be with you again.*

John shook his head when the bus pulled to a stop a few hundred yards down the highway. "Foolish *Englischer*. In a hurry to get nowhere fast."

He settled his hat on his head and glanced back at

his cargo. Thankfully, the restored antique sleigh carefully wrapped in a heavy tarp hadn't shifted. He could ill afford another delay in getting it to its new owner.

His entire trip had been one misadventure after another. He'd left home in plenty of time to complete the two-day journey, but a wrong turn in unfamiliar country had taken him five miles out of his way. One of his tie-downs had snapped, forcing him to lose time rigging another. Then a broken wheel had taken three hours to repair, time he didn't have to spare. This simple trip could end up costing him as much if not more than a hired hauler would have charged and he was already half a day late for his appointment. He hoped his *Englisch* client was the understanding sort.

Putting his team in motion, John reached the rear of the bus before it moved on. According to the directions in the letter from his customer, he needed to turn right at the rural intersection just ahead. He waited for the bus driver to move out of the way. After several minutes, he leaned to the side trying to see what the holdup was. A woman in a red coat with a purple backpack slung over her shoulder finally stepped off with two little children in tow. The bus pulled away, belching black fumes that made his horses snort and toss their heads. He spoke softly to quiet them.

The woman stood at the edge of the highway, looking first north and then south as if expecting someone who hadn't shown up. The roads were empty in all directions except for the bus traveling away from them. The children, both girls about three years old, were clinging to her legs. One rubbed her eyes, the other cried to be picked up. The family's clothing and uncovered heads told John they weren't Amish.

He slapped the reins against his team's rumps and turned his wagon in front of them, glancing at the woman's face as he did. She looked worried and worn-out, but she smiled and nodded slightly when she met his gaze.

One of her little girls pointed to his team. "Horsey, Mama. See horsey?"

"I do, sweetheart. They're lovely horses, aren't they?" Her smile brightened as she glanced down at her daughter. The love in her eyes shone through her weariness. Why wasn't anyone here to meet them?

"Horses bad," the other child said, stepping behind her mother.

The woman dropped to one knee and pulled the child close. "No, they aren't bad. They may look big and scary, but they won't hurt you. This man tells them what to do. I'm sure they mind him far better than you mind me sometimes."

The child muttered something he couldn't make out, but the young mother laughed softly. It was a sweet sound. "No, precious. They won't step on you and squish you."

The child latched on to her mother's neck and muttered, "I tired. Want to go home now."

He should keep moving. He'd told his client to expect him four hours ago, but it didn't feel right to drive away and leave this young mother standing alone out here even if she wasn't Amish. He pulled the horses to a stop and looked down at her. "Do you need help?"

Detaching the child from her neck, she stood up and smoothed the front of her coat with one hand. As she did, he noticed a bulge at her waist. Was she pregnant?

"I'm trying to get my bearings. I haven't been out

this way in years. Do you know an Amish farmer named Ezekiel Lapp?"

Her voice was soft and low. He heard the weariness underlying her tone. The wind blew a strand of her shoulder-length blond curls across her face. She brushed her hair back and tucked it behind her ear as she looked at him with wide blue eyes.

She was a pretty woman. Her daughters, identical twins by the look of them, were the spitting images of her with blue eyes and curly blond hair. Some man was fortunate to have such handsome children and a lovely wife to come home to at night.

She placed a hand on each little girl's head in a comforting or perhaps protective gesture, her fingers moving gently through their hair. She raised her chin as she faced him.

The gesture reminded him of his wife, Katie, and sent a painful pang through his chest. Katie used to give him that exact look when she was determined to do things her own way. The woman at the roadside wasn't physically similar to his wife. She was tiny where Katie had been tall and willowy. She was fair where Katie had been dark, but the two women shared the same stubborn set to their chins and the same determination in their eyes. He smiled in spite of himself.

Katie would have been a good mother, too…if only she had lived.

He shut away his heartbreaking memories. Katie May was gone, their unborn child laid to rest with her. It had been four years since their passing, but his grief was as sharp as if it had been yesterday. Most folks thought he had moved on with his life. He'd tried to, but he couldn't forgive God or himself for her death.

He looked away from the young woman and her children. "I don't know him. I'm not from this area."

Realizing how gruff his voice sounded, he gestured to the tarp on the flatbed wagon behind him. It had taken him eight weeks to restore the sleigh and two days to haul it this far. He was anxious to drop it off and head home. "I'm delivering this sleigh to Melvin Taylor. The directions he sent said he lived four miles south of this intersection. Does that help?"

Her face brightened. "I remember Melvin. He lived a half mile south of Grandfather's farm. We can find our way now. Thank you. Come on, girls." She repositioned the backpack on her shoulder and took each girl by the hand as she started down the road.

John didn't urge his horses to move. A three-and-a-half-mile walk was a lot to ask of such small children, and the woman if she was pregnant. It would be dark before they arrived at their destination. The mid-November day had been pleasant so far, but it would get cold when the sun started to go down.

He didn't normally concern himself with the affairs of the *Englisch*, but something about this young woman kept him from driving away. Maybe it was the worry he had glimpsed on her face when he first saw her, or how she spoke so caringly to her girls. Perhaps it was the way she squared her shoulders, looking as if she carried a great weight upon them. He didn't know what it was, but he couldn't leave without offering her assistance.

Maybe it was because she reminded him of Katie.

This is foolish. They'll be fine on their own. An Amish family wouldn't think twice about walking that far.

However, an Amish mother and her children would be properly dressed with heavy coats and sturdy shoes.

The thin white shoes on this woman's feet didn't look as if they would last a mile. He sighed heavily and urged his team forward to catch up with her.

He pulled his horses to a halt beside her. "It's a long walk, *frau*. I can give you a lift. I'm going in the same direction."

She stopped walking and eyed him with obvious indecision. "That's very kind of you, but I don't want to put you to any trouble."

"It's no trouble." It was, but it would trouble him more to leave her.

"We'll be fine." She started walking again.

Stubborn woman. "It will be dark before you get there. The *kinder*, the children, already look tired."

She glanced at her girls and then at him. "You're right, they are tired. It was a long bus ride from… home." Her gaze slid away from his.

He didn't care where she was from or why she didn't want to share that information. The more time he spent reasoning with her, the longer his client would be waiting. He leaned toward her. "Then hand the children up to me and save them a long walk."

She hesitated, chewing on the corner of her lower lip.

Exasperated, he was ready to leave her and get on with his journey. "You'll be safe with me, *frau*, if that is what worries you."

"That's exactly what a serial killer would say."

He scowled at her but noticed the twinkle in her eyes as she tried to hide a smile. "Are you teasing me?"

She grinned. "I was trying to, but I fear I have offended you."

The *Englisch* were a strange lot. "I take no offense. Give over your *kinder*."

He took each child she lifted to him and settled them on the bench seat, knowing he would likely be sorry for his generosity before long. The children would whine and cry, and the woman would probably talk his ear off. He offered her his hand.

A blush stained her cheeks rosy pink. "I'm not as light as the girls."

He almost laughed at the absurd notion that she was too heavy to lift. "I can get you up here without undue effort…unless your pockets are full of bricks. Are they?"

A smile twitched at the corner of her lips. "They aren't, but you may think so."

Her sweet expression pulled a chuckle from him in return. "I doubt that."

She slipped her hand in his. Her fingers were soft and dainty compared to his big calloused paw. He'd almost forgotten what it was like to hold a woman's hand, how it made a man feel strong and protective. Gazing into her upturned face, he was drawn to the humor lingering in her blue eyes. Sunlight glinted on her hair as the breeze tugged at her curls. He easily pulled her up to the wagon seat. The delicate scent of jasmine reached him. Was it her perfume?

Amish women never wore perfume. It was considered worldly to do so and was thus forbidden, but the fragrance of this young woman reminded John of summer evenings spent on his grandmother's porch as the bees hummed around the hanging plants she had cherished. Perhaps he would buy a plant in the spring to remind him of his grandmother and of this young mother.

He slowly released her hand and forced himself to concentrate on his horses. "Walk on, Jake. Get along, Pete."

* * *

Willa Chase glanced from under her lashes at the man beside her. Her Amish Good Samaritan had amazing strength. He had lifted her pregnant bulk with one hand as easily as he had lifted her three-year-old daughters. Seated beside him, she felt dwarfed by his size, but, oddly, he didn't intimidate her. He had spoken gruffly at first, but there was a gentle kindness beneath his teasing that put her at ease.

It was an unusual feeling for her. Before her husband died, he had taught her not to be the trusting sort. Perhaps she'd made an exception because this man was Amish. She had been Amish once, too. A very long time ago. To keep her children safe, she would become Amish again. Then Willa Chase and her daughters would disappear forever.

"I like horsey. Like horsey man," Lucy said, giving their driver a shy smile.

"Horse bad. Man bad." Megan glared at him and stuck out her lower lip as if daring him to argue with her.

"No, he isn't bad, Megan." Willa slanted a glance at the man beside her. As was typical of married Amish men, he wore a beard but no mustache. "I'm sorry about that, sir."

He shrugged. "Little ones speak the truth as they see it."

Relieved that he wasn't offended, she smiled her thanks. "You must have children of your own if you know how embarrassing they can be."

His expression hardened. "*Nee, Gott* has not blessed me with *kinder.*"

His tone said the conversation was over. Remembering how much her Amish grandfather had disliked idle chitchat, Willa whispered to her girls, "We must be quiet so we don't scare the horses or annoy our new friend."

She settled them against her sides, hoping they would fall asleep again as they had on the bus. Willa remained silent, too. The less she said, the better. She couldn't believe she had let slip that she was going to her grandfather's farm, but at least she'd caught herself before she blurted out where they were from.

God had been looking out for her when He sent this man to aid her. Unlike some of the talkative, nosy people on the bus who were full of questions about the twins, an Amish person was unlikely to be inquisitive. Most believed it was impolite to question strangers. Others worried they might be speaking to a shunned former member and would choose silence out of caution. Either way, it worked to her advantage now.

Soon they would be safe with her grandfather. She refused to think about what would happen if he turned them away. He wouldn't. She had to believe that.

The rocking of the wagon, the jingle of the harnesses and the steady clip-clop of the horses' hooves slowly soothed the tenseness from her muscles. She closed her eyes to rest them just for a minute.

The moment she opened the door and saw a police officer standing in the hall outside their apartment in a run-down section of Columbus, Willa knew something terrible had happened. An accident, the officer said. A hit-and-run. Glen was dead. They were still looking for the driver. At least the police officer didn't take her daughters away from her.

Willa stumbled through the following days of grief

with leaden feet. After writing to inform Glen's parents, she moved again. Glen had always been the one to say when and where they went. He knew how to erase their trail—only no matter how often they moved, he would inevitably come home one day and say they had to go again. His parents were closing in. She shared Glen's deep-seated fear without knowing why. She knew only that his parents had the power and the money to take the children away. They said she was an unfit mother. She had been, but she was better now. Glen was the one who knew what to do. How could she fight his parents without him? She was pregnant, broke and on her own against their terrible scheme. She could think of only one way to keep her children safe. She had to run.

Someone grabbed her arm. Willa jerked upright. It took her a few seconds to gather her foggy wits. The wagon had stopped moving. She found her Amish Good Samaritan staring at her.

"You were asleep. I feared you'd *falla* out *da* wagon."

She checked her daughters and found them awake, too. "I guess I was more tired than I thought."

He released her. "Is this your grandfather's place?"

She looked past him and saw a mailbox for E. Lapp. A glance up the lane proved she had arrived at her destination, for she recognized the farm where she'd grown up. "It is. Girls, we are here. Thank the nice man for giving us a ride."

Lucy did. Megan only glared at him. Willa got down and lifted them off the wagon without his help. He touched the brim of his hat and drove on. He glanced back once. Willa knew because she was still standing by the mailbox looking after him. She raised her hand in a simple wave. He did the same and then turned back to the road.

The Amish were quiet, kind, peaceful people. Willa had forgotten how unassuming they could be during the years she had been away. Her Good Samaritan hadn't asked a single question about who she was or why she was in the middle of nowhere with two little children. She was glad he hadn't. She hated the idea that she might have had to lie to him.

She watched the burly man drive away with a sense of loss, almost as if she were losing a gentle giant of a friend. Although he was a stranger, she had felt safe in his company. For the first time since her panicked flight from Columbus, she felt hopeful about her decision to return to her Amish grandfather. It had to be the right choice. She didn't have another option.

She cupped a hand over her abdomen and raised her chin. Time was short, but she would find a safe place for her daughters and her unborn baby before it was too late.

Adjusting her bag on her shoulder, she shepherded her tired girls up the dirt lane. When she drew close to the house, she saw an elderly man standing on the farmhouse steps. It had been ten years since they'd last met. It wasn't a time she liked to recall. She stopped a few feet away. "Hello, Grandfather."

Ezekiel Lapp's weathered face gave no indication of what he was thinking. His dark Amish clothing, full gray beard and black hat added to his somber appearance, but he was frailer and thinner than she remembered. Her daughters clung to her legs as they peered at him from behind her.

"Why have you come?" he asked.

"I wanted you to meet my daughters. This is Megan and this is Lucy." Willa placed a hand behind their heads and urged them to step forward. Lucy faced him, but Megan spun around and retreated behind Willa again.

"Hi." Lucy opened and closed her fingers to wave at him.

"Where is your *Englisch* husband?" Ezekiel asked, ignoring the child.

"Glen passed away six months ago."

"It was *Gott*'s will, but I am sorry for your loss," Ezekiel said softly in Pennsylvania Deitsh, the language of the Amish.

Willa blinked back tears. The pain was still fresh in her heart. "*Danki*. Thank you."

"Mama is sad," Megan said.

"I sad," Lucy added. "I'm cold, Mama."

The early fall wind had a bite to it. Willa shivered despite the coat she wore. It wasn't heavy enough, but it was the only one she had that she could button across her pregnant stomach.

"Come inside." Ezekiel turned and went in the house without waiting for them.

Relief made Willa's knees weak. *So far, so good.*

She had no idea what she would do if he turned them away. She had spent the last of her money to get this far. Unless her grandfather took them in, they would be sleeping in a barn or under a bridge tonight. She climbed the steps with the girls close beside her.

Inside the house, little had changed since the day her parents walked away from their Amish life with her in tow. The wide plank floor of the kitchen had been scrubbed clean. A simple table with four chairs sat in the center of the room. The windows were free of shades or curtains, for an upright Amish family in her grandfather's ultraconservative church had nothing to hide from the outside world. A single plate, cup and fork in the dish drainer by the sink proved her grandfather still lived alone. The room smelled faintly of bleach and stout coffee. The scent transported her to the past the way nothing else had done.

She had been fifteen the last time she stood in this room, completely confused by the family quarrel taking place. One day she was Amish and knew her place in the world. She knew what was expected of her. She had been a week away from her baptism. The next week she was an awkward, shy, frightened girl trying to fit into the perplexing English world her parents had chosen.

Her Amish childhood had been filled with hard work, but she had been happy here. If her grandfather took them in, she could be happy here again. Nothing mattered as long as she had her children with her.

She led her girls to the heavy wood-burning cookstove and held out her hands to the welcome heat. "Don't touch. It's very hot," she cautioned them.

"Are your children hungry?" her grandfather asked, speaking *Deitsh*.

"I'm sure they are."

"Have them sit." He walked to the counter and opened a drawer.

Willa helped the girls out of their coats and seated them at the table. She hung their coats on pegs by the front door and then stood behind her daughters, not daring to assume the invitation included her.

He scowled when he turned around. "Sit. I will not

eat with you, but I am permitted to feed the hungry as our Lord commanded us. Then you must go."

Willa's heart sank, but she held on to the hope that he would change his mind when he learned the details of her situation. She took a seat at the table and waited while her grandfather prepared church spread for her daughters.

A mixture of peanut butter, marshmallow cream and maple syrup, the tasty treat was often served on bread or used as a dip for apples or pears. He spread it on thick slices of homemade bread and set it on plates in front of them. It was just as good as Willa remembered...

The girls loved it. When they were finished eating, she led them to the stark living room and settled them for a nap on the sofa.

When she was sure they were sleeping, she returned to the kitchen. Her grandfather sat at the table with a cup of coffee in his hands.

She stood across from him and laid a protective hand on her stomach. "I have no money. I have no job. I don't have a place to live, and my baby is due the second week of January."

Willa thought she glimpsed a flash of sympathy in his eyes. "Your husband's family will not help you?"

A chill slipped over her skin. She crossed her arms to ward it off. They were the ones claiming she was an unfit mother because of her mental breakdown. According to Glen, they had paid an unscrupulous judge to grant them custody of the twins while she was in the hospital. Willa knew nothing about the law, but without money and without Glen to help her, they would succeed in taking her children away. She couldn't allow that. "*Nee*, you are my last hope."

* * *

Her grandfather took a sip of his coffee. "I have no money to give you."

"I don't want money. I wish to return to the Amish faith." She held her breath, hoping he believed her.

He was silent for a long time. She waited and prayed for his forgiveness and for his understanding.

He shook his head. "I can't help you. You must go."

She couldn't bear to hear those words. Not after she had come so far. Tears sprang to her eyes, but she blinked them back. "Please, I'm begging you. I have nowhere else to go. Don't turn us away. We are your flesh and blood."

His brow darkened. "You come to me wearing *Englisch* clothes, with your shorn hair and your head uncovered. I see no repentance in you. I have heard none from your lips, yet you say you want to be Amish again. You share in the shame your father brought to this house."

"I was a child. I had no choice but to go with my parents."

"You chose to remain in the *Englisch* world all these years, even after the death of my son and his wife. You could have come back then. I would have taken you in. *Nee*, I will not help you now. This suffering, you have brought on yourself." He rose, put on his hat and coat and went out the door.

Willa sat at the table and dropped her head on her crossed arms as she gave in to despair. Gut-wrenching sobs shook her body. Why was God doing this? Hadn't she suffered enough? How much more would He ask of her?

Chapter Two

"I'm sorry I'm late. I had a few unexpected delays." John stepped down from his wagon as Melvin Taylor came out of the house to meet him.

"You said you'd be here today. It's still today." Melvin pushed the brim of his red ball cap up with one finger and grinned.

Relief made John smile. Melvin appeared to be the understanding sort and a rare *Englisch* fellow in John's book—one who wasn't in a rush. His hopes for more work from the man rose.

"Can't thank you enough for taking on my little project."

"I enjoyed restoring it." He loved re-creating useful things from the past.

Melvin rubbed his hands together. "Well, don't keep me in suspense any longer. How did it turn out?"

"I'll let you be the judge." Moving to the back of the wagon, John untied the ropes and lifted the tarp covering his load. The antique blue-and-gold sleigh had made the journey unharmed.

"I knew she was a beauty under all that neglect."

Melvin drew his fingers along the smooth, elaborately curved metal runner. "I'm right pleased with your work, John Miller."

"Danki."

It had taken John weeks to duplicate all the missing pieces in his forge and assemble it. After he replaced the tattered upholstery with a plush blue tufted fabric, the result was well worth his time and effort. The Portland Cutter would glide through the snow as neatly now as it had a hundred and fifty years ago.

He had managed to turn back the hands of time for the sleigh. If only he could change one hour of the past for himself.

Such a thing wasn't possible. He had to spend the rest of his life knowing his pride had cost the life of the only woman he would ever love. His penance was to go on living without her. Hard work at his forge was the only way he kept the long hours of loneliness at bay.

Melvin stepped back from the wagon with a big grin on his face. "Would you be willing to take on another project for me?"

John tried not to sound too eager. "I'd have to see it first and we would have to agree on a price."

"Sure. I think you'll like my latest find."

John followed the childishly eager man to a large shed. Melvin pushed open the sliding door with a flourish to reveal a half dozen sleighs. Five were in pristine condition. Only one needed restoration work. A lot of work.

Melvin patted the faded front seat, sending a small cloud of dust into the air. "I found this vis-à-vis sleigh at a farm sale about an hour north of here."

John walked around the vehicle, assessing what

needed to be fixed. Vis-à-vis sleighs were easily recognizable. They consisted of a raised coachman's seat and two lower passenger seats behind the driver that faced each other. They had originally been used in cities where well-to-do people were driven about during the winter to parties and such.

He checked the floorboards first. They were rotten. That was to be expected. Three of the ornate lantern holders were missing, but he could duplicate them from the one remaining. The runners looked sound. They must have been repaired at some time in the past. The upholstery definitely needed replacing, but the wooden frames of the seats looked in good shape. "I can have it ready in three weeks, maybe less."

He could finish it in two weeks, but he didn't want to lock himself into a shorter time frame. More pressing work might come up. Better to finish earlier than promised rather than later.

"Awesome. To have it finished before Christmas, that will be great. Let's hope for plenty of snow." They agreed on the price and the men shook hands.

"Shall I ship it to you?" Melvin asked as they walked toward the door.

"I figured the cost of transporting it home and bringing it back myself in my estimate. If I have to hire someone to ship it back, that will be an additional charge."

"Agreed. I'll help you get the other one unloaded and this one strapped on, and then we can have a cup of coffee. The missus put on a fresh pot when she saw you drive in." The two men walked toward the house.

Unbidden, the thought of the young mother he'd met earlier entered John's mind. He should have asked her name. Melvin might know. Although her business was none of his, John's curiosity got the better of him. He glanced at Melvin. "I met someone on my way here who said she knew you."

"Oh? Who might that be?"

John unstrapped one side of the sleigh and tossed the lines to Melvin. "She said Ezekiel Lapp is her grandfather. I gave her a lift to his place."

Melvin's bushy eyebrows shot up in surprise. "Willa Lapp has come home?"

"She didn't give her name."

"It has to be Willa. Ezekiel only had one son and one grandchild. I haven't seen that sweet girl in years. How is she?"

So her name was Willa. "She looked fine. She had two daughters with her. Twins about three years old." He and Melvin lifted the sleigh down and carried it to the shed.

Melvin put down his end and leaned on the upholstered back. "Little Willa is a mother, if that don't beat all. I sure can't imagine her grown and married with kids. I hope Ezekiel has the good sense to let bygones be bygones. He's a lonely old man. His wife passed on years ago. Then his son left the Amish and took his wife and Willa with him. I heard Ezekiel's church shunned them, so I reckon he had to, as well."

That brought John up short. Was Willa an excommunicated member of the Amish church? If so, her relationship with her grandfather was much more complicated than a non-Amish person like Melvin realized. To willingly take the vow of baptism and then break that vow was a serious offense. John started to wish he hadn't asked about her.

"It broke the old man's heart. He wouldn't even speak

his son's name. I thought the Amish forgave everyone. Don't they forgive their own for leaving?"

"If a person leaves before they are baptized, they are not shunned. If a baptized member repents and confesses their sins, they will be forgiven and welcomed back into the church." Perhaps that was why Willa had returned after so many years.

"And if they don't repent, they have to be shunned forever?"

"That is our belief."

Melvin shook his head. "The Amish folks around here are fine people and good neighbors, but I don't expect I'll ever really understand them."

Embarrassed that he had pried into Willa's personal life when she hadn't shared anything, he decided to dismiss her from his mind and changed the subject. "How did you get into collecting sleighs?"

Melvin happily shared the story of his passion while the men loaded the vis-à-vis.

An hour later, John left Melvin's farm with his thermos full of coffee and a dozen oatmeal cookies in a box under his seat. He would spend the night again with his cousins near Berlin and be home by late afternoon on Monday. As the mailbox for Ezekiel Lapp came into view, John slowed his team and looked toward the house.

His own sister hadn't joined the faith, choosing instead to marry a non-Amish fellow. Many Amish families had *Englisch* children and grandchildren who were accepted and cherished. He prayed that Willa and her daughters would find kindness and acceptance, too.

He slapped the reins to get his team moving faster. It was a long way to Bowmans Crossing. He had no cause to worry about a stranger and her family. He would never see them again. They were in God's hands.

Willa raised her head and saw it was almost dark outside. She must have fallen asleep. Her head hurt from crying. She rose stiffly and stretched her aching back, then wiped her damp cheeks as she looked around. Were the girls still sleeping? That would be unusual.

She checked in the living room. The sofa was empty. She called their names, but neither of them answered. Where were they? Panic uncoiled inside her. Their coats were gone from the pegs where she had hung them. She yanked open the front door and saw them come out of the barn walking beside her grandfather.

Lucy saw her first and came running. "Mama, I saw a cow."

Willa's pounding heart slowed with relief. She dropped to one knee and hugged Lucy. "Did you? Was she a nice cow?"

Lucy nodded. "She licked her nose like this." Lucy stuck her tongue out and tried to touch it to her nose.

"Cows poo in the dirt," Megan said with a look of disgust.

Willa held back a chuckle as she rose to her feet. She stepped aside as her grandfather carried a red pail of fresh milk up the steps. From under the porch, half a dozen kittens came out meowing for their supper. Her grandfather handed Megan the pail. "Pour this in the pan for the kittens."

"I help." Lucy grabbed the side of the pail. The two girls poured out the milk while the kittens tumbled around their feet and into the aluminum pie pan.

She left Megan and Lucy to play with the cats and followed her grandfather inside.

"Thank you for watching the girls and letting me sleep."

"You were worn-out."

"I was. It has been a long time since I've had a peaceful night's rest."

He was silent for a long moment, then he glanced toward the porch. The girls were still playing with the kittens. "Out in the barn Megan told me that bad people are looking for her and Lucy. What did she mean?"

Willa decided to tell him and took a seat at the table. After all, what did she have to lose? "My husband, Glen, had a falling-out with his parents before he met me. He would never talk about it except to say that they wanted to lock him up. He was a good man. I can't believe he did anything wrong."

Even as she defended him, she knew it wasn't entirely true. Glen found it easy to assume new identities and fabricate stories about where they came from without remorse, but he had been good to her.

"Go on," her grandfather said.

"He was always worried that they would find us. We moved three times the first year we were married. Then the girls were born."

Shame burned in Willa's throat, but she forced herself to continue. "Trying to take care of fussy twins wore us down. I'm not making excuses, but it was hard. We didn't have any help. Glen had to work and I was home alone with the babies. I never got enough sleep. I became…sick."

Her grandfather wouldn't understand the terrible things she had done. How could he when she didn't understand them herself. She should have been stronger. The doctors at the hospital had called it postpartum psychosis. The voices telling her to hide her babies from Glen hadn't been real. They had been delusions, but she had done all they told her to do, even wading into the cold, rain-swollen river with the babies in her arms. They all would have died that night if not for the quick-thinking intervention of a stranger.

Willa realized she had been staring into the past, trying to remember all that had happened, but so much of her memory was blank. "I spent four weeks in a hospital. Glen couldn't manage alone. He contacted his parents, believing they would help for the sake of their grandchildren. They came, but they only wanted to take the girls away from us. They said we were unfit parents and that the law was on their side."

Tears slipped down Willa's cheeks and she brushed them away. Tears wouldn't help anything. She had to be strong. It was up to her now. "Glen managed to get away with the babies before the police came. He picked me up at the hospital and we left town with only the clothes on our backs. We tried to start over, but we had to move so many times I lost count. After Glen died, I didn't know what to do except to come here. If his parents find me, they will take the girls away and I'll never see them again."

"Will the *Englisch* police come here?"

"Maybe, I can't be sure. I was careful not to tell anyone where I was going. I purchased a ticket for the next town down the road, but I got off the bus before then. People on the bus may remember us. An Amish fellow gave us a lift here, but he wasn't from this area. I do know Glen's parents won't stop looking for the girls, but it will be hard to find us among the Amish."

He stared into his coffee cup for a long time. Finally, he glanced at her. "Up in the attic you will find a black trunk. There are clothes that you and the girls can wear in it. They will be warmer than what they have on now. They are *goot* Amish clothes. If you mean to rejoin the faith, you must dress plain."

"Does this mean we can stay?" She was afraid to hope.

"With me, *nee*. Go to my sister, Ada Kaufman. She was also shunned by our church, but I hear she has kept to the Amish ways in a new church group in Hope Springs."

Willa had fond memories of her great-aunt Ada, a kindly and spry woman with a son and daughter a few years older than Willa. A flicker of hope came alive inside her chest. She still had family she could go to.

The thought of spending Christmas with her aunt and cousins Miriam and Mark made Willa smile. They'd had some fine times together in the old days. Her cousins might be married with children of their own by now. Her daughters could have cousins to celebrate the holidays with the way she once did.

"Do you think Ada will help me?"

"That, I cannot say. I have an old buggy and a horse you can use to travel there."

"How far is it?" Willa had never heard of Hope Springs.

"Three days' travel to the east, more or less."

Three days by buggy with the girls. It would be next to impossible. Where would they stay at night? What would they eat? She had no money. And yet, what choice did she have except to go on faith? There was no going back now. "*Danki, Daddi.* What made you change your mind?"

"Your children deserve the chance to know our ways. I pray *Gott* opens your heart and that you seek true repentance. When you do so, you will be welcomed here."

"I'll send you money for the horse and buggy when I can," she promised.

"I want no money from you. They are a gift to your children. You may all sleep upstairs in your old room, but you must leave at first light on Monday."

It wasn't what she had hoped for, but she wasn't beaten yet. Perhaps her great-aunt's family would be like the kind Amish man she had met that afternoon. The memory of his solid presence and quiet kindness filled her heart with renewed hope. She wished she had been bold enough to ask his name. She would remember him in her prayers.

Three days after delivering his restored sleigh, John was home and hard at work on his new project. The coals in his forge glowed red-hot with each injection of air from his bellows. Sweat poured down his face. He tasted salt and ashes on his lips, but he didn't move back. The fire was almost hot enough. Using long tongs, he held a flat piece of iron bar stock in the glowing coals, waiting until it reached the right temperature to be shaped by his hammer. A black heat would be too cold. A white heat would be too hot. A good working heat was the red-orange glow he was waiting on. The smell of smoke and hot metal filled the cold air around him.

Movement out on the road that fronted his property

caught his attention. He let go of the tongs and shaded his eyes with one hand to see against the glare of the late-afternoon sun. Was his mother coming home from the quilting bee already? He didn't expect her for another hour.

A buggy approached the top of the hill, but it wasn't one he knew. He didn't recognize the skinny horse between the shafts, either. He'd put shoes on nearly every horse in the area. He knew them and their owners on sight. This was someone new, and he or she was driving erratically.

The horse trotted up the road veering from side to side in a tired, rambling gait. Its black hide was flecked with white foam, but it kept going. The road led uphill to where his lane turned off at the crest. Just beyond that, the road sloped downward for a few hundred yards before it ended in a T where it intersected the blacktop highway that skirted the edge of the river just beyond. The tired horse crested the hill and stumbled but didn't turn in John's lane. As it went past, John realized there wasn't anyone in the driver's seat.

It was a runaway. Without someone to stop it, the horse was likely to trot straight across the highway into traffic and perhaps even into the river.

John let go of the bellows, sprinted up his lane and out into the road after the buggy. Had the horse been fresh, he wouldn't stand a chance of catching it, but it was tiring. The steep climb had slowed it.

"Whoa there, whoa," he shouted, praying the horse was well trained and would respond to the command. It kept going. Sprinting harder, he raced after the vehicle, his lungs burning like his forge. There was traffic below on the highway. A horse-drawn wagon loaded with hay slowed several cars, but one after the other, they pulled out and sped around him. The buggy was unlikely to make it across without being hit.

Running up behind the vehicle, John realized it was a Swartzentruber buggy. The most conservative group among the Amish, the Swartzentruber didn't fit their buggies with the slow-moving-vehicle sign, windshields, mirrors or electric lighting. One rear wheel wobbled heavily. He finally drew close enough to grab the rear door handle. Yanking it open, he gave one final burst of effort and threw himself inside, no easy task for a man of his size.

The buggy wasn't empty. There were two little girls in black bonnets holding on to each other in the back seat. They started screaming when they saw him.

"Shush, shush. *Ich bin freind.*" He spoke in *Deitsh*, telling them he was a friend. He quickly climbed over the seatback. An Amish woman lay slumped on the floorboards, her face obscured by the large black traveling bonnet she wore. The reins had fallen out of her hands but not out of the buggy. He glanced out the front and saw the horse was nearly at the bottom of the hill. The highway was less than ten yards away.

John grabbed the reins and pulled back as he stomped on the buggy brake. The foam-flecked black mare stumbled to a halt and hung her head, her sides heaving as a car zipped past. The poor horse didn't even flinch.

John quickly checked the woman on the floor. She was dressed in a heavy black winter coat, gloves and a black traveling bonnet. He could see she was breathing. He tried rousing her without success by shaking her shoulder. He had no idea what was wrong. The girls in back kept crying for their mama.

After lifting the woman onto the seat, he spoke to the girls again in *Deitsh*. "What are your names? Do you live near here? What is your papa's name?"

They were too frightened or too shy to answer him. As he pulled his arm from behind the woman's head, he noticed a smear of blood on his sleeve. He untied her bonnet and removed it. Her *kapp* came off with it and her blond curls sprang free. His breath caught in his throat as he recognized the woman he'd given a lift to several days before.

What was Willa Lapp doing here?

The side of her head was matted with dried blood, but the wound under it was only a shallow gash. Had she struck her head hard enough to be knocked unconscious, or had she hurt herself when she fell? He had no way of knowing.

He asked the children what had happened, but they only stared at him fearfully without answering. He would have to wait until the woman could answer all his questions when she came to.

Leaving her settled more comfortably on the seat, he stepped forward to check on the horse and noticed a piece of harness hanging loose. It had been repaired with a loop of wire at some time in the past. The wire had snapped, leaving a sharp point sticking through the leather. The flapping piece of harness had been jabbing the mare's side with each step she took, forcing her to keep moving even as she was close to exhaustion.

Now what? John pulled on the tip of his beard as he looked around. He couldn't ask the trembling, exhausted horse to pull the buggy back up the steep hill. He didn't want to leave two crying children and an unconscious woman at the side of the road until he could return with a fresh horse. The mare had to be walked until she cooled down or she would sicken in this cold. It left him with only one option. He had to take them all together.

The girls had stopped crying and were huddled behind their mother. She hadn't stirred. He found a horse blanket beneath the back seat, unhitched the mare and covered her with it. Leading her back to the buggy door, he opened it and held out his hand to the nearest child. "*Kumm*, we *lawfa*."

She pushed his hand aside. "Bad man. Go away."

The other girl patted her mother's face. "Is Mama sick?"

He switched to English. "*Ja*, your mother is sick. I will take you to my house. Come, we must walk there."

They looked at each other with uncertainty. He slipped his arms beneath their mother and lifted her out of the buggy. His suspicion that Willa was pregnant proved to be true. Starting up the hill with his burden, he glanced back. The children climbed down and hurried after him, giving a wide berth to the horse he was leading. They reached his side and stayed close, holding hands with each other as they struggled to keep up with his long strides. He slowed his pace.

One of the girls caught hold of his coat. "Horsey man, wait."

He stopped walking. "I'm not horsey man. My name is John, John Miller."

"Johnjohn." She grinned at him.

"Just John, and what is your name?"

"Lucy. Is Mama okay?"

"You are all okay thanks to God's mercy this day." He had stopped this woman's buggy from running into traffic and being hit by a car. Why hadn't someone stopped Katie May's buggy before it had been smashed to bits and her life snuffed out?

Why hadn't he stopped his wife from leaving that day? It was a question that haunted his days and nights.

The woman in his arms moaned, pulling his mind from the past. He started walking again. She wasn't heavy, but his arms were burning by the time he reached the front steps of his house. He dropped the horse's reins and hoped she was too tired to wander off until he got his unexpected guests settled. This was costing him valuable time away from his forge and wasting fuel. He didn't like interruptions when he was working.

He carried her into the living room, laid her on the sofa and then knelt beside her. The little girls pressed close to him.

"Mama's sleeping," whispered the one who'd told him her name was Lucy. The only way he could tell them apart was that Lucy still had her bonnet on. The other sister had taken hers off somewhere between the buggy and his front step.

He gazed down at Willa's peaceful face. Her dark blond eyelashes were fanned against fair cheeks framed by golden curls. She was even prettier than he remembered.

He shook off his unusually fanciful thoughts and gave her injury closer inspection. The gash wasn't deep, but the fact that she hadn't roused had him worried. He unbuttoned her coat to check for other injures and found none. He pulled his hands away. He had no idea what to do with an unconscious pregnant woman.

Lucy tugged on his coat sleeve. "I'm hungry."

The other child crossed her legs. "I need to go potty."

He sat back on his heels in consternation. Where was his mother when he needed her?

Chapter Three

W illa heard voices she didn't recognize. Were they real, or was she hallucinating? The psychosis wouldn't start before her baby was born, would it? Her hands went to her stomach. Reassured by the feel of her unborn child nestled there, she opened her eyes. She was in a room she'd never seen before. Where were her girls? She tried to sit up. Pain lanced through her head, sending a burst of nausea to her empty stomach. She closed her eyes, hoping it would recede. She needed to find her children.

"Take it easy," a man's voice said close beside her.

She turned her head to see someone looming above her. She blinked hard, and he swam into focus. He was a mountain of a man with broad shoulders and a black beard that covered his jawline and chin. He knelt beside her and slipped an arm under her shoulders to ease her upright. His dark brown hair was cut in a bowl style she remembered from her youth. He was Amish or perhaps Old Order Mennonite. The beard meant he was a married man. His eyes were a rich coffee brown with crow's feet at the corners. She thought she read sympathy in their depths. The longer she looked at him, the more convinced she was that they had met before, but her mind was so fuzzy she couldn't remember where.

She clutched his arm as she struggled to get up. "Where are my daughters?"

His muscles were rock hard beneath her fingers. The feel of his steely arms was reassuring. It triggered her memory. She did know him. This was the man who had kindly given her a ride to her grandfather's farm.

"Relax. Your children are with my *mudder*. She is getting them something to eat." He patted her hand, and she let go of him. He sat back on a chair at the end of the sofa.

Willa had to see them for herself. "Lucy, Megan, come here!" A deep, harsh cough sent burning pain through her chest. Her cold was getting worse.

The pair hurried through the open doorway. "Mama, you awake?" Megan asked.

Her little worrier. Older than her sister by five minutes and a hundred years. Willa pulled both girls to her in a fierce hug. "Yes, I'm awake."

Megan scowled and took Willa's face between her hands. "Don't fall down!"

"I'm sorry I frightened you." She kissed Megan's hair and noticed her Amish *kapp* was missing. Willa had had trouble keeping the unfamiliar head covering on the girls. They didn't like them.

"I got peanut butter and jelly." Lucy offered her half-eaten sandwich to her mother. "Want some?"

Willa shook her head, ignoring the pain the movement caused. "I'm fine. You finish it."

"Okeydokey." Lucy didn't need further urging. She bit into her food with relish and was soon licking her fingers. The girls hadn't eaten since yesterday morning when they'd finished the last of the bread her grandfather had grudgingly given them. Willa hadn't had anything for two days, not since leaving her grandfather's farm. Her stomach growled loudly.

An elderly woman in Amish garb came to the doorway. "*Kinder, kumma* to the *dish* and let your *mamm* rest."

Megan leaned in to whisper in Willa's ear. "She talks funny."

The man seated beside Willa cleared his throat. She had almost forgotten that he was there. "My *mudder* doesn't speak *Englisch* often, so it is *goot* for her to practice."

Lucy hurried after the woman. "I want another sandwich, please."

Megan followed her. "Me, too."

Lucy frowned at her sister. "My sandwich, not yours!"

"I want one!" Megan fisted her hands on her hips.

"Lucy, Megan, you can each have your own sandwich," Willa said to end the mutiny she saw brewing. Their normal bickering relieved her mind. They didn't seem traumatized by what had happened.

Now that she knew her girls were safe, she turned her attention to the man at the end of the sofa. "How did we get here, and where is here?"

He scowled at her. "I have many questions for you, too. I happened to notice your buggy going past my lane with no one driving. I assumed it was a runaway and ran to catch it. Your girls were in the back seat and you were unconscious on the floorboard up front. What happened to you?"

She raised a hand to her aching head. She found a bandage above her temple. "I must have fainted and hit my head. I haven't been feeling well." She didn't tell him she hadn't eaten. Another deep cough followed her words and left her head spinning.

"You don't remember what happened?"

They'd slept in the buggy again last night. Rather, the girls had slept. Willa's nagging cough had kept her awake. She had a vague memory of hitching up the horse at dawn. After that, only bits and pieces of traveling along the winding roadways came to mind. Nothing about how she had hurt her head.

"I don't remember much after starting out on the road this morning."

He eyed her intently. "You are not Amish and yet you and your children are dressed in our way and traveling by buggy. Why? What are you doing here? How did you find me?"

She scowled at his rapid-fire questions. "I wasn't looking for you."

"You told me you were visiting your grandfather, Ezekiel Lapp."

"I did see Grandfather. He gave me the horse and buggy so that I could visit other family members." Even with this kind man, she couldn't bring herself to share information about her destination. She'd spent too many years hiding where she was from and where she was going.

She knew the Amish bonnets would fool the casual observers, but not the real deal. Willa Chase and her children had to disappear. Someone looking for them wouldn't look twice at an Amish woman traveling with two children in a buggy. This man already knew she wasn't Amish, so she decided to tell him the truth, just not the whole truth.

"My parents left the church when I was young. I have decided to return to the faith and raise my children to be Amish, but I wanted to get reacquainted with my other relatives and spend Christmas with them before I decide where to settle."

"You are not shunned?"

She looked at him in surprise. "No. I wasn't baptized when my parents made the decision to leave. They were shunned by our congregation, but my parents are both gone now."

He studied her for a long moment, then nodded. "Our ways are *goot* ways to raise *kinder*. This is also the wish of your husband?"

Willa stared at her hands clenched together in her lap. "He died last May."

Her life had been a constant struggle since the horrible moment she received the news that Glen had been killed. Now that her grandfather had turned her away, she had one slim hope left—that her Amish great-aunt Ada or perhaps her cousin Mark or her cousin Miriam would take them in.

"I am sorry you lost your husband. I know it must have been difficult for you," the man said softly.

The compassion in his voice touched her deeply. *"Danki."*

She put aside her grief and focused on the present. "And thank you for stopping my runaway carriage. You have come to my rescue twice now and I don't even know your name."

"John Miller. My mother is Vera Miller."

"I'm Willa Lapp." She gave her maiden name, unable

to look John Miller in the eyes as she did so. "You have already met my daughters, Megan and Lucy. Where are we?"

His mother came in and handed Willa a steaming bowl of chicken soup and a spoon. "Eat. Your babe needs nourishment."

Willa took a sip and the hot, delicious broth drove away her nausea. "This is good. *Danki.*"

"Eat it all." The woman went back to the kitchen.

"You are at my home near Bowmans Crossing," John said.

The soup was warming Willa from the inside out. The chunks of chicken were tender and the noodles were the thick homemade kind her mother used to make. The name of the town he mentioned didn't ring a bell. "Is that close to Hope Springs?"

He shook his head. "You are a long way from there and traveling in the wrong direction if that is where you're headed."

She digested this unwelcome news. She had hoped to find her great-aunt before dark. She didn't want to spend another night on the open road. "Thank you for your help, but I must get going."

"Your horse needs rest and your buggy needs repairs. I can fix it, but it will take some time."

Disappointment weighed her down. She was so tired. Why couldn't one thing go right? "I'm afraid I can't pay you for any repairs."

"I have not asked for payment."

He rose and took the empty bowl from her hands. "You need rest, Willa Lapp. Don't worry about your *kinder. Mamm* will look after them. She also is not a killer of serials."

Willa had to smile at his mistaken turn of the phrase. "The term is *serial killer*."

She remembered how difficult it could be to translate the Pennsylvania Deitsh language of her youth into English. An Amish fellow might say he would go the road up and turn the gate in.

John frowned slightly as he repeated her words, "Serial killer. *Danki*. She is also not one of those. She has fixed a bed for you."

Willa wanted to protest, but she could barely keep her eyes open. She did need rest. Just a short nap while he fixed her buggy, then she would be on her way. She prayed her great-aunt would be as kind to her as this man and his mother had been.

Her eyes drifted closed. She barely noticed when John's mother came back into the room. "Bring her, John, she's too worn-out to walk."

John lifted Willa in his arms. She wanted to protest, but she didn't have the strength. Her head lolled against his shoulder. For the first time in months, she felt truly safe, but it was only an illusion. Someone wanted to steal her daughters away. She was their only protection. She couldn't let down her guard.

John waited until his mother pulled back the covers, then he laid Willa gently on the bed in the guest room and took a step back. He hooked his thumbs through his suspenders, feeling ill at ease and restless. This woman brought out his protective instincts and he didn't want to feel responsible for her or for her children. He needed to get back to work. The forge would be cooling by now. He'd have to fire it up again. More time and fuel wasted.

His mother began removing Willa's shoes. "What did she say about pretending to be Amish?"

"She said she was raised Amish but her parents left the church. She wants to return and raise her children in our faith."

"Then we must do what we can for her. Does she have people nearby?"

"Near Hope Springs, I think. That's where she was heading."

"That is a long trip from here with such little ones. Joshua Bowman's wife, Mary, is from there. Perhaps they know each other. Did you tell her she was welcome to spend the night with us?"

"*Nee.* I did not, and why should I? She wants to leave." He didn't want them here another hour, let alone overnight.

His mother made shooing motions with her hands. "Your work will keep, but go if you must. I will see to her. You can keep the *kinder* occupied for me. Outside is best, for I want this young mother to get plenty of rest. I am worried about her babe."

He took a quick step back from the bed. "You think she might give birth here?"

"If the *bobli* wants to come, nothing we do or say will stop it, but there is no sense hurrying his or her arrival for lack of a little rest. Go along. You won't be any help if she does go into labor."

She was right about that. He was a volunteer firefighter along with many of his neighbors, but running into a burning house was not as scary as a woman giving birth. "Call me if you need me."

"I can handle this. Get out from underfoot."

Mamm was a tiny thing and crippled with arthritis

that twisted her hands, but she was still a force to be reckoned with when she set her mind to something.

He found the twins sitting at the table in the kitchen. They watched him warily. He could see subtle differences in their features, but he wasn't sure which was which. Both of them were without their *kapps*. "Come outside and help me with my chores. Your mother is taking a nap."

"Will we see a cow?" The girl closest to him asked.

"Which one are you?"

"Told you. I'm Lucy."

"That's right, you did."

Her sister licked a smear of jam from the back of her hand. "Cows yucky. I'm this many." She held up three fingers.

Lucy nodded and folded her fingers into the correct number. "I'm this many."

Megan pointed to him. "How old are you?"

"Older than all your fingers and toes together."

"I can count. One, two, four, five, three." Lucy ticked off each finger.

"That's very good. Put on your coats. Would you like to feed the goats?"

"Same as at the zoo?" Lucy nodded vigorously.

John had no idea how they fed goats at a zoo, but he figured it couldn't be much different than what he did. He helped Lucy into her coat.

Megan pulled away from him when he tried to help her. "I can do it."

She got her coat on but couldn't manage the buttons. It was getting cold outside, so he buttoned her coat in spite of her protests and held open the door for them when he was done. Megan hung back until Lucy went out, then she hurried after her sister.

"Where's my horsey? Give him back." Megan narrowed her eyes as she looked up at him. She pointed to her mother's buggy sitting beside the barn. He'd fetched it after his mother arrived home and stabled the tired horse.

"I didn't steal her. She is resting in the barn just as your mother is resting in the house."

"What's a barn?" Lucy waited for his answer.

"That big red building."

He figured that was enough information. He was wrong. He wasn't prepared for the barrage of questions a pair of three-year-olds could ask, but he soon learned their curiosity was endless. Most of the time he understood only half of what they were chattering about and he couldn't keep the two of them straight when they darted every which way so quickly.

"Why are cows brown?"

"God made them that color."

"What do cows eat?"

"Hay." He forked some over the stall to his milk cow Maybell.

"What's hay?"

"Dried grass."

"You have a funny hat, Johnjohn."

"It's just John."

"Can cow come in the house?" one asked.

He quickly shook his head. "*Nee*, the cow can't come in the house."

The other child parked her hands on her hips. "Cow come with me!"

"No," he repeated sternly.

A mutinous expression appeared on her face and she shook a finger at him. "Don't tell me no!"

He leaned down to look into her eyes. "No!"

Tears welled up and quickly spilled down her cheeks. "You bad man."

He raised his eyes to the barn ceiling. How did they know at this young age that tears could turn a man's resolve into putty? "I am not bringing a cow into the house."

"I see kitty," one said and ran toward the yellow tabby perched on the window ledge.

Her sister's tears vanished, and she went running toward the animal, too. The cat didn't care for the sudden attention. She jumped down and scampered out the door.

Both children turned toward him. One scowled. "Kitty ran 'way."

"I don't blame her. I'd like to do that myself." He decided the frowning one was Megan and decided to test his theory. "Megan, do you like goats?"

She nodded. Okay, he had that right. "Come, we will feed them now."

He gave each child a pail of grain. His small herd crowded around the children, eager to reach the feed. Lucy petted the head of each goat that came to investigate her. "Me like goats."

"They can't come in the house," he said quickly to forestall another episode of tears.

"Okeydokey," Lucy said.

"Where did you girls come from?" he asked, hoping to get more information about them.

Lucy pointed toward the road.

"What town did you come from?" he asked to be

more specific. He was more curious about their pretty mother than he cared to admit.

Megan sighed deeply. "Our town."

Lucy's lower lip trembled. "Me want to sleep in my bed."

"You will sleep in a warm bed tonight, I promise." He laid a hand on her head. To his surprise, she wrapped her arms around his legs.

She looked up at him. "You nice, Johnjohn."

"No! Bad man," Megan yelled. She yanked Lucy away from him, making Lucy wince at the tight grip on her arm.

John leaned down to frown at Megan. "That was unkind. You must tell your *shveshtah* you are sorry and ask her forgiveness."

For a second he thought she would defy him, but she put her arms around Lucy and pulled her close. "I'm sorry."

Lucy pulled away and sniffled. "It's okay."

John stood up straight. "*Goot.* Your family is second only to God in your life. You must care for each other always. Let's go milk the cow. Maybe your mother will be awake by then and I can get back to work." His first order of business was to see what was wrong with the rear wheels of their buggy. His mother was insistent that they stay overnight, but he wanted them on their way first thing tomorrow.

His attempt to milk the cow proved far more difficult than he had imagined. In spite of his cautions, Lucy tried to catch Maybell's tail as Megan crawled under her belly to see what he was doing. The cow jumped and almost upset his milk pail when Lucy squealed loudly. She had spotted Maybell's twin calves in the next pen.

The girls climbed the wooden fence and jabbered to each other and to the curious calves in a steady stream of words he couldn't hope to keep up with.

They squealed again. He grabbed the pail as the cow kicked nervously. His chores had never been so nerve-racking. A glance over his shoulder revealed five kittens had come out of the hay to get their supper portion of fresh milk. The cats beat a hasty retreat when the girls rushed them.

"Johnjohn, why kitties run away?" Lucy demanded.

"You scared them by being too noisy. You must be quiet around the animals."

"Why?"

"Because all creatures enjoy peace and quiet. Including this blacksmith."

"Kitties!" Megan said, pointing toward the top of the hay bales where the litter had taken refuge.

"Leave them alone, and they will come down." He poured a portion of the milk into a small wooden trough.

He walked to the barn door and held it open. "Come, we must take the *millich* to *Mamm* so we can have fresh cream on our oatmeal tomorrow morning."

They were halfway across the front yard when the door of the house flew open, and Willa came rushing out. Her cheeks were bright red and her eyes were glassy. "I've slept too long. We have to be on our way. Get in the buggy, girls. Where is my horse?"

His mother came out of the house and took hold of Willa's arm. "You are feverish, child. You can't travel today."

"I have to go. You don't understand. I have to go or they will take my babies away from me." She staggered closer to John. "I need a horse. Please, get my horse."

He looked at his mother, and she shook her head. He spoke softly to Willa. "You can't go until you are better. The girls are fine. See?"

He stepped aside so she could see them. "No one is going to take them. They are safe here. Go back into the house, where it's warm."

She clasped her arms across her chest. A shiver racked her body. A second later, her eyes rolled back in her head and she collapsed. He managed to catch her before she hit the ground.

He headed toward the house with her in his arms. By the time he reached the steps, her eyes fluttered open. She pushed against his chest. "I'm fine. Put me down."

"You aren't fine and you aren't going anywhere except back to bed. You will stay there until my mother tells you that you may get up. Is that understood?"

"I need to get to Hope Springs tonight. I can't let the children spend another night on the road." He barely heard her hoarse whisper.

"You can't get to Hope Springs before nightfall. It's a two-day trip from here."

"That can't be."

"Your horse must have carried you many miles out of your way. You can send a letter to your family, telling them that you have been delayed. Or I can use the neighborhood phone and call them if you will give me a number. That way they won't be worrying about you."

She closed her eyes and shook her head. "They aren't expecting me."

He stood aside so his mother could open the door for him. "That's *goot*. They can be just as surprised and happy to see you when you are well. Now, back to bed with you."

She closed her eyes. "You are very bossy."

He fought back a smile. "And you are very stubborn."

"So I have been told," she whispered before her head lolled to the side, and he knew she was asleep again.

She didn't rouse when he laid her on the bed. He stepped back and thrust his hands in his pockets. Her daughters crept in behind him. Lucy tugged on the hem of his coat. "Mama sick?"

Willa looked small and vulnerable lying beneath the thick quilt. He wanted to see her standing strong with that stubborn chin jutting out. He nodded. "*Ja*, I think she is very sick."

Megan squeezed past him, grasped her mother's hand and tugged on it. "Mama get up."

His mother scowled at him and leaned down to reassure Megan, slipping her arm around the child's shoulders. "Your *mamm* just needs to rest. *Kumm*, we must let her sleep. You are all going to stay with us for a few days. Won't that be nice?"

"Feed cows again?" Lucy asked.

"*Ja*. Tomorrow John will let you feed all the animals again. Now it's time to make our own supper. Go into the kitchen. I'll be there in a minute. You may each have a cookie from the plate that is on the counter."

The girls reluctantly left the bedroom. John followed his mother down the hall. "You sound positively delighted to have this family of strangers stay on for days."

"I am."

"Well, I'm not. I haven't been able to get a single piece of work done today."

She stopped and turned to face him. "You have done nothing but work yourself half to death for the past four years."

"You speak as if that is a poor thing."

"Work is all well and good, but you've forgotten how to have a little fun now and again."

"I know how to have fun." His mother was being ridiculous.

"What was the last thing you did simply for the fun of it?" She stared at him with her arms crossed.

"I enjoy my work. It is fun to me."

"You can't think of anything, can you?"

He shook his finger at her. "If they do stay another day, you will keep the chatterboxes occupied while I get caught up on my work. A forge is no place for such wild *kinder*."

"They aren't wild."

"Maybell will disagree with you."

"I will keep them. All you had to do was ask." She smiled sweetly, and he saw exactly how tomorrow was going to turn out. It would be a repeat of today.

"The first thing on my list will be repairing their buggy so they can leave."

"If *Gott* wishes them to go, they will go. If He wishes them to stay, they will stay." His mother turned away and walked into the kitchen.

Chapter Four

❧

Willa stretched her stiff and aching muscles, then snuggled down beneath the warm quilt again, reluctant to open her eyes. If only she could stay asleep for a few more minutes. Just a few more.

"You're awake, I see."

The familiar voice put an end to Willa's wishful thinking. She turned her head and found John's mother sitting in a rocker beside the bed. There was daylight pouring through the window. "What time is it?"

Pushing to her feet, Vera patted Willa's shoulder. "Time to eat something. I'll be back in a minute with your tray. I hope you like strong tea. I never could drink coffee while I was pregnant."

"You don't need to coddle me," Willa said, but Vera was already out the door.

Willa sat up in bed and pushed her hair back from her face. Her chest ached from coughing and her throat was scratchy, but she didn't intend to stay in bed another day as much as she wished she could.

"This is not coddling. It's plain common sense," Vera said as she returned with a tray of tea and cinnamon toast. "The more you rest, the sooner you will be well enough to travel. Perhaps tomorrow."

When Vera finished propping pillows behind Willa, she placed the tray on her lap.

Willa smiled her thanks. "A good night's sleep has done wonders for me. I won't trouble you any longer."

"Eat and then we shall see."

"Where are my daughters?" Willa looked past Vera to the empty hall. She wasn't used to having the girls out of her sight. She couldn't rest easy until she saw them.

"They are helping my son John with the chores. I believe they are gathering the eggs and feeding the chickens."

Willa bit her lower lip. "I'm not sure they will be much help."

Vera chuckled. "I'm sure you are right, but John needs a lesson in patience. *Kinder* are often the best teachers of that virtue."

"I don't want them to annoy him."

Vera moved to the window to look out. "I hope they will. My son has become a stuffy fellow. It will do him good to see the world through the eyes of little ones for a change."

Willa moved the food tray aside. The last thing she wanted was to cause John trouble. He'd been more than kind. "I can't thank you enough for all you've done for us, but I must be going. I still have a long way to travel. Has John had a chance to repair my buggy?"

Willa stood. The room spun wildly. She closed her eyes and pressed a hand to her head as Vera steadied her.

"Sit before you fall down."

"It will pass. I stood up too quickly, that's all."

"*Nee*, this is your babe's way of saying you need more rest. Back in bed and don't try getting up again unless John or I am close by. I don't want to have to pick you up off the floor."

Willa's legs trembled, forcing her to sit on the side of the bed. As much as she hated to admit it, she wasn't going anywhere until she had regained more of her strength. She meekly allowed Vera to tuck her in again. When the dizziness subsided, Willa opened her eyes to find Vera watching her with a worried expression. It had been a long time since anyone had worried over her.

"I'm fine now. Truly I am."

"You will drink your tea and eat your toast, and not another word about leaving. Is that understood?"

"It is," Willa answered, feeling like a scolded child. Vera Miller was clearly used to giving orders and being obeyed.

"*Goot.* Rest today and tomorrow you will feel much better."

After Vera left the room, Willa sipped the tea and nibbled on the toast as she took stock of her situation. She couldn't leave today, and it wouldn't do her any good to argue. She shuddered to think what could have happened yesterday when her horse was trotting unguided along the roads. They were safe for now. The children were being fed and looked after, something she couldn't do herself.

Leaning back against the headboard, she drew a deep breath, pleased that it didn't trigger a coughing fit. The tea was soothing, and it was making her sleepy.

Another day's rest would see her stronger, but she couldn't stay longer than that. Time was growing short. She had to learn if her great-aunt or her cousins would take her and the children in. Her baby was due in less than two months. She had to have a safe place for the girls and her babe before she gave birth. Nothing mattered but protecting them, even from herself.

"How is she?" John asked his mother when he came in. His two terrors followed right behind him. He hoped Willa Lapp was able to travel. Keeping an eye on her two energetic children was exhausting. How did women do it? Between answering their endless questions and keeping them out of harm's way, he was ready to cart them all to Hope Springs himself.

"Willa is resting at the moment, but she is in no shape to travel. She stood at the side of the bed and almost fainted."

He stifled a groan. That wasn't what he wanted to hear. He wanted her to be on her way, but he could hardly push a sick woman out the door. "Then the *kinder* must stay with you the rest of the day. I have work to do and I cannot have them underfoot. They court disaster at every turn."

His mother frowned at him. "That's a harsh thing to say about such darlings."

"Johnjohn's mad," Lucy told her.

John pointed at her. "This one almost tumbled out of the hayloft door. I barely caught her in time. Megan dropped the basket of eggs and broke half of them. And someone left the henhouse door open. I spent the last hour hunting down and catching our chickens."

His mother actually smiled, making him feel foolish for allowing two children to get the better of him. "I wondered what was taking so long. Accidents happen. It's not as if they are going out of their way to annoy you, but I will keep them with me for the rest of the day. Does that make you happy?"

"It does. Very, very happy."

"*Kumm* and *redd-up*, girls."

Megan cocked her head to the side. "What's *redd-up*?"

"It means to clean up. I can't believe John let you get so dirty."

His mouth dropped open. "I let them? I don't know how I could stop them. They crawl under and over and into everything."

"Never mind. A little dirt washes off easily enough. Shall we go in and see your *mamm*? She's been missing you."

"I miss Mama. Need a hug." Megan followed his mother to the kitchen sink and allowed her to wipe her dirty hands and face.

Lucy stood beside him, looking up with sad eyes. "Johnjohn mad at me?"

He blew out a cleansing breath. "*Nee*, I'm not mad at you. Go wash your face."

She smiled brightly. "Okeydokey."

When she wasn't being a bother, she had an engaging way about her. He watched as his mother led them down the hall to the guest room. He had plenty of work waiting but found himself following them instead. He wanted to see for himself that Willa couldn't travel. He wouldn't put it past his mother to keep her abed just to annoy him.

From the doorway he saw Willa propped up in bed. She had her eyes closed, and it looked as though she were sleeping. She was pale with dark circles under her eyes and bright spots of color in her cheeks. Was she still running a fever? Guilt replaced his annoyance. She did look ill.

Her eyes opened as her daughters climbed onto the bed with her. The transformation on her face was amazing. He had seldom seen such radiant joy. It was as if the sun had come out after a fierce storm.

She stretched out her arms and pulled the girls to her sides. "This is what I need to make me feel better. Lovebug hugs."

She gave her affection so freely. He wasn't used to seeing that. Most Amish women were very reserved. Public displays of affection were frowned upon.

Willa caught sight of him. "I hope they haven't been troubling you, John."

"Not a bit." He shoved his hands in his pockets, unsure why he didn't tell her the truth.

"They can be a handful. Two handfuls." She kissed each child on the head. "I see you have your *kapps* on. That's good."

"Where yours?" Megan asked.

Willa brushed a strand of her hair back from her face and looked around. "I'm not sure. Where is my dignity?"

Her tousled curls caught the sunlight shining in and glowed with a warm light that made him want to stretch his hand out and touch them. It wasn't proper for a man to see a woman with her head uncovered. A woman's hair was her crowning glory, meant to be seen only by God and by her husband.

"Here it is," John said, picking up the covering where it had fallen to the floor. He handed it to her, looking away in embarrassment as she finger combed her hair and settled the *kapp* on her head. He shoved his hands in his pockets again.

"Johnjohn's mad at me," Lucy said with a pout and a mournful look in his direction.

"He is? What did you do?" Willa asked.

Lucy cupped a hand to her mother's ear and whispered loudly. "I let the chickies go bye-bye. I'm sorry."

"Oh, dear. I'm sure John has forgiven you. You won't do it again, will you?"

Lucy solemnly shook her head. "Megan broked the eggs."

"On accident." Megan glared at him.

Willa clapped a hand over her mouth. "Oh, John, I'm sorry. You have had your hands full."

He shrugged. "They didn't mean any harm."

"Of course they didn't," his mother said as she slipped past him with a sly grin on her face.

"Rest up," he said to Willa, backing away. "Your horse is fine, and I'll have your buggy fixed in no time."

"Thank you, John. Girls, why don't you stay with me for a little while?"

"Play games?" Megan asked with a bright smile. "Hide-and-seek?"

"Not today. Lucy, there is a book in my backpack on the floor by the window. Will you bring it here, please?"

"I'll get it," John said, quickly crossing the floor. He grasped the backpack by the strap and laid it on the bed beside her.

"Thank you, John. Lucy, you pick the first story. Megan, you can pick the second one. Okay?"

The girls nodded. Lucy peered into the bag and pulled out a tattered children's book. "This one."

"The story about the kitten who lost her mittens. We like this one, don't we?"

Lucy nodded vigorously. "We saw kitties. They runned away."

"Sometimes it takes a while for kittens to learn to like a new person. If you are kind to them, they will soon warm up to you."

"Bad man scared them," Megan said.

John was shocked to see fear widen Willa's eyes. "What bad man? Did you see him?" she demanded.

Megan pointed to John. "Him."

Willa visibly relaxed. "John isn't a bad man. He's a nice fellow."

Megan frowned. "Nice?"

"Very nice." Willa glanced at him and quickly looked away.

He couldn't be sure, but he thought she might be blushing.

Megan didn't look as if she believed her mother.

John pondered Willa's reaction to Megan's words as he walked back to the kitchen. His mother was busy mixing something in a bowl. He checked the stove and found there was still coffee in the pot. He poured himself a cup and leaned his hip against the counter. "Has Willa told you much about herself?"

"*Nee*, and I haven't asked. Why?"

"Something Megan said. She said the bad man scared the kittens. She meant me, but I saw fear on Willa's face."

His mother stopped stirring. "What do you think it means?"

"I don't know. Maybe she is running away from someone."

She started stirring again. "I don't like to think that, but I reckon it's possible."

"Yesterday she said someone was trying to take her babies away."

"She had a high fever, John. She might have been out of her head."

"Maybe, but her fear was real." He took a sip of coffee and grimaced. It was cold.

"What can we do about it?" his mother asked.

He walked to the sink and poured out his cup. "I'm going to fix her buggy so she can leave. We don't need outsider problems."

"I will see what I can find out. If she is in trouble, we must help her."

"If she is in trouble, she must take it with her when she leaves," he insisted. She and her children had disrupted his life enough.

"I don't know how I raised such a hard-hearted man. Your wife would have wanted to help this poor woman."

He cringed inwardly. "Katie's gone."

"So is your father, but you and I are here until *Gott* calls *us* home. What we do with the rest of our lives is important. Hiding in your smithy isn't the way God wants you to live. You are young. You still have time to find love, a wife, a family, if only you would open your heart."

"I tried it your way, remember? It didn't work out."

"Your father and I pressured you to court Rebecca, I admit as much. That was a mistake on our part. It was too soon for you, but because Rebecca loved another is no reason for you to give up on finding happiness."

"I'm happy enough. I don't need a wife. I had one

and God took her from me. What I need is to get back to work." He stormed out of the kitchen, slamming the door behind him.

Chapter Five

Willa cupped her hands over her belly as her baby kicked hard enough to make her wince. "Please don't be in a hurry to arrive," she whispered. "If you give me enough time, I promise to make sure you are safe. I love you so much already."

She looked up to see Vera standing in the doorway. "Is everything all right? I thought I heard the front door slam."

"My son gets tired of my prodding ways and balks like a stubborn mule at times. At least when he does, I know he is paying attention to my ramblings."

"Is he upset because we are here?"

Vera dismissed her suggestion with a wave of her hand. "All things in the world are by the will of *Gott*. You are here because He wishes it. My son will come to that conclusion in time."

Willa smoothed a wrinkle from the cover over her lap. She needed to believe God would protect her, but doubts crept in when she was alone. "I want to believe in His great goodness, but sometimes I wonder how He can allow such sadness in the world."

"His ways are beyond our understanding. His plan is too large for us to see more than a tiny portion of it, but He has a plan for us all."

"Mama, more story." Lucy pushed the book toward Willa.

"In a minute, darling."

Vera sat on the edge of the bed. "I happen to have a box of toys in my bedroom across the hall. It's a big brown wooden box under the window. Would you girls like to look for something to play with? I'm sure I have a doll for each of you in there."

"Yeah." Megan slid off the bed and Lucy quickly followed her.

Vera watched them go and then turned to Willa. "What kind of trouble are you in?"

Taken aback by Vera's bluntness, Willa tried to stall until she could decide what to say. "Why do you ask that?"

"So you *are* in trouble."

"I didn't say I was."

"You didn't say you weren't. Tell me about it. I want to help."

"I'm not— It's not— It's nothing that involves you." Willa stared out the window.

"John and I will help if we can."

Willa looked at the kindly face of the woman beside her. "I believe you would. If there was a way for you to help me, I would tell you, but there isn't anything you can do."

"I could be the judge of that if I knew what was wrong. What are you afraid of? Is it your husband? Not all men are kind."

"My husband was a gentle man. He'd never hurt anyone."

"So who brings the fear to your eyes that my son says he has seen?"

John was more perceptive than Willa expected. Maybe it was because she was still so tired, but she found she needed to confide in someone. "If you must know, my husband's parents want to take my daughters away from me. They say I'm an unfit mother."

Vera drew back. "How can they do such a thing?"

"They have money and influence. They say the law is on their side. I'm not a bad mother. I'm not." She was too ashamed to tell Vera about her past illness. Tears welled up in Willa's eyes. It all seemed so hopeless. She couldn't even get out of bed, let alone protect those dearest to her.

"The *Englisch* lawmen look for you, also?"

Willa nodded.

"Is this why you are pretending to be Amish?"

"I didn't know what else to do. I had very little money. I bought bus tickets for us to the town near where my grandfather has a farm. I got off before we reached it. That is where I first met John."

Vera's eyes widened. "You have met my son before?"

"Just once. It was after we left the bus. He was kind enough to give us a ride on his wagon so the girls didn't have to walk so far."

"I wonder that he didn't mention this," Vera said more to herself than to Willa. "Why didn't you stay with your *daddi*?"

Willa looked away. "Grandfather wouldn't take us in. He didn't believe that I wanted to become Amish again. He said I should have returned sooner."

"That is shameful. We are to welcome those who wish to return to us. The Lord will judge his actions one day. He should remember that."

Willa gave her a watery smile. "Don't think too harshly of him. He gave us these Amish clothes and told me to go to his sister, who lives near Hope Springs. He said if I truly repent and join the faith, I may return to him."

"At least he had some kindness for you. Will your great-aunt take you in?"

"I don't know." Willa's voice broke. She pressed her hands to her mouth to hold back a sob. Crying wouldn't help. It never helped.

Vera sighed heavily. "This is a difficult situation. It will take much prayer to see the path our Lord wishes us to follow. It is not right to keep your *kinder* from their grandparents, but I understand why you feel you must. Have you spoken with them? Are you sure of their intentions?"

"My husband spoke to them. He told me he couldn't change their minds. They have a man searching for us, a private detective. He was always able to find us, and each time we were forced to move again. I don't know how he found us in Columbus, but he did. I went out to buy some milk for the girls, and when I came back to the apartment, the woman next door said the police and this man had been there looking for me. She had promised to call them when I returned, but she said she didn't promise to call them right away." Willa laughed at the memory of the elderly Mrs. Kramer's daring, but her laugh held an edge of hysteria. She had come so close to losing her babies.

She thanked God for a half gallon of milk and the

unconventional spirited old woman who had lived beside them. In some ways, Vera reminded Willa of Mrs. Kramer. She had the same sharp look in her aged eyes. "You and your son have been kind to me, as well. I can never repay you."

"Your prayers for us are repayment enough. God moves in strange ways, but He has brought you here for a reason," Vera muttered.

She stood and laid a hand on Willa's cheek. "This detective will not find you. We Amish are in the world, but we are not a part of this world. We have our own ways and they serve us well, for we serve *Gott* first."

"I hope and pray he doesn't find us. I have to believe my great-aunt will help. I want my children to celebrate this Christmas and many more with my family."

"One of the Bowman sons is married to a woman from Hope Springs. She may know your family. This man is looking for an *Englisch* woman and her daughters, *ja*?"

"He is."

Vera patted Willa's arm. "Get some rest. No one will take your *kinder* while you sleep. There is only an Amish *frau* and her daughters visiting us if anyone should ask."

Willa rubbed her face with both hands. "I'm afraid we won't pass for Amish if anyone looks closely."

"Then no one must look closely. In time you will become more Amish and so will your little ones."

Time wasn't on Willa's side, but her daughters were safe for now. Her body and mind craved rest. She snuggled down under the quilt again. She heard Megan and Lucy arguing over a doll in the other room, but be-

fore she could get up, Vera intervened and the squab-
ble ended.

What would John make of Willa's story when his
mother filled him in on the details? She knew Vera
would tell him. Among the Amish, the man was the
head of the house. All important decisions were made
by men. Women had their say, to be sure, but it would
be up to John to allow Willa to stay or to inform the
police of her whereabouts.

It was a relief to have that much of her past out in
the open, but she didn't dare try to explain why Glen's
family feared for the children's welfare. Willa wouldn't
hurt them, not knowingly, but what might happen if the
voices came back after her baby was born? Someone
had to keep them safe if she wasn't able to care for them.
The Amish valued God first, family second and then
the community. They cared for their own. She prayed
her great-aunt's family would provide all she needed.

John came in from the outside and wiped his feet
on the mat. His mother was standing beside the table
staring at him with a deep frown etched between her
brows. She tapped one foot as she waited for him to
speak. Whatever she was upset about, he was sure it was
something to do with that woman. The one he couldn't
stop thinking about. The one with golden curls who
gave lovebug kisses.

"I know that look, *Mamm*. What is on your mind?"

"Why didn't you tell me you had met Willa before?"

"It didn't seem important." He took off his coat and
hung up his hat. When he looked her way, she hadn't
moved.

"Not important? The Lord places this stranger, this

desperate young mother, into your care twice in a single week, and you don't think that is important enough to mention?"

"I admit it is a strange coincidence, but that's all. She's leaving. Her own family will take care of her as soon as she reaches them. What's for lunch?"

"Don't change the subject."

"The subject of that woman and her children is closed. Her buggy has been repaired. Her horse is rested, but the poor creature isn't up to a long trip. I will send the family on their way with one of our horses."

"You have more concern for an animal than you do for that poor child. She is not up to a long journey, either."

"What do you want me to do? She needs to be with her own family during this time. I can't spare four days away from my work to drive her to Hope Springs and then drive back. I'm not going to pay for a driver to take her. We can't afford it."

"You may be right about that."

He hadn't expected her to give in. "I am."

"She can write to her family and ask if they will send the money. In the meantime, she can get plenty of rest and regain her strength, and I will have the chance to enjoy her darling daughters. It shouldn't take more than a week."

"*Mamm, I* don't want her here."

"And why is that?"

Did he have to spell it out? He clenched his jaw until his teeth ached. If his mother needed the hard truth, he would give it. "She's a reminder."

"A reminder of what?" his mother asked gently.

"That Katie and I could have given you grandchil-

dren by now if God had spared her life. She is a reminder of how unfair life is."

"My poor son, I know your grief is deep. So is mine.
So is Willa's. Life seems unfair because we do not understand God's great plan for us. We grieve and that is
as it should be, but life must be more than grief and sorrow. If that is all you look for, that is all you will find."

She was wrong. He wanted to feel anything but this
crushing sorrow. There simply wasn't room in his heart
for joy. Willa and her daughters were painful remind-
ers of that fact every time he saw them.

He wasn't narrow-minded enough to think he was
the only person to have suffered the loss of a loved one.
His mother didn't need to point that out. He pitied Willa,
for her loss was as great as his. How did she face each
new day? How did she find the strength to get out of
bed each morning? Was it because of her daughters? It
was something he'd never be able to ask her.

In truth, he didn't want to know anything else about
her. He didn't want to feel sorry for her or know she
struggled as hard as he did to keep his feelings hidden.
He didn't want to like her children or listen to Lucy tell
him "okeydokey" with that silly, adorable grin on her
face. He didn't want Megan to like him even a little. He
wanted to be left alone.

He yanked his coat off the hook and put it on, then
jammed his hat on his head. "Don't worry about making me anything for supper. I'll be in the workshop. I
parked Willa's buggy close to the house. Make whatever
preparations you need to see that they can travel comfortably, but they are leaving in the morning."

John pulled open the door without waiting for his
mother to reply. A few snowflakes drifted lazily down

around him. The weather forecast in the newspaper that morning had called for occasional flurries. Hopefully it wouldn't amount to much, and his guest could leave as planned.

He spent the next six hours sweating over his forge and shaping the lantern housings he needed for Melvin's sleigh. He finally managed to finish one he was happy with. He should have known better than to try to work when his mind was filled with thoughts of Willa and her problems. At his current rate of speed, it would take him a full year to finish all the work the new sleigh needed. He was bone tired and hungry. He took a deep breath and prepared to go in. He was sure his mother would be waiting up for him. She would be asleep in her chair in the living room, but she never failed to wake up when the door opened.

Opening his workshop door, he saw a light layer of snow coated everything. Streams of it snaked across the ground in the wind and piled up against the side of the buildings, but it wasn't falling at the moment. Willa's buggy sat near the front gate, topped with a white crown. He took the time to brush it off before he went in.

To his surprise, his mother wasn't waiting up. He had braced himself for another argument for no reason. He found a plate of roast beef sandwiches in the refrigerator along with a slice of pumpkin pie topped with fresh whipped cream. It was his favorite. He chuckled as he recognized his mother's way of apologizing.

On his way to bed, he passed his mother's bedroom door and heard the sound of her snoring. He paused outside Willa's door to listen but didn't hear any movement within. He opened the next door softly and looked inside. His mother had made up two cots for the twins, but they were both asleep in one bed with their arms around each other. He closed the door and went to his room at the end of the hall. In spite of his fatigue, he barely slept. A little before six o'clock he rose and got dressed. His mother was in the kitchen. The smell of coffee and frying bacon filled the morning.

Willa sat at the table with a white mug in her hands. She blushed and looked down when she caught sight of him. "Good morning, John."

"Guder mariye," he muttered. She looked more rested, but he couldn't say she looked well. There were still dark shadows beneath her eyes and a hollow look to her cheeks.

"We will be on our way as soon as we have finished eating. Hurry up, girls."

"I'm done," Lucy announced, holding both hands in the air.

John waited for his mother to make some comment, but she didn't. He put on his hat, determined not to feel like he was tossing a bird with a broken wing out into the snow. "I'll hitch up the horse."

Outside, he brought out his best and gentlest buggy horse, a black mare named Clover. She was reliable and steady in traffic. He backed her into place and hitched her to the buggy. He turned to see his mother coming out of the house with a wicker hamper over her arm. Lucy followed her, chatting away and skipping. His mother put the basket down and motioned to him. "Give me a hand with this, John. It's heavy."

His mother was probably sending a week's worth of food with the family for a two-day trip. He started to lead Clover toward her when he heard a loud crack.

Clover jumped forward. The front wheels of the buggy pulled completely out from under it. The cab toppled to the ground as he looked on in astonishment.

Lucy clapped both hands to her cheeks. "Oh, no! Johnjohn broked it!"

His mother smothered a laugh. "He certainly did."

"This isn't funny." He struggled to control the confused horse.

"Lucy, go back inside and tell your *mamm* that you'll all be staying a little longer."

"Okeydokey." Lucy whirled around and ran into the house.

His mother looked up and held out one hand. "I do believe it's beginning to snow."

Chapter Six

"So this is where you've been hiding."

Willa stepped inside John's workshop and shook the snow from her shawl. It had been coming down heavily since early morning, big fat flakes that stuck to everything and piled up fast. Warmth surrounded her inside the building with a low ceiling and tools of John's trade everywhere. The smell of smoke and hot metal filled the air. She peeled off her gloves and tucked them in the pockets of her apron.

John sat at a small desk near the south-facing window with an open ledger book in front of him. "I'm not hiding."

"Perhaps not, but I feel as though we have driven you out of your own house." Willa tightened the black shawl across her shoulders. He hadn't come in since her buggy came apart that morning. The buggy pieces had been moved into the barn, but John hadn't offered any information on the repairs that were needed or how long it might take. Vera had sent Willa to check on him as it was almost time for supper. It was easy to see he didn't want their continued company, but she and the girls wouldn't be able to travel until her vehicle was fixed. Maybe not even then if the snow kept up much longer.

He closed the book he had been writing in. "I've had a lot of work to catch up on, that's all."

"Have you fixed our buggy?"

"Not yet. I seem to be missing the exact parts I need. I'm sure I had some of the same size carriage bolts last week. I can't imagine where they have gone."

"Can't you make some?"

"Not easily. They have to be the right size down to the millimeter."

She looked around the room. Horseshoes of every size hung from pegs on one wall. Assorted tools were lined up in a metal rack. A huge anvil stood near the furnace. The forge itself was a brick structure that resembled a large table with a hood over it and which had a depression where a low fire burned. At the rear of the building were open wooden shelves that held stacks of long steel rods. "I'm afraid I don't know much about the blacksmith trade. A blacksmith's shop is called a smithy, am I right?"

"You are." He busied himself choosing a round steel rod from the stack.

"I see you use coal for your fire. Why not propane? Vera mentioned your church approves the use of some propane appliances and generators."

"A few blacksmiths use propane. I prefer coal or coke as it is called. I get better heat and a coke forge has an advantage because it can be scaled easily."

"What does that mean?"

"It means I can make the fire larger or smaller depending upon my needs."

She moved closer to the forge, where a bed of coal

glowed bright red. She had to take a step back as the heat scorched her face. "How hot does it get?"

"Very hot. About fourteen hundred degrees, but there are times when I need it hotter or colder."

"Hotter than fourteen hundred degrees?"

"Welding requires more heat."

"No wonder you don't allow the girls out here. Lucy is quite brokenhearted that she can't watch you work."

"It's too dangerous. Her pouting will not sway me."

She walked over to the anvil and ran her fingers along the curved surface. "Thank you for that. It must feel good to pound away your frustrations out here."

"If I am frustrated, I clean my shop and go do something else. A clear mind means good work. If I make something when I'm distracted, it often goes in the scrap barrel for another day." He gestured toward a fifty-gallon drum in the corner.

She saw a number of metal pieces sticking out of it. "I hope we are not the cause of these failed projects."

He ignored her comment. "Blacksmithing is about control, not about power or strength. Sometimes I must hit the metal hard, but it is more important to hit the metal as accurately as I can. When I first started working beside my father in this shop, he drew an X on the anvil. He said, 'Strike here only. Move your work, not your hammer. Chasing it around the anvil will result in a ruined piece.' He was right."

"It sounds difficult to me."

"Like everything worthwhile, it comes with time and practice."

"What happens if you make a mistake?"

"There are no mistakes."

It was her turn to smile. "Are you that good?"

He shook his head. "Metal can be reused. If I botch a piece, I simply give it another chance as something else." He crossed to the forge and pumped the bellows, making the coals glow hotter.

"What are you making today?"

"Cabinet pulls. I sell them at Luke Bowman's hardware store. He has ordered twenty of them."

"Will it annoy you if I watch?"

He shrugged. "I don't mind."

"Explain to me what you are doing?" He definitely seemed more relaxed out here among his tools.

"A blacksmith needs four basic things. A way to heat his work. A way to hold his work. Something to put under his work and a way to apply forces to his work."

"Let me guess. The forge is for heating things."

A smile tugged at the corner of his mouth. "Very *goot*. I heat my work with a forge. Forges need fuel and air, lots of air, hence the bellows."

She gestured to the array of long-handled tools. "These pincher things are for holding your work."

"Tongs, and you're half right. I hold things with tongs but also with vises or clamps. There are a number of different tongs for holding various shapes."

He picked one up. "This tong is made for holding a half-inch square rod, but it won't work if I try to hold a round rod. A flat piece of stock requires that one." He pointed to the tong on the end. "I have to be able to hold tight to the hot steel when I hit it. A good vise is also an important tool. Not a cheap one that you can buy in an *Englisch* store, but one made for heavy-duty work."

She patted the anvil. "I assume since this is bolted down that it goes under your hot metal."

"Right once again. This is a finely designed tool. It

also belonged to my father. You'll notice it has two holes in it. They are called the pritchel and the hardy hole. A pritchel is used for punching through a piece of metal. It also holds the work steady so it doesn't distort when I start punching. The hardy holds cold tools. I use a V-block to put a bend in a piece or make a curved shape. The horn, the pointy end of the anvil, is used for curving metal around it."

It was much more information than Willa really wanted to know, but she was interested because he was interested. She could tell it was more than his job. It was his passion.

He brought a length of steel rod to the table and placed one end in the fire. In a matter of minutes, he had cut the glowing metal into several shorter lengths. Then he twisted them into a spiral pattern and punched out the screw holes for a set of nearly identical cabinet pull handles.

"You make it look easy."

"A piece this size is easy."

"So you say. Thank you for the demonstration. It was very interesting." She picked up several of the horseshoes. "My husband would have loved this place," she said softly.

"What did he do? Does it bother you to talk about him?" he added quickly.

She smiled softly. "Talking about Glen doesn't bother me. He was an amazing person in my life. I can't pretend he didn't exist because he's gone now. The pain of his loss is with me if I talk about him or not. Does that make sense?"

"It does."

"Glen didn't have a craft the way you do. His passion

was horses. Funny, isn't it? He wasn't Amish, but he loved working around the trotters and pacers we use to pull our buggies. Whenever we had to move, he always went to the local racetracks to find a job. He could talk for hours about this horse's stats or why that horse's jockey wasn't the best fit. And horseshoes. He knew a lot about horseshoes and how they make a horse run better, the same way a good pair of track shoes makes a human sprinter run faster."

She noticed John watching her closely. "I'm sorry. I haven't had anyone I could talk to about Glen since he died. The girls won't remember him in a few years. I don't know how to keep his memory alive for them except through my memories. He went out to the corner store to pick up a loaf of bread because I had forgotten to get some that afternoon."

She had just learned she was pregnant after a visit to the local free clinic. She'd been too upset to remember the bread. She'd never got up the nerve to tell Glen he was going to be a father again.

"What happened?"

There was so much compassion in John's voice that it brought tears to her eyes. She turned away so he wouldn't see them. "He was struck and killed by a speeding car as he crossed the street. They never found the driver."

"You miss him." It was a statement of fact, not a question. She appreciated that.

She took a deep breath. "I do. Every day. Just as I know you must miss your wife."

He nodded. "As you say, every day."

Willa saw the pain in his eyes and wanted to offer any comfort she could. "What was she like? I know the

Amish don't normally talk about the loved ones they have lost, but I'm willing to listen."

A hint of a smile touched his lips. "She was a little like you."

"Like me how? Short with blond hair and big feet?"

"*Nee*, she was tall and willowy with thick glossy brown hair and gray-green eyes, and I don't think you have big feet."

"Then why do you say she was like me?"

"She had your...attitude. I think that is the word I want."

"What kind of attitude do I have?" She expected him to say small and timid.

"I've seen you stick out your chin like you are daring the world to stand in your way."

His answer surprised her. "My husband called it my stubborn streak."

"*Ja*. That's exactly what I called Katie's attitude when she wanted something done her way. I think she would have liked you, Willa Lapp."

It was an unexpected compliment. "It's a shame you didn't have children. They make it easier sometimes. When I want to lie down and weep, I can't because I have to take care of my girls."

The smile vanished from his face. He stared at the fire in his forge. "Katie was pregnant with our first child when she was killed."

Willa pressed a hand to her chest. Her heart actually ached for him. There were no words to express her sympathy, so she remained quiet. The only sounds were the crackle of the fire and the moaning wind rising outside.

After a few moments, John spoke again. "We had an argument that afternoon. She wanted to go to an ice-skating party with some of our friends. I thought it was a bad idea. I forbade it. She ignored me. She hitched up her pony cart and drove away. I should have stopped her. I should have reasoned with her instead of putting my foot down. I knew how stubborn she could be."

He held his hand toward the fire. "I should have gone with her. Her cart was struck by a pickup at the end of our lane. I saw it happening, and I couldn't do anything to stop it."

Drawn to his pain, Willa stepped close and gently pulled his hand away from the heat. "I'm sorry. It is a terrible thing to endure."

John fastened his gaze on her small fingers where they rested on his arm. She didn't tell him it was God's will. She didn't say his wife and child were in a better place and that he would see them again if he lived a devout life. He didn't want to hear those words. He'd heard them so often they no longer held any meaning.

Willa simply said she was sorry. She understood—he felt it in the gentle touch of her hand. She didn't make light of his pain or his guilt. How could this stranger understand him so well?

His mother had lost a son and her husband of forty years not long afterward, but she carried on. He knew her grief was real—he grieved for them, too—but she faced it differently. He didn't have his mother's strength. Maybe he didn't have her faith.

He looked at Willa. "You should get back to the house. *Mamm* will start to worry about you if you are gone too long. The weather is getting worse. You might not be traveling for a day or two even after I fix your buggy."

"I'm sorry you are stuck with us, but we will be leaving sooner or later. I need to reach my great-aunt and her family before this baby arrives." Her expression grew somber, and he wondered why. He thought all mothers looked forward to the arrival of their children with joy.

"Is everything okay with your babe?"

She placed a hand on her belly and rubbed in slow circles. "I pray it is. I pray every day and night."

He longed to chase the worry from her eyes and reassure her. "God hears your prayers, and He will answer them."

"I know." She looked up and smiled. "Your mother wants you to come in for supper. I'm to drag you there by the ear if I must."

He laughed. "I would like to see you try. You're no bigger than a mouse."

She flexed her arm. "I have more muscle than you think. Don't forget, I've been picking up two toddlers for ages. That's a workout. Hammering a horseshoe is nothing compared to the strength it takes to stop Lucy from bolting. Hauling you in by the ear would be a piece of cake compared to managing those two."

"I won't put you to the test, although I might challenge you to arm wrestle in the future just to prove you wrong."

"Not on an empty stomach, please. I'm starving. Come in the house."

"As soon as I've put out my fire."

"I'll wait for you." She raised the heavy shawl over her head and pulled on her gloves.

A familiar beeping broke the stillness in the room.

"What is that?" Willa asked.

"My pager." He pulled the device from the waistband of his pants and read the scrolling message it displayed.

"Blacksmiths need pagers?"

"They do if they are part of the volunteer fire department," he said.

"Is there a fire?"

"*Nee*, it was only a message telling me they have rescheduled our meeting with the county emergency management folks for Saturday afternoon."

"That's a blessing. It would be rough weather to fight a fire."

"There is no good weather for a fire." He clipped the pager back on his waistband and tidied his shop. After making sure the fire was out, he held the door open for Willa. A fierce gust of wind hit, knocking her back against him. He caught her by the shoulders and steadied her. He could barely make out the light from the window across the way. "Take care. This is worse than I thought."

She turned her face away from the wind. "I can't see the house. We might become lost if we go out into this."

He grasped her gloved hand. "We won't. I can see the light in the kitchen window. Hang on to me. I don't want us to get separated."

She tucked her chin into the folds of the shawl. "Promise you won't let go."

He squeezed her hand. "I promise. You are safe with me."

She tightened her grip and nodded. "I trust you, John Miller."

Willa woke the next morning to the sound of the wind roaring outside and snow hissing against the window in her bedroom. The storm was still in progress. She smiled as she sat up, feeling more rested than she had in ages. No one would find her today.

Her son or daughter kicked against her ribs, making her sit up straighter. She smiled and patted her belly. "Someone else is feeling better, too."

Her stomach rumbled, and Willa realized she was famished. "Maybe you're trying to tell me you are hungry. You're going to be a roly-poly little thing if we stay here much longer. Vera's roasted chicken and biscuits last night were the best I've ever had."

Tossing back the quilt, she slipped out of bed and dressed quickly in the cold room, grateful for the woolen leggings Vera had loaned her. Willa paused to pray that her own family would be as welcoming and as kind as the Millers had been.

After checking on her daughters and finding them sleeping, Willa made her way to the kitchen by lamplight. The rest of the house was quiet. Neither John nor Vera appeared to be up yet. Willa lowered the chain that held the pair of ceiling lamps and lit their mantles with long matches from a holder on the wall. She raised the lamps again and a warm glow illuminated the room.

Rubbing her hands together to warm them, she turned her attention to food and began rummaging through the kitchen cupboards and refrigerator. She came up with the ingredients for a Spanish omelet. She hummed as she whipped the eggs, diced the potatoes and dried peppers, and heated the oil in a skillet. It was wonderful to be free of worry—at least for a day.

She had shelter and warmth, her daughters were sleeping snug in their beds and she had the run of a well-stocked kitchen. It had been so long since she'd had these most basic elements that she refused to think about what the future held and simply enjoyed the moment.

She was slipping the omelet onto a plate when John walked into the room. "Something smells good."

"Would you like a Spanish omelet? It will only take me a few minutes to make you one." She considered offering him hers but couldn't bring herself to do it.

"Eat yours before it gets cold. I'll have coffee for now."

She was too hungry to argue with him. "I'm afraid I haven't made any. Coffee doesn't agree with me now. This is sad because I normally love coffee."

"Will it bother you if I make some?"

"Not at all."

"*Goot*, because I need a cup or four." He ran a hand through his hair, leaving it sticking up every which way.

Willa was tempted to smooth it for him but resisted the urge. "Did you figure out how to fix my grandfather's buggy?"

"I need to replace several large bolts that are missing from the frame and fifth wheel, the mechanism that allows the front wheels to turn in the same direction that the horse does. I wonder how my mother managed to get them off?"

Willa paused with her fork halfway to her mouth. "You don't really think your mother crawled under the buggy and loosened those bolts, do you? We could have been hurt if it had come apart while we were traveling. She wouldn't risk that."

"It wouldn't have rolled a foot the way it was. Someone knew what she was doing. I know Lucy and Megan couldn't have done it. That leaves my mother or you, and I'm willing to give you the benefit of the doubt considering your condition." He began spooning coffee grounds into the percolator.

"Couldn't they have simply worn out over time and fallen off yesterday? It is an old buggy. My grandfather never was one to invest in equipment upkeep. Is there any ketchup?"

He opened the refrigerator door, pulled out a bottle and handed it to her. "That possibility exists, but I didn't find any broken bolts on the ground. As I said, it wouldn't have rolled more than a few inches before coming apart. I drove it over beside the house myself after I fixed the loose rear wheel. It seems unlikely that my mother removed the bolts and hid the ones I keep in my shop, but I can't put it past her. She was adamant that you and the children stay longer."

"She has been very sweet to us. The girls have taken a great liking to her." Willa squeezed a liberal amount of ketchup onto her eggs.

"Is that good for the baby?"

"Is what good for the baby?" She forked a bite into her mouth and closed her eyes. Delicious. She cut herself another piece.

"That." He pointed to her plate. "The peppers and onions and all that ketchup."

She shrugged. "Plenty of babies are born in Spain, so I assume Spanish omelets are safe for pregnant women."

"There are some antacid tablets in the medicine cabinet if you need them later."

She sat up straight and burped. "Thanks. I may need them, but it tastes so good I can't stop."

"I don't see how you have any room left for food after the way you ate last night. I've never seen a woman eat so many biscuits. You had six after eating half a chicken."

Her mouth dropped open. "In case you haven't noticed, I'm eating for two!"

"Are you sure there aren't more? Like five or six?"

"That's an awful thing to say."

"What are you two quarreling about at this hour of the morning?" Vera asked as she came into the room.

John gestured toward Willa. "She's determined to eat us out of house and home. Lock the cellar and hide the key so she can't get to the canned produce."

Willa finished her eggs and pushed back from the table. "Do you have canned peaches? Oh, that sounds so good."

Vera chuckled. "I do, and John will fetch them for you."

He headed toward the cellar door. "Shall I bring up a dozen jars, or do you think you'll need more?"

"A dozen will do for a start," she said with a chuckle.

"I have some material in my sewing room that I want you to look over to see if you can use any of it," Vera said.

Willa was still smiling at John's teasing as she followed Vera down the hall. To her surprise, she saw several framed photographs on Vera's dresser as she glanced through the open door to Vera's bedroom. Stepping inside, Willa saw the photographs were all family portraits of parents with four children, three boys and one girl who looked to be the same age as her daughters.

"Those are my *Englisch* daughter, her husband and their children," Vera explained.

"Does your bishop allow photographs?" Willa had never heard of such a thing.

"As long as I don't keep them on public display, he allows it. My daughter's family lives on the West Coast and I seldom get to see them, but she makes sure that I get at least two family photographs each year."

"Your church group is very progressive. My grandfather's church would shun anyone who kept photographs."

"I don't allow photographs to be taken of myself, but one of the girls at the local school is a talented artist. She has sketched likenesses of John and me. I plan to give them to my daughter. They are coming the week after Christmas and plan to stay for two weeks this year. I'm so excited to see them. It's been four years since I last saw all of them." Her smile faded and sadness filled her eyes. "Not since my oldest son's funeral."

"You lost a son? I'm sorry, I didn't know."

"No reason why you should."

"John told me about his wife last night and how she died."

Vera set the photograph back on the dresser. "Did he? That is a surprise. I knew you needed to stay with us for a reason."

Willa tipped her head to the side. "You didn't rig our buggy to break so we couldn't leave, did you?"

"What a silly question. I'd better get started on breakfast for everyone. Look through the material in the next room and let me know if you can use any of it. We will have to buy snow pants and boots for the children. Ana Bowman stocks a small selection in her gift store."

"I don't have any money to buy their clothing. I can't accept more charity when you have already given us so much."

"That is your *Englisch* pride speaking. Shame on you. An Amish woman is humble before the Lord and the world, and she accepts help without quibbling. The girls need warm clothing. We are commanded to care for widows and orphans by our faith. You shall have what you need. I don't want to hear another word about the cost. The day will come when you are able to help someone in return. Is that understood?"

Being humble was harder than Willa remembered, but she nodded.

"*Goot.* I think I have enough green worsted wool to make the girls overcoats and I know I have enough white organdy to make several *kapps* for you and the girls. If you are going to become Amish, you and your children must have more than one set of Amish clothes to wear. You will have to help me with some of the sewing. My hands ache something dreadful today."

Willa realized Vera hadn't answered her question about the buggy, but she didn't press the issue. After all, she and her girls were safe and being well cared for, at least until the storm was over. Soon they would have to move on, but not today.

Willa remembered John's teasing that morning and realized she was going to miss him as much as his mother when she did leave. Maybe more.

When had she come to like him so much?

Chapter Seven

"Johnjohn, will you play with me?"

John looked up from his magazine that afternoon to see Lucy standing in front of his chair staring at him. "I'm busy. Play with your sister."

He started reading again. He hadn't seen Willa or his mother for several hours, but he had been out plowing the lane after the wind had subsided. Nick Bradley would have had a hard time getting in to pick him up for the meeting even with his four-wheel-drive vehicle. Some of the drifts had been four feet deep, but Pete and Jake had no trouble breaking through them.

He glanced out the window. The winter landscape was brilliant and sparkling under a thick layer of pristine snow. The sky was clear and blue without a trace of clouds. The snowstorm had ended before dawn after blowing for two days. His mother and Willa had vanished into his mother's sewing room for much of that time. He had spent most of the gray daylight hours in his workshop and had accomplished a goodly amount of work. He had an hour to catch up on his reading before the fire department meeting this evening.

Lucy tapped his knee. "Read me a story, please," she said again with added emphasis on the *please*.

He chose the safest answer he could think of. "Go ask your mother."

"Mama is sleeping. Story, please."

Willa was sleeping. That was a good thing. She needed her rest. "Then go ask my mother."

Lucy gave an exasperated sigh.

Megan was lying on the oval rug in front of the sofa stacking wooden blocks. "She say ask you."

He hadn't seen anything in his blacksmithing journal he felt would interest a three-year-old. "Lucy, I don't have a storybook for you."

"No story?" Lucy stuck out her lower lip. Were tears next?

Please, not that. Maybe he didn't need a book. "I reckon I could tell you a story instead of reading one. Will that work, Lucy?"

"Okeydokey." She crawled onto his lap before he could think of a way to stop her.

She held out her hand to Megan. "Sissy, come listen to story."

Megan eyed him with distrust and shook her head.

John gave her the distance she seemed to need. "Megan can hear the story just fine where she is." Now all he had to do was think of one.

"See my new dress?" Lucy smoothed the vibrant blue material that matched her eyes. He hadn't noticed before, but Megan was wearing an identical new outfit, as well. Their old dresses had been oversize and a dull gray color.

"I see, and Megan has a new dress, too. You both look very nice and very plain."

It was true. Their hair was parted in the middle and held back with blue plastic clips that peeked from beneath their snowy-white *kapps*. Their *kapps*, which were the right size, and for once they were both wearing them. They were two very Amish-looking children.

Lucy folded her hands together and gazed up at him. "Once upon a time…"

She was persistent if nothing else. He chuckled. "Who is telling this story, you or me?"

"You. Once upon a time…"

He leaned back and looked at the ceiling. He'd never told a child a story before. Where did he start? Perhaps with something they would recognize.

"Once upon a time…" He paused to grin at Lucy. She smiled back.

"Once upon a time there were two little girls who came to visit an Amish farm. They were sisters. The Amish word for sister is *shveshtah*." It wouldn't hurt for them to start learning the language if their mother intended to raise them in the faith.

Lucy rolled the strange word around on her tongue. John smothered a smile. "The sisters came to the farm in a buggy pulled by a *gual*, a horse. The sisters decided to visit the animals in the barn. What animals do you think they saw?"

"A cat!" Lucy shouted.

"That's right. They saw a fluffy yellow *katz*. They wanted to pet her, but she ran away to chase mice. What else did the girls see?"

Megan crept closer and leaned on the arm of his chair. "A cow."

"They did, they saw a milk cow. Our word for milk cow is *milchkuh*."

"Baby cows, too," Lucy added.

"A calf, a *kalb*. In fact, the sisters saw two. The *kalbs* were twins just like the sisters. What is the Amish word for sister, Lucy?"

"*Shveshtah,*" Megan answered.

"*Da shveshtahs kumm* to the farm in a buggy pulled by a *gaul*. On the farm they saw a *katz*, a *milchkuh* and *kalbs* in the barn. The cat ran away, but the cow stayed to eat hay. The sisters looked at each other and said 'We want hay for supper, too.'"

Lucy shook her head. "We don't want hay."

"What about you, Megan? Would you like hay for supper?" he asked, hoping to draw her out.

She almost smiled but quickly made her yucky face. "No!"

"Me, neither," he said. "I want apple pie and ice cream, and that is the end of our story about sisters visiting an Amish farm."

"Are you *kinder* ready for supper?" his mother asked from the kitchen door. Willa stood behind her, smiling softly at him. She, too, wore a new dress out of the same blue material with a black apron over it. Like her daughters, the color matched her lovely eyes. She looked rested and pleased with him.

Warmth filled his chest at the approval in her gaze.

Lucy slid off his lap and grabbed Megan's hand. "I hungry."

"Good. I hope Vera fixed enough hay to feed everyone," Willa said as she turned away.

The girls skidded to a halt in the doorway. His mother burst out laughing. "She is teasing you. We are having ham and potato soup, not hay. Go wash your hands and then come to the *dish*."

"*Dish* is the Amish word for table," Willa said. "Put your toys away in Vera's room and then wash up."

The children went down the hall. His mother turned to John. "I had no idea that you were such an entertaining storyteller."

"It's a newfound skill. One born of desperation. Save some soup for me. I'll eat later. Nick should be here any minute to pick me up for the meeting."

Willa placed glasses on the table. "Now that you have told the girls one story, you will have to tell them more. Once is never enough with my daughters. Fortunately for you, we will be on our way as soon as you get our buggy back together."

He realized he wasn't as happy about that as he should be. He would miss them when they were gone. "I will get the nuts and bolts I need from Luke Bowman's hardware on the way home tonight"

"But you won't be able to work on the buggy tomorrow, and Willa can't travel. Tomorrow is church Sunday. She's coming to the prayer meeting with us."

Willa tipped her head to the side. "I'm not sure the girls are ready for an Amish church service."

"They will learn our ways as all Amish children do, by the example of their parent."

Vera folded her arms over her chest. "If you truly wish to rejoin our faith, you must start somewhere."

"You are right, of course."

John could see Willa was worried about their behavior or perhaps something else. "They are sweet children and young enough that much will be forgiven them."

"It's only that I hate to expose them to so many strangers at once. I know they will be uncomfortable, especially Megan. I have always stressed stranger danger. Megan takes it to heart. Lucy has never met a stranger."

Maybe he could get to the bottom of the mystery about her fears. "Why are you so worried about strangers?"

Willa cast his mother a sharp look. "Didn't you tell him?"

Vera turned her attention to the pot on the stove. "I may have forgotten to mention it."

"You forgot to tell me what?" he asked, not certain he wanted to know. Willa had her gaze fixed on the floor. His mother began ladling soup into the bowls lined up on the counter. The tension in the air was as thick as smoke. Something wasn't right.

The tromping of heavy boots on the porch caught John's attention. The outside door opened and Sheriff Nick Bradley walked in. John was surprised to see him in uniform. He pulled his trooper's hat from his head. The bright gold star on the front glinted in the lamplight. "Evening, folks."

The world rocked under Willa's feet as she struggled to draw breath. It wasn't possible. How had the police found her here? Had John told them? Had Vera? She had to get to the girls. They had to get away. She took a step back, but Vera grabbed her arm with a painful grip, forcing her to stand still.

"Good evening, Nick. Have you time for a bowl of my potato soup before you and John head out to your meeting?" Vera's cordial tone cut though Willa's panic.

The tall man pulled his trooper's hat off his head. "I wish I did, Vera, but I've got another fella to pick up and these roads are slow going."

"Then don't let me keep you."

He gestured toward Willa with his hat. "I don't believe I've met your visitor."

"I'm sure you haven't. She is visiting us for the first time. *Frau* Lapp, this is Sheriff Bradley. He is a fair-minded fellow and a *goot* friend to the Amish."

He smiled. "It's nice to meet you, ma'am."

Willa couldn't speak. She simply nodded once. *Please, God, don't let the girls come out until he is gone.*

It seemed God wasn't listening, for she heard giggles and pounding feet in the hallway, but only Lucy came in. At the sight of a stranger she rushed to hide behind Willa. Willa prayed Lucy wouldn't speak. Her English would give them away for sure.

The sheriff grinned and squatted to Lucy's level. He asked her name in flawless *Deitsh*. Willa swallowed hard. John stepped between her and the sheriff as he pulled on his coat. "She is a shy one. She barely speaks to me. We should get going."

Standing upright, the sheriff settled his hat on his head. "It was nice meeting you, *Frau* Lapp. You've got a mighty cute *kinder.*"

"Danki." She barely managed to utter the word.

The sheriff touched the brim of his hat and followed John out the door.

Willa's knees began shaking so hard she could barely stand. Vera pulled her toward a chair. "It's all right now."

Willa dropped onto the seat. "What shall I do? What do I do now?" She grabbed Lucy by the shoulders. "Where is Megan?"

"Putting toys away," Lucy whispered and then started crying.

Megan came in and quickly put her arm around Lucy. "Don't cry."

"Bad man," Lucy said between sobs.

"Willa, you are frightening your little ones," Vera said in a stern tone.

Pulling her daughters close to comfort them, she said, "The man is gone. We're fine." Willa looked at Vera. "Did you know he was coming?"

"I did."

"Why didn't you warn me? We could've stayed in my room until he left."

"And then you would have been more afraid, if that is possible. He saw you, and he saw Lucy. What did he see? An Amish *frau* with a child."

"I could've given myself away."

"You did not. *Gott* was with you. Now let us have supper before the soup gets cold."

"I don't think I can eat." Willa's hands were still shaking.

"Nonsense. Think of the *boppli*. You both need nourishment."

"Do you really think we fooled him?" Willa stared at the door, expecting the sheriff to return at any moment.

"Of course we didn't fool him. That would be dishonest. He saw exactly what I see. He saw a friend of mine and her little girl. Tomorrow is church. You will worship as one of us. You will sing the hymns you learned as a child and have not forgotten. More people will meet *Frau* Lapp, a sad young widow with two small children. No one will see an *Englisch* woman pretending to be Amish...because she does not exist."

"I'm not sure I can do it."

"You can if you do it for the right reason. Seek and

you shall find comfort listening to the preachers as they share the word of *Gott*. Salvation is yours if you accept *Gott*'s will. Then you will know peace. You are safe here."

Willa wanted to believe her, but she couldn't take her eyes off the door.

John sat stiffly in the front seat of Nick's SUV. He didn't know what Willa was afraid of, but he would find out before this night was over. He'd seen the fear in her eyes when the sheriff came in. Her fingers had been clenched so tightly her knuckles stood out white against the blue of her dress.

Nick hadn't spoken since they got in the SUV. He turned into the lane of Stroud's horse farm. Noah Bowman, a neighbor and another Amish volunteer firefighter, lived on the stable grounds with his new wife. Nick stopped the car in front of their house and turned in his seat to face John. "*Frau* Lapp seemed upset to see me. Know any reason why she should be afraid of me?"

John expected his question. Nick was too good at his job not to have noticed Willa's reaction. John was glad he didn't know what was wrong. He shared what he knew to be the truth. "Her husband was recently killed in an automobile accident. The police brought her the bad news. I didn't think to tell her that an officer of the law was coming to the house tonight. Perhaps she feared more tragic news when she saw you."

"That explains a lot. Thank you. Please give her my condolences when you speak to her again and tell her I didn't mean to frighten her or dredge up bad memories."

"I will."

Nick started to open the car door, but Noah had seen

them and hurried out of the house. He slid into the back seat. "*Guten nacht*, John. Evening, Nick. I appreciate the lift. What's new in the big bad world of law enforcement?"

"Same old thing. Drunk drivers, drug busts, drag racing, buggy racing, two missing-person reports. Oh, there was a report of a rabid squirrel trying to get in someone's front door last week. Turned out to be a pet that belonged to the man in the next apartment."

"Who has gone missing? Some of our Amish kids?" Noah asked.

It was sad, but some youth who didn't wish to join the faith felt so pressured to do so that they saw running away in the dead of night as their only way out.

Nick turned the SUV around. "One was a boy from Bishop Troyer's church. Your brother Luke still runs a counseling group for kids who want to leave, doesn't he? Ask him if he knows anything about the boy."

"I will, but you know Luke deeply respects the privacy of those who come to him."

"I appreciate that. The number of runaways in this area has gone down 50 percent since he started his group. The other missing people aren't Amish. It's a woman from Columbus with three-year-old twin daughters. They were last seen getting off a bus outside of Millersburg, and then they vanished into thin air."

"That doesn't sound good," Noah said.

Nick shook his head. "We don't suspect foul play. According to the Columbus police, the woman is involved in a custody situation. They think she disappeared on purpose."

"Millersburg is quite a ways from here," John said. "Any reason to think she is in our area?"

"None, but we're conducting a statewide search. We take missing children seriously. I wish we had posters to put up, but strangely there aren't any photographs of this woman or her children."

"They must be Amish," Noah joked.

Nick chuckled. "They aren't Amish. Her husband was wanted for embezzlement before he was killed about six months ago. She's about five feet two inches tall with blond hair and blue eyes. The twins are blonde with blue eyes, too. The woman was last seen wearing a red coat and carrying a purple backpack. That's all we know."

Noah leaned forward. "Is she a criminal, too?"

"Let's just say we want to talk to her."

John remained silent. Nick had just described Willa the first day they met. No wonder she looked frightened when Nick came through the front door. Why were they looking for her and her children? What had she done? He was tempted to ask Nick but decided he owed Willa the chance to explain.

The men arrived at the fire station a short time later. John put his concerns about Willa aside and concentrated on the meeting he was required to attend. The safety of his community and his fellow firefighters might depend on the information that was shared by the emergency preparedness officers. It wasn't until they were on their way to Noah's later that evening that John wondered exactly how he was going to question Willa.

Nick's cell phone rang as he turned into the horse farm. He pulled it from his pocket and listened to the caller for a minute before he said, "I'm heading home now. I'll pick up Joshua and Mary. We'll meet you at the hospital in thirty minutes."

He hung up. Noah leaned forward in the back seat. "Is something wrong?"

"My wife thinks her mother is having another heart attack. It doesn't look good."

Noah laid a hand on Nick's shoulder. "Let us know if we can help."

"I will. I need to get going."

Nick drove John home and then took off with his red lights flashing as soon as John was out of the car. John climbed the steps slowly and opened his front door with reluctance.

Willa was waiting at the kitchen table when John walked in. Her face was pale, but she looked composed. She clutched a mug of coffee in her hands. Before he could speak, she said, "I have some explaining to do, but would you like your supper first?"

"Our fire chief brought pizza for everyone, so you don't need to fix me anything."

She took a deep breath and raised her chin. "That's too bad. I was hoping for a short reprieve. What did Sheriff Bradley say about me?"

"He noticed that you were frightened, and he asked me if I knew why."

She pressed her lips tightly together. "What did you tell him?"

"Only what I know, which isn't much. I told him that your husband died recently, that a police officer brought you the news and that you weren't expecting to see another officer at our door tonight. He also mentioned there is a missing-person report for a woman with twin daughters who got off a bus outside Millersburg."

Willa rubbed her hands up and down her arms as if

she were cold. "I can't believe they tracked me to the bus station so quickly."

He took a seat opposite her at the table. "Willa, who is looking for you?"

She gripped her mug again and lifted her chin to meet his gaze. "My husband's parents are looking for me. They want custody of my daughters. They want to raise them as their own and to make sure I never see them."

He didn't understand. "How would such a thing be possible? Have they told you this?"

"I have never met them, but that is what they told Glen. My husband said they filed a police report claiming we were unfit parents a month after the girls were born and that a judge had granted them temporary custody. Glen said we could never fight them in court. They have too much money and too much influence, so we took the babies and ran. If his parents or the police locate us, they will take the girls away from me and I may never see them again. I could even go to jail for disobeying a court order."

John read the sincerity in Willa's frank gaze. He raked a hand through his hair. He didn't know what he had been expecting, but it wasn't this.

She took a sip of her coffee and waited for him to speak. He had no idea what to say. He couldn't imagine his friend Nick taking the twins away from their mother. "Your husband's parents have been looking for you since the girls were newborns?"

"They have a private investigator looking for us. My husband spent the last three years trying to keep our whereabouts a secret, but we were always discovered.

Many times we had to leave at a moment's notice to avoid being caught."

"That must have been a difficult way to live."

She lowered her gaze. "It was. It took money and planning to hide from those looking for us. Glen was the one who did all that. I simply followed him. I discovered how difficult it was after he was gone. I couldn't do it alone."

"Why go to your grandfather? Surely his family would know to look for you among your relatives."

"Glen told them I was an orphan when he called them to tell them he had gotten married. He thought they would stop hounding him if he proved he was starting a new life. As far as I know, Glen's family has no idea I was raised Amish. He was ashamed of my backward ways, my odd speech, my ignorance of modern technology. I tried very hard to become English enough for him."

John could tell by the sadness in her eyes that she hadn't been able to accomplish her mission. "So you came to hide among us."

"I didn't know what else to do. I prayed my family would take us in. My grandfather wouldn't. He didn't believe I sincerely wanted to return to the faith, but he told me to go to his sister in Hope Springs. He loaned me the horse and buggy for the trip. You know the rest of the story."

"Your plan is still to continue to Hope Springs?"

"It is. I'm hoping and praying that no one will look for me there. I love my daughters more than my own life. I will do anything to keep them with me. The question now is what will you do with this information?"

John hadn't known Willa long, but she wasn't an

unfit mother. He was certain of that. "Nick Bradley is a friend, but he is an outsider. The *Englisch* ways are not our ways. We have our own laws laid down by God and the church. The law that says you are a poor mother is an unjust law."

She breathed a deep sigh of relief. "It means a lot to hear you say that."

"I'm pleased you feel you can confide in me."

A pink flush stained her cheeks. "You and your mother deserve to know the truth."

He rose to his feet and crossed to the sink, not wanting her to see how moved he was by her trust in him. After years of hiding and then finding out he was friends with the sheriff, it had taken courage for her to reveal her story. He poured out his cold coffee.

Willa brought her cup to empty it into the sink, too. "Do you think the sheriff will come back? That he will guess who I am?"

"He said he isn't looking for an Amish woman. He has met you and he has no reason to doubt you are anything but a visiting Amish friend of ours."

They stood shoulder to shoulder in the silence of the still house. He looked down at her bowed head. The top of her *kapp* wouldn't reach his chin unless she stood on tiptoe. She was such a tiny woman to bear such a large burden. It would be easy to put his arm around her and draw her close.

The thought shocked him. He never imagined he would want another woman in his arms after Katie died, but he did. He wanted to hold Willa and not just to comfort her. He wanted to be comforted by her. The urge was overwhelming. He had to grip the edge of the sink to keep his hands from doing just that.

He had no right to touch her and no reason to think she would welcome his embrace. "You are a brave woman, Willa Lapp. I've never met anyone quite like you."

"I don't feel brave." She slanted a glance up at him. "Will you tell your bishop about me?"

"Since you are leaving, I don't see the need to inform him about this, but I urge you to do so when you reach your family in Hope Springs. It is always wise to seek the council of holy men."

"I'm sorry I put you in a difficult position with your friend. It is a poor way to repay your kindness. I did tell your mother all of this. I assumed that she would tell you."

"It makes me wonder why she did not."

"You don't think it simply slipped her mind?"

He gave her a wry smile and shook his head. "Not for a minute."

Chapter Eight

The sound of tires crunching through the snow outside brought Willa bolt upright in bed later that night. Car lights shone through the window. Had the sheriff come back? Was he going to take her children?

She jumped out of bed, pulled a robe over her nightgown and rushed into the hall. John came out of his room fully dressed. He carried a flashlight in his hand. The beam illuminated a circle on the floor, but it gave enough light for her to see his face. "It's all right, Willa. Go back to bed. I'm being called out for a fire."

The painful hammering of her heart slowed. "I thought the sheriff had returned."

"It is only the *Englisch* neighbor who collects Amish volunteers in our area." He spoke softly.

As her panic receded, she realized he was heading out to fight a blaze in frigid conditions. Would it be dangerous for him? "What kind of fire is it?"

He stood inches away from her. "I don't know the details. I'll learn more when I reach the fire station."

"Be careful, John."

He touched her cheek. "I trust God to keep me safe as you should, too."

She wanted to grasp his hand, but she didn't. "I sometimes think He is busy elsewhere and isn't paying attention to me."

"Never think that. He is with us always. Go back to bed." He slipped past her and went out the door, letting in a blast of cold air.

She pulled her robe more tightly around her. She hadn't realized how much she did doubt God's mercy until this instant. The faith that had sustained her since childhood hung by a thread. What kind of life would she have if she lost it?

Unable to go back to bed, she went into the kitchen and made a sandwich for herself and one for John in case he was hungry when he returned. Spreading the mayo, she realized she hadn't given a thought to the people affected by the fire. Laying down her knife, she folded her hands and asked God to watch over John and the other firefighters. The lives or livelihoods of a family somewhere might be in peril. She prayed for them, too.

Picking up her knife again, she finished cutting the sandwich and carried her plate into the living room, where the window looked out toward the lane. She settled in a chair, ate a few bites and kept watch for John's return.

The clouds in the east held the barest hint of pink when a red pickup turned into the lane and stopped by the house. John got out, and the vehicle drove away. She couldn't help but notice the tired slump of his shoulders as he approached the house.

He looked surprised when she opened the door for him. "What are you doing up so early?"

Willa stretched her stiff neck as she took in his grime-covered face. "I couldn't sleep. You look tired. Was it a bad fire?"

"Bad enough." He walked into the kitchen, turned on the water and began to wash his face.

She waited until he finished washing and drying off. "Was it a family you know?"

He shook his head. "A gasoline tanker truck missed a corner and overturned on the highway about four miles south of here. The truck caught on fire. We managed to get the driver out before the truck exploded. It was a near thing. Then we had to keep the fire from spreading to a nearby house. We did with the help of another fire crew. The driver had some injuries, but the paramedics said they thought he'd be okay."

"That is a wonderful blessing."

"Some family will have a much happier Christmas, that's for sure."

"I made you a sandwich, but would you like me to cook something?"

"A sandwich is fine. I'm going to try to catch a few winks before we have to leave for church. You should do the same."

"I will."

She started down the hallway but stopped when he spoke. "Thanks for waiting up for me."

"I knew I was going to worry, so there was no point in trying to sleep."

"To worry is to doubt God."

"Perhaps, but it's a skill I have perfected." She walked on down the hall and wondered if that would ever change.

* * *

John woke when the sunlight brightened his room. A glance at the clock showed it was time to get his chores done before church. He swung his legs over the side of the bed and sat up. Had Willa gotten any sleep? She needed to take better care of herself.

He dressed quickly in the cold room. As he started to make the bed, he realized he hadn't thought about Katie for almost an entire day. Missing her beside him had been his first thought each morning and his last thought at night since her death. This morning his first thoughts had been for Willa.

He sat on the side of the bed and waited for the sharp pain of grief to return, but it didn't. He missed Katie. He missed her friendship and her smile, but he remembered those things with a gentle sadness. What had changed? He knew the answer as soon as the question formed in his mind.

Willa and her daughters had brought a new energy into his home, and if he admitted the truth, she brought a special light into his life. He saw himself more clearly. He saw how crippling his grief had been. He would always miss Katie, but perhaps it was time to lay his sorrow to rest.

An hour later John stomped the snow from his boots on the front porch and stepped onto the rag rug inside the kitchen. Willa was wiping strawberry jelly from Lucy's face. He noticed the dark circles under her eyes had reappeared. She had been too worried about him to sleep. Did that mean she cared about him?

Today was her last day with them. A few days ago, he had been eager to see the last of her. Now he didn't want to think about her leaving. When had he become such a fickle fellow?

He knew the answer. When Willa had slipped her hand in his and said that she trusted him. He wasn't sure he had earned her trust, but it pleased him to know she gave it freely.

"We're almost ready." She turned to wipe Megan's face next and lifted her from the booster seat his mother had unearthed from somewhere.

"Bundle them up well. It'll be a cold ride. Are you sure you are up for this?"

She straightened and pressed a hand to the small of her back. "Ask me in an hour. Can we make it through this much snow with the buggy?"

"The roads have been plowed. We won't have any trouble. You may want to put some bricks in your pockets today as long as they are hot ones. You'll need them."

She gave him a sad smile. "At least you won't have to try to lift me up onto the wagon the way you did a little over a week ago."

Was that all it had been since he'd met her on the road to her grandfather's farm? Sometimes he forgot she was little more than a stranger. It felt as if he had known her for ages.

She grimaced and bent from side to side. "My aching back is not looking forward to the drive. I didn't have this kind of pain during my pregnancy with the girls until I went into labor."

He reeled with shock. "Are you in labor now? Shall I get the midwife? Where is my mother?"

She had the nerve to laugh at him. "I'm not in labor, John. I know what that feels like. This feels like I've been lifting twenty-pound sacks of potatoes all morning."

He strode past her to lift Lucy out of her high chair, hoping to hide the red tide he felt rising up his neck. "Perhaps too many *rundlich boppli* like this one."

Willa took Lucy from him and balanced the girl on her hip. "She is not a plump baby. She is exactly where she should be for her age." She scowled at his feet. "And you are getting my clean floor dirty."

He looked at the trail of melting snow and barn muck he'd left as he crossed the kitchen. "It is my floor. I will get it dirty if it pleases me."

Her eyebrows shot up. "I hope it pleases you to mop it. I've already done that once this morning, and I need to get the children ready for church. The mop is on the back porch." She tipped her head toward the door and walked out of the room.

John allowed a smile to slip free as he watched her carry Lucy to the back bedroom. Megan followed after her.

"What are you grinning about?" his mother asked as she came in from the living room. She carried several flannel-wrapped bricks that she placed in the oven.

"Willa is sadly lacking in *demut*. Have you noticed that?"

"*Nee*, I have not noticed a lack of the humbleness in her, but why should that make you smile?"

"Because it is my kitchen floor."

"You aren't making any sense. Are you sick?" She reached up to lay a hand on his forehead.

"*Nee*, I'm not sick. Make sure Willa and the girls are bundled well and you do the same. I don't want you coming down sick."

"Don't worry about me. I feel fine." She glanced toward the back bedroom. "It is our last day together. I will miss them when they go. This house hasn't felt so alive in years."

"*Kinder* have a way of doing that," he said softly. Having the twins and their mother around had been as disruptive as he'd feared, but he was growing used to them.

"I wonder what frightens her so much," his mother said softly.

He frowned. "I thought she was afraid her husband's parents will take her children away."

"There is that, but she is safe with us and she knows it. I feel something else has her deeply worried. I wish she would confide in us."

His mother enjoyed gossip, as much if not more than the next person did, but she wasn't given to imagining things. If she believed Willa was afraid of something else, she probably was.

Turning to face him, his mother laid a hand on his chest. "John, will you drive Willa to Hope Springs when the weather clears? I don't want her traveling there by herself. I hate to think of her out on the roads alone in the winter. Her horse could slip and fall. Anything could happen."

He had been thinking the same thing. "I have a sleigh to finish. I can't take four days away from my work to drive to Hope Springs and back."

It was a poor excuse and he knew it.

"Please, son, for my peace of mind."

He didn't want to endure a lingering goodbye. A quick break was the best. "I'll arrange for a driver to take her there in a comfortable car. Will that make you feel better?"

His mother frowned. "I thought we couldn't afford to hire a driver."

He couldn't afford it, but with the money he had been promised for his work on the vis-à-vis, he could pay part of it and perhaps barter for the rest with one of the local drivers. "I'll work something out. Willa will be much more comfortable and can make the trip in a few hours."

"If you think that is best, I agree. We're going to be late for church if I don't hurry up and get ready. The food hamper is packed. Will you take it out for me?" She started down the hallway to her room, but she didn't look or sound pleased.

"I will as soon as I finish mopping the floor," he called after her.

She stopped and turned back. "What did you say?"

"Never mind. Don't forget to bring the bricks."

She gave a slight shake of her head and walked into her room. John mopped his way backward from the door to the counter where the hamper sat and then out the kitchen door. He left the mop leaning against the porch railing.

After placing the hamper on the back seat, he walked up to stand beside Clover and scratched the mare under her chin. "This should be an interesting church service. I am guessing that Lucy and Megan will have a hard time sitting still on our wooden benches. Let's pray the bishop and the preachers give short sermons today."

Vera was already in the back seat of the buggy when Willa finally made it out the door with both the girls dressed in their new Sunday clothing. It had been a fight to keep Megan's bonnet on her head and Lucy's shoes on her feet, but they looked sweet and very Amish in their deep purple, ankle-length dresses and *eahmal shatzli*, the long white aprons worn by little girls. Willa was especially pleased with their forest green woolen coats. She and Vera had worked hard to get them finished in time. Both girls wore black traveling bonnets over their *kapps* to keep their heads warm on the ride. She and Vera wore bonnets, too.

John stood patiently beside the horse. He looked quite handsome in his black Sunday suit and his flat-topped, wide-brimmed black hat.

Willa mentally corrected herself. He looked very plain. His eyes brightened as he met her gaze. If only she could find a way to still the flutter in her midsection when he smiled at her. His kindnesses the previous evening made her respect and admire him even more. It was a good thing that she was leaving tomorrow, because she was becoming very fond of him. Too fond.

"I'm sorry if I have made us late." She hoped he attributed her breathless tone to battling with her daughters.

"I know who to blame for your tardiness." He leveled a stern look at her girls. "The next time you disobey your *mamm*, you will have extra chores to do."

"We'll be good," Lucy said, her eyes round as saucers.

"And you, Megan? Will you do what your mother tells you?"

She nodded. "Hat's on. See?" She smoothed the sides of her bonnet.

He crouched down to their level and smiled at them. "*Goot.* When you honor your mother, you please God and that pleases me."

"Okeydokey." Lucy patted his cheek.

He lifted the girls into the back seat with his mother. She already had the hot bricks on the floor to warm their feet and spread a quilt over their legs. Willa looked in and frowned slightly. "Don't you want to ride up front, Vera?"

"I'm fine here with the girls to keep me warm. It's best that you sit up front. Sitting in the back when I was pregnant always made me queasy. I don't want you feeling sick during the service."

In that instant Willa realized John's mother was trying to foster a romance between the two of them. The elderly woman was going to be sadly disappointed if she hoped to sway Willa from leaving. She might have gotten away with loosening the wheels of Willa's buggy, but she wasn't going to be able to pull the same stunt again. The very idea of his mother's meddling would have been funny if not for the fact that Willa already liked John far too much. She liked Vera, too, and the girls adored her, but a relationship with John wasn't possible.

Willa had to leave. She had to have her family around her when her baby was born.

John took hold of Willa's elbow to steady her as she climbed in the buggy. Willa smiled her thanks, but she wasn't smiling inside. Love and marriage were out of the question for her no matter how much she might wish it could be otherwise.

He tucked the thick lap robe around her. "Are you warm enough?"

"I'm fine." She looked away from the concern in his eyes. He climbed into the front seat and slapped the reins to get the horse moving.

They arrived at the home of Hank Hochstetler and

his family about forty minutes later. They weren't late. The service hadn't started, but they were the last to arrive. Vera got out with Willa and the girls as John parked his buggy among the two dozen other vehicles that lined the lane and unhitched his horse.

Vera took Willa's arm. "Be careful on this ice. Hank runs a small engine repair business. The service will be held in his shop. His home is too small to accommodate all of us."

Willa entered the metal building and almost backed out when she saw the number of people inside. She closed her eyes and drew a deep breath. As nervous as she was, she knew she couldn't let it show. The twins clutched her coat and looked at her in concern.

"It's okay," she whispered to them.

Vera took them both by the hand. "There are only friends here, so there is nothing to be scared of."

"Let's sit near the back in case I need to take the girls out," Willa said, knowing it was unlikely her girls could remain quiet for three or more hours of preaching in *Dietsh* with Bible readings in High German. Amish children were expected to mirror their parents and elders with a somber devout demeanor during the service, but exceptions were made for children as young as the twins.

Willa followed Vera into the building and felt the weight of all the eyes watching her. A new person at church was always a cause for curiosity.

The inside of the workshop was spotlessly clean. She knew the family and friends of the owner would have spent days making sure every surface was cleaned inside and out. The workload for hosting a service was such that each family in the congregation was expected to host only once a year.

The backless wooden benches were lined up either side of the center aisle. Men and boys sat on one side while women and girls sat on the other side. Around the perimeter, a few padded chairs had been carried out from the house for some of the more elderly members. The room was a sea of black on the men's side. Black coats and pants were the standard Sunday dress code. Identical black hats hung from a long row of pegs on the back wall.

The women were more colorful. Their long dresses and matching aprons were an assortment of solid colors, blue, green and mauve. Vera took her place on one of the benches and patted the seat beside her, indicating the girls should sit next to her.

From the men's side, the *volsinger*, the hymn leader, began the first song. He had a fine, steady voice. After the first line, the rest of the congregation joined in. The slow and mournful chanting reverberated inside the steel building as members blended their voices together without musical accompaniment. The opening song, like all Amish hymns, had been passed down through the generations for more than seven hundred years. Willa picked up the heavy black songbook, the *Ausbund*. It contained the words of the song but no musical notations. Every song in the book has been learned and remembered by members of the faith down through the ages.

The second song of an Amish church service was always the same hymn. *"Das Loblied,"* a song of love and praise. Willa was astonished at how easily the words and melody came back to her. It was as if she had last sung it yesterday instead of ten years ago.

She had kept God in her heart, but there was something special about worshipping with others. The bishop was an eloquent speaker who filled his sermon with praise for God, his great works and his unending mercy. His heartfelt words sparked a ray of new hope in Willa. Vera had been right. Willa drew deep comfort from the preaching and the songs. She didn't have to be alone. She could become part of a larger community bound together by faith and a commitment to each other.

This prayer meeting was the first step in her journey back to that faith. Not to hide among the Amish, but to become one of them again if God so willed it.

She prayed fervently that it was His will. That her family would welcome her and that the sheriff would never discover her real identity.

Chapter Nine

Twice during the service Willa took the girls out when they became restless. Once when Lucy needed to use the bathroom and again a half an hour later when Megan decided she needed to go.

Willa walked the girls up to the house and saw she wasn't the only mother missing part of the preaching. A tall woman with unusual violet-blue eyes and blond hair was changing a fussy baby in the bedroom across from the bathroom.

"Mama, baby cry," Megan whispered. A worried look filled her eyes.

"He will be fine in a minute," the mother said as she finished wrapping her son in a blanket before lifting him to her shoulder. As promised, he quieted immediately.

Willa sent Megan into the bathroom and waited outside with Lucy.

The woman walked toward Willa, her eyes sparkling as she smiled at Lucy. "I have two, but they are a year apart. I'm not sure I could manage twins. How old are your girls?"

"They turned three last month. How old is your son?"

"Two months. I'm Rebecca Bowman, and this is Henry."

"I'm Willa Lapp, and this is Lucy. Her sister is Megan."

"I was surprised to hear such a little one speaking English. You aren't from this area, are you? Do you have family here?"

Willa had known this would happen. With so many people around, someone was bound to overhear the girls speaking English. She gave a carefully edited version of her circumstances. "My husband wasn't Amish. He only wanted the girls to speak English, so I never taught them *Deitsh*. He passed away a few months ago, and I returned to my Amish family. The girls and I were on our way to visit my great-aunt, but my buggy broke down near John Miller's place. He and his mother took us in during the storm."

"Vera and John are *goot* people. I know them well. I was married to Vera's oldest son. Like you, I became a widow at a young age, but God smiled on me and now I have a new *wunderbar* husband and two busy boys." She kissed the head of her infant. "When is your baby due?"

"The second week in January." Willa pulled her coat closed. She had hoped to keep her pregnancy a secret, but Rebecca had sharp eyes.

"That makes you about thirty-three weeks along?"

"Almost."

"I remember how much I wanted those last weeks of pregnancy to fly by. I felt like a fat waddling goose by the end."

The fear of a relapse left Willa wishing she could

stay pregnant forever. "I'm not in a hurry. I have so much to do first."

"If only they would listen to our wishes, but babies often show up at the most inconvenient times. If your family is in the area, Janice Willard is an excellent nurse-midwife. She isn't Amish, but she could be. I can give you her phone number."

"My family lives several days from here and I will be leaving tomorrow, but thank you."

"I washed my hands," Megan said, coming out of the bathroom and holding her palms up for Willa to inspect.

"That's very good."

"Goot," Megan said. She gazed up at Rebecca. "Can I see baby?"

"They will pick up our language quick enough." Rebecca smiled and dropped to one knee. She opened the blanket so Megan could gaze at the baby's face.

"I like baby," Megan said softly.

Rebecca looked up at Willa. "That bodes well for your new addition."

"It does. I hope it is a boy."

Rebecca rose and spoke to Megan. "Henry has a brother named Benjamin. You can meet him after church is over."

Willa took both her daughters by the hand. "We should get back to the service."

"No, me tired." Lucy pulled away and stuck out her lip.

Rebecca chuckled. "I feel the same way. It won't last much longer, and then you can get something *goot* to eat. Do you know what church spread is?"

Lucy brightened instantly. "Yes, yummy."

"I think it's yummy, too." Rebecca winked as Willa

held her hand out to Lucy. "Let's go see if the bishop is done talking."

"Okeydokey." Lucy smiled brightly at her new friend.

The bishop was finished, but another of the preachers was just getting started when they returned to their seats. All in all, Willa was pleased with how well her daughters behaved. They conducted themselves much better than the young boy of about three who roamed back and forth between his parents, going the long way around the room each time at a run. From the looks cast his way by several of the elders, Willa suspected the boy's father would hear from them after the meeting.

Following the church service, Vera walked beside Willa to the house, where the meal would be held. "I didn't see Mary, Joshua or Ana Bowman in church. They must be visiting somewhere. I wanted you to meet Mary and find out if she knows your family in Hope Springs."

"I met Rebecca Bowman a little while ago."

"Did she tell you she was once my daughter-in-law?"

"She did."

"She is a fine woman. I had hoped that she and John would make a match of it, but *Gott* had different plans for them. Come, I want you to meet some friends of mine."

Inside, the house was a beehive of activity as women unpacked hampers and arranged food on the counters. Vera introduced Willa to many of the married women and a few of the single women in the congregation. It surprised Willa how friendly the women all seemed.

The benches were quickly carried in and restacked to form tables and seating for the meal. Since there wasn't enough room to feed everyone at once, the ordained and eldest church members ate first. The youngest among the congregation would have to wait until last. Few of the youngsters seemed to mind, for they were all busy playing with their friends.

Rebecca won Megan's heart when she had the girl sit in a chair and hold Henry for a little while. Lucy wasn't interested in the baby, but she did watch some of the other children closely. Willa could tell she wanted to play with them, but she wasn't willing to leave her sister. When Rebecca took Henry back, the twins were drawn away by a pair of school-aged girls who had been charged with looking after the younger children while the women prepared and served the noon meal.

Willa began unpacking the hamper of food the Millers had provided. There was bread, cold cuts, pickles and homemade pretzels along with the traditional church spread of peanut butter and marshmallow cream. Other women unpacked cheeses, pies, cookies and assorted baked goods. It was far different Sunday fare than had been served in the Swartzentruber group where Willa grew up. She recalled everyone eating bean soup from a common bowl along with bread, beets and pickles.

She heard her girls laughing and looked up to see them enjoying a game of tag with the other children. A pang of regret hit her hard. She pressed a hand to her mouth.

"What's wrong?" Vera asked.

Willa didn't realize she was being watched so closely. "Glen and I never stayed in one place long enough for the girls to make friends. It's nice to see them having fun with children their own age. I wish he were here to see it."

"Your *kinder* will have many chances to make friends when you settle into a new community. Is your heart set on going to Hope Springs? You could always remain here. You would be most welcome."

The idea would be tempting if she weren't afraid of her illness returning. "My heart is set on getting to know my family again."

"Of course. Still, it is something to consider after your reunion with your relatives. You might not like them."

Willa laughed out loud. "If they are anything like you, I will love them. I can always return to visit you."

"You must promise to do so. I've grown fond of you. John has, too, although he doesn't like to show it."

Willa's grin faded and she looked away. "John is a kind man."

"Is he the kind of man you might consider as a husband?" she asked hopefully.

Willa quickly shook her head. John would make a fine husband, but not for her. Marriage would mean more children and more chances to hurt them. "I won't marry again."

"You are too young to say this. Forgive the meddling of an old woman who would like to see her son happy again."

Willa managed a half-hearted smile. "You are forgiven. What can I do now?"

Rebecca appeared at her elbow. "You can help me set the tables."

"I can do that." Willa jumped at the chance to escape Vera's watchful eyes. If only she could escape the sudden longing Vera's suggestion had unleashed in her heart.

Willa followed Rebecca's lead and began setting a knife, fork, cup and saucer at each place. Vera came along behind them pouring coffee into the cups. Some of the women were rolling up their sleeves, ready to wash the plates and cups as soon as the diners were done with them; others were cutting cakes and desserts. Everyone was chatting and laughing.

Willa was amazed at how natural it felt to be doing such ordinary tasks with Vera and her friends. For a little while, she forgot about being discovered or needing to constantly look over her shoulder. Everyone accepted her at face value. Much of the talk among the women was about the fire the previous night and how thankful they were that it hadn't been worse. A few talked about visiting family for Thanksgiving, but the conversation soon turned to Christmas and everyone's plans.

Lillian Bowman, one of the teachers, announced the school program would be held twice this year because of the number of people expected to attend. The children would perform at two o'clock and again at six o'clock on Christmas Eve. Willa's school Christmas programs had been some of the highlights of her childhood, as they were for all Amish children. She thought of her girls and knew she wanted them to experience the same excitement over the true meaning of Christmas as she had when she was young.

Returning to join the Amish might have been an act of desperation on her part, but Willa began to believe it was also the best decision. She had been one week away from making that choice when she was fifteen. So much had changed in the intervening years, but now that she was twenty-five, she was free to make her choice again.

Rebecca and her sister-in-law Fannie Bowman told

the women they had plans to take several groups caroling on December 19. Everyone who wanted to join them could meet at the Stroud Stables at three o'clock. The bishop's wife called for everyone's attention and said she planned to hold a cookie exchange on the twenty-third as long as she could keep the bishop from eating all the cookies until everyone arrived.

Willa was laughing with the others when she looked across the room and met John's gaze. He had come in to eat. He gave her a small smile and a nod. She felt the color rush to her cheeks, but she smiled back.

Looking down, she laid another knife by a cup and saucer. She could almost pretend this was her family and her church group and that this was where she belonged. That the plans for Christmas included her and her children. When she looked up again, John stood across the table from her. He said, "It's nice to see you looking happy among us."

She glanced toward the women gathered in the kitchen. "I have missed this feeling of belonging and sharing. I didn't realize how much until today."

"I pray you find it again where you are going."

It seemed as if he wanted to say more, but he didn't. He took his plate to the table and left shortly afterward.

Had John come to care for her as his mother had suggested. She was flattered, but she hoped his mother was mistaken. Willa didn't want to hurt his feelings. He had suffered so much loss in his life already. She didn't want to add to his sadness.

Willa looked for him outside after she had eaten lunch and helped the women clean up. She scanned the farmyard and quickly located him. He was easy to pick out in the sea of black suits and hats for he stood a good head taller than most of the men standing outside in the cold sunshine. He was joking and smiling as he visited with them. The mood in this community was so much brighter and happier than the church group where she had grown up. Wouldn't it be wonderful if her great-aunt's congregation were like this one?

A group of teenage girls passed Willa on their way to the large shed now empty of benches. There would be volleyball and other games held inside the spacious building. Most of the youths in their *rumspringa* would remain for the singing that would be held after supper that evening. After that, many would pair up for a buggy or sleigh ride home with a date. Willa had looked forward eagerly to her *rumspringa*, her running around time, when she was growing up, but her father's decision to leave the faith had prevented her from having a normal Amish teenage life. How different would her life have been if he hadn't made that choice?

She didn't blame him. He had his reasons for leaving. Willa's mother had suffered from deep bouts of depression, something the community and others in the family didn't understand. His attempts to get her help from outside had been met with firm disapproval. Her father left to get her mother the help she needed, but in the end, it didn't matter. Her mother accidently took too many of the pills Willa's father was sure would help. Willa knew he simply gave up on life after his wife's death. They were both gone before Willa turned nineteen. If not for meeting Glen, Willa had no idea what she would have done. He became her rock. In spite of the sorrow that had touched her life, Willa knew she was blessed. She wouldn't have Lucy and Megan if she hadn't married Glen. She wouldn't trade being their mother for anything.

John noticed her and nodded in her direction. She gestured to the empty hamper she carried and then to the buggy so he knew what she was doing.

She was looking about for the twins when John approached with an older man he introduced as Isaac Bowman. "Isaac has some news about his daughter-in-law Mary."

Willa brightened. "I looked forward to meeting her today. I understand she is from Hope Springs. I have family in that area that I haven't seen in many years. I was hoping she might know them."

"Mary, my son Joshua and my wife left here late last night to go to the hospital in Millersburg. We had received word that Mary's grandmother had fallen ill. She used to live with Joshua and Mary, but she moved in with her daughter in Hope Springs last fall. I learned a short time ago that she passed away. Our family will be leaving to attend the funeral in Hope Springs later this week. I'm sure Mary will be happy to visit with you about the folks she knows when she returns."

Willa hid her disappointment. "I'm sorry for her loss. I'm leaving tomorrow, so I won't have the chance to meet her."

Vera came to join them beside the sleigh. "I just heard about Ada. What a shame. I know how much she loved Mary and how she adored little Hannah. Many people will miss her. Do we know what happened?"

"Only that she passed away," Isaac said.

Vera shook her head. "It's so sad, but Ada Kaufman lived a long life. We grieve for you and your family, but we also rejoice in the knowledge that she is with our Lord in heaven."

Willa's breath caught in her throat. Ada Kaufman was her great-aunt's name. They couldn't be talking about her, could they? Surely not. Kaufman was a common Amish name. Willa didn't want to believe that she had traveled all this way only to have her refuge crumble before she reached it.

John took the hamper from Willa's hands and stowed it under the back seat. "Nick Bradley got the call last night when he took me home after the safety meeting. He said his wife thought Ada was having another heart attack. He left my place to pick up Joshua and Mary and take them to the hospital."

"Miriam would want her daughter with her at such a time," Vera said.

Willa's hope that it wasn't her great-aunt faded. Ada had a daughter named Miriam and a son named Mark, but how was the sheriff involved with her family? Willa looked at John. "Is the sheriff related to them?"

"He is Miriam's husband. Mary is their adopted daughter," Isaac said.

"I don't understand." A chill settled in Willa's chest. How could her cousin Miriam be married to the English sheriff?

Isaac slipped his hands into the pockets of his coat. "It's an unusual story. Ada's daughter, Miriam, left the Amish and became a nurse after her brother died. The way I understand it, Ada and her husband were shunned by their church group because of Miriam's choice. They were members of an ultraconservative Swartzentruber church. I'm not sure where Ada came from originally. I think it was Millersburg, but Mary will know. Ada moved to Hope Springs and joined a more progressive Amish church so that she could see her daughter. When Ada's health began to fail, Miriam came home to take care of her. One night, someone left a baby on Ada's doorstep. Can you believe that?"

Willa pressed a hand to her throat. Had some other poor woman heard the voices that weren't real and done something she regretted? "Perhaps the babe's mother was ill and didn't know what she was doing."

Isaac shook his head. "She knew. Mary was a homeless and destitute child herself, barely sixteen years old. She thought she was doing what was best for her child by giving her away. Miriam and Sheriff Bradley tracked down Mary and reunited her with her baby. Not long afterward, Miriam married the sheriff and they adopted Mary. A few years later our son Joshua met and fell in love with both mother and daughter. That is how Mary and Hannah came to us, and we thank *Gott* daily for that blessing."

Willa struggled to keep her expression blank. Her great-aunt and her cousin Mark were both gone. Miriam was all the family Willa had left, and she was married to the sheriff. Willa didn't dare go to them.

Willa slowly backed against the buggy door as the conversation continued around her. What did she do now? There was no one left to help her.

She was truly alone.

Chapter Ten

Something was wrong.

John saw Willa shift to the back of the group as more people heard the news about Ada and gathered around Isaac for information. John worked his way to her side. Her starkly pale face frightened him. "Willa, are you all right?"

Her hand trembled as she grasped his arm. "Can we go?"

"What's wrong?"

"I have a headache."

It looked like more than a headache to him. Did this have something to do with the death of Ada Kaufman, or was it the baby? The wildness in her eyes worried him.

"I'm tired, that's all. I need to lie down," she said before he could voice his questions.

He grasped her elbow. "I will take you inside, and you can lie down there."

"I'd rather go home unless you wish to visit longer."

"*Nee*, I'm ready to leave." He opened the back door of the buggy and helped her inside.

He caught Samuel Bowman by the arm and spoke quietly into his ear. "Willa needs to return home. Can you help me hitch up?"

His eyes widened in alarm. "Of course. Should I send Rebecca to you?"

Samuel's wife, Rebecca, was widely known as a lay nurse. "*Nee*, Willa wants to go back to the house. She has been ill recently, and I think she is overtired."

"I'll go get your mare."

Vera seemed to notice what was going on and came to John. "Is Willa okay?"

"She says she has a headache and is tired. Will you fetch the girls?"

She nodded and made shooing motions to the people standing in front of the buggy talking to Isaac. They quickly made way and Samuel soon came trotting up with Clover. He and John made short work of hitching the mare. John climbed into the driver's seat as Vera reappeared with Megan and Lucy. He held his door open. "Sit up here with me, girls, and I'll let you drive after a while."

"Bless you," his mother said in relief.

She got in back and John slapped the reins against Clover's rump. The mare trotted quickly down the lane.

John glanced over his shoulder frequently as he drove home. Willa kept her face turned to the window. He couldn't be sure, but she looked on the verge of tears. He wanted to help, but he had no idea what to do. His mother patted Willa's hand and spoke softly to her. Willa answered but kept her face turned away. He couldn't hear what they were saying.

"Are you feeling better, Willa?" he asked after they had traveled a mile.

"I'm sorry to ruin everyone's day."

"You didn't ruin anything," his mother assured her.

Megan tugged on his sleeve. "I drive horsey?"

He had promised the child only to keep her and her sister quiet so they wouldn't bother Willa, but he didn't mind showing Megan what to do. Some of his earliest memories were of his father helping him to hold the reins on the way home from church.

"You will have to sit on my lap so that I can help you and you can see where you are going."

"Okay." He was surprised that she agreed. He lifted her up and settled her against his chest.

She eagerly reached for the reins and he showed her how to hold the lines properly. "You must keep the right amount of tension on them. Not too firm and not too slack."

Her hands weren't big enough to hold them correctly, but she concentrated on doing exactly as he instructed. When their first turn was coming up, he said, "Check your mirrors. Is there any traffic behind us?"

She stretched her neck to do so. *"Nee."*

He glanced back at Willa to see if she had heard her daughter use a *Deitsh* word. She didn't appear to be paying attention. That was unusual. She was always aware of what her children were doing and saying.

He helped Megan guide the mare around the corner. When they were straightened out again, Megan beamed a bright smile at him. "I did it, John. I drive *goot*. Clover *es goot gaul*. Right?"

It was the first time Megan had sought his attention or his approval. The tender emotions that flooded his chest pushed a lump into his throat. He swallowed hard before he could speak. *"Ja, liebchen,* you drive *goot."*

"I wanna do it," Lucy said, standing up to crawl into his lap with Megan.

"One at a time," he said. "Megan, can Lucy have a turn?"

For a second he thought she would argue, but she relinquished her place without a word. Lucy took the reins and jiggled them. "Giddy up, giddy up."

He stopped her from shaking them. "*Nee*, we are going fast enough. The horse has a long way to go. She will be tired if you make her run."

Lucy sat quietly for a while, but she soon lost interest in driving and wanted to sit with her mother. Willa leaned forward to lift her over the seatback. She held her hand out to Megan, but the child shook her head and remained beside John.

"I hold baby Henry," Megan said, looking up at him.

He would have liked to see that. "Did he cry?"

"*Nee*. Him *goot* baby. John like baby?"

"Sure, I like babies, when they aren't crying. Did you meet other new children today?"

Megan was soon telling him all about her friends and the games she had played. He was amazed at how talkative she had become all of a sudden. Was this the same distrustful child who'd called him "bad man" before today?

"Don't bother John, Megan," Willa said in a low, tired voice.

"She isn't bothering me," he assured her quickly.

Willa fell silent and continued to stare out the window as she held Lucy. When they arrived at the house, Vera took charge of the twins while Willa went inside. John put away the buggy and stabled the horse. When he entered the house a short time later, he found his mother in the kitchen alone.

"Can you open this for me?" She handed him a pint jar of canned chicken.

He twisted the lid enough to loosen it and handed it back. "Where are the girls?"

"I put them down for a nap. I'm making some chicken and noodle soup for supper. It will perk up Willa in no time." It was the meal she always fixed when someone in the family was under the weather.

"And where is Willa?" he asked.

"She went out the back door just a minute ago. Will you check on her?"

That was exactly what he needed to do. He opened the door at the rear of the kitchen and looked out. Willa, wrapped in a quilt, sat in the white wooden rocker at the far end of the porch with her head back and her eyes closed. She looked small, sad and vulnerable. A powerful urge to take her in his arms and kiss away her sadness made him realize how much this woman meant to him. He'd never expected to feel this way after losing Katie. He wasn't even sure his feelings were real. He wanted to believe it was just sympathy for the sad young mother, but he knew it was something more.

Willa rocked back and forth trying to calm her churning thoughts. Her headache had become a throbbing reality.

Dear God, what do I do? Help me, I beg You.

"Are you feeling better?" John's voice startled her.

She opened her eyes to see him sitting on the porch railing, watching her. The concern on his face tempted her to lie, but she couldn't. "Not really."

"Want to talk about what's wrong?"

Looking out over the snow-covered ground, she shook her head. "Not really."

He folded his arms across his chest. "Are you going to make me guess? Because if I had to guess, I'd say that Ada Kaufman was the great-aunt you were on your way to see."

Her gaze snapped to his. "How did you know?"

"You aren't very good at hiding your feelings."

That almost made her laugh. "I'm better than you think I am."

Otherwise he would see how much she had come to care for him.

"Why didn't you say something to Isaac about being related to Ada? I know Mary and Joshua. They would welcome a long-lost cousin with open arms."

"You are forgetting one thing. Mary's mother, my cousin Miriam, is the wife of the sheriff. I can't tell them who I am. He will enforce the *Englisch* law that says I'm an unfit mother and give my daughters to Glen's parents."

"You can't know that. Nick has great respect for our Amish ways."

"He isn't Amish, and neither is my cousin now. I can't trust that they will help me." Her voice caught in her throat.

"What will you do now? Will you go back to your grandfather?"

"I can't unless I know it is safe. The private detective employed by Glen's parents is an expert at tracking people down. According to what the sheriff told you, he has already discovered that I left the city by bus. He may have discovered where my grandfather lives and that I went to see him."

She had tried not to draw attention, but people noticed her daughters because they were twins. Their white-blond hair and vivid blue eyes made them memorable. She had tried keeping their heads covered with knit caps whenever they went out, but Megan was forever pulling hers off. The ticket agent at the bus station must have remembered them. The woman had commented that she had twin granddaughters about the same age.

Willa had seen the detective only once. Glen had spotted him loitering near their apartment building and pointed him out. She'd seen a small nondescript man with dark glasses, not the monster Glen told her was after them.

Glen had been furious because he had landed a good paying job at the local racetrack only two weeks before. They hadn't been able to return to the apartment until well after dark. They'd crept in, packed up their things and left that night. Glen died a month later. She had moved twice after his death, but it became much more difficult without him.

John scuffed one boot back and forth on the porch floor. "Nick told me that your trail disappeared where you got off the bus. I could ask him what more they know about you."

She shook her head. "It would only make him wonder why you're curious."

"I will finish the sleigh for Melvin Taylor before long. I could speak to your grandfather after I deliver it."

Willa sat up straight. "Would you? When will you go? It has to be soon. My baby will be here shortly after the New Year. I have to have a home for my children before then."

"I can have the sleigh finished in a little over a week. I will hire a truck to haul it next Wednesday and bring me back the same day."

She laced her fingers together. "John, that would be wonderful. I pray he has changed his mind and will shelter us."

"You must remain with us until I speak to your grandfather and return with his decision."

"It seems I have no choice. I'm sorry to impose on your kindness. I hope you know I'm grateful. Please let Grandfather know about Ada's death, too. They were estranged, but she was his sister."

John cleared his throat. "There is something else to consider."

"What's that?"

"You could stay in Bowmans Crossing permanently and make your home here. You already have friends in our community, for I consider myself your friend and so does my mother. God went to a lot of trouble to bring you to us. If your being here is His will, perhaps you should accept it."

John had no idea how tempting his suggestion was. To live in this community, among friendly and caring people, it was everything she had dreamed of finding for herself and her daughters.

She rubbed her hands up and down her arms. The one problem with the plan was that she had to confide in someone about her condition. As much as she wanted to tell John the whole truth, she couldn't bring herself to reveal what she had done in the past. She glanced at him. He wouldn't understand and she couldn't bear to see the revulsion on his dear face if he learned how she had tried to harm her babies.

"What do you think of that idea?" John asked.

She read the hope in his eyes and turned away. "It's a temping thought, but I want my children to be with family this first Christmas without Glen."

"Of course."

She heard the disappointment in his tone. It mirrored her regrets. If only there was a way for her to stay.

Maybe she didn't have to reveal those details. Maybe it would be enough to tell him she had been ill after the twins were born and that she could become ill again and might have to go away for a while. Would he accept that? She knew without a doubt that he and Vera would take care of the girls.

The midwife would have to know. Willa was prepared to share her history with a medical caregiver. The psychosis had come on with no warning last time. Someone needed to be ready to step in if it happened again. The midwife might even know of a place Willa could stay after the baby came if the worse happened.

Since the Amish didn't use insurance, Willa wouldn't have to provide proof of her identity if she had to be hospitalized again. The hospital would take the word of a midwife and treat the Amish woman Willa Lapp. The church would cover any medical bills she couldn't pay.

Then she remembered there would have to be a birth certificate filled out for her child. She would have to list the father's name or say he was unknown. To deny Glen was the father of her baby was unthinkable. How could she do that to his memory? How could she do that to her son or her daughter? Yet the detective might know about her pregnancy. Were birth records public records? Could he find the name she was using and the area she lived in by searching them? She wasn't sure. She wasn't even sure whom she could ask. Perhaps the midwife would know.

Willa rose to her feet and crossed the porch to lean on the railing beside John. Maybe he was right and this was God's will. Her detour to Bowmans Crossing may have been a blessing in disguise. She wasn't sure that the detective knew about her Amish upbringing, but in the event that he did track her as far as her grandfather's home, the trail would end there.

Her grandfather wouldn't offer information to an outsider, but he wouldn't lie for her. The detective might learn from her grandfather that Willa Chase had gone to Hope Springs, but Willa Chase had never arrived at her great-aunt's home. Ada Kaufman was gone now. Only her daughter, Miriam, knew Willa. If questioned, Miriam would say she hadn't seen or heard from her cousin. The detective would believe her because it was the truth and because Miriam was married to the sheriff.

Willa was afraid to give voice to the hope that she might be free at last. "If my grandfather won't take us in, I'll consider staying."

John took her gently by the shoulders and turned her to face him. "As a friend I only want what is best for you and for your children."

"To have your friendship means a great deal to me, John. I cherish that gift, and I hope you know that you have my friendship, too." He was dearer to her than a friend, but she couldn't let it become anything more.

He smiled and gently covered her hand with his own. "Friendship is a gift meant to last a lifetime. For my lifetime, you shall have it."

He nodded toward the door. "Let's go tell my mother you are staying until I can return from delivering the sleigh. She's going to be thrilled. She might even tell me where she hid the carriage bolts."

Willa chuckled; thankful he could change the subject so easily. "I'm still not convinced she took them. I wouldn't know which ones to remove."

"She was married to a blacksmith for forty-seven years. She knows exactly which ones to take out and which ones to leave. She could probably make them for you."

"Now you are exaggerating."

"Actually, I'm not. She made all the cabinet pulls in the house because she didn't like the ones *Daed* made for her. Are you feeling better?"

"Much better, *danki*."

"Don't tell *Mamm* that until after you have had some of her special chicken and noodle soup. She thinks it can cure anything."

Willa smiled, but she knew chicken soup wasn't going to mend the ache in her heart. She cared deeply for John, but she could never allow herself to love him or any other man.

Chapter Eleven

Vera's eyes sparkled when she heard the news from Willa. "This is *wunderbar*. I have so much to do before Christmas and now I will have you to help me."

"Only for another week or so," Willa cautioned her.

"If that is *Gott*'s will. I must ready my Christmas cards to send and I need to get this house clean before my daughter and her family arrive. I'm not sure I have enough time even with your help, Willa."

John shook his head. "Christmas is a month away."

"You are right. I don't have a moment to waste. Where did I put the cards I got last year? I don't want to overlook anyone. My poor fingers ache at the thought of all those notes I must write."

Willa smiled indulgently at John's mother. "Perhaps I can assist you with that."

"You are a sweet child. I appreciate any help you can give this old woman. *Gott* will reward you for your kindness. I think I left the cards in a shoebox under my bed." She went off to search for them, leaving Willa and John alone in the kitchen.

"I knew she would be happy about it," he said.

"Her attitude makes me feel less like an intruder in the family."

"Never feel like that. There are many things you can do that will make her life easier. I have been thinking about hiring a girl to help her. Are you interested in the job?"

"Perhaps for my room and board, but not for a salary."

"I think a salary might be cheaper than feeding you. I've seen how much you can eat."

She was happy that he could tease her. She wanted to remain friends. "That reminds me, I'm hungry, John-john. Where is that ham you promised me?"

"I can see I'll have to slaughter another hog before the New Year."

"That would be wonderful, but what about right now?"

He tipped his head to the side. "Do you really want some ham? I can go down and bring it up."

She laughed. "No, I want pickles and peaches."

"Are you serious?"

"Very. Never make fun of a pregnant woman's cravings. I could want fresh bananas. How long would it take you to fetch some of those?"

"The local market isn't open on Sundays. You would be out of luck until tomorrow. That is if they had any fresh produce delivered in the snowstorm."

"Aren't you glad I only want canned peaches?"

"Good thing I brought up a half dozen jars of them yesterday. How many are left?"

"One."

His mouth dropped open. "You ate five quart jars of peaches?"

"Don't be silly. Your mother made two peach cobblers to take to church this morning. I've only had two jars."

"That's a relief. I was afraid I'd have to put a lock on the cellar door."

"You know we Amish believe in sharing everything."

Vera came back into the room with a shoebox in her hand. "That's the first time I've heard you refer to yourself as Amish. Are you ready to commit wholeheartedly to the faith?"

Was she? Could she take her vows with a pure and sincere heart?

"It can't be about hiding, Willa," John cautioned.

"Pray about it before you decide and let *Gott* guide you," Vera said, setting the box on the table.

"Either way, you will be welcome to remain with us," John said.

"I think I would like to speak to the bishop as soon as possible." Baptism was a serious undertaking, and she didn't want to enter into it lightly. From having listened to his sermon, Willa was hopeful that Bishop Beachy would prove to be a wise spiritual advisor.

"And the midwife," Vera said, taking a slip of paper from her pocket. "I took the liberty of obtaining her phone number for you. Our phone hut is a few hundred yards south of our lane. John can show you."

Willa inclined her head and took the paper. "I will visit the midwife here if I can't return to my grandfather's home, but I would rather wait until I know something for certain. I will write to Bishop Beachy tomorrow and ask him to see me. Will you be able to watch the girls for me if he can? I want my grandfather to know I'm seeking baptism."

"I would love to have them to myself," Vera said. "They can help me make Christmas cards."

Willa looked at John. "May I borrow your buggy?"

He leaned close to his mother. "She wouldn't have to use ours if her own could be fixed."

His mother lifted the lid off her shoebox. Four long metal grease-covered bolts lay on top of a sheet of newspaper. "Will you look at this? How do you suppose these got under my bed?"

Willa pressed a hand to her lips to hold back a laugh.

John plucked the bolts out of the box. "Someone who should confess her deception to the bishop put them there. You may take your own horse and buggy wherever and whenever you wish, Willa. I'll have it fixed first thing in the morning. I'll add a slow-moving-vehicle sign on the back as well as reflectors, turn signals and lights while I'm at it."

As he went out the door, Willa clasped her hands together and tried to look stern. "Vera, how could you do such a thing?"

The elderly woman gave her a smug smile. "It's quite easy if one has the right tools."

Over the next few days, Willa and the girls fell into an increasingly comfortable routine. They had breakfast with John and Vera. After John went out to work in the smithy, Willa and the girls helped Vera with the household chores. If the weather was nice, Willa let the twins play outside. Every hour that went by without the return of the sheriff allowed Willa to relax a little more. Often Vera would teach them new Amish words as they helped her with her cleaning or cooking. In the evenings after supper, John would read aloud from his

Bible. The girls enjoyed climbing onto his lap and help-ing turn the pages. Willa caught him staring at her one evening and smiled at him. He looked away quickly as a dull blush crept up his neck. He was such a kind and gentle man. His easy way with her daughters endeared him to Willa as little else could do.

The following afternoon, the girls came running into the kitchen and grabbed Willa's hands. "Come play hide-and-seek, Mama," they said together.

It was their favorite game: a game with a purpose Willa hoped would someday be a part of the past. She was tired of running and hiding. "All right, we'll play."

"Can *Mammi* Miller play, too?" Lucy asked.

Willa looked at Vera. "What about it?"

"I thought you would never ask." She put her hands over her eyes and started counting.

John was in his smithy making a list of things he needed to finish Melvin's sleigh when the outside door opened. He looked up to see Willa come in. "What are you doing out here?"

She quickly closed the door behind her and grinned at him. "I'm hiding."

He chuckled. "Hiding from your girls?"

"From your mother."

"What is she up to now?"

"We're playing hide-and-seek with the girls. Your mother is very good. She has found me four times al-ready."

"I didn't know she possessed such skill."

Willa crossed to the window to look out. "Neither did I or I wouldn't have invited her to join the game. Here she comes. Where can I hide?"

He moved his chair aside. "Quick, get under my desk if you can."

"I may be pregnant, but I'm still flexible." She dropped to her knees and crawled under it. He sat down and picked up his pen.

The outside door opened and his mother charged in. "Come out, come out, wherever you are."

He kept his head down, knowing he would burst out laughing if he looked his mother in the eyes. "Have you lost one of the twins?"

"I haven't lost anyone. I know Willa is in here." She moved around the room, looking into the corners and behind the forge. "Where is she?"

He turned in his chair to face her. "That's for me to know and you to find out."

His mother arched one eyebrow and leaned to the side to peek under his desk. "Like that, is it? Very well, she may win this round, but I'll win the game."

Chuckling, she left the smithy closing the door softly behind her. John held out his hand and helped Willa climb out from under the desk. Her face was flushed, and her eyes were sparkling as she stood. John didn't release her hand. Instead, he pulled her closer, driven by the need to kiss her. He stopped himself just in time. This wasn't the way a friend behaved.

Her smile vanished and her eyes widened as she gazed up at him. John stepped away from her quickly. "You can make it home safely now."

"*Danki.* You are always coming to my rescue." She sounded breathless.

"That's what friends are for."

"I'm grateful, my dear friend." She pulled her hand

free, slipped around him and was out the door before he could think of anything else to say.

John kept busy over the next few days, working long hours on the sleigh for Melvin. Work in the smithy also kept him away from Willa except at mealtimes and in the evenings when the girls and his mother were present. Willa saw him as a friend, and he was determined to be that friend without asking for more. The problem was that he wasn't sure he wanted to settle for friendship. His feelings for Willa were growing stronger every day. It was foolish of him, knowing she could be gone in a few days.

He hammered home the brass tacks that lined the edge of the red velvet seat. It was the last thing he had to finish before he left in the morning.

For a long time he'd been unable to come to grips with losing Katie and their child. The arrival of Willa and her daughters had helped him do that. They had opened his heart to new relationships. If only a relationship other than friendship was possible with Willa. He wanted to ask her if there was a chance for something more, but in his heart he knew it was too soon.

The outside door opened and his mother came in. "I wanted to see this project before you hauled it away. It's beautiful. You have done a fine job on it."

"Danki." He looked over her shoulder. "Where is Willa?"

"I sent her to take a nap with the girls. She has been cooking and cleaning all morning. How are you getting along?"

He frowned. "What do you mean?"

"How are you and Willa getting along?"

He thought that was what she meant. "Fine."

"Fine as in you like her and she likes you, or fine as in it's none of my business?"

"You aren't very subtle."

She waved one hand. "I'm old. I don't have time to be subtle."

He sighed. She was like a dog with a bone. "Willa isn't a member of the Amish faith. I am. She still mourns her husband. Even if I were ready to consider remarrying, which I'm not, it wouldn't be possible."

"She is considering baptism. She wrote to the bishop and he has agreed to see her next week."

John put down his hammer. "She is not considering marriage."

"So she says. I wish she could see you for the *goot* man you are."

"She sees me as a friend."

"Many a marriage has started with friendship and grown into love."

"Don't hold your breath, Mother. You're old. You might not be able to hold it long enough."

"You make jokes, but I see your unhappiness."

He wished she wasn't so observant. "All things are as God wills. I leave it in His hands."

Willa watched John leave with the sleigh when it was finished with mixed emotions. She wasn't sure what news she wanted him to bring back. Was she to leave this place, or was she to stay? She kept busy during the day, but her eyes were frequently drawn to the window and the view of the lane. Near sundown she saw the truck turn in and went out to meet him. He waved to the truck driver as the man pulled away, and then he turned to her. A smile lit his tired face. Her heart grew light at the sight of it. How had she come to care so much for him in such a short time?

"Have you news for me?"

"I have plenty to share."

The front door of the house opened and his mother stepped out. The twins came charging around her and attached themselves to his legs, forcing him to walk forward swinging each of them along as they giggled and shouted their welcome.

His mother wiped her hands on her apron. "You made good time. I have beef stew on the stove that is ready when you are."

"Sounds *wunderbar*. I will be in as soon as I have finished my chores."

She spoke to the children. "*Kinder*, leave the man alone and let him finish his work. Come inside and we will show him all the Christmas cards you have made after he has something to eat."

Willa stayed outside after the others went in. Her smile quickly turned to a worried frown. "Did you see my grandfather?"

"I did. Come into the barn while I finish my chores."

"Is my grandfather willing to take us in?" Willa asked.

"He has not changed his mind." John looked down. "To my way of thinking, it is for the best. I can't see the twins growing up in Ezekiel Lapp's dour household."

Willa sighed and followed him to the barn. "I thought he might change his mind after he learned that his sister is gone. Has anyone been there to ask about me?"

John stopped inside the door to face her. "Melvin said an *Englisch* fellow visited all of the farms in the neighborhood. Melvin knew I gave you a lift to your grandfather's place."

Her eyes widened with fear. "Then he will come here looking for you."

"He won't. Melvin didn't care for the man's attitude and decided not to tell him anything. He said the man was pushy and rude to Mrs. Taylor. Melvin was happy to hear you are safe with my family."

"I remember Melvin as a kind man."

"Is Chase your real name?"

"It was my married name. I went back to using Lapp after Glen died. Maybe that wasn't very smart, but it's a common enough name among the non-Amish, too. Did the *Englisch* man speak to my grandfather?"

"He tried, but your grandfather wouldn't talk to him. According to Melvin, that was the reception the man got at most of the Amish farms he visited."

"What did my grandfather say when you told him about Ada?"

"Sheriff Bradley and his wife had already been there to inform your grandfather of his sister's death. Your grandfather did ask Miriam about you. When she said she had not seen or heard from you, he assumed you had gone back to your *Englisch* life. He didn't tell her that he had sent you to Ada."

"When you told him I hadn't returned to my old life, was he happy about that? Did you tell him that I'm considering baptism?"

"I did. He said he no longer has a granddaughter, and he asked me to leave."

She turned and leaned against Clover's stall. So that way was closed to her forever.

John moved to stand behind her. "You know what this means?"

"It means I have no family."

He laid his hands on her shoulders. "It means you may stay among us without fear of discovery. No one knows you are here."

She turned around and wiped the tears from her cheeks with both hands. "I will always fear discovery. Glen's parents won't stop looking. The sheriff is a friend of yours. We will run into him somewhere someday. He'll overhear the girls talking and realize they aren't Amish children. It's a short leap from that to wondering if I'm the missing woman with twins that he's been looking for."

"Have faith, Willa. God is with you and your children. He led you here for a reason."

Willa wanted to believe John. She wanted to believe God brought her to these people to find sanctuary among them, but she couldn't let go of her fears.

Her baby would be born in a few weeks. She had nowhere else to go. She needed somewhere to live and someone to protect her children. "Is the invitation to stay with you and your mother still open?"

"You know it is. You have a home with us for as long as you want it."

"I don't have a choice. I'm sorry."

"My mother will be over the moon."

"And you?"

He placed one finger under her chin and raised her face to look at him. His lopsided grin tugged at her heartstrings. "I'm getting used to having you and the children underfoot."

She looked away from the affection shining in his

eyes. "I need to make an appointment with the local midwife, and I need to find a job."

She would need money if she had to run again, but she had no idea where she would go.

If the midwife couldn't shelter her, then John and Vera would have to know her secret. She prayed that would never happen.

Vera was delighted with the news. The following morning found her busy taking inventory of her baking supplies for the upcoming cookie exchange. "I must make plans for Christmas. It will be *wunderbar* to have *kinder* in the house on Christmas morning. There is so much to do. I'm sorry your grandfather has rejected you, Willa. I may write him a letter and tell him what I think of his coldheartedness, but I will wait until after Christmas to do so."

"I have forgiven him. He has suffered much in his life, and it has made him bitter."

"You put me to shame for my un-Christian thoughts of the man, but I may write anyway. Would you mind cleaning my good dishes in the hutch?"

Willa hid a smile. "Not at all."

Megan tugged on Willa's dress. "*Mamm*, can we play outside?"

"*Ja*, but stay on the porch."

Willa finished wiping off the good dishes displayed in Vera's hutch and paused to listen. The girls had been playing outside on the porch after their nap, but the sounds of laughter and chatter had stopped. She glanced out the window. They were nowhere in sight, the pail and spoons she had given them to play with lay on the steps. Pulling a black shawl from a peg by the door, she wrapped it around her shoulders and stepped outside. She couldn't see them.

"Megan, Lucy, where are you?" They didn't answer.

She walked around the side of the building to check the garden. They weren't there, either. A seed of worry sprouted in her chest. Where were they? She scanned the snowy landscape. All she saw was a yellow barn cat hunting along the garden fence.

She called again. The cat stopped and glanced her way before leaping over the fence and running off. Willa started to turn back to the house but noticed two sets of twin-size footprints in the undisturbed snow beside the fence. They led through a side gate in the garden.

Perhaps they had gone down to John's workshop. She hoped that they weren't annoying him. He had been surprisingly patient with their questions and pestering.

The snow between the house and the barn had been churned by numerous horses and boots during the past two days. Willa couldn't distinguish the children's footprints, but she suspected they were heading to the barn to look for the kittens. They liked to feed them milk when John did his chores. Gray clouds drifted across the face of the sun, blocking much of the warmth. She pulled her shawl tighter around her, wishing she had chosen her heavy coat instead.

John's workshop was empty; however, the glow of coals in the forge proved he had been working there recently. Both buggy horses were still in their stalls, so he had to be nearby. She started to call out to him but paused when she caught the distant sound of childish laughter.

She moved through the dark barn toward the far door. It was open and she stepped through. The sun came out from behind the clouds. The dazzling brightness momentarily blinded her. She cupped a hand across her brows to block some of the light.

Her girls were both with John. He didn't look annoyed in the least. He stood with her daughters on top of a low earthen dam at the head of a small pond in his pasture. Each of her daughters was seated in a shiny aluminum grain shovel. They squealed with delight as John pushed first one and then the other down the snow-packed incline and out onto the ice, where they whirled around a time or two before falling over.

"Again," Megan shouted as she jumped to her feet.

Lucy tried to stand but slipped and sat abruptly, giggling all the while.

Laughing, John walked out onto the ice to set Lucy upright and onto her shovel. Then he pulled both girls back up to the top of the dam.

Willa leaned her shoulder against the doorjamb to watch them. The shovels were the same kind of make-shift sled her father had used when she was small. Spinning across the ice in one was among her fondest winter memories. When she was older, her father had given her a real sled. It might have gone farther and faster, but it never twirled her around until she was too dizzy to stay upright the way her father had done.

"There you are. You'll catch your death out here in nothing but a shawl." Vera draped a coat across Willa's shoulders.

Willa snuggled into the warmth. "I just stepped out to check on the girls. I didn't intend to be out here long."

"Did you find them?"

"They are with John. They seem to be having a very good time." She nodded toward the pond.

Vera stepped to the barn door and stood beside Willa. "*Gott* be praised. I was beginning to think I would never see that again."

"A child on a scoop shovel?" Willa grinned as John folded his large bulk onto one shovel and let Megan and Lucy try to pull him across the ice. They didn't make any progress until he helped by pushing with one hand.

"*Nee.*"

Willa heard the catch in Vera's voice and glanced at her. "Then what?"

"My son happy and laughing the way he was before Katie died." Vera pressed a hand to her trembling lips as tears glinted in her eyes. "I'm so glad you and your *kinder* came to us."

Not knowing what to say, Willa slipped her arm around Vera's shoulders and hugged her close. The two women stood watching the merrymakers for another few minutes, then Vera pulled away. "You should get back to the house before you freeze."

"I will in a minute." Willa didn't want to go in. She wanted to watch her little girls being carefree and happy. They were probably too young to remember this day when they were her age, but maybe God would allow this happiness to stay with them and outweigh the sadness they had known.

Vera leveled a stern look at Willa. "If you aren't back in the house in ten minutes, I'll send you to bed without your supper."

"I'll come in, I promise."

"See that you do." Vera's expression grew serious. "Don't hurt my son. He's grown fond of you and your girls."

Willa looked at her in surprise. "Vera, I would never knowingly hurt either of you."

"I reckon it's the unknowing hurt that I'm most worried about."

She walked away, leaving Willa to stare after her wondering what she had meant by her cryptic remark.

Chapter Twelve

It snowed heavily during the night, and the following morning arrived overcast and cold. Willa knew she had put off calling the midwife long enough. After breakfast she bundled up the twins and trudged with John to the end of the lane and down the highway to where a small red building sat back from the road in front of a stand of cedar trees. A solar panel extended out from the south side of the roof. Through the window in the side of the building she could see it was unoccupied. She opened the door and stepped inside.

The shack held a phone, a small stool and a ledge for writing materials along with an answering machine blinking with one message. She looked at John. "Shall I listen to it?"

"Sure. I use it for my business, as do my neighbors. Just don't erase it if it isn't for me."

It was for him. Melvin Taylor had referred a man to John for an estimate on restoring a wooden bobsled. John wrote down the man's number. "I'll call him when you're done."

A local phone directory hung from a small chain at

the side of the ledge, but Willa didn't use it. She had the number for the midwife on the piece of paper Vera had given her. The woman answered on the second ring. Willa answered a few questions, made an appointment and hung up. Afterward, she and the girls threw snowballs at the cedar trees while John conducted his business. When he came out, they all started home together.

The girls ran ahead of them, stopping occasionally to throw a snowball at unsuspecting objects. Lucy threw one and a rabbit darted out from beneath a clump of grass at the base of the fence post. She squealed in delight. "Mama, see bunny run? Johnjohn, what's bunny called?"

"The bunny *es der haas*."

"I see *der haas*," Megan said, looking to him for confirmation.

He took his hat off and plopped it on her head. *"Ja, der schnickelfritz saw der haas."*

Willa laughed. "*Schnickelfritz* is the perfect description. A mischievous child is exactly what she is. They're both mischievous children."

His smile was warm as he looked down at her. "I think they must take after their mother in that way."

"Perhaps a little," she said as Megan ran down the road with his large hat wobbling on her head.

"Perhaps a lot. When do you see the midwife?"

"She can see me Saturday at noon."

"I can drive you if you'd like."

"That won't be necessary," she said quickly.

"I don't mind. You shouldn't go alone."

She hated to point out the obvious problem with his offer. "I appreciate that, but it wouldn't be wise. I don't want to start any talk about us."

He looked taken aback, then blushed a deep shade of red. "I see your point. My mother will drive you."

"I will drive myself. End of discussion."

The girls came running back to them as Lucy tried to snatch John's hat from Megan. "Help me, John," Megan shouted.

"I want hat, Johnjohn." Lucy pouted when she couldn't catch her sister.

John stood up straight and raised his hands like claws. "The big bad *beah* wants his *hut*. Grrr." He charged toward them, sending them shrieking as they dodged away from his swinging arms. Finally, the make-believe bear snatched them both up, whirled around once and toppled backward into a snowbank.

Willa chuckled as she picked up his hat from the roadway where Megan had dropped it. John had an amazing way of lifting her spirits and making her want to laugh aloud. He could make her grin without even trying. What was it about this man? She tried to put her finger on it, but she couldn't. Happiness had been such a foreign emotion since Glen's death that she almost didn't recognize it.

Looking away from his infectious grin, her gaze traveled to Megan and Lucy. Not only could John make her smile, but her daughters appeared to be falling in love with him.

Willa bowed as she handed his hat to him. "Your *hut*, sir *beah*. Please don't eat my *schnickelfritz*."

"Oh, that sounds delicious. I will have *schnickelfritz* for lunch." He snapped his teeth at first one twin and then the other.

The girls scrambled out of reach and ran toward the house, calling for Vera to save them. Willa extended her hand to help John to his feet. He got up without assistance and began to brush the snow from his clothes.

Willa folded her arms and watched him. "I want to thank you, John."

"For what?"

"For befriending my daughters. They miss their dad. You are making it easier for them." She reached up to brush a lingering patch of snow from his shoulder.

"I'm glad I can help. Have I made it easier for you?" His voice held a low breathy quality that made her look at him sharply.

"I can't think about me. I have to think about them and what they need." She started to turn away, but he caught her by the arm.

"You will have to think of Willa Lapp sooner or later."

"Perhaps, but not now." She gently pulled away from him and followed her girls into the house.

A little after eleven o'clock on Saturday morning, Willa hitched up her horse and drove over to her appointment with the midwife. The midwife's home was a modest old farmhouse painted white just off the highway four miles from the Miller farm. If not for the power lines running to the house, it could have been the home of an Amish family.

Willa liked Nurse Willard as soon as she met her. A tall, big-boned woman with short gray hair, Janice, as she insisted on being called, was a no-nonsense woman who valued plain speaking. She wasn't happy with Willa for waiting so long to consult her and for failing to bring her medical records.

After Willa's exam, Janice wrote in a manila folder

while Willa got dressed. "If your prepregnancy weight is accurate, you could stand to gain a few more pounds."

"John says I eat all the time."

"Ignore him. Is that your husband?"

"I'm a widow. My husband passed away last May. I'm staying with John and Vera Miller."

Janice folded her hands. "I'm sorry for your loss."

"Thank you."

She went back to writing. "Your official due date is January 11, is that right?"

"Yes."

"That makes you thirty-four weeks and a few days. Are you sure about your dates?"

"Pretty sure."

"Don't be surprised if you don't go to forty weeks. You mentioned you have twins. Were they delivered by C-section?"

"I delivered them naturally."

"You were a fortunate woman. Twins can be tricky to deliver, especially for a first-time mother. Any complications during your pregnancy?"

"None."

"What about afterward?" Janice asked without looking up.

"Is this conversation confidential?"

That caused the midwife to put her pen aside and face Willa. "It is. So are your medical records and personal information. I'm a nurse-midwife, and I'm bound by the laws of this state to keep what you tell me in strictest confidence. I can't share any of your information without your written consent."

Willa couldn't look the woman in the face. She stared

down at her clenched hands. "I had an episode of postpartum psychosis after the twins were born."

"I see. You must have been terribly frightened by that."

"I didn't know what was happening. I don't remember much, only what I was told."

"Did you receive psychiatric care?"

Willa nodded, unable to speak.

"Were you hospitalized? What treatments did you receive, what drugs?"

"I don't have any of those records."

"If you tell me where you were hospitalized, I can get them."

"I'd rather not say."

"Mrs. Lapp, you have had a serious complication that could reoccur. I am not an expert on this illness. I have to know how to help you. I understand you are staying with Vera and John Miller. Are they aware of your condition?"

Willa looked up. "I don't want them to know. They won't understand."

"You aren't giving them enough credit. The Amish in this area are progressive. Bishop Beachy has openly urged his congregation to seek help for mental health issues, both from within the church and from outsiders if need be."

"The stigma is still real no matter what they claim. I've seen it. My parents were driven out of their church because of my mother's depression."

"I'm sorry that has been your experience. Willa, what were your symptoms? How did your psychosis present?"

"I would rather not say."

"Okay, but you are going to have to work with me. When did they start?"

"When the twins were two weeks old."

Janice sat back in her chair. "A home delivery is not out of the question, but you will need close monitoring for several months. Have you thought about how you will explain that to the family you are staying with? This is a small community. Word gets around."

"I was hoping to deliver here and stay here. If the Millers or the community have to be told anything, I will tell them I became sick after the twins were born and I might become sick again and have to be hospitalized."

"I do have a delivery suite and a recovery room where mothers and fathers can stay overnight, but I'm not equipped to have a long-term patient here. You would need around-the-clock observation."

"I have to stay somewhere. I can't burden Vera Miller with my care."

"She can arrange for mother's helpers to stay with you. You won't burden Vera."

"And then everyone in the community will know I'm being watched in case I turn crazy." Willa couldn't keep the bitterness from her voice. How many whispers had she heard about her mother? How many pitying looks had she endured even after they left the Amish? The English world had been no better in spite of her father's hopes. She didn't want to put her girls through that. She didn't want to put John through the same confusion and pain Glen had endured as he tried to cope with her insanity.

Janice crossed her arms and leaned back in her chair. "I'd like your permission to speak to several of my colleagues about your case. One is the doctor I practice under, Dr. Marksman. He will have to be informed. The other is also an RN, so your privacy will be protected. Her name is Debra Merrick. She is the public health nurse in our district. I'm going to ask her to line up professional mental health help for you in the event it is needed. We will find a place for you to stay. Although you aren't an abused spouse, we do have a home for women in need that's run by a Christian women's charity. I'll speak with them. We'll work something out."

"Thank you." Willa forced herself to relax.

"Try not to worry. I'll have Dr. Marksman and Debra here to meet you at your next appointment, which will be the twenty-first of this month. That will put you at thirty-six weeks. I see all my mothers weekly for the last month, so plan on coming in weekly until you deliver. We will figure out the best thing to do for you and your baby."

Janice walked Willa to the door. Before she opened it, the nurse-midwife turned to Willa. "I strongly advise you to confide in someone. You can't do this alone. Your condition is not your fault. You shouldn't be ashamed. You would not be ashamed if you broke your arm after falling on the ice or suffered an attack of appendicitis."

How could it not be her fault? There was some flaw in her that she should have been able to control. "My mind is made up. I don't want anyone outside of the doctor and the other nurse to know."

"Then that is what we will do."

Willa walked outside and climbed into her buggy. If she managed to get past this delivery without people learning about her condition, she would be safe from then on out. There would not be another pregnancy because she would never remarry. At least not until she was past her childbearing years. Then and only then would she be able to think about her own desires. About her feelings for John.

He was attracted to her. She would have to be blind not to see it. Would he be willing to wait for her? It would mean he'd never have children of his own. No, she couldn't do that to him.

John was waiting just inside the barn for Willa when she drove up. He came out to take her horse, impatient to know that she and her baby were okay. "How did your visit with the midwife go?"

"The baby and I are both well, but she said I need to gain more weight before I see her again."

"That must have made you happy. I'm going to get a lock for the refrigerator."

Willa smiled, but it didn't reach her eyes.

"What else did she say?"

Willa got out of the buggy. "Not a lot. I have to see a doctor next time."

"A doctor? Why?" He stared at her over the back of her horse.

"When the twins were born, I became very sick and had to be hospitalized. There is chance that could happen again. The midwife wants to take some precautions."

"What kind of precautions?" How serious was it?

"I may have to stay near a hospital for a few weeks after the baby is born."

"A few weeks?" He'd never heard of a new mother needing to stay away from home for so long.

"Just to be on the safe side."

It was odd that she didn't look at him. Was she embarrassed to speak of such things? "I'm sure she knows best. Have you spoken to my mother about this? *Mamm* may know of some remedy for this ailment."

"I haven't. As I said, it's a precaution and my worry may be for nothing. You know how I like to worry. You have told me to have faith. I want you to know I'm trying. I'm going to go see the bishop tomorrow evening to talk about getting baptized. I'd rather not go alone. Would you come with me? I would ask your mother, but I'm hoping she will watch the girls for me."

He was pleased that she wanted him beside her. If she chose to join the faith, there wouldn't be anything keeping them apart. He would be free to tell her how much he had grown to care for her. "I'd be happy to drive you."

Willa had a hard time concentrating on the preaching during the church service on Sunday morning. Was she making the right decision? She prayed that she was. Happily her girls were well behaved, and she had to take them out only once. At the meal, she barely picked at her food, sparking a frown from Vera. The long morning was finally over, but Willa's soul searching continued.

She hid her nervousness as she rode beside John in the buggy on Sunday evening. She wanted to make the right decision, but she wasn't sure what that would be.

If she chose to join this church, she would be bound by their rules for a lifetime. Living without electricity wasn't the most difficult part of being Amish, although she did still reach for the nonexistent light switch when she entered a dark room. Living without the convenience of a phone, traveling by horse and buggy, and wearing plain clothing didn't trouble her. Opening her home to any Amish person who needed assistance would be a chance to repay the kindness she had received. What did trouble her was the knowledge that she might be making her decision based not on her love of God but on her fear of discovery.

The true meaning of becoming Amish wasn't in the outward signs of the faith. It was about committing her life to God as a member of a pious community. It was about giving her life over to His will.

The sheriff hadn't returned. That gave her hope that she had been accepted at face value and he wouldn't come looking for her again. The midwife had a plan to make sure Willa and her new baby would be safe if the need arose. If bringing Willa to Bowmans Crossing was God's plan for her sanctuary, then she had to let go of her lingering fears. If only it wasn't so hard.

The bishop's wife showed them both into her husband's study and returned a short time later with refreshments. Willa had her choice of coffee or spiced apple cider and a number of delicious-looking cookies and cakes. She chose the spiced cider and a pumpkin roll.

The bishop came in a few moments later. "I see my wife, Ellie, is already plying you with food and drink. Welcome, Willa Lapp. I see by the note you sent that you are interested in joining the faith. Can you tell me why?"

Willa drew a deep breath and started her story. "My *Englisch* husband passed away, and I am alone in the world except for a grandfather who will not accept me and my children into his home because my parents were shunned. I thought I had other relatives in

Hope Springs, but I have recently learned that they have passed on or have left the church."

"I'm sorry to hear this. We welcome you to get to know our community. I'm sure you have learned a great deal about us from John and Vera."

She smiled at John. "I have. Their kindness to me and my children is a big part of my decision to remain in Bowmans Crossing. Everyone I have met only reinforces those feelings."

"I'm pleased to hear that. Tell me about your Amish childhood."

"I was raised in a Swartzentruber Amish community. I had completed my baptism classes but had not yet been baptized when my parents left the community. I was only fifteen and my mother was ill. I thought we might come back, but my parents wouldn't allow me to return. My parents died within a year of each other. Mother died first. I still thought we would go back to our community then, but my dad wouldn't consider it. He became ill a short time later. I stayed to take care of him. When he died, I wrote to my grandfather, but he never replied. I was alone."

The bishop listened to her, nodding occasionally.

"I soon met and fell in love with a good man and we married. We had twin daughters the following year. Then my husband was killed in a hit-and-run car accident."

Ellie reached over to cover Willa's hand with her own. "God has given you many trials."

"Your path back to us was not an easy one," John said quietly.

It hadn't been easy, but he was right. Every turn in Willa's life had brought her closer to this place and these people. And to God. If she believed that, she had to believe that this was where she belonged. This was God's plan for her. This was where she was meant to serve Him. A deep calm spread across her mind as she opened her heart to His will.

The bishop took a sip of his coffee before speaking. "We normally hold baptism classes twice a year. In the fall and in the spring."

"I am aware of those practices," Willa said.

"Candidates attend nine meetings with our church leadership over a two-and-a-half-month period leading up to the baptismal ceremony."

"Since I have already completed the baptism classes, would it be possible for me to take my vows without repeating my instructions? I would be happy to allow the church leadership to test my knowledge and my conviction." She laid a hand on her belly. "This child is due in January, and I wish to be baptized before he or she is born."

Shaking his head, the bishop held up a hand to caution her. "This is not a decision to be rushed."

"I am not rushing into it. I made my choice many years ago. The right to take my vows was denied me. I lost my way because of that. I ask only for the chance to make my vows before God and the church so that I may bear my child with a cleansed soul and a joyful heart."

The bishop looked from Willa to John and then to his wife. He folded his hands together and considered her request. Finally, he nodded once. "This is a very unusual request, but I see no reason why I can't discuss this with our church elders. Your desire to serve God is heartfelt. I see that in your eyes. The ministers and I are meeting tomorrow evening to discuss another issue. I will give you our decision the following day if we arrive at one."

Willa didn't realize she had been holding her breath until she had to speak. "*Danki*, Bishop Beachy."

"Are you planning to attend our cookie exchange?" Ellie asked.

"I am. May I have another piece of your delicious pumpkin roll? I do need the recipe."

Mrs. Beachy smiled brightly. "I'll write it out for you right now."

When Willa left with John a half hour later, snow had begun to fall. Willa's breath rose into the air in a frosty cloud. She couldn't remember the last time she had felt so lighthearted and free. She held her arms wide and opened her mouth to catch snowflakes.

"Was it the right decision?" John asked.

She clasped her arms around herself to hold on to her joy. "Oh, John, it was. I've never been so sure of anything in my life. Even if I can't be baptized before my baby arrives, I will be baptized with the next class in the spring."

"I'm happy you can consider staying until spring."

Willa drew another deep breath. "I wish I could say I'm not worried about being discovered. I am. But each day brings me more peace of mind. Can you feel Christmas in the air?"

"What?"

"Christmas is coming. The night our Savior took the form of a tiny baby to bring Salvation to us all. Isn't it glorious?"

"You are making me wonder what Ellie Beachy puts in her pumpkin roll."

Willa chuckled. "Offhand, I would say she adds a

generous dose of Christmas spirit. Let's get home. I want to make some tonight."

He opened the buggy door for her to climb in. "As long as you promise not to eat them all yourself."

"John Miller, you begrudge me every bite I take."

"I don't, but Clover may. She's the one that has to pull you around." When he climbed in, the buggy sagged in his direction. He outweighed her by over a hundred pounds.

Willa folded her arms. "No pumpkin roll for you."

On Friday afternoon, a buggy carrying four members of the church leadership arrived at the Miller home. Willa waited patiently in the background as Vera made them welcome and settled them in the living room. When he was ready, the bishop beckoned Willa to take a seat on a chair facing the men.

One by one, they took turns asking her questions about the faith and about her understanding of the eighteen articles of the Dordrecht Confession and if she had read them. She had when she took her baptismal classes, but the German words had carried little meaning for her at fifteen. She had read them again from the prayer book Vera loaned her with an English translation. It left her with a better understanding and respect for the traditions of the Amish church and an abiding belief in the articles of faith.

They then asked her if she understood what was expected of her according to the church's *Ordnung*. Vera and John had spent many hours detailing the church rules for her. She didn't remember them all. She stumbled when she listed them and thought her hopes of being baptized were lost, but Bishop Beachy simple smiled. "Some members are better than others at knowing the rules and following them. The congregation is reminded of the *Ordnung* twice a year."

"Can you live by these rules?" one of the ministers asked.

"I have lived with them and I have lived without them. I freely choose to live by them for the rest of my life."

When asked if she could shun a wayward member by the deacon, Willa hesitated.

"I understand the need to shun a person who willfully disobeys the church laws. It is done out of love, to make them see they have sinned and to bring about a change of heart. I would have to be sure they had been given every chance to repent and return before I voted to place them under the *Meidung*. Having seen how deeply it can divide a family, I would, but I would never be eager to do so."

After two hours, the men retired to John's bedroom for a discussion. Willa's hands were shaking when she went to the kitchen sink for a drink of water.

"How is it going?" John asked from the back door. Willa read the encouragement in his eyes. He had the girls with him. They looked tired.

"I have no way of knowing. Are you girls ready for a nap?"

Megan nodded. Lucy shook her head but rubbed her eyes with both hands.

John leaned against the doorjamb. "They may not be tired, but I am. I can't swing a shovel around one more time without my arms falling off."

"You are good to keep them occupied."

"You must know I will do whatever I can to aid you."

The tenderness in his voice brought tears to her eyes. "You are the best friend I've ever had."

"The look in your eyes says you see more than a friend just now. Why can't you admit it, Willa?"

"I have to put the girls down for a nap." Willa headed them toward their bedroom, determined not to look at John again. She did see more than a friend. She saw in him the man she was growing to love. As hard as she had guarded her heart against him, he had found a way in. As she opened the door to the girls' bedroom, the door to John's room opened, too, and the men came out.

Bishop Beachy leaned down to speak to the girls. "Who have we here?"

"I'm Lucy. Megan's my *shveshtah*." Lucy rubbed her eyes again.

"I see you have learned one *Deitsh* word since you have been with us."

Megan gave him a sour look. "*Der katz, a milchkuh* and her *kalbs* stay in barn. What's bunny called?"

Bishop Beachy laughed heartily. "The bunny *es der haas*."

Megan smiled at him. *"Ja ver goot."*

He chuckled as he looked at Willa. "It seems that I have been tested and have passed, as have you. Because of your heartfelt desire, you will be baptized on Sunday the nineteenth before the service."

When the men left, Vera wrapped Willa in a big hug. "I'm so happy for you."

"I can't believe it."

Vera stepped back and rubbed her hands together. "We have very little time. We must take you around and introduce you to as many families as we can before Sunday so everyone feels comfortable with you joining us. Those who meet you will love you as much as John and I do. Isn't that right, John?"

"It is hard not to love her." He opened the back door and went out.

Chapter Thirteen

"I'm going to need a job." Willa kneaded the bread dough while Vera looked on with a cup of coffee in her hand. Willa found the rhythmic movements were soothing. Over the past two days, she and Vera had been in and out of the buggy too many times for Willa to recall. She had met over two dozen of the local families. Once they finished the bread, they would be on their way to Isaac Bowman's home for a meeting with his family, as they were hosting the service where Willa would be baptized.

"You have a job. You take care of me, your *kinder* and John."

"I don't take care of you or John. You can both take care of yourselves. Besides, I need a paying job. I will need to get a place of my own someday. Any suggestions?"

"Add a little more flour to the dough if it feels sticky."

Willa sprinkled a handful on the table. "I don't mean the dough, I mean about finding work."

"I think the bread dough has been kneaded enough. Go ahead and divide it into the pans."

"I'm serious about finding work, Vera." She would need money if she had to get away quickly. For now, she had to pray God would be merciful and keep her hidden, but she wanted to be prepared if someday she had to leave.

"You know you are welcome to stay with us. You can't leave until after the babe is born."

"I know." She didn't want to leave. Every day she discovered some new thing about John that made her care for him more. Harder still was knowing he cared for her, but she didn't dare return his affections. Perhaps living apart would lessen her affection for him.

"If John is the reason you don't want to stay, you can tell me now."

Willa shrugged. "Maybe he is part of it."

"He's a stubborn man. Sometimes he can't see what is right under his nose, but he will make a good husband. If you gave him a little more encouragement, it might make a difference."

Willa shaped the dough in the pans and turned to face Vera as she wiped her hands on her apron. "You mistake my meaning. I'm fond of John the same way I'm fond of you, but I don't want to encourage him. I'm not looking for another husband."

"You should be. You're young. You have children to care for. You don't have to remain alone. Would your husband want that for you? I think not."

Glen would have wanted her to be happy, but that was beside the point. She wasn't able to be a wife. "I'm content to raise my children and live a good life. I don't need a husband for that."

"Harrumph," Vera said in disgust as she pulled open

the oven door so Willa could slide the bread pans in. "John isn't the only stubborn one in this house."

"Who says I'm stubborn?" he asked from the doorway. Neither of the women had heard him come in.

"I do," his mother said, shooting a sharp glance at Willa. "And so is this one."

"I thought that the first time I met her. I'd like to show you something, Willa. Can you come out to the workshop?"

She couldn't think of a good excuse not to go with him. "Sure."

He looked over his shoulder. "Where are the girls?"

"Playing with their dolls in their room. Shall I get them?" Willa was already moving in that direction. With the twins around, she could avoid the pitfalls of being alone with John.

"*Nee.* I don't want them following us. I need your opinion on something."

Willa had no idea what he was talking about, but she put on her coat and followed him out to the smithy. He checked behind them, then he picked up a bundled object from the corner and carried it to the forge. He pulled off the burlap wrapping. "What do you think?"

It was a toddler sled. Only, this one was big enough for two. The curved rails around the back that kept a small child from rolling off backward were metal and painted bright red.

"John, it's lovely. Did you make this?"

"The base is pine. It should hold up through a few years of use. They will outgrow it quick enough, but your next child can use it, too."

"The girls will love it."

"Do you think it's too fancy for a Christmas present?"

"With the red paint? A little, but they are so young they won't know any different. You are always doing something kind for them."

He stepped close. "It's because I like their mother. I'm trying to win her affection by currying favor with her children."

She looked away. "I wish you would stop. It won't do you any good."

"I was afraid you would say that. Perhaps this will change your mind." He placed a hand beneath her chin and lifted her face to his. Slowly, he bent low and kissed her.

Willa had time to move away, but her feet wouldn't listen to her brain. The tenderness of his lips against hers made her respond in kind. Her mind stopped shouting that it was a mistake and her heart took over. She cupped his face with her hands and lost herself in the sensations his touch brought to life. It was a wonderful, tender kiss unlike any she had known before.

He groaned and pulled her close. It wasn't until her belly bumped against him that her foggy mind started working again. She pushed against his shoulders and turned her face away. "You must not do this."

"Not do what? Not show you that I'm falling in love with you? I've been trying to hide how I feel, but it's a losing battle."

"I have to go in."

He gripped her arms. "Why must you run away? I know you mourn your husband, but I am the man you were kissing seconds ago. You can't tell me otherwise."

"Please, John. I can't do this. Do I care for you? Yes, I do, but there can never be anything between us."

"Why? What is holding us apart? Your children? The

babe you carry? Is that what worries you? Willa, I can love them because I love you."

She shook her head and gazed into his eyes. "I don't need to explain myself to you. I'm sorry to hurt you. I never intended to do that, but you have to forget this happened."

He dropped his hands to his sides, freeing her. She stumbled toward the door, brushing away the tears that sprang to her eyes. Behind her he said, "I'll forget this kiss the day after you do, Willa Lapp."

Willa went in the house and straight to her room. She didn't want Vera's eagle eyes to see the traces of tears on her face. When she had washed her face and regained her composure, Willa came out of her room and saw Vera taking the last loaf out of the oven. Lucy and Megan sat at the table enjoying warm slices of bread with butter and sugar sprinkled on it.

Vera glanced at Willa. "Oh, *goot*, you are ready. John is bringing round the buggy."

Willa's heart sank. "John's not coming with us, is he?"

Vera's eyes narrowed. "He is. Does it matter?"

"Not at all," she said with a forced smile.

When the girls were finished with their snacks, Willa helped them into their coats and sent them out to sit up front with John. She took her spot in the back seat and avoided looking at him for the short drive to the Bowmans' home. She pressed a hand to her mouth as she remembered the feel of his lips against hers. Why had he kissed her? Why had she kissed him back? It had been foolish.

The Bowman house was set back near the river. A small shop boasting Amish gifts and crafts above the door was located just off the highway. Past the gift shop, a large metal building contained the woodworking and furniture-making business the Bowmans were renowned for.

Of the Bowman family, Mary and Joshua were still gone, but Isaac and Anna welcomed Willa, as did the rest of their sons and their wives.

Isaac slipped his thumbs through his suspenders. "So you have decided to stay in our district. What made you change your mind? I thought you were on your way to Hope Springs."

Willa looked down. "I learned my family no longer lived in the area. It had been many years since I was in touch with them. Since I was really looking for somewhere to settle with my daughters, I felt Bowmans Crossing was as good as any and better than most."

"It is indeed." Isaac turned to John, who was standing by the buggy. "I have some work for you if you are interested. Can you look at the shaft on my lathe and tell me what it will take to fix it? It's out of balance."

Anna and Vera went inside. Rebecca gave Willa a hug. "Have you met our nurse-midwife yet?"

"I did. I see her again next week."

"Isn't she a fun lady?"

"We haven't gotten to know each other well enough for me to say. She was nice and seems to know her job." Willa was still hopeful that Janice would be able to secure a place for Willa to stay after the baby was born. Knowing she might have to stay with Vera and John weighed heavily on Willa's mind, but at least she knew Lucy and Megan would be well cared for.

"I forget you haven't known Janice as long as I have. If you haven't already arranged for a mother's helper, I can give you the names of a couple of local girls. They were both wonderful during the month after Henry was born. I didn't have to lift a finger if I didn't want to."

Willa followed Rebecca inside the house. "More than a mother's helper, I need a job."

"Are you serious? Isn't your baby due in a few weeks?"

"Yes, but I can work until then, take some time off and return after the baby arrives. I have no money of my own, and I have lived off the charity of the Millers far too long already."

"I might be able to help."

"Really?"

"We are short-handed at my mother-in-law's gift shop. The holidays are our busiest time of the year, and with Mary still in Hope Springs, we have been struggling to cover for her."

"I've worked in retail before."

"Can you run a computer?"

"Until I'm baptized. Was the computer question a test?"

"Not at all. We have permission from the bishop to use computers for our businesses only. They are powered by our generator and use Wi-Fi to connect to the internet by satellite. It sounds like I know what I'm talking about, but I can't even turn the thing on, let alone fill orders. Isaac has an *Englisch* teenager that handles most of it, and she's barely seventeen. Are they born knowing this stuff now?"

"Do you honestly think I could get a job here?"

"I'm almost sure of it. Let's go see what Anna has to say. I think she'll jump at the chance to hire you." Rebecca led the way to the kitchen, where Vera and Anna were chatting with several other women.

Willa stopped Rebecca before she went in. "Will I be able to bring my daughters to work with me? They are only three years old, but they are well behaved." She didn't feel safe leaving them alone all day. It would take time to adjust to having them out of her sight.

"I take Benjamin and Henry with me and they are not well behaved. Your children will be welcome."

As Rebecca predicted, Anna was thrilled to have an experienced worker offering to hire on for Christmas and even afterward. She went out to get Isaac to decide on a salary. His offer was generous by Willa's previous work standards, but Rebecca assured her that all of them earned the same amount. Willa had a job starting tomorrow. Everyone congratulated her.

Anna clapped her hands together. "Enough chitchat. We have work to do."

"What work?" Willa asked, looking at the smiling women around her.

"We are going to make your baptismal dress and there is no time to waste."

Together, the women measured, cut and stitched together a new black dress, a black organdy *kapp*, a lovely new white cape and a long white organdy apron for the occasion. Willa was overwhelmed and grateful for their generosity.

She waited for John's comment about her job as Vera told him on their way home later that afternoon. He looked at her for a long moment. "If this is what you wish, I'm happy for you."

He didn't sound happy. She avoided facing him across the supper table during what would surely be an awkward meal by pleading a headache and staying in her room. The next morning, he was gone by the time she got up. She dressed and fed the girls. Vera made them a lunch to take and handed the brown paper bag to Willa. "Don't spend the whole day on your feet. Put them up when you can and drink plenty of water."

"I will. Don't worry about me."

"You girls mind your *mamm*," Vera told them. "I don't want to hear bad reports about you. Are you sure you don't want to leave them with me?"

"They have never been away from me for so long. I want them to feel comfortable and see what I'm doing before I leave them with you for the day."

"They would be fine, but you are their *mudder*. Get a move on, girls."

"Okeydokey," Megan said.

Lucy whirled on her. "I say okeydokey. Not you."

Megan pouted but didn't talk back. Vera shook her finger at them. "This is not the way to start your mother's first day on the job."

Willa wondered at the tension between the girls but didn't have time to deal with it. She left Vera to get them into their coats and went out to hitch up her horse.

John had her mare hitched and waiting when Willa stepped outside. He tipped his hat to her and went inside the smithy without a word.

She had allowed her weak will to destroy their friendship. She should have found a way to avoid his kiss without hurting his feelings.

The store was busy, but Willa had no trouble keeping up with the flow of customers. Many of the Amish ones just wanted to visit with each other. Many of the *Englisch* ones bought items, but most wanted to snap pictures of the twins in their *kapps*, which Willa discouraged. All day long as she worked, Willa wondered what the coming evening was going to be like when she returned home. She couldn't very well plead another headache and continue to hide in her room. Vera would march her off to the doctor if she did. Would John remain aloof? Would he avoid spending time with the girls?

When she reached home an hour before suppertime, the girls charged through the door ahead of her. John was waiting in the living room with his paper open. He quickly folded it shut and held his arms wide. "My *schnickelfritz* are home. *Kumma*, tell me about your day."

They crawled into his lap and began chattering about the store and how baby Henry threw up on his *mamm*'s shoe. Willa was so grateful for his continued friendship with the girls that she couldn't speak until she swallowed the lump in her throat. "You have a *goot* friend in John, girls."

"I know." Lucy nodded vigorously, kissed his cheek and snuggled against his chest. Willa turned away and went down the hall because that was exactly what she wanted to do, too.

"Have you forgotten our moment together? I have not," John called after her.

She paused with her hand on the doorknob of her room and sighed. "Try harder."

Chapter Fourteen

John had no idea how to break through the wall of Willa's reserve except to pound away at it as he did with the hardest steel in his shop. Brute force wasn't the answer. Metal had to be tempered, heated to the melting point and worked before it grew too weak or too hard again. He already knew he had to melt Willa's resistance, and her daughters were the fire he would use.

"Can the girls stay home with me today?" he asked at breakfast two days later. Willa had those dark circles under her eyes again. She wasn't sleeping well. Part of him was glad and part of him hated to be the cause of her discomfort.

"That will be fine. I think they are getting bored with playing behind the counter. Even baby Henry is losing his luster."

"Where women are concerned, it happens to all men," he said sadly. "Some of us sooner than others."

He was rewarded with a hint of a smile. "Some men never had much luster to begin with."

"True. When do you have an appointment with the midwife?"

"Next Tuesday."

"Will you have trouble getting off work to go?"

"*Nee*, for Rebecca has said she will cover for me."

"Have you gained enough weight to make the midwife happy, or should I put a brick in your pocket?"

That brought out a real smile. "One brick or two? I have the feeling she will scold me if I gain too much."

"One brick, then, or another jar of peaches?"

She met his gaze for the first time in days. "I do have a craving for peaches."

"I'm glad to hear that. I'll loan you the money to buy some at the gift shop. I don't want the midwife to think I'm starving you."

He heard her laughter behind him as he walked out the door to hitch up her horse, feeling exceedingly pleased with himself. They might not be back to where they were before the kiss, but this was a start.

When the second hymn finally came to an end on Sunday, Willa entered the house of Isaac and Anna Bowman and took the seat reserved for her near the minister's bench. She sat with her head bowed on this most solemn occasion. She was vowing to reject the world, accept Jesus as her Lord and live a humble life in a community governed by God's word.

The ministers and the bishop entered the room from behind her. For the next several hours Willa listened to the sermons delivered first by the ministers and then by the bishop. She tried to absorb the meaning into herself. She closed her eyes and breathed deeply. This day she felt the warmth of God's presence. She gave thanks for the goodness He had bestowed upon her and begged His forgiveness for all her doubts.

The bishop finally ended his sermon and turned to Willa. "The solemn vow you make today is not made to me. It is not made to any of the congregation here with us today, for we are only witnesses."

He raised his hand and pointed to the ceiling. "This vow you make unto God Himself. Let there be no misunderstanding. Let no doubt remain in your heart."

The deacon came forward with a pail of water and a cup. The bishop looked at Willa. "Is it your desire to become a member of the body of Christ?"

"It is my heart's desire," she answered firmly.

The bishop's wife came forward and untied the ribbons of her *kapp*. The bishop then laid his hand on Willa's head. "Upon your faith, which you have confessed before God and these witnesses, you are baptized in the name of the Father and the Son and the Holy Spirit. Amen."

The bishop cupped his hands over Willa's head. The deacon then poured the water into the bishop's hands. It trickled through his fingers and over Willa's hair and face.

The bishop then extended his hand to her. "In the name of the Lord and the Church, I extend to you the hand of fellowship. Rise up and be ye a faithful member of our church."

Willa stood. The bishop gave her hand to his wife, who greeted her with a Holy Kiss upon her cheek.

Facing the congregation, Bishop Beachy said, "It is the duty of everyone present to aid this new member as we would each other. We must be ever watchful that none of us strays from the path God has set before us. All must conform to the *Ordnung* of this church without question. Though these rules are sometimes difficult, they are made for the good of the many and not of the one. Obey them and never depart from them."

Willa glanced at John and saw tears upon his face as he smiled with joy for her.

On their way home late that afternoon, Willa heard Vera speak softly to John. "She is baptized. I've held my breath long enough. I'm not getting any younger."

The following afternoon, John came in from finishing his chores to find his mother spooning cookie dough onto a baking sheet and singing a Christmas carol. Slightly off-key but with enthusiasm. The twins sat on the kitchen floor banging on pans with wooden spoons and occasionally joining in with a word or two. Loudly and very off-key.

"O Holy Night" had never sounded quite so bad. John stood in the doorway to the kitchen and stared at his mother in amazement. He couldn't remember the last time he had heard her voice raised in song outside of church services or the last time she had looked so happy.

She caught sight of him and fell silent. Her smile faded. When she stopped singing, the girls stopped banging. She pushed the last spoonful of dough onto the sheet. "I thought you were out in your workshop."

"I just came in to see if there was any coffee left from supper."

"Johnjohn, we go carol."

"That's right. We are going caroling tonight."

The cellar door opened, and Willa came up with several quart jars of fruit in her hands. "Are these the ones you wanted?"

His mother took the jars from her. "They are. There

isn't any *kaffi* left, but I'm sure Willa can fix some. I wouldn't mind having a cup myself."

"I would be happy to make some," Willa said quietly, keeping her eyes averted.

"Don't go to any trouble on my account." He wished she would look at him more often.

"Sing more, *Mammi* Miller," Lucy said, banging her pot.

"That's all the singing for now. Put your pots away," his mother said.

Megan frowned. "Aw, do we have to?"

"Yes, you have to." Willa held out her hand for the spoon.

He had certainly put a damper on their impromptu concert. His first thought was to leave and let them resume their fun, but something held him in place. He leaned his shoulder against the doorjamb. "I would like to hear more singing, *Mammi* Miller."

His mother folded her arms over her chest, leaving smears of flour on her sleeves. "You may choose the next song as long as you join in."

If she expected him to back out, he decided to disappoint her. She knew he didn't like to sing. "I will if Willa will. How's that for a tongue twister?"

He caught a hint of a smile before Willa subdued it. "Willa will if John joins in willingly. Say that three times fast."

"I think I'll just sing." He drew a deep breath and began, "Joy to the world, the Lord is come." His voice was often compared to a bullfrog, but he was going caroling tonight no matter what.

He motioned to Willa and his mother, and they joined in. The twins started banging, and by the second verse they were adding a stream of *joys* to the lyrics. He glanced at Willa and found she was smiling at him. Today it reached all the way to her eyes. They sparkled with amusement, and it made him feel that he was making headway. Painfully slow headway, but they were moving in the right direction. Toward each other.

Two hours later, John waited beside Samuel's sleigh and tried unsuccessfully to curb his excitement. He was almost as giddy as Megan and Lucy. A sleigh ride with Willa at his side was his idea of the perfect winter evening, especially since he didn't have to drive. Lucy was the first one out of the house. She quickly claimed her spot in the front seat beside Samuel. Megan came out next and scrambled up beside her sister. He'd never seen them so delighted.

"Are you sure you don't want to sit in back with your mother?" John asked, praying they would say no.

Samuel winked at John as he covered the pair with one of the lap robes he held. "They will have a better view up here, and it won't be so crowded in the back seat. I remember what it was like to go caroling before I became an old married fellow."

John was thankful the darkness hid the blush he knew was staining his cheeks red as he climbed in the back seat. He would owe Samuel a favor for arranging this. *"Danki."*

"Don't mention it."

Rebecca came out followed by John's mother and Willa. Rebecca settled on the front seat with the twins between her and her husband. Willa stepped aside to let Vera get in beside John.

"I'm afraid I can't tolerate sitting in the middle," his mother said without a hint of shame. "I hope you don't mind."

"*Nee*, of course not." Willa took John's hand as he helped her in. He gave her gloved fingers a quick squeeze and saw her smile before she looked down.

Samuel handed several quilts to John. His mother got in but shifted uncomfortably. "Can you scoot over a little more, Willa? I'm practically hanging out the side."

John wanted to kiss his mother's cheek. He heard Samuel's laugh quickly change into a cough. John lifted his arm and placed it over Willa's shoulders as she moved closer. "Don't worry. I will keep you warm," he said in a low voice as he spread the robe over her.

Willa remained stiff as a metal rod beside him. As much as he wanted to pull her closer, he knew it would only make her more uncomfortable. It took time for heat to bend steel, and he was becoming a patient man.

"Is everyone ready?" Samuel asked. Five confirmations rang out. Samuel slapped the lines and the big horse took off down the snow-covered lane. Sleigh bells jingled merrily in time with the horse's footfalls. The sleigh runners hissed along over the snow as big flakes continued to float down. They stuck to the hats of the men, turning their brims white before long. Megan and Lucy tried to catch snowflakes on their tongues between giggles.

John leaned down to see Willa's face. "Are you warm enough?" She nodded, but her cheeks looked rosy and cold. John took off his woolen scarf and wrapped it around her head to cover her mouth and nose.

"*Danki,*" she murmured.

"Don't mention it. In spite of the cold, it's a lovely evening to go caroling, isn't it?" The thick snow obscured the horizon and made it feel as if they were riding inside a glass snow globe. The fields lay hidden under a thick blanket of white. Pine and cedar tree branches drooped beneath their load of the white stuff. A hushed stillness filled the air, broken only by the jingle of the harness bells and the muffled thudding of the horse's feet.

Their first destination was only a mile from John's house. They reached it all too soon. As they drew close, he saw several sleighs parked in front of the home already. The other members of the Bowman family were waiting for them. They all got out and walked toward the house. The porch light was on. The front door opened to reveal his neighbors Connie Stroud and her daughter Zoe waiting for them. As Lucy and Megan scrambled down from the sleigh, John offered Willa his hand to help her out. When she took it, he gave her an affectionate squeeze. She graced him with a shy smile in return.

"Was this what you imagined Christmas would be like when you decided to return to your Amish family?"

She shook her head. "I never imagined anything like this. Do you do it every year?"

"We do."

"You aren't going to actually sing, are you, John?"

He threw back his head and laughed. "*Nee*, but I will hum along."

"Softly, dear, softly," she suggested.

He wondered if she realized that she had called him *dear*. It was turning out to be an even more wonderful night than he had hoped for. He squeezed her hand as the song began and softly hummed close to her ear.

They made stops at various English and Amish homes as the group made a circuit around the farms in the area. Wherever they stopped, they were greeted by cheerful people with hot drinks and mounds of cookies. Samuel called out the song titles and began each one as the group followed his lead. They sang five songs at each home before bundling into the sleighs again. Calls of Merry Christmas and *Frehlicher Grischtdaag* followed them when they left. Lucy and Megan were worn-out before the sixth house. John and Willa remained in the sleigh with the girls bundled under the quilts while the others sang.

He looked over at Willa. "I hope you don't mind missing out on the cookies."

"I don't when I have something so sweet in my arms." She adjusted Lucy's hat to cover her ears.

"I feel the same way." He hefted Megan to a more comfortable hold. "What will we do when we have three? We don't have enough arms between us."

"You should have children of your own, John," she said, looking away.

"I like yours. I can't wait to meet the next one. Are you hoping for a boy or a girl?"

"I would like a boy."

He pulled the quilt up higher around Megan and knew it was now or never. He had to share his heart, or he would burst. "I've become mighty fond of little girls and of one grown woman who happens to be their mother."

"I know the girls are fond of you, too."

"And their mother? How does she feel?"

"She likes you."

"There's a problem, then."

She glanced his way. "What problem?"

"I more than like you, Willa Lapp. In fact, I'm in love with you. What are we going to do about it?"

* * *

I'm in love with you. What are we going to do about it?

The question echoed through Willa's mind as she stared at the hope in his eyes. What could they do about their growing feelings for one another? She was in love with John. He loved her. She didn't doubt him, but what future was there for them? How could she make him see how hopeless it was unless she told him the truth? The whole terrible truth. She had tried to kill the little girls he loved.

She could do the same to another child. To the child she carried.

Show me the path I need to take, Lord.

John waited patiently for her answer.

She looked away. "I can't change how you feel, but I can't give you the love you seek."

Megan raised her head. "Can we go home now?"

"We'll go home soon," Willa assured her.

"Willa, talk to me," John said. "I know you care about me."

"Not here. Not in front of the girls."

"Then tomorrow. We need to talk without interruptions."

"I have to work until noon, then I see the midwife."

The carolers came back to the sleighs. Vera settled herself in the back seat and glanced at the girls. "These two won't be up in time to go to work with you, Willa. They can stay home with me. Anna has invited some of the schoolchildren and their families over tomorrow for treats. I'll bring the girls in to meet the children at noon and they can stay and play with the others."

"I'll bring them," John said. "That way you can get

your grocery shopping done, and I can drive Willa to her midwife appointment."

"Wunderbar," Vera said, patting Willa's hand.

Willa forced a smile. She had until tomorrow to think of a way to let John down without breaking his heart. And hers.

Willa sighed as she dusted the jars of jam on the gift shop shelves. A sleepless night had provided only one answer. She had to tell John about her condition. Perhaps with the support of the midwife, Willa could make him see that loving her was pointless.

The bell over the front door jingled. "I'll only be a minute, Nick. I just want to grab some hard candy for Hannah."

Willa turned around, happy for the distraction. An English woman with dark auburn hair and bright green eyes walked across the floor toward her. She wore jeans and an emerald green parka that brought out the color of her eyes. There was something familiar about her.

"Do you have root beer candy? The kind that looks like little barrels?"

Her voice gave her away. Willa stared, unable to believe her eyes as her cousin Miriam Kaufman stood smiling in front of her. She was Miriam Bradley now. The sheriff's wife. Miriam hadn't changed much in ten years.

"We are out of root beer candy." She wanted to shout at her to go away.

The woman pointed to the display case. "No, you aren't. I see a bag right here." She tipped her head to the side. "Don't I know you?"

"I'm new here." Willa looked away, resisting the urge to run.

"Willa? It is you. Willa Lapp. Little cousin Willa. You are the spitting image of your mother. How long has it been?"

"Ten years, I think. How are you, Miriam?" Willa saw the sheriff step out of his vehicle as a tour bus pulled up beside him. He waited as a dozen tourists got off.

Dear God, please don't let him take my babies.

"It's been a hard month so far. My mother passed on a few weeks ago. Did you know that?" Miriam asked.

"I heard. I'm sorry." *Please go away. Stop talking to me.*

From the corner of her eye, Willa saw John pull up in his wagon. *No, no, no. Take the girls home, John.*

Willa wasn't sure she wasn't screaming the words aloud. Miriam turned and pointed out the door. "That's my husband. He's the sheriff. I never joined the Amish, but I guess you can see that for yourself."

The back door opened and Rebecca came in. "I see John is here. I'll take over for you, Willa."

"Danki." How could this be happening? John lifted Megan out of the back of the wagon. He hadn't seen the sheriff. Willa stripped off her apron and grabbed her coat from behind the counter. She couldn't meet her cousin's eyes. "Good to see you, Miriam. I have to go."

"We'll see each other again. My daughter lives here."

Willa wanted to run to the wagon, but she forced herself to walk. She passed the sheriff on his way into the building. He stepped aside and tipped his hat. "Good day, *Frau* Lapp. Nice to see you again." After what seemed like an eternity, she reached John's side. "I have to take the girls with me. Lucy, Megan, get in the buggy."

"I thought I was taking you to the midwife."

"My plans have changed. I have to go home." She untied the horse from the railing at the side of the building.

"Willa, what's wrong?"

"I can't talk." She got in her buggy, and as soon as she was out of sight of the gift shop, she whipped the horse into a run.

John got home as fast as he could. Willa's sweaty horse stood in front of the house. He had no idea what was wrong. He moved through the house calling her name. She didn't answer. He stopped at her bedroom door and saw her bundling clothes together.

"Willa, what are you doing?" John stared at the purple backpack on her bed.

She emptied the pegs on the wall and the drawers of her bureau and stuffed everything into her bag. "I have to go. They are going to find out where I am if they don't know already. I have to protect the girls."

"Who do you have to protect them from?"

"From Glen's parents. They will know where I am soon if they don't already."

"What are you talking about?"

She closed the bag and faced him. "My cousin Miriam came into the gift shop. She recognized me. She will tell the sheriff and he'll come for me and take the girls away."

"You aren't a bad mother. We will show Nick the truth."

She turned her back to him. "You don't understand. I once did something very wrong."

He stepped close behind her and laid his hands on her shoulders. "What are you saying?"

She leaned back into his arms for a brief instant. Then she straightened. "I have to go."

He turned her around. "Go where?"

Cupping his face in her hands, she shook her head sadly. "You can't help me. I can't tell you where I'm going. They will come here looking for me, and I don't want you to have to lie for me. But I want you to know that I do love you, John. Please forgive me. If you love me, you won't try to stop me."

"That's not fair."

"I do love you. Never doubt that. No matter what you hear about me, know that I love you with all my heart."

"You're coming back, aren't you? When these people find you aren't here, they will go away."

"I wish it were that simple. They won't stop looking for us."

"What about Megan and Lucy? How will you explain this to them? They have grown to love me as I love them. They have grown to love my mother. She adores them. Taking them away will break her heart."

"Please, John, this isn't easy for me. Don't make it any harder."

He caught her hand. "I don't want it to be easy for you. I want it to be impossible for you to walk away from me."

Willa's heart ached for the pain she was causing him. "If only you knew how close to impossible it is. I'm sorry." She barely choked out the words.

Picking up her suitcase, she pressed past him and into the hall. Her daughters were playing with their dolls on the living room floor. "Get into the buggy, girls."

A sharp pain cut across her abdomen. Willa gave a muffled moan and leaned against the chair back. "Not now."

"Where we going?" Lucy asked.

"We have to take a little trip." When the contraction let up, she knelt and helped Lucy button her coat.

Megan touched her cheek. "Mama is sad."

Willa sniffled once and wiped away the tears that slipped down her face. "I'm not sad. I was just out in the cold too long."

Megan looked over her shoulder. "John sad. Need hug, John?"

"Yeah, I need a hug." He dropped to one knee and drew both girls to him.

"You're squishing me." Megan pulled back in protest.

Lucy wrapped her arms around his neck. "Love you, Johnjohn."

"I love you, too." His voice trembled. He kissed the top of her head and then kissed Megan. "*Gott* be with you."

Willa pressed her hand to her mouth to keep from sobbing. Why had God brought her to this wonderful man only to tear her away from him? It was so unfair.

"Let's go, girls." She struggled to her feet and swung her backpack over one shoulder. If she waited another minute, she wouldn't have the strength to walk away from him.

She opened the door but didn't look back. "Tell your mother goodbye for me."

He didn't say anything. She stepped out and closed the door behind her.

Chapter Fifteen

John wanted to smash his fist into the door. How could she do this? How could she turn her back on what they had? On her vows to the church? What had she done that was so terrible?

He sank to the floor as tears rolled down his face. Why did she make him love her and then leave?

He couldn't imagine life without her or her wonderful children. He was starting to think of her baby as his own child. In his mind they were his family. It had been a foolish daydream and nothing more.

He was sitting alone at the kitchen table when his mother came in half an hour later. She pulled off her coat and bonnet and hung them up. "I'm sorry I'm so late. I was talking with Belinda at the store and the time just slipped away. Where is Willa?"

"She has gone." Saying the words aloud made them even more painful.

"Gone where?"

He looked up and met his mother's puzzled gaze. "She wouldn't tell me."

"John, what are you saying?"

He drew a deep breath and sat up straight. "Willa has taken the children and has left us. She won't be coming back."

"*Nee*, that can't be."

"I wish with all my heart that it wasn't true, but it is."

"Why?"

"Miriam Bradley recognized her. Willa fears Nick will take the girls away."

"And you let her go?"

He stared at the floor. "What could I do?"

"Anything but sit alone in an empty house."

He rose slowly to his feet. "You're right. I will be out in the smithy."

His mother took hold of his suspenders with both hands. "*Nee*, you won't!"

"*Mamm*, stop it." He tried to free her grip, but she held on.

"I won't stop until you hear me. You locked yourself in your smoldering world of grief and hammered away until you had a shield of iron around your heart—until Willa and her children broke through it. Your great regret was letting Katie drive away that day after your argument without trying to stop her."

"It's not the same."

"You're right. It's not. You can't change the past, but you can find Willa and the children before she disappears with them forever."

"How am I going to find her? She wouldn't tell me where she was going?"

"Use your brain. She will need a car to get far away quickly. Who would drive her? She has no money."

His mother might actually be right. "The public

health nurse and the midwife both have cars. They might help her."

"Debra Merrick doesn't have a well-baby clinic today. She won't be at the school."

"Willa had an appointment with the midwife this afternoon."

"Go there. If you fail to find her, at least you will know you tried."

He bent and kissed his mother's cheek. "I'll find her and I'll bring her home."

John didn't bother with a buggy. He bridled Clover and swung up bareback. The shortest distance to the midwife's was through the woods by the river. He nudged the mare to a gallop and prayed his mother's guess was right.

Twenty minutes later, he saw two cars in the driveway along with Willa's buggy.

Please, God, let her be here.

He jumped off his horse, charged through the front door and skidded to a halt in the midwife's living room. Willa sat weeping on the sofa with Debra Merrick holding her hand.

Debra smiled at him. "Willa, I think you know this man. Lucy has mentioned you a lot, Johnjohn."

His racing heart slowed as he gazed at Willa's puffy eyes and tear-streaked face. He took off his hat, dropped to one knee in front of her and took her other hand. "No more running away, no more secrets. I'm here. I'm going to stay no matter what you tell me because I love you and I don't want to live without you."

Willa swallowed hard as she stared at his beloved face. "You won't feel that way when I tell you everything."

Janice came in from the other room. "The children are watching TV. You must be John Miller. Thank you for coming. Willa needs all the support she can get. Unfortunately, Dr. Marksman had an emergency."

John squeezed Willa's hand. "I'm listening."

She looked into his eyes, knowing the love she saw there would soon die, but he deserved to know the truth. "Two weeks after the twins were born, I developed what the doctors call postpartum psychosis. I started hearing voices. They weren't real. I know that now, but they were as clear to me then as your voice is today."

He raised one eyebrow. *"Narrish?"*

"I was crazy, yes."

"We don't use that word," Debra said. "You had a psychiatric illness."

Willa didn't take her eyes off John. "It's rare, but this illness happens only to new mothers. I never knew such a thing was possible. I was tired and depressed. The girls were fussy all the time. I felt like a failure as a mother. Glen said it was just the baby blues, but it turned into something much worse."

"Go on," John urged gently.

Willa drew comfort from his acceptance so far. "The voices told me to take my infants to the river and hide them in reed baskets so Glen couldn't hurt them. That shouldn't have made sense. He would never have hurt them, but I believed the voices. I don't remember what happened after I reached the riverbank. I was told I waded into the water with the babies strapped in their car seats, not in reed baskets. If I had let go of them, they would both have drowned. Do you understand? They would have died if a stranger hadn't stopped me from dropping them into the water. I was going to kill them, and I didn't even know it." She buried her face in her hands and started sobbing. Every day she gave thanks for the woman who had saved the lives of her daughters.

Debra spoke again. "Postpartum psychosis is caused by hormonal changes in a woman's body after she gives birth. It affects about one out of a thousand women. Sadly, we know little about how the brain is affected. We do know that approximately half of women who have had one episode will have another episode with their next pregnancy."

"But half of them will not be crazy again," John said.

"As I said, *crazy* isn't a word we use, but that's correct. The good news is that this condition can be treated. As I have been telling Willa, now that you and she are aware of the possibility of a reoccurrence, you can take steps to minimize the risks."

"What kind of steps do we take?" he asked.

Willa's gaze snapped to his. "We?"

His troubled expression faded. "You are not alone. You do not have to face this without help."

"You heard what I said. What I did."

"I heard you, and I have heard these women. The burden God has given you to bear is beyond my understanding, but not beyond my love."

Janice laid her hand on Willa's shoulder. "John is right. You aren't alone. That is the beauty of belonging to an Amish community. The incidence of postpartum depression is lower among Amish women. Studies suggest the reason is because Amish women have so much help after a new baby is born. Family members and mother's helpers arrive to take over the new mother's chores and leave her free to rest and focus on her baby. Getting adequate rest is one way to decrease the risk of a psychotic episode occurring. Another way is the use of antidepressant medication. The third step is to decrease your stress. Part of that means accepting help. This isn't something you have to hide. We will all help you."

Willa wiped her cheeks with both hands. "I can't stay. My husband's parents are trying to take my children away from me. They claim I am an unfit mother. They may know where I am by now. I have to get away."

Janice pulled up a chair and sat beside Willa. "You are not an unfit mother. I had no idea you were dealing with such an emotional issue. You must be terrified. Have you spoken to an attorney?"

Willa shook her head. "My husband didn't trust them. He said we had to keep moving so that his parents couldn't find us."

Debra patted Willa's hand. "I'm not one to speak ill of the dead, but he was wrong about that. It is difficult for grandparents to gain custody of their grandchildren in this state. Our courts are very reluctant to remove children from their biological parents. It is unlikely that your in-laws have been granted custody without an investigation and documentation of abuse or neglect."

The first bit of hope sprang to life in Willa's heart. "Are you sure? Glen said they have the money and influence to take the children from us."

Debra sat back. "I can't be positive, but I am certain of one thing. You are not an unfit mother and you should welcome the chance to prove it. I know several child welfare workers in this county. They can assess the children's home situation and prepare a report for your attorney. You do need a lawyer, and I can recommend a fine one. She's a friend of mine. With your permission, I will speak to her about your case. I'm sure she will help."

Willa looked to John. "Is that acceptable?"

He nodded. "It is to me."

Debra and Janice exchanged pointed looks. Janice said, "There is a way to make certain they can't remove the new baby after he or she is born."

"How?" John asked quickly.

Janice glanced from Willa to John. "In Ohio, when a woman marries, her husband is recognized as the legal father of her unborn child even if he is not the biological father. Your in-laws would not have a claim on the baby when he or she is born. Adoption is the only way you can gain legal rights for the twins."

John rose to his feet and paced across the floor as he considered Janice's words. If he proposed to Willa now, would he be placing undue pressure on her to wed him? He wanted her to marry him because she loved him, not because it would put her baby beyond the reach of her in-laws. He turned to gaze at her. God willing, they would have many years to sort out their feelings on the subject. "Willa Lapp, will you marry me?"

John didn't wait for her answer. He closed the distance between them and took her hands in his. "Let me do this."

She pressed a hand to her forehead. "I don't know what to say. I need to think."

"*Nee*, don't think." He wrapped his arms around her and gently kissed her, savoring the feel of her in his embrace. A rush of love for her pushed away his doubts and left him overwhelmed with tenderness for the courageous woman he held.

She pulled away. "I love you, John, but I can't let you do this."

"I love Lucy and Megan. You know that. I couldn't love them more if they were my own. Your babe is already the child of my heart. Why not let me give him or her my name?"

"I don't want you to marry me in haste and regret your decision for years."

"I won't regret it."

"What if I become ill again? What if I say terrible things and do terrible things each time I have a baby? You would soon learn to hate me."

"Never." He gripped her hand. "Marriage is for better or for worse, in sickness and in health. We don't know what God has planned for us, but I want a future with you if He allows it. A future we'll face together. I can speak to the bishop right away. We have both been married before, so we may wed at any time. This must be your decision, Willa. Place your trust in God and in me, and do not allow fear to rule your heart."

He watched the struggle going on behind her eyes. She closed them and bowed her head for so long he began to lose heart.

Chapter Sixteen

"I don't deserve your love, John." Willa looked up and smiled at him. "But I have never been more grateful for anything in my life."

"Will you marry me?"

"I can't believe you still want that."

He gathered her in his arms. "I will never stop wanting you, Willa darling. Give me the right to keep you by my side for as long as God wills. Give your children the right to call me their father."

"What if we lose them?"

He kissed her cheek. "We won't. I have faith in God's mercy. He has brought me all that my heart desires. Say yes."

Lucy came flying into the room and grabbed his arm as she grinned at him. "I heard you, Johnjohn. Did you miss me?"

Megan was close behind her sister and grabbed his other arm. "Can we go home, please? I think the kitties are missing me."

He rose to his feet, lifting both girls in his arms. "I

have missed you both and your mother most of all. What do you say, Willa? May we go home now?"

"Yes."

"Will you marry me? With these two witnesses, will you promise to love and cherish me for as long as we both shall live?"

Willa drew a deep breath and rose to her feet. "Yes."

She raised her face for his kiss and her daughters squealed in delight.

After two nerve-racking days without hearing from the sheriff, Willa started to relax. Perhaps Miriam didn't know Willa was the woman her husband had been looking for. Debra left a message on the machine at the phone hut, telling them her friend was willing to take their case at no cost and would be out to see them after the first of the year but to call if they needed her before then.

John spoke to the bishop and made plans to marry her on the Tuesday after Christmas. She could barely believe John was willing to wed her after all he had learned, but he constantly reassured her that he was.

On the morning of the third day, Willa was filling the coffeepot with water when she looked out the kitchen window and saw a white SUV with the county sheriff's logo printed on the side. It pulled to a stop in front of the house. A second unmarked black car stopped behind it. Her newfound faith in God's mercy was about to be put to the test.

John moved to stand behind her and laid his hands on her shoulders. "I know Sheriff Bradley. He is a *goot* man."

"But he must obey the law." It was too late to run. Where could she hide?

"We must have faith in God's goodness."

"That's easy for you to say. They aren't your children."

He turned Willa around to face him. "Those words are painful to hear. I love the girls as if they were my own. To see them taken away from us would break my heart into tiny pieces. The will of God can be difficult to accept, but even in our sorrow He is with us. This is our faith."

She wrapped her arms around him. "I'm sorry. Forgive me. I'm afraid."

"I know you are, but I have seen you be very brave for the sake of your children. Be brave now."

Vera came into the room. "Did I hear a car?" At Willa's nod, she said, "I'll keep the girls in their room until you send for them."

John led Willa to the front door, opened it and stepped outside still holding her hand. Nick Bradley and her cousin Miriam got out of the SUV.

"Good morning." The sheriff nodded at them.

"What brings you out this way, Nick?" John asked.

Miriam came around the vehicle to stand beside her husband, but her gaze was fixed on Willa. "Hello, cousin. We have brought Gary and Nora Chase with us. They have asked Nick to make a welfare check on their grandchildren. Are the girls here?"

Willa was trembling so hard she thought she might fall down. She couldn't speak. John slipped his arm around her shoulders and pulled her against his side. "They are. Come inside. It is too cold to stand out here and we have much to talk about."

The doors of the black car opened, and Willa got her first look at her in-laws. They didn't look like evil people. The man bore a stunning resemblance to his deceased son. He had graying hair and wore glasses, but she would have known him as Glen's father anywhere. The woman with him was blonde and slightly plump. She gripped her husband's arm tightly. Willa saw an odd mixture of hope and fear cross her face as she looked up at him. He covered her hand with his own in a gesture of comfort.

Willa turned away and went inside. She could hear the girls laughing in their room. She wanted to fly to them and gather them into her arms.

Please, God, I trust You to be with them and with me whatever Your plan is for us, but don't destroy their happiness. They are so young and innocent.

She moved into the kitchen and sat in the rocker by the stove. She clasped her hands together. Her fingers were ice-cold. John stood by her side with his hand on her shoulder.

The sheriff and Miriam took seats at the table. Willa's in-laws remained standing awkwardly in the center of the room. Miriam said, "I don't believe you have met these people."

Willa raised her chin. "My husband wanted nothing to do with them."

Glen's mother turned to hide her face in her husband's shoulder. His arm went around her. He cleared his throat. "We are aware of our son's feelings. I assure you it was one-sided. We loved Glen. We only wanted to help him."

Willa hardened her heart. "You chased him away from every job, from every home we tried to make. We lived in terror that you would find us and take our daughters away. How was that helping?"

Gary flinched but faced her. "Glen became a compulsive gambler as a teenager. It only got worse no matter how often we tried to help him. The break in our relationship came after my son stole a large amount of money from my business after I gave him a job there. I had no choice but to press charges. That's when he started running."

Willa bristled. "I never knew Glen to gamble."

Nora patted her husband's arm and faced Willa. "Our private investigator was often able to locate Glen by having the gambling windows watched at the larger racetracks."

Willa frowned. "He worked at the racetracks."

Gary nodded. "He did, but never for long because of his gambling."

Willa didn't want to believe him, but it explained so much: the large sums of money that disappeared quickly and the weeks without any pay. "You told him you were going to take the children away."

Nora stepped closer. "We were overjoyed when Glen called us to help with the babies after you became ill. We saw a chance to reconcile with our son. While you were hospitalized, I was home alone with the babies when a man Glen owed money to came to collect. It was so frightening. He left, but when Glen came home, Gary and I told him we wanted temporary custody of the children while he got help for his compulsive gambling addiction at an inpatient facility."

Gary moved to stand beside Nora. "We wanted to make sure both he and the girls were safe. Glen agreed and signed the papers, but before he went into treatment, he took the girls to visit you and disappeared. After we learned of his death, we continued looking for you because we want to help and because we love our grand-daughters. We don't want to take them away from you."

Miriam leaned forward on the table. "It's true, Willa. Nick checked out their story."

Willa looked at them in disbelief. "Glen lied about everything."

"Not everything," Nora said. "He loved you and his daughters very much. May we see the girls?"

John said, "Come with me and I'll reintroduce you to Megan and Lucy. They will be delighted to have a new *mammi* and *daddi*, but first I must tell you that Willa and I plan to marry. I will raise Willa's children as my own."

Nick chuckled. "We heard the news from Debra and your new attorney early this morning. Nora and Gary had plenty of questions about having Amish grand-children."

Miriam smiled at Willa. "Fortunately, we were able to answer most of those questions, since we have an Amish granddaughter, too. If your girls are anything like Hannah was at three, watch out."

Gary grasped his wife's hand. "We just want to be a part of their lives."

Glen had wronged his parents and lied to her, but she knew he had been genuinely afraid of losing the girls. She glanced at John. He nodded and said, "Perhaps you would like to spend Christmas with us so we can get to know each other."

Gary looked at his wife. "We'd love that."

"You should come to the school's Christmas program tonight," Miriam suggested. "It will give you a feel for the kind of education your grandchildren will have."

"Plus, Hannah has a major part in the play they're putting on," Nick said with a knowing smile for his wife.

The girls were shy of their new grandparents at first, but by midafternoon they were showing Gary and Nora the kittens and cows in the barn and introducing them to the horses. John came into the house while they were exploring. Willa was washing dishes. "Are you all right?" he asked.

She sighed heavily. "All these years of fear for nothing. I still can't believe it. I was wrong to doubt God's mercy so long. I can't imagine how Nora and Gary must have suffered."

"We will make it up to them. Shall we take the sleigh or the buggy to the school program tonight?"

She touched a soapy finger to his nose. "I have a fondness for sleighs, as one brought us together."

"Fond enough to name our boy Melvin? It was his sleigh."

"I have always liked that name."

He rubbed his nose on her *kapp* and kissed her forehead. "Then the sleigh it is."

They attended the late performance. Vera was in her element as she explained their Amish customs and answered Nora's questions. Afterward, the family rode home slowly along the snow-covered country road as the brilliant stars came out overhead. The only sounds were the hissing of the runners over the snow and the jingle of harness bells. Willa snuggled against John and leaned her head on his shoulder. The peace of Christmas Eve seeped into her heart and healed the wounds of Glen's betrayal.

God had brought a fine man into her life, and she was a fool if she didn't hold on to him.

When they reached home, Willa and Nora put the girls to bed and had to read only one story before the twins were both fast asleep.

John leaned back in his chair and glanced up as Nora and Willa came into the kitchen, where he and Gary had been enjoying a cup of coffee after having decorated the mantel and window ledges with pine boughs.

Willa drew a deep breath and smiled. "It smells wonderful in here."

Vera came in with several large candles and holders in her hands. "It finally seems like Christmas. Willa, will you place the candles in the windows so the world may see them shining brightly and know the light of the Christ child is found in this household?"

John's heart overflowed with love for Willa as he watched her place a candle in the kitchen window and light it. In a few more days she would be his wife. Suddenly, her face grew pale. Her knuckles turned white as her fingers tightened on the window ledge. He sprang to his feet. "What's wrong?"

Willa started panting. "It's time."

"Are you sure? Could this be false labor?" his mother asked.

"*Nee*, this is the real thing. My back has been aching for a while." She drew a deep breath and stood upright.

"It's too soon." Fear clutched John's chest.

Willa shook her head. "The midwife said this one might come early. My dates could be off."

His mother turned to him. "Fetch the midwife."

John felt as if his feet had turned to lead. Willa's baby was coming, and he wasn't yet her husband. "I will fetch the bishop, too."

"You don't have to, John," Willa said softly.

"I don't need to, but I want to." How much time did he have? "I'll hitch up the buggy."

Gary took John by the arm. "It will be faster if we use my car. It has four-wheel drive."

As the men rushed out the door, Nora took Willa by the arm. "Are you ready to lie down, or do you want to walk?"

"I'll walk. I hope they hurry."

They did. Willa was standing in the living room holding on to the fireplace mantel when John and Gary rushed in with a sleepy and slightly grumpy bishop.

"Where is the midwife?" Nora demanded, looking past them.

"I called her. She is on her way," Gary assured her.

Willa gritted her teeth as another contraction hit. "I hate to rush you, Bishop Beachy, but I don't think we have much time."

The flustered man motioned to John. "Take her hand. Maid of honor stand at Willa's side and the groomsman stand beside John."

Nora stepped back to allow Vera to stand beside Willa, but Willa shook her head and held out her hand. "Nora, I would be most pleased if you would stand up with me."

"Are you sure?"

"You are part of my family. I'm sure."

"Don't you need rings?" Gary asked, working his wedding band off.

"*Nee*, we do not use such worldly symbols," the bishop said kindly.

Willa grasped John's hand and felt him tremble. "Are you sure?" she whispered.

He squeezed her fingers as he smiled at her. "I am

the happiest man on earth at this moment. I'm sure. Are you?"

Willa thought she knew exactly how he felt. "There is not a doubt in my heart."

Together they listened to the solemn words of the ceremony and answered "I do" in strong, sure voices.

The bishop raised his hand to bless them. "I pronounce you husband and wife and what *Gott* has joined together let no man put asunder."

The outside door opened, and Janice Willard came in with a large black bag. She paused as she saw the gathering. "What did I miss?"

"Not the most important part," John said. He turned to Willa, gently pulled her into his arms and kissed her. A second later another, stronger, contraction hit, and she bowed her head against his shoulder. She couldn't stifle the moan that rose to her throat.

"I know that sound," Janice said as she moved John out of the way and took Willa's arm. "Let's get you into bed."

In the early hours of Christmas morning, Melvin John Miller made his appearance in the world, and Willa wondered how so much pure love and joy could arrive in a six-pound-two-ounce bundle.

The twins were excited to find a new baby had arrived in the night, but they worried it might have to go back home later. Willa assured them baby Melvin was theirs to keep.

At John's suggestion, Gary invited the girls outside to see another gift. The sled John had made sat on the front porch. Megan and Lucy soon had Gary pulling them around the yard on it until he was red in the face. When he tired, Nora took over, laughing like a kid herself.

John sat on the edge of the bed beside Willa and gazed in awe at the child sleeping in her arms. "You have a beautiful son."

Willa looked tired but happy. "We have a beautiful son."

John reached out and drew his fingers along the curve of her cheek. "I have received a pair of *schnickelfritz*, a newborn son and a *frau* I love with all my heart as my Christmas gifts. I'm afraid I will wake and find it has all been a dream."

She captured his hand and pressed a kiss into his palm. "I am not a dream. I love you, husband, with all my heart."

"It was hard for me to believe in love again, but you and your children have convinced me that God wishes us to be a family." He leaned his forehead against hers and whispered, "I will never stop giving thanks for your love."

"I trust God to make our lives joyful. I trust that he will give us more children to love and years to work together side by side. I know we shall have obstacles to overcome and trials to endure, but I will do my best to make you a good wife."

John's lips touched hers with incredible gentleness, a featherlight touch. The sweet softness of his lips moved away from her mouth. He kissed her cheek and then her brow. It wasn't enough. She cupped his face with her hand and brought his mouth back to hers. To her delight, he deepened the kiss. Joy clutched her heart and stole her breath away.

Slowly, he drew back. Willa wasn't ready to let him go. She would never be ready.

"I love you, Willa," he murmured softly into her ear.

"You made me whole again. I was brokenhearted and on the edge of despair. You and your beautiful daughters found a way to mend me."

"I lived a life ashamed of what I had done. I thought I was beyond help. I thought I didn't deserve the wonderful babies God had given me. And then you came into my life and I saw hope and I found faith."

He kissed her again and then leaned down to kiss the baby's head. There was a knock at her door. Gary and Nora came in with Vera and the twins. The girls edged close to the bed to admire their new brother.

"I like him," Megan said, touching him softly.

"I like him more," Lucy added, taking hold of his little hand. She looked at John. "Are you sure we can keep him?"

John smiled. "I'm sure."

"Are you our daddy now?" Megan asked.

He nodded solemnly. "*Ja*, I am your *daed*. Is this okay?"

Megan stared at him a long moment. "Does this mean we're your Amish daughters?"

"*Ja, Gott* has given me Amish Christmas twins as a gift. I love you and your little brother very much."

The girls climbed on the bed and put their arms around his neck. Lucy kissed his cheek. "We love you, too, Johnjohn."

In that moment, Willa thanked God for the mysteriously twisted path that had brought them all to this place. It was exactly where they belonged.

* * * * *

HER AMISH
CHRISTMAS CHOICE

Leigh Bale

To my very own Rose, who has brought me more joy
than I ever thought possible.

I returned, and saw under the sun, that the race is not to the swift, nor the battle to the strong, neither yet bread to the wise, nor yet riches to men of understanding, nor yet favour to men of skill; but time and chance happeneth to them all.
—*Ecclesiastes* 9:11

Chapter One

"*Hallo?*"

Julia Rose jerked, startled. The two nails she'd been holding between her pursed lips dropped to the wooden planks of the front porch and bounced off into the weedy flower bed.

She swiveled around on the rickety ladder and caught a glimpse of a tall man standing directly behind her. She didn't have time to return his greeting. The leather gloves she wore were overly large and caused her to lose her grasp on the heavy hammer. It followed the nails, thudding to the wooden porch below. The ladder wobbled and she fought to retain her grip on the tall post she'd been holding upright with her left hand. For fifteen minutes, she'd struggled to get it in just the right spot so she could nail it into place. Now, it slid sideways. Without its support, the heavy canopy above sagged dangerously near her head. The overly stressed timbers gave a low groan and she widened her eyes.

"*Acht gewwe!*" the man called in a foreign language.

A sickening crack sounded above and Julia scrambled down the ladder. Like a zipper coming undone, the nails holding the awning to the side of the building pinged into the air as the canopy tore away from the outer wall and knocked her to the ground. She gasped in pain as the ruined wood continued its descent toward her.

With a cry of alarm, she curled against the side of the wall, protecting her head with her arms. She was vaguely aware of the man shielding her, taking the brunt of the weight against his own back.

"Oof!"

She glanced up and found his face no more than a breath away. She gazed into his eyes, catching the subtle scent of licorice. His muscular arms held her tight as another piece of the canopy bludgeoned him with a shocking thump. He jerked at the impact but made no sound. For several seconds, they both held perfectly still. She felt uncomfortable with his close proximity but couldn't move away just then.

"*Alles fit?* Are you all right?" His voice sounded low and calm, like the approach of thunder off in the distance.

"I think so." She stared in fascination, captivated by his piercing blue eyes... The kind of eyes that could see deep inside a person's heart and know exactly what they were thinking. In those brief moments, she took in his plain clothes, his angular face, short auburn hair and a faint smattering of freckles across the bridge of his nose. No doubt he spent hours working outside in the sun.

"Mar-tin! Mar-tin, are you okay?"

Julia looked up and saw a boy of approximately fifteen years standing in front of the ruined porch. Dressed identical to the man, his short, stocky build was accented by plain black pants, a blue chambray shirt, black suspenders and a black felt hat.

They were Amish!

"*Ja*, I'm okay, Hank." The man holding onto Julia let her go and moved back with a slight grimace.

She scurried to safety, standing beyond the reach of the broken canopy. With her out of the way, the man jerked to the side and let the remaining boards sag to the ground. They hung there like a great, broken beast.

"It'll be all right now. You'll be okay." The boy named Hank patted Julia's arm, looking directly into her eyes as he earnestly searched her expression for distress.

Hank was a stranger and again she felt uncomfortable by the invasion of her personal space but saw no guile in his dark eyes. He looked genuinely concerned for her welfare. His brown eyes slanted upward and he had an open, childlike expression. As she took in his reddish-blond hair and small, flat nose, she recognized instantly that Hank must have Down Syndrome.

"Y-yes. I'm fine," she said.

He smiled wide, pushing his wire-rimmed spectacles up the bridge of his nose. He looked so innocent and sincere that she had to return his infectious smile.

"Mar-tin, she's okay. How about you? Are you okay?" Hank asked, his accent heavy.

"*Ja*, I'm all right," the man named Martin said.

But Julia had her doubts. He stood slowly and sidestepped the rubble, stumbling before he regained his footing. As he rubbed his left arm, a flash of pain crossed his face. He clenched his eyes closed for a brief moment but didn't utter a single word of complaint. His black felt hat had been knocked from his head. He opened his eyes and glanced at her, a look of worry creasing his handsome forehead.

"You are not injured?" he asked, his voice tinged with an edge of authority.

She shook her head. "No, thanks to you."

She coughed and waved a hand at the dust filling the air. Martin had used his own body to shield her from the heavy boards. She considered what might have happened if he hadn't been there.

He stood up straight, his great height a sharp contrast to Hank's. "You should rope off this area so no one walks by unaware and puts themselves in danger."

"Yes, I'll do that. Th-thank you," she said, still breathless and amazed by the ordeal.

"You're *willkomm*." He brushed the dust off his clothes.

"Mar-tin, I saw what happened and came to help." Hank's face was lit by an eager expression.

"*Ach*, you sure did. I'm glad you were here." Martin rested a hand on Hank's shoulder and the boy smiled at the man with adoration. The two looked alike, yet Martin didn't seem old enough to be Hank's father. Perhaps they were brothers?

"Thank the *gut* Lord no one was seriously injured today." Martin flexed his right arm as if testing it for soundness. He arched his waist, his blue chambray shirt stretching taut across his solid chest.

Hmm, very odd. Though she understood his comment, she realized he was mixing English with some other language.

He looped his thumbs through his black suspenders. The tips of his heavy work boots were almost covered by the hem of his plain gray pants. A brisk October wind ruffled his short hair, but he didn't seem to feel the chill. Within two weeks, it would be November. Julia pulled her own jacket tighter in front of her, ever conscious that winter was fast approaching.

When the man reached to scoop up his hat and placed it on his head, she tried to look away. Since she'd never seen an Amish man before—even when she'd lived in Kansas, where she knew a few settlements existed—she couldn't help staring. When she and her mom had recently moved here to Riverton, Colorado, she hadn't expected to find any Amish. But more than that, she wondered what he was doing here at her place.

"Who are you?" she asked, trying not to sound rude.

He bent over and tossed the heavy post aside, his movements strong and athletic. "I am Martin Hostetler and this is my younger brother Hank. Carl Nelson, the attorney in town, told me you are looking for a handyman to fix up your place. I've done work for Carl in the past. If the owner of your business is available, I'd like to speak with him about a job."

Him. He thought the owner of the store was a man.

A stab of pain pierced Julia's heart. Her father had never owned this rundown hovel; he'd died just eleven months earlier after a valiant battle with pancreatic cancer. Both Julia and her mother missed him more than they could say.

"I'm the owner, Julia Rose," she said, lifting her chin higher and trying to force a note of confidence into her voice.

After her father became sick, she'd supported her parents off the proceeds of her handmade soap. Mom had lupus and couldn't help much. As an only child, Julia had stepped in to care for them. It had been a meager living but Julia was grateful her mother had taught her the craft. She'd learned to make lotions, creams, facial masks and lip balms, too. But if they didn't get the soap store up and running within the next six weeks, she wouldn't have time to make more soap, which could jeopardize her wholesale contract.

"*Ach*, you are the owner? But I thought Walter Rose still owned this building." Martin blinked, gazing at the drab brown structure with surprise.

"That's right. He was my grandfather. But he died a couple of months ago and left everything to me."

"*Ach*, I didn't know. Mr. Nelson didn't tell me that. My condolences."

"*Ja*, my condenses, too," Hank said, struggling to pronounce the word with his thick tongue.

Julia couldn't hold back a small laugh, to which the boy smiled. It was a blunt, open smile that sparkled his dark eyes and lit up his face with joy.

She glanced at Martin, seeing the genuine compassion in his eyes. She also felt sad for her grandfather's passing but couldn't really miss him. Not when she'd never met the man. Now that she was twenty-three, she mourned the fact that she'd never gotten to know her grandpa. As an only child, she had lived a rather lonely life and longed for family and friends. She thought she'd found that when she became engaged to Dallin almost two years earlier. But it didn't last. And all she knew about her grandfather was that he had not gotten along well with her father. At all. The two had a falling-out years before her birth and hadn't spoken since. She had no idea why.

"Mr. Nelson sent you here?" she asked.

"*Ja*, he said you need a handyman to help with repairs."

Carl Nelson was the only attorney in town and had contacted Julia after Grandpa Walt died. Located at the end of Main Street, the store was rundown but spacious, with lots of potential for growth. Her grandfather had lived in the two-bedroom apartment upstairs, which included a small bathroom and kitchen-living area. But they had no electricity in spite of having turned the power back on. Julia wasn't sure, but she thought there was a problem with the fuse box. Apparently, the same situation had existed while Grandpa Walt had lived here. She and her mother had arrived in town two weeks earlier and were still using the gas and kerosene lamps he'd left behind.

"I definitely need a handyman," Julia said as she explained the situation to Martin. "With my father being sick and not enough money to pay the bills, we had to shut off the power back home in Kansas. I've contacted an electrician here in Riverton, but it'll cost a lot to replace the fuse panel and upgrade the system. We need to wait until I have more funds. But it's no matter. We kind of got used to doing without electricity. We live a simple life."

He nodded. "You are better off without it and I don't need it for my work."

"That's good. Paying you is my priority right now, so I can get my studio and store up and running. Do you know carpentry work?" she asked, wondering how he could do the job without a power drill and electric saw.

Another nod, a slight smile curving his lips. "*Ja*, and plumbing, but I don't use electricity."

Though she'd never met an Amish person, she'd

heard the use of electricity was against their religious values, or something like that.

"But there's just one thing you need to know... Hank works with me. I promise he won't be a bother or slow me down. Is that okay?" Martin asked.

As he listened to this exchange, Hank's eyes widened, his mouth hanging slack. His expression looked so intense that she didn't have the heart to say no.

"Of course. That will be fine," she said, realizing she had no one else to hire. Not in a town this size. Thankfully, the money Grandpa Walt had left her would allow her to pay a handyman.

Hank's eyes sparkled with pure delight. "*Ach*, I work hard, too. I help a lot."

She returned his smile, a feeling of deep compassion filling her heart. She liked this boy and his brother. All her life, she'd wished she had a brother or sister of her own. Someone to help look after her ailing parents. Since her breakup with her lying ex-fiancé, she'd felt so alone and it warmed her heart to see how kind these two brothers were to each other.

"*Gut.* What needs to be done?" Martin asked.

Julia shrugged, brushing at her faded blue jeans. "As you can see, the front porch is falling apart, there are two gaping holes in one of the walls of my workroom, and I need to install counters, cabinets and shelving in the area where I plan to make and sell my soap."

Martin nodded, seeming to mentally calculate how to accomplish these tasks. "You make soap?"

"Yes, among other things. I sell my products nationwide. But since the soap needs to cure for four or five weeks, I'm eager to get some made before my next contract comes due the first of February. I supply hand-made soaps to KostSmart."

He looked at her without recognition. Obviously, this Amish man didn't get out much if he'd never heard of the giant supermarket chain. But since they didn't have a KostSmart here in Riverton, she figured it was unimportant. As long as the town had a postal service, she could ship her goods anywhere in the world.

"Follow me." Julia slipped through the front door. "The porch is the first thing I need repaired, so we can walk inside without fearing for our lives."

"*Ja*, I see that." Martin showed a wry smile as he trailed after her. Upon entering the spacious room, he pulled the hat off his head. Hank did likewise, copying his brother's every movement.

Wow! They sure were polite. Dallin, her ex-fiancé, had never treated her so courteously. Never said *please* or *thank you*. Never asked how she was. How it hurt to discover he was coming over not to spend time with her, but to be near her former best friend, Debbie. But Dallin had loved kids. Julia had longed for a family of her own and thought she would have it with him. Losing her fiancé and best friend all at once had broken her heart and left her feeling more alone than ever before.

She mentally shook her head. No! She was not going to think about Dallin. She'd already cried buckets of tears over him. She and Mom had a fresh start and it didn't include her two-timing fiancé and ex–best friend. But he'd taught her one important lesson: never trust a man.

"Exactly how skilled a carpenter and plumber are you?" she asked.

"I am skilled enough for the work you need done."

Martin's voice was filled with confidence and a sweeping honesty. But Dallin's lies had taught her to question everything.

"Can you expand on your experience, please?" she asked.

"Ja..." Martin took a deep breath. "I have helped the men in my *Gmay* build seven barns, nine houses, a variety of sheds and outbuildings and many pieces of furniture in my father's home."

"What is a *Gmay*?" she asked.

"The Amish community here in Riverton. Members of our congregation follow the same *Ordnung* and attend church together. We also rely on one another in all facets of everyday life," he said.

"Ordnung?" she asked, enthralled by his use of new words and curious to know their meaning.

"The unwritten rules that govern our community."

"Oh. Then, I suppose you are skilled enough," she said.

Still, a lance of skepticism speared her. Although the building she owned was quite shabby, Julia had a vision of a happy place to live. Some nails and paint could transform this store beautifully. She was determined to make it work. Determined to secure a future for her and Mom. She must! She was alone now and had promised her father before his death that she'd look after her mother. After all, Mom was the only family she had left.

Martin glanced around the enormous room filled with boxes, broken furniture and piles of junk.

"Except for the old woodstove, I'd like everything hauled off to the dump," she said.

"Ja, I can do that. Hank will help me," Martin said.

Hank nodded eagerly. Julia didn't see how they could carry everything off without a truck, but she didn't say so. She had already cleared tons of debris from their living quarters upstairs and stacked it neatly in the backyard until they could haul it off. When she considered the bit of money Grandpa Walt had left her, she didn't want to spend it on a car. Although she had a driver's license, they'd sold their broken-down truck to pay bills many months ago. When she and Mom had moved to Colorado, they'd shipped their few possessions here, then traveled to town via bus. The general store, post office and bank were within walking distance, so they shouldn't need a vehicle.

"What do you charge?" She braced herself, but there was no need. Martin requested such a low hourly rate for himself and Hank that she was compelled to offer more.

Martin shook his head. "*Ne*, the price I have asked is sufficient for our needs."

"But…but I don't want to cheat you," she said.

"You won't. I trust you. It is a fair price for both of us," he insisted, his gaze never wavering.

Hank didn't say a word, just gawked at his brother with complete confidence.

"All right. When can you start?" she asked, hoping he didn't let her down.

"Right now. But we don't work on Sundays. I'll get my tools."

He headed outside with Hank. She watched them through the grimy windows that desperately needed cleaning. While many people worked or played on Sunday, she figured Martin and his family must go to church. With her father's death and mother's illness, she'd been thinking about God quite a bit lately. She'd been hungering to know and understand His place in her life. She'd even considered going to church, to see if she could learn more about Him, though she hadn't had time to act on that goal yet.

It was then she noticed a horse and buggy-wagon, tied beneath the tall elm tree that edged the five-space parking lot in front of the store. Martin reached into the back of the wagon, lifted out a large wooden toolbox with a handle on it, then headed back toward the store with Hank trailing after him like a waddling duck.

With a measuring tape, Martin calculated the expanse of the porch and made some notes with a pencil and notepad. Placing his hands on his narrow hips, he studied the wreckage. Hank copied his brother's stance, his pudgy hands on his thick waist. Standing side by side, the two brothers looked endearing. When Martin jerked on a pair of leather gloves and started stacking debris off to the side of the building, Hank did likewise.

Soon, Martin appeared at the front door. "I'm afraid the lumber is rotted clear through." He met Julia's gaze.

"What do you recommend?" she asked.

"I should install new lumber and then paint it to match the rest of the store. It'll be more sound and last you for years to come."

Again, she was struck by his self-confidence. "All right. If you'll go to the building supply store, just tell Byron Stott what you need and to put the charge on my account. I've already made arrangements with him and he knows I'll have someone coming in to buy supplies for me."

She didn't tell him that she'd also warned Byron not to let her new handyman cheat her. Byron knew he must provide her with a receipt. She'd trusted money to Dallin once and it had quickly disappeared. She wouldn't do that again.

Martin nodded, then turned on his boot heels and went outside. Hank was poking the dirt with a long stick but came running when his brother called him. As the two climbed into the buggy, Julia folded her arms, thinking it was much too cold in the shop. Soon, the snow would fly. She should speak with Martin about obtaining firewood for the old black stove. Hopefully he would know where she could buy fuel at the lowest price.

Turning, she glanced out the window, noticing the horse and buggy had disappeared from view. Trust. It wasn't a new notion to her, but something she no longer freely gave to everyone she met. Dallin had betrayed her trust, but she was willing to try one more time. She just hoped Martin Hostetler didn't let her down.

Martin stood inside the building supply store and gazed at the stacks of two-by-fours he intended to buy. Wearing his heavy leather gloves, he lifted several boards onto his flat cart and thought about the woman who had just hired him.

Julia Rose was pretty, with a small upturned nose, a stubborn chin and soft brown eyes that showed intelligence and an eagerness to succeed but also a bit of self-doubt. With her russet hair pulled back in a long ponytail and no makeup, she looked almost Amish. But not in the blue jeans and shirt she was wearing. And most definitely not without the white organdy prayer *kapp* that all Amish women wore.

She was *Englisch*. A woman of the world. Yet, Martin couldn't help admiring her spunk. The way she'd stood on that rickety ladder and gripped the hammer told him she was determined. In fact, she reminded him of his *mamm*, who had raised six children and still worked beside his *daed* after twenty-eight years, doing whatever needed to be done without complaint.

"Whatcha gonna make?" Hank asked in Deitsch, the German dialect his Amish people used among themselves.

Martin turned and found his brother standing beside him. He was as sweet and sincere as they came. The Amish only went to school through the eighth grade. Now that Hank was too old for that, Martin had taken him under his wing. Both his parents tended to lose their patience with Hank and his penchant for getting into trouble, but Martin had deep compassion for his younger brother and had recently started taking the boy with him.

"Remember, we're making a porch overhang for Rose Soapworks?" Martin said.

"*Ja*, that's right. I remember now," Hank said, his thick voice filled with a happy lilt. Nothing seemed to ruffle the boy's feathers. He was always in a good mood.

Pushing his cart, Martin headed toward the aisle where sheets of metal siding were stacked in tidy order. He was careful not to buy too much. He'd been pleasantly surprised when Julia Rose had told him to come pick out the supplies he would need and he didn't want to betray her trust.

"Julia's gonna like the porch we make, huh, Mar-tin?" Hank said, speaking his name as if it were two words.

"*Ja*, I hope so. But you should call her Miss Rose."

"How come? I like her name. Julia. Julia. Julia," Hank repeated in his heavy staccato voice.

"It's not good manners for you to call her by her first name. She's a grown woman and you're still a youth. It's proper for you to call her Miss Rose." Martin stepped past the boy, pushing his cart as he went.

With dogged determination, Hank hurried after him. "I like her last name, too. Rose. Rose. Rose. How come she's got two first names?"

"I don't know but Rose is her last name." Martin didn't try to overexplain as he rounded the corner and quickly filled a paper sack with nails and lag bolts. He was used to his brother's incessant chatter and didn't let it bother him. He selected several pieces of flashing to sieve off water during rainstorms.

Hank grinned and slid his dirty fingers beneath the suspenders crossing his shirtfront. He'd removed his leather gloves and tucked them into his waistband. "We're gonna get enough money to build your barn, huh?"

"We're working toward that goal and a little extra so *Mamm* can make you a new coat and vest for Church Sunday," Martin conceded.

"*Ach*, a gray coat 'cause I look *gut* in gray. Julia sure is *schee*. Don't you think so?"

"Miss Rose," Martin corrected.

"*Ja*, Miss Rose sure is *schee*," Hank said.

Yes, Julia was pretty, but Martin didn't say so. It wouldn't be proper, especially since she was *Englisch*. Even now, he couldn't forget the soft feel of her during those few scant seconds when he'd held her in his arms, or the fragrance of her hair, a subtle mixture of citrus. And the moment he'd looked into her beautiful brown eyes, he'd felt something shift inside his heart like the cracking of a giant oak tree's trunk beneath a bolt of lightning.

No! He mustn't think such things. Julia wasn't Amish and he didn't want to do anything unseemly that might get him into trouble with his parents or church elders.

Hurrying to the front of the store, he set the bag of nails on the counter. Byron Stott, the proprietor, stood behind the cash register. He pushed a jagged thatch of salt-and-pepper hair out of his eyes and glanced at Martin.

"Anything else you need?"

"*Ne*, this is all. Please put everything on Julia Rose's account," Martin said.

Byron lifted a bushy eyebrow in curiosity. "So, she hired you as her handyman, did she?"

Martin nodded.

"And me, too," Hank chimed in.

Byron grunted. "She told me someone would be coming in."

Martin stood silent. Though he had lived in this community over ten years and knew the townspeople quite well, he was Amish and understood the expectations of his faith. He should keep himself apart from the world and not become too friendly with the *Englisch* townsfolk.

Moving around Martin's cart, Byron lifted and moved each item to access the price tag. The beep of the scanning gun filled the air in quick repetition.

"You gonna ask Julia to drive home with you from the singings?" Hank asked his brother.

Noticing that Byron was watching him with amusement, Martin's face flushed with heat and he quickly turned away. "*Ne*, of course not."

The singings were usually held after church services and included all the young people who were of dating age. As a group, they spent the evening singing or, if weather permitted, playing volleyball outside. They enjoyed refreshments afterward and frequently the young men drove the young women home in their buggies. Alone. This form of Amish dating frequently resulted in marriage. But at the age of twenty-five, Martin had long ago stopped attending such events because the girls were too young and immature to hold his interest.

"How come?" Hank persisted.

"Your kind can't marry outside your church." Byron Stott spoke as if it should be obvious.

"Oh." Hank's mouth rounded in confusion. He stared at the man, the tip of his tongue protruding between his lips. "But what if she becomes Amish? Then it would be okay. Right?"

Martin didn't respond but he saw Byron's curious stare. This wasn't the first time that Hank had embarrassed him in public.

"Since you don't want her, I'm gonna invite her to the singing. We can make her Amish and then she's gonna be my girl," Hank said in a happy voice.

Byron flipped a lever and opened the till on the cash register as he laughed out loud. "A grown woman like Julia Rose isn't gonna join the Amish and she definitely won't be your girl."

Martin bristled at the proprietor's unkind words but remained mute.

Hank scowled. "How come? I'd treat her real *gut*.

Just like my *vadder* treats my *mudder*. She is his queen. And that's how I'd treat Julia. Like a queen."

Byron just snorted and looked away.

Martin didn't say a word. He didn't want to hurt his brother's feelings. *Familye* and marriage meant everything to the Amish people. Telling Hank that he would probably never marry and have a *familye* of his own wouldn't be nice.

Not when Martin had failed to secure a wife for himself. He knew he should have wed long ago. It was the expectation of his people. He'd stepped out with every eligible Amish woman here in Riverton and those living in the nearby town of Westcliffe, too. A couple of years ago, he'd spent several months with his relatives in Indiana, seeking a suitable Amish wife. But he'd failed miserably. It seemed either the woman didn't want him or he didn't want her, with nothing in between.

He thought about Julia Rose again and the way the sunlight gleamed against her russet hair. Wouldn't it be ironic if he finally found someone he wanted to marry… and she happened to be *Englisch*? Such a relationship would never work. Either Martin would be shunned for marrying outside his faith, or his wife would have to convert. He couldn't see either scenario happening between him and Julia Rose. Besides, his faith was too important for him to give up.

His thoughts were ridiculous and he almost laughed out loud at his silly musings.

Byron completed the tally, made some notes on a ledger, then handed a long receipt to Martin.

"Give this to Julia. She'll be expecting it," Byron said.

With a quick nod, Martin folded the receipt and tucked it inside his black felt hat since he had no pockets.

"*Ach*, I don't see why I can't invite Julia to the singings just because she isn't Amish. I'm gonna ask her to be my girl. You just wait and see," Hank mumbled as they headed outside.

Martin was not going to comment. Not in a million years. Hank saw mostly the good in other people and didn't always understand social mores. Although their mother was accepting of Hank's Down syndrome, she had confided to Martin once that she feared she had been punished by *Gott* for doing something wrong. Martin had comforted her, believing it was just the way Hank was. The boy was so eager to please and rarely showed anger or malice. He brought so much joy into their lives that Martin thought he was a blessing, not a punishment.

The buggy-wagon was parked off to the side where Byron Stott had constructed a hitching tether for his Amish clientele. Hank skipped along beside Martin, stopping to inspect an ant crawling across the pavement. Martin quickly loaded his purchases into the back of the wagon, waited for Hank to get inside the buggy, then took the lead lines into his hands and slapped them against the horse's back. As he turned onto the street and headed toward Rose Soapworks, he let the rhythmic clop of the horse's hooves settle his jangled nerves.

For some reason, Hank's senseless chatter upset him today. It had never bothered him before. Martin usually had a quiet heart. But somehow, meeting Julia Rose had unsettled him more than he'd realized.

He'd recently purchased sixty-five acres of fine farmland just two miles outside of town. In the spring, he planned to build a barn and raise horses and a *familye* of his own. But just one problem: he had no wife. No one to build a house for. No one to love and dote on the way he longed to do. No reason to work so hard for the land he'd just acquired. And no one to love him in return.

But he was determined to change all of that. And soon.

Chapter Two

"Who is that?"

Julia turned and found her mother standing beside her in the spacious workroom at the front of the store.

It was lunchtime and Julia was getting ready to make sandwiches when she thought perhaps she should ask her new workmen if they were hungry. Gazing out the wide windows, she'd been watching Martin and Hank tap-tapping with hammers as they rebuilt the front porch. Or rather, Martin did most of the work while Hank hopped around in a circle, chased a stray dog and laughed out loud at absolutely nothing at all.

"They're our new handymen. The man's name is Martin Hostetler and that's his younger brother Hank. Mr. Nelson recommended them to us," Julia said.

Her mother frowned. At the age of forty-four, Sharon Rose was still fairly young but she had lupus and not much stamina. Though she never wore makeup and insisted on keeping her long, graying hair pinned in a tight bun at the back of her head, she had a pretty face with soft brown eyes. Dressed like Julia in blue jeans and tennis shoes, Sharon took a deep breath and let it go.

"But they're Amish," she said.

"Yes, that surprised me, as well. But Martin rescued me when the porch canopy fell on top of me and he says that he's an experienced carpenter and plumber. Apparently, he's helped build numerous structures."

The scowl on Sharon's face deepened. "I have no doubt that's true. The Amish always help each other build their own homes and barns. But isn't there someone else you can hire?"

Julia figured Mom had acquired knowledge about the Amish sometime during her life. But her mother's doubt caused a lance of uncertainty to spear Julia's heart. She was trying so hard to be a savvy businesswoman and to keep her promise to her father. Had she made a mistake by hiring Martin without knowing more about him? No, she didn't think so.

"Not that I know of. Mr. Nelson told me he would send us one of the best carpenters in the area. He said the man would work hard and wouldn't cheat us," she said.

"That's probably true. The Amish are brutally honest. At least they have that quality going for them." Mom said the words with contempt, as though it was a failing rather than a virtue. That piqued Julia's curiosity even more. Since Dallin had lied to her on several occasions, she was glad to hear that she could trust Martin.

"How do you seem to know so much about them?" Julia asked.

Mom shrugged and continued to gaze out the filthy windows, her eyes narrowed and filled with doubt. "I knew some Amish people once. They were some of the most cruel, judgmental people I ever met. I don't want anything to do with them again."

Julia flinched. Wow. That sounded a bit harsh.

"Surely that was an isolated case. There are good and bad people in all walks of life, right?"

Mom hesitated several moments. "I suppose so."

"Besides, I've already hired Martin. I can't fire him now without just cause," Julia said.

Mom didn't reply, which wasn't odd. She was a quiet woman, keeping most of her thoughts to herself. Instead, Julia faced her mother and gave her a brief hug. "Don't worry, Mom. It's going to be fine."

Mom nodded and showed a tremulous smile. After all, she was still mourning Dad. "Yes, of course, you're right. I'm just being silly."

"Ahem, excuse me."

The two women whirled around and found Martin standing in the doorway, hat in hand.

"Oh, Martin. I want you to meet my mother, Sharon," Julia said.

"Mrs. Rose." He nodded courteously, his gaze never wavering.

Mom just looked at him with a sober expression. Julia didn't understand. It wasn't like her mother to be unkind or to disapprove of someone without knowing them first.

"Hank and I are gonna take a brief lunch break, if that's all right," Martin said.

"Yes, of course," Julia said. "In fact, I was just coming to ask if you'd like a sandwich."

"*Ne, danke.* We brought our own lunch." Without waiting for her reply, he disappeared from view.

Mom stepped closer to the door. A blast of sunlight gleamed through a small patch of glass that wasn't covered by grunge and Sharon lifted a hand to shade her

eyes. She and Julia watched for a moment as Martin retrieved a red personal-size cooler from his buggy. Hank
joined him as the two sat on the edge of the porch. Had
Martin been so certain that Julia would hire him that
he had packed a lunch? Or did he always come into
town prepared?

"What's troubling you, Mom?" Julia asked.

Maybe Mom feared Martin might try to steal from
them the way Dallin had done. It hadn't been much
money but enough that it had made their lives more difficult. Mom had loved Dallin and Debbie, too. They'd
become part of the family. Or so Julia had thought.
They'd eloped just three weeks before Dad's death. Because he'd been on so much pain medication, Dad didn't
know what Dallin had done. But the final blow was
when he didn't even attend her father's funeral. Dallin and Debbie's betrayal had devastated her and Mom.

"No, of course not. I have no doubt he'll do a fine
job. It's just that…"

"What?" Julia urged.

Sharon waved a hand and showed a wide smile.
Reaching out, she caressed Julia's cheek. "Oh, it's nothing. I'm just missing your father, that's all. In the past,
he always dealt with such things. But you're doing a fine
job. I'm sure it'll be okay. And now, I'd better return to
work. That back room isn't going to clean itself out."

"Mom, why don't you go lie down for a while? I
know your joints are hurting and I don't want you to
overdo it."

"I'm fine, dear." Sharon limped toward the hallway
leading to the back of the building. Julia watched her
go, worried about her despite her assurances.

When she looked back at Martin, Julia saw that he'd

laid a clean cloth on the porch and pulled out several slices of homemade bread, ham, two golden pears and thick wedges of apple pie. After compiling the bread and meat into sandwiches, Hank eagerly picked one up and almost took a bite. Martin stopped him with a gentle hand on his arm. Without a word, Martin removed his hat and bowed his head reverently. Hank did likewise. For the count of thirty, the two held still and Julia realized they must be praying.

She envied the close sibling relationship they shared. There was something so serene about their bent heads that she felt a rash of goose bumps cover her arms. Then Martin released a breath and they began to eat. While Martin chewed thoughtfully, Hank's cheeks bulged with food and he glanced around with distraction.

At that moment, Martin looked up and saw her. Julia's face flushed with embarrassed heat. How rude of her to stand here and watch them. Yet, she couldn't move away. She felt transfixed with curiosity. Especially when Martin gave her a warm smile. With his back turned, Hank didn't notice her. Taking his sandwich, he hopped up and ran to climb the elm tree. Some unknown force caused Julia to step outside to speak with Martin.

"Um, I hope you don't think me impolite but can I ask what you were doing a few minutes ago?" she asked.

Martin tilted his head to the side and blinked in confusion. "You mean when I was working on the porch?"

She shook her head. "No, before you ate. You bowed your heads for a long time. Were you praying?"

He nodded and bit into his pear, chewed for a moment, then swallowed. "*Ja*, we always pray before a meal. To thank the Lord for His bounty and to ask a blessing on our food. Don't you do the same?"

How interesting. How quaint, yet authentic.

"No, I'm afraid not. I wasn't raised that way," she answered truthfully.

But even as she spoke, she wondered why not. It seemed so appropriate to thank God for all that He had given her. Rather than being odd, it seemed right.

She stepped nearer. "What do you say in your prayers?"

"That depends." He indicated that she should sit nearby on the porch and she did.

"On what?"

"*Ach*, sometimes we say the Lord's prayer before a meal. If there is trouble brewing at home or a special blessing we need, I often mention that to *Gott* and ask for His help. Other times, we pray at church meetings as a congregation and as a *familye*. And still other times, we say personal prayers in private. Most of our prayers are silent but they all differ, depending on their purpose and what is in my heart."

Yes, she could understand that. She'd oftentimes carried a prayer inside her heart but had never spoken one out loud. Because frankly, she didn't know how to do so.

"Do you pray often?" she asked.

"*Ja*, many times each day. Why do you ask?"

With her father's death, Mom's illness, Dallin's betrayal, financial problems and their recent move to Colorado, she'd needed to know God was nearby. To know that He was watching over them and she wasn't alone. But her prayers were always in silence, spoken within.

She shrugged. "I was just curious. I wasn't really

raised with prayer in my daily life. But there are times when I speak to God in my heart."

He lifted his eyebrows. "You believe in *Gott* then?"

"Yes, I do." Giving voice to her belief deepened her conviction. That God lived and was conscious of His children now in modern times, just as He had been in ancient times. She'd never really gone to church, yet she had decided for herself that she believed in a loving creator who was conscious of her needs. But unfortunately, she knew very little about Him.

Martin flashed a gentle smile. "I often carry a prayer in my heart, as well. *Gott* is perfect and knows all things. He hears all prayers, even those we don't speak out loud. Although He doesn't always answer us on our timetable. When was the last time you prayed?"

She took a deep inhale and let it go. "Yesterday, but I prayed most the night my father died. I couldn't understand why God had abandoned us. But it's odd. Instead of anger, I felt a warmth deep within my chest and an unexplainable knowledge that God was with us even during that dark time. And Mom became sick with lupus even before Dad was diagnosed with cancer. She helps with the soap making but she can't do a lot. Still, I knew I'd find a way to take care of her. And then, a few months later, Carl Nelson called to say that my Grandpa Walt had passed away and left me this store. That's when we moved here. So it seems the Lord heard and answered my prayers after all. I just wish my father hadn't died."

Now why had she told Martin all of that? She didn't know him. Not really. Yet she had confided some deeply personal things to him. She stiffened her spine, hoping Martin didn't make fun of her.

"I'm sorry you lost your *vadder*," he said. "You and your *mudder* must have gone through a very difficult ordeal. But I'm so glad you recognize how the Lord has blessed you. I believe when we think all is lost, that is when *Gott* is testing us, to see if we will call on Him in faith or in anger. Yet, He doesn't leave us comfortless. He is always with us if we seek Him out."

Martin's words touched her heart like nothing else could. For a moment, she felt as though God truly was close to her. That He wasn't a remote, disinterested God, who was withdrawn and didn't really care about her and Mom.

"Hank, don't climb so far. *Komm* down now. It's time for us to get back to work," Martin called to his brother.

Turning her head, Julia saw that the boy was high in the elm, clinging to a heavy branch. The boy looked over at them, saw Julia and immediately scrambled down.

The enchanted moment was broken. Although she'd like nothing better, Julia realized she couldn't sit here all day chatting with Martin. She had plenty of work to do. Honestly, she was stunned that Martin was so easy to talk to.

"Well, I'd better get inside and help Mom. Thank you for answering my questions." She came to her feet, dusting off her blue jeans.

"Anytime," he said.

Hank came running, a huge smile on his face. "*Hallo*, Julia. Did you see how high I climbed?"

"Miss Rose," Martin corrected the boy with a stern lift of his eyebrows.

Hank ignored his brother, focusing on Julia. "I went higher than ever before. I could even see the top of your roof. You have a big hole up there where the shingles have blown away."

Julia blinked, then glanced at Martin. "Oh, dear. A hole in the roof? And winter is coming on."

"Don't worry. As soon as I've completed the porch, I'll take a look at it," Martin said.

"But there are so many other chores needing to be done. I didn't even think about the roof." A feeling of helpless dread almost overwhelmed her.

"Never fear. The Lord will bless us and it'll all get done."

Martin sounded so confident. So sure of himself. So filled with conviction. She couldn't help envying his faith. His words of reassurance brought her a bit of comfort, but what if he was wrong? What if they didn't get the workroom set up in time?

She had been making single batches of soap up in the tiny kitchen of their apartment almost every evening but that would only satisfy the grand opening of their store on December 1. It would take her four weeks of making super batches of soap to satisfy her wholesale contract, and the soap required four to five weeks to cure after it was made. She must ship her orders by the end of January in order to meet her next contract deadline the first of February. So much was riding on her being able to make soap by the end of November. By the end of December, she had to have most of the soap made.

As she went inside, Julia hoped Martin was right.

The pressure was on. Martin knew Julia was worried. He could see it in her eyes. He'd heard the urgency in her voice and could feel the apprehension emanating from her like a living thing. If Hank was right and there was a big hole in the roof, it would need to be repaired before the autumn rains began, which was any day now. Depending on what needed to be done, it could suck up precious time he needed to build the shelves and countertops for her workroom.

It was Martin's job to get it all done in time for her to open her shop. He felt the seriousness of the situation as though his own livelihood depended on it. His reputation was on the line. He'd been doing a lot of carpentry work for people in the community and wanted to increase his business as a side job for more income to build his barn and, one day, his new house. He also wanted to make Julia happy and ease her load in any way possible.

Working as fast as he could, he built the framework of the awning first. Standing on the rickety ladder, he affixed the lag bolts. Satisfied with his labors, he looked down at Hank, who had wandered over to peer through the store windows. No doubt he was looking for Julia.

"Hank!"

The boy jerked, looking guilty. Martin resisted the urge to smile.

"Hand me up those two-by-six boards," he called.

Hank lifted a four-by-six board instead.

"*Ne*, that's the wrong one. I need the two-by-six." Martin forced himself to speak gently, although he felt impatient for his brother's mistake. It was costing him precious time.

Hank laid a hand on the smaller boards and looked up at him with a questioning gaze.

"*Ja*, those are the right ones. That's *gut*. Hand them up."

Martin reached out a hand as Hank lifted the boards one by one so he could nail them into place. By the time he'd laid the furring strips over top of the frame, it was almost dinnertime. He'd accomplished a lot today but should soon start for home. *Mamm* would be expecting them. He would finish up tomorrow. The weather should hold for a couple more days so he could repair the roof. For now, it was time to leave.

"You've done a fine job today."

He turned and saw Julia standing off to the side of the porch, looking up at him. Hank immediately raced over to stand beside her, gazing at her with adulation.

"I helped," Hank said.

She blessed him with a smile so bright that Martin had to blink. "Of course you did."

Hank beamed at her. "Do you like to sing?"

Martin stiffened, knowing what his brother was about to ask. "Not now, Hank."

Hank threw a disgruntled glare at his older brother. "But I want to ask her—"

"It's not the right time," Martin said.

Julia hesitated, looking back and forth between the two. In a bit of confusion, she spoke to Martin as she inspected his work with a critical eye. "I didn't expect you to get the porch finished today, but it looks almost complete."

"*Ja*, it has come together well. I'll put on the finishing touches and paint it first thing in the morning. I hope it is satisfactory," he said.

"It's more than satisfactory. It's beautiful. If I didn't know better, I would say it was never damaged. You've cleaned up every bit of mess, too. I can't even tell you worked on it today."

As her gaze scanned the porch and awning, he could

see her searching for any imperfections. He climbed down and set the ladder aside for his use tomorrow.

"My *daed* taught me to tidy up after work," he said.

She tilted her head. "Your dat?"

"*Ja*, my dad."

"Oh, your father," she said.

"*Ja*, my *vadder*."

He'd swept up the sawdust and discarded nails and placed them in a large garbage can. *Mamm* told him that his fastidiousness was bothersome to some of the Amish girls, which was one reason they didn't want to marry him. But instead of being irritated by his meticulous work, Julia seemed to approve. For some crazy reason, that delighted Martin like nothing else could.

She nodded with satisfaction. "I do like it very much. With a coat of paint, it'll look perfect."

While Julia watched, he packed his tools away in the toolbox. When he was finished, he faced her again. "We'd better get going. We'll see you in the morning."

"Yes, see you tomorrow." She waved and turned away, going back inside.

Martin climbed into the buggy with Hank and directed the horse toward the main road. He'd worked hard today, yet he didn't feel tired. No, not at all. Instead, he felt rejuvenated and eager to do a good job for Julia Rose.

When he pulled into the graveled driveway at home, his father was just coming from the barn, carrying two buckets of frothy white milk. His mother, sisters and other brother had just finished feeding the chickens and pigs.

"Martin! Hank! You're finally home." His mother waved, a huge smile on her cheery face.

Emily, Susan and Timmy came running, surrounding him and Hank as they hopped up and down with excitement.

"Did you get the job?" thirteen-year-old Emily asked, her face alight with expectation.

"You must have got the job because you've been gone all day," little eight-year-old Timmy reasoned.

Martin laughed as he swung seven-year-old Susan high into the air. The girl squealed with delight. Their greeting warmed his heart. How he loved them all. He thought about Julia having only her mother to come home to. It must be so lonely for her.

"Supper's about ready. *Komm* inside and tell us about your day." His father stepped up on the porch, his words silencing the children's incessant questions. At the age of forty-nine, David was the patriarch of the home and still strong and muscular from working long hours of manual labor.

"I'll just put the road horse in his stall and toss him some hay," Martin said.

Linda, his mother, waved an impatient hand. As the matriarch of the *familye*, she was just as confident in her role as David was. "*Ne*, Timmy can do that. You and Hank *komm* inside now. I want to hear all about your day."

"Ah, don't say anything important while I'm gone," Timmy called. But the boy obediently took hold of the horse's halter and led him into the barn.

Once they were inside, they washed and sat down at the spacious table in the kitchen. *Mamm* had already laid out the plates and utensils. The room was warm and smelled of something good cooking on the stove. With six hungry children and a husband to feed, Linda always made plenty. Only Martin's nineteen-year-old sister, Karen, was missing. She was newly married and lived back east with her husband.

"*Ach*, did you get the job?" His father sat down and looked at him expectantly.

"*Ja*, we got the job," Hank answered for him. The boy beamed with eagerness and Martin didn't have the heart to scold him for speaking out of turn. After all, the job was his, too.

Martin smiled with tolerance and purposefully waited until Timmy returned from the barn before speaking. Because they prayed before eating, they had to wait for the boy anyway.

Once everyone was assembled, David beckoned to his wife. "*Mudder*, *komm* and sit."

David pointed at her chair and Martin watched as his mother sat at the opposite end of the table, nearest the stove. As each member of the *familye* bowed their head to bless the food, he couldn't help loving this nightly ritual. His mom was always up and buzzing around the table to see to everyone's needs. But during evening prayer, she sat reverently with her *familye* for these few minutes while they gave thanks to the Lord.

When they were finished, everyone dug in and she hopped up to pull a pan of fresh-baked cornbread from the oven.

"Hank and I will be doing handyman work." Martin speared two pork chops and laid them on his plate. The clatter of utensils and eating filled the room, but no one spoke as they waited to hear every word he said.

"What kind of handyman work?" David asked as he spread golden butter across a hot piece of cornbread.

Martin sliced off a piece of meat and popped it into

his mouth. He chewed for several moments before swallowing, then explained his tasks and asked his father's advice on how to assemble the cabinets in Julia's workroom. The conversation bounced around various topics but kept coming back to his new job.

"Julia's nice, too. She's real *schee*." Hank spoke with his mouth full of cooked carrots.

David's bushy eyebrows shot up and he looked at Martin. "Julia?"

"*Ja*, Julia Rose. She's my new boss," Martin said. "She lives with her *mudder* in that old building Walter Rose owned. Apparently, Julia was his granddaughter. It seems that old Walt died a couple months back and left the place to her. She's renovating it so she can sell handmade soap."

"Soap?" David said the word abruptly, like it didn't make sense.

Martin shrugged and took a long drink of fresh milk. "*Ja*, she sells it to stores across the nation."

"Humph, I guess the *Englisch* don't make their own so they have to buy it somewhere," David said. "But I thought you'd be working for a man. How old is this Julia?"

Martin took a deep breath, trying to answer truthfully while not alarming his father. After all, it wasn't seemly that an unmarried Amish man should be working for a young, attractive *Englisch* woman. "She's twenty-three but she stays in the house most of the time while Hank and I work outside. The job is only for six or seven weeks, so it'll be over with soon enough."

His father's gaze narrowed and rested on him like a ten-ton sledge. Martin felt as though the man were looking deep inside of him for the truth. Linda also paused in front of the counter where she was slicing big wedges of cherry pie. She didn't say anything, waiting for her husband's verdict on this turn of events, but Martin could tell from her expression that she was worried.

"*Ach*, I guess you've got Hank with you all the time, so you're not alone with this woman," David finally said. "And once it's done, you'll have enough money to build your barn in the spring. But don't forget who you are and what *Gott* expects from you, *sohn*. Always remember your faith."

"I will," Martin assured him.

"But she's *Englisch*. Are you sure this is wise?" Linda asked, her brow furrowed in a deep frown.

"*Mamm*, don't worry," Martin reassured her with a short laugh. "I'm a grown man and know how to handle myself. Besides, it's only for a short time. It isn't as if I'm going to fall in love and leave our faith or something crazy like that, so rest your fears."

"And besides, Julia's gonna be my *maedel*, not Martin's," Hank said.

David and Linda shared a look of concern, to which Martin quickly explained the boy's desire for Julia to be his girl. "I've already told Hank that Julia isn't Amish and she's too old for him anyway."

Without missing a beat, Martin's sister Emily handed him a bowl of boiled potatoes. Martin forked several onto his plate. The whole *familye* knew the drill, having discussed issues like this a zillion times before.

"Why does it matter if Julia isn't Amish?" Hank asked with a frown.

Linda shook her head and shooed Hank's question away with her hand. "She's not of our faith. She's not one of us." Handing plates of pie to Emily to pass around the table, she leaned against the counter and faced Martin again. "So, tell us something about this woman boss of yours."

Taking a bite of buttered potato, Martin kept his voice slow and even, trying not to say anything that might overly alarm his mother. "She and her *mudder* live a simple life like us. They don't wear makeup or fancy clothes. Nor do they own a car or use electricity. Julia has even asked me a couple of questions about our faith. And she's devoted to her *mudder*, who is sickly."

Linda winced with sympathy. "What's wrong with her?"

"She has lupus. Julia's father recently died of cancer. Julia's been earning a living for them and taking care of her parents. From what I can see, she's a *gut*, hard-working woman."

"But she's not Amish," David said, his bushy eye-brows raised in a stern look that allowed for no more discussion on the matter.

Linda stepped near and rested a hand on Martin's shoulder. "*Ach*, you'll be careful not to be drawn in by her, won't you, *sohn*? I couldn't bear to lose you. You'll remember what your *vadder* and I have taught you and stay true to your faith."

He met his mother's eyes, his convictions filling his heart. He could never stand to hurt her by chasing after an *Englisch* woman. "You don't need to worry about me, *Mamm*. I will only marry someone of our faith. This I vow."

"*Gut*. It's too bad you can't convert Julia to our faith." Linda showed a smile of relief and finally sat down to eat her own supper. The conversation turned to what the younger children were learning in school.

Martin ate his meal, listening to the chatter around him. He'd done his best to alleviate his parents' concerns but knew they were worried. And he agreed that it was too bad Julia wasn't Amish. If she were, his parents would have no reservations about him working with her.

As he carried his dishes over to the sink for washing, he listened to Hank's incessant chatter and a feeling of expectancy built within his chest. He couldn't wait to return to work in the morning and be near Julia again. And though he refused to consider the options, he knew deep inside that it had little to do with the money he would earn and more to do with his pretty employer.

But he meant what he'd said. He would marry an Amish woman or not at all.

Chapter Three

The following morning, Julia glanced at the clock she'd hung on the wall in her spacious workroom. She blinked, hardly able to believe it was barely five o'clock. She'd been up for two hours already. Like many mornings, she couldn't sleep, so she'd started work early.

After she completed several tasks, faint sunlight filtered through the dingy windows, highlighting the bare wooden floors with streamers of dust. She really must wash the windows today, before she painted the walls. That should brighten things up quite a bit. With the delays from yesterday, she feared Martin might not have time for everything needing to be done. Careful not to let Mom work too hard, Julia had helped her clear most of the boxes and junk out of the room, stacking them in the backyard. Above all, her priority was to get the soap room operational. But a hole in the roof could create worse problems down the road.

Squinting her eyes, she worked by kerosene light. She'd acquired an old stainless steel sink from the discount store in town and wanted it ready once Martin built the cabinets she required. Using a mild cleanser, she scrubbed at a particularly grimy spot. The sink's two spacious tubs would accommodate the big pots she used for soap making.

Martin would be here in a few hours to finish the porch. Then he'd check the condition of the roof. After that, she wanted him to—

Tap-tap-tap.

She looked up, thinking the sound came from above. Had Mom awakened early and was doing something inside their apartment? She caught the deep timbre of a man's voice coming from outside but wasn't sure. It came again, followed by Hank's unique accent. She glanced at the wall clock and discovered it was almost eight. Ah, her handymen were already here and the sun was barely up.

"Be careful with that paint, Hank. You don't want to spill any." Martin's muffled voice reached her ears.

Sitting back, Julia set aside the soft sponge. In her warm slippers, she padded over to the window and peered out.

Martin and Hank stood side by side in front of the porch as they perused their handiwork. Each of them held a brush that gleamed with white paint. Martin also clutched the handle of a paint bucket. No doubt they'd been trimming the porch and front of the building. A feeling of elation swept over Julia. She couldn't wait for it all to be finished.

Martin had rolled the long sleeves of his shirt up his muscular arms. A smear of white paint marred his angular chin. Hank also wore several smatters of paint on his forearms and clothes. In the early morning sunlight, Julia caught the gleam of bright trim on the post nearest to the window but couldn't see the rest of the porch from this angle. And all that work had been done while she was cleaning the new sink.

Hmm. Dallin had never worked this hard. He'd rather laze around and borrow money from Julia, which he never paid back. Maybe it was a blessing she hadn't married him after all.

Walking over to the front door, she flipped the dead bolt, turned the knob and stepped out onto the porch. In that short amount of time, Martin had climbed to the top of the rickety ladder leading up to the roof. Hank held the ladder steady from below. Busy with their labors, they hadn't noticed her yet. She watched as Martin dipped his brush into a bucket of paint he'd set on the pail shelf, then touched up a spot high on the side of the awning. As he concentrated on his work, he pressed the tip of his tongue against his upper lip.

The ladder trembled.

"Hold it steady, Hank. Just a few more spots and we'll be finished. Then we can start on the roof." Martin spoke without looking down.

Fearing she might break his concentration, Julia didn't say anything. A tabby cat crossing the road caught Hank's attention. Julia knew the animal was named Tigger and belonged to Essie Walkins, the elderly widow who lived two houses down. Tail high in the air, the feline picked its way across the abandoned street. No doubt it was hoping to cajole Julia out of a bowl of milk. She'd fed the cat many times, much to her mother's chagrin. Sharon didn't like strays.

Seeing the feline, Hank abandoned his post and hurried toward Tigger. Without the boy's weight to hold the ladder steady, it shuddered uncontrollably.

Julia gasped as Martin grabbed on to the gutter to

keep from falling. She rushed over and gripped the sides of the ladder, staring up at him with widened eyes. The ladder stabilized but too late. The bucket of paint plummeted to the ground with a heavy thud. Julia scrunched her shoulders, hoping she wouldn't get hit in the head by the falling object. Spatters of white struck the outer wall of the building, the mass of paint pooling in the middle of the wooden porch.

"Oh, no!" Julia breathed in exasperation.

Martin stared down at her with absolute shock. Likewise, Julia was so stunned that she was held immobile for several seconds. Then, Martin hurried down the ladder, his angular face torn by an expression of dread.

"*Ach*, Julia! Are you all right? The bucket didn't hit you, did it?" He rested a gentle hand on her arm, his dark eyes filled with concern as he searched her expression.

She shook her head. "No, it missed me. I'm fine."

Satisfied she was okay, Martin stepped away. She could still feel the warmth of his strong fingers tingling against her skin. As he perused the mess, his lips tightened. Then, his gaze sought out his recalcitrant brother.

Hank stood in the middle of the vacant street, clutching the tabby cat close against his chest as he stroked the animal's furry head. Tigger looked completely content as the boy walked over to them, smiling wide with satisfaction.

"*Ach*, look at this *bussli*. Isn't she beautiful? I saved her from being hit by a car," the boy crowed, his eyes sparkling.

"Him," Julia corrected. "The cat's name is Tigger and he's a boy."

Hank's expression lit up with sheer pleasure. "*Ach*, Tigger. What a fine name."

"Hank, there are no cars coming at this time of the morning. You were supposed to be holding the ladder for me, not chasing after *die katz*." Martin's voice held a note of reproach but was otherwise calm. He wore a slight frown, doing an admirable job of controlling his temper. In that moment, Julia respected Martin even more.

"I know, but I saw Tigger and didn't want him to get hit by a *kaer*," Hank said.

Julia glanced at the empty street. Since it was so early, there wasn't a single car, truck or person in sight. But being an agricultural community, Julia knew that would soon change as farmers came into town early to transact their business. Since Tigger freely roamed the streets at all hours of the day, she wasn't too worried he'd be struck by a car.

"You know how fast motor vehicles go," Hank continued. "Remember what happened to Jeremiah Beiler last year when an *Englischer*'s car hit his buggy-wagon and broke his leg? It nearly kilt him and his *dechder*."

"Killed, not kilt," Martin corrected the boy.

"His deck-der?" Julia asked, confused by some of their foreign words.

"Daughters," Martin supplied. "They were riding with him in the buggy when the car struck them from behind."

"Oh," Julia said.

"*Ach*, I couldn't let this sweet kitty get hurt." Hank nuzzled Tigger's warm fur, completely oblivious that his efforts to protect the cat had endangered his brother's life and created a big mess that would now have to be cleaned up.

Meeting Martin's frustrated expression, Julia showed an understanding smile. "It's okay. No harm was done. We'll just tidy it up."

Martin rested his hands on his lean hips and gazed at the splattered paint with resignation. He certainly wasn't a man who angered easily. That was another difference between him and Dallin. Julia's ex-fiancé had raised his voice at her numerous times while kicking things and slamming doors. She hadn't liked it one bit. In retrospect, she was so grateful he was out of her life. But who would she marry now? Would there ever be a kind, hardworking man for her to love? She wasn't sure she'd ever be able to trust another man.

"How exactly do we clean up the paint?" she asked, wondering if a thinner from the hardware store might remove the white stain from the wood.

"You don't need to do a thing. I'll get this straightened out as fast as I can and reimburse you for the waste," Martin promised.

Again, she was impressed by his integrity. "There's no need for reimbursement. The porch is all but finished and it doesn't look like we lost much paint. In fact, everything looks great, except for the spill. Let me help you clean it up." She reached for a bucket of rags sitting near the front door, grateful when Martin didn't refuse her aid.

While Hank snuggled the cat, they shoveled the drying pool of paint into a heavy-duty plastic bag and set it in the waste bin to be disposed of later. Julia held the dustpan for Martin, wondering how they would get the streaks of white off the wooden porch. Since Martin was so good at his job, she decided to let him handle the problem.

"You're up early," Martin spoke as they worked.

Julia smiled. "I was thinking the same about you. There's no need for you and Hank to come to work so early."

He shrugged. "We're always up early. I usually milk the cows and feed the horses before the sun rises. I had my chores at home finished and decided to get an early start here. I'm determined to repair your roof by the end of the day, although I didn't expect this added chore."

He chuckled and Julia stared. She thought the Amish were a very stern, serious people. She had no idea they laughed and was glad he found the situation amusing. After all, her mother had taught her there was no use crying over spilled milk. It was better to just clean it up and move on. It seemed that Martin was of the same inclination.

She laughed, too, suddenly so grateful he was here. Since her broken engagement and her father's death, she'd felt so alone in the world. It was nice to have someone capable to depend on.

"Well, accidents are bound to happen now and then," she said.

"You're very understanding."

He stood to his full height and she gazed up into his eyes. With the early morning sunlight gleaming at his back, it highlighted his red hair and seemed to accent the shadows of his handsome face. She was caught there, mesmerized for several moments. Then, she mentally shook herself. After all, Martin was Amish and she wasn't. They could never be more than friends. It was that simple.

"How will we clean the wood siding?" she asked, forcing herself to look away.

"I believe I have some sand paper in my toolbox. If I'm careful, I can take off just the bare layer of paint without damaging the wood and no one will know it was ever there." He indicated the box sitting nearby.

Opening the lid, he pulled out a sheet of gritty paper and a hand sander. While Julia swept up the dust, he sanded the porch just enough to get the paint off. The work delayed them by an hour but Martin didn't say a word when it came time to climb up and check the roof.

"Martin, I'm grateful for your dedication, but I'd like to suspend your next task for thirty minutes, please," Julia said.

Poised at the bottom of the ladder, his forehead furrowed in a quizzical frown. "What do you need me to do?"

She smiled, resting a hand on the side of the ladder so near to his own. "I think it's time we retire this rickety old thing. Would you mind going to the supply store and purchasing a good, solid ladder that will ensure our safety?"

A low chuckle rumbled inside his chest and she stared, mesmerized by the sound.

"*Ja*, I'd be happy to do that. I'll go and hurry right back," he said. "Come on, Hank."

He stepped away from the porch, tugging on Hank's arm to get the boy to follow him.

"But I want to stay here with Tigger." The boy stuck out his chin, refusing to release his hold on the cat.

"If it would make things easier for you, Hank can wait here with me. He can help me fix breakfast," Julia offered. Surely Hank wouldn't get into as much trouble if he remained behind, and Martin would be quicker with his errand, too.

"We have already eaten at home. Our *mamm* fixed us a big breakfast before we left," Martin said.

"Then perhaps Hank can help me finish cleaning out the workroom. I'm going to paint the walls today," she said.

Martin hesitated, a doubtful expression on his face. "You're certain you don't mind watching him while I'm gone? He can be a bit of a handful at times."

She waved Martin on. "Of course. We'll see you in a while."

Turning toward Hank, she indicated that the boy should follow her. "Come on, Hank. Let's go upstairs and see if we can get a bowl of milk for Tigger."

"*Ja*, I'm sure he's hungry," Hank said.

Smiling happily, the teenager followed her inside, carrying Tigger with him. Julia didn't look back to see if Martin was still watching her, but she didn't have to. She could feel his gaze resting on her like a leaden weight. And as she led Hank upstairs, she wasn't sure why her chest felt all warm and buoyant inside.

Martin was gone a total of twenty minutes. Driving his horse and buggy, he pulled up in front of the supply store and whipped inside to peruse the selection of ladders. After choosing one that was sturdy but not too costly, he asked Byron Stott to put it on Julia's account, then hurried back to Rose Soapworks.

He didn't disturb Julia to find out where Hank was. Hoping to get some work done, he set the new ladder against the side of the house and scrambled up to the rooftop with his tool belt strapped around his waist.

Bracing himself so he wouldn't fall, he sat against the chimney and analyzed the problem. Sure enough, there was a hole in the roof. Not too bad. The tar paper and shingles had blown off and the wood beneath was starting to rot away. Martin knew he could fix it with little effort. And while he was up here, he'd replace the missing shingles in other areas before they became a bigger problem, too. When he was through, Julia's roof would be ready to face winter.

Using the claw of his hammer, he pried up the decayed fragments and tossed them over the side of the house where they fell harmlessly to the ground below. Wouldn't Julia be surprised when he finished the project by midday? Then he could build the shelves in her workroom.

"Martin?"

He jerked, startled from his task. Julia stood at the top of the ladder, holding on to the edge of the roof. Her eyes were wide and anxious, her face drawn with worry.

Something was wrong.

"You shouldn't be up here. You might fall," he said, wondering why he cared so much.

She blinked. "I… I need to speak with you on an urgent matter. It's about Hank. Could you come down, please?"

Oh, no. What had Hank done now? Martin hated to think ill of his younger brother but feared the boy may have done something bad during his absence.

"*Ja.* I'll climb down now."

Her head and shoulders disappeared from view. Moving carefully, Martin scooted over to the eave so he could grasp the top of the ladder and place his booted feet on the rungs. Julia had already scampered to the bottom and was looking up at him expectantly. Climbing down, he stood next to her. One glance at her ashen face told him that she was quite upset. She wrung her hands in front of her, her movements increasing his own urgency.

"What is it? What's wrong?" he asked.

"It's Hank. He...he's missing," she said.

Missing!

A flush of dismay swept over Martin. This wasn't the first time Hank had taken off by himself. Usually it was harmless and they found him easily. But once, the boy had gotten himself so lost that it took a day and night with the entire *Gmay* searching to find him. Still, Martin didn't want to panic needlessly.

Taking a deep, settling breath, he held out a calming hand. "First, tell me what happened."

"I... I don't know," Julia said. "We were upstairs in the kitchen with Mom and I was getting a bowl of milk for Tigger. One minute, Hank was there with us and the next minute, he was gone. We've searched everywhere. Upstairs, downstairs and even outside. We can't find him."

"Don't worry. We'll find him. Can you show me where you last saw him?" he asked, determined not to give in to the alarm coursing through his body.

"Come with me." She hurried toward the front door and he followed as she swept through the spacious workroom, down a long hallway to the back of the building and then hurried up a flight of stairs to the apartment above.

Once inside, Martin removed his hat, his heavy boots thudding against the bare wood floors. The landing upstairs opened into a small but comfortable living area.

The spacious rugs covering the floors looked clean but threadbare. Sharon Rose stood before the kitchen sink, holding a dish towel as she dried a plate. Tigger sat on the floor nearby, his tail curled around him as he sat licking his paws in smooth, languid motions. An empty bowl rested beside the cat and Martin figured Tigger had already lapped up his milk.

Martin nodded a respectful greeting to Sharon. "*Hallo*, Mrs. Rose."

"Hello, Martin." The woman didn't smile and spoke rather stiffly before turning to reach for another plate in the dish drain.

He didn't have time to consider why Mrs. Rose didn't seem to like him. Maybe the woman was just nervous having strangers in her home.

"May I take a quick look around?" he asked Julia.

She released a pensive sigh. "Of course. Maybe you can find him."

With Julia tagging along behind, he called for his brother as he headed toward the back bedrooms. "Hank! It's Martin. Where are you?"

Embarrassed to be wandering through Julia's home, he peered behind each door and under each bed. The furnishings were sparse and excruciatingly tidy. Except for an occasional clock or picture of a landscape hanging on the walls, the rooms were devoid of all the worldly clutter that invaded so many *Englisch* homes.

As if sensing his thoughts, Julia gave a nervous cough. "We didn't bring much with us from Kansas. We sold all but the necessities."

Martin nodded, hating to invade Julia and her mother's privacy like this. Her comment gave him a bit of insight into what they'd been through. He imagined losing her father and moving to another state hadn't been easy on them. In fact, he remembered when his own *familye* had moved here over ten years ago. He'd been fifteen years of age. Old enough to wonder if his father's plan to start over in a strange place with little water for their crops and a short growing season might be a huge mistake. But it had worked out. His family was happy and doing well. If only he could find a good Amish woman to marry and start a family of his own, his life would be perfect.

"You see? There's no sign of him. It's like he just disappeared." Standing in front of a narrow walk-in closet, Julia lifted her hands in dismay.

"Maybe he is outside."

Julia shook her head. "I don't think so. The stairs creak and I'm certain I would have heard him go down. He must still be up here but I don't know where."

"May I look behind your clothes? Once, Hank hid beneath a quilt in an armoire. He could be hiding anywhere," he said.

"Yes. Whatever it takes." Julia stepped aside.

He slid the closet door open and reached in to push the clothes away. A panel of wood with a latch affixed at the top was set into the back wall… A small doorway.

"That's just the crawl space up to the attic. It's quite dark in there. Surely he wouldn't have gone inside?"

Martin shrugged. "I'm not so sure. I've learned from past experience not to bypass any possibility."

"Oh. Well, I haven't been in there yet, though I've been meaning to check it out once the electricity is turned back on. The door is still closed. Wouldn't it be open if Hank had gone in?" Julia asked.

"Who knows?" Martin said.

Without asking permission, he tugged on the pull and the panel swung open. It had a knob on the inside, which would make it easy to close. As he hunkered down, Martin was conscious of Julia joining him in the bottom of the closet. She crouched beside him, so close that her shoulder brushed against his arm and her sweet, clean fragrance filled his nose.

Peering inside, Martin blinked to adjust his eyes to the dim interior. Just beyond the doorway, a stair with a splintered handrail led up to the attic. Scrunching his shoulders so he could fit past the slim doorway, he climbed the few steps, conscious of Julia following. The railing wobbled, the stairway narrow and rickety.

"Be careful on these stairs. They feel like they're about to give way. It might be best if you wait here," he told Julia.

She nodded, staying where she was. He figured he'd have to rebuild the stairs when he had more time.

The attic was cramped and he had to stoop over because of his great height. As the room opened into view, he saw the skeletal structure of bare rafters intersected with gray sheets of insulation. No plywood had been laid across the beams of lumber so that a person could walk safely across the room. The thin drywall that made up the floor also provided the false ceiling for the apartment below but it wouldn't support much weight. A heavy layer of dust covered the entire room. Vague sunlight gleamed through a vent set high in the outside wall.

"Hank! *Ben je er?*" he called loudly.

A faint whimper came from across the expanse of the room. Glancing into the shadows, Martin saw his brother huddled in a far corner, his face contorted with fear. He must have walked across the rafters. Otherwise, he could have fallen through the floor to the apartment below.

"Mar-tin," the boy whispered, as though he didn't dare speak any louder.

"Hank!"

"Oh, he's here! I'm so glad," Julia breathed the words with amazement.

Relief flooded Martin. He'd found his brother. Hank was safe. "What are you doing in here? Could you not hear us calling you? Why have you not come out?"

He spoke in Deitsch, trying to keep his voice calm in spite of the irritation coursing through his veins.

An expression of guilt crossed the boy's features. "I… I feared you might be angry with me for coming up here."

Martin took a deep inhale and let it go. His poor, sweet brother. Did he not understand how much he loved him? A spear of compassion pierced Martin's heart. Right now, he just wanted Hank out of here and on safe ground.

"*Ne*, I am not angry," he spoke gently. "It was wrong for you to *komm* here and you must not do it again but no harm has been done. Now, take my hand."

Martin stepped out onto one of the strong rafters and lifted his arm, waiting for his brother to move toward him.

Hank stood away from the wall, holding onto the beams of timber that stretched overhead. As the boy did so, he walked on the narrow beams crisscrossing the floor like a gymnast negotiating the balance beams. Unfortunately, Hank was not light on his feet and tottered on the narrow boards. Losing his balance, he stepped on the insulation and his foot promptly crashed through the flimsy flooring.

Julia gasped, her body going tense.

"Hank!" Martin yelled.

The boy sprawled among the scratchy insulation. He wrapped his arms around one of the strong floor planks, his left leg disappearing below.

"Hold on. I'll *komm* to you," Martin said.

A feeling of dread pulsed through his veins as he stepped out onto the narrow joists. He had no idea how solid the timbers were and didn't want Hank to fall through to the apartment below.

"Be careful." Julia spoke the warning softly, but there was no need. Martin's senses were on high alert as he crossed to his brother.

Reaching out, Martin pulled Hank up, careful not to jerk on the boy's leg and cut him on the jagged pieces of drywall. Like a little child, Hank wrapped his arms around Martin's waist and pushed his face against his chest as he held on tight.

"Mar-tin, I fell," Hank cried, his eyes wide with terror, his voice vibrating with tears.

"*Ja*, but you're all right now. Step only on the beams of lumber. They are strong. The insulation is supported only by drywall and won't hold your weight," Martin warned.

Within moments, he had Hank back at the stairway and Julia pulled the boy into the safety of the closet. She hugged him tight.

"Oh, I'm so glad you're all right. I was so worried about you," she told the boy.

Hank gave a startled laugh. "*Ja*, me, too."

"Thank the Lord you're all right," Martin said.

"Mar-tin, you saved me," Hank said, clutching his brother.

"Is he okay?"

Martin turned and saw Sharon standing in the bedroom, her eyes wide with concern.

"*Ja*, he is fine," Martin said.

"Good, that's all that matters. But now we have another small problem. There is a big hole in my bedroom where Hank's foot came through the ceiling," the woman said.

Martin froze, hardly able to believe what he heard. Oh, no. Because of Hank, it seemed he now had another repair job to rectify. Maybe it hadn't been such a good idea to bring Hank along with him on this project. It seemed he just created more work.

Stealing a quick glance at Julia, Martin tried to gauge her expression. Hopefully she wouldn't fire him on the spot. But her face was curved into a smile. And then she started to laugh. A high, lilting sound that caused a warming pleasure to flood Martin's chest.

"This day seems full of surprises. What else could go wrong?" she asked, her shoulders shaking with amusement.

Sharon smiled, too, but then seemed to catch herself. With a frowning glare tossed at Martin, she turned and walked out of the room.

"Shall we go take a look at the latest development?" Julia asked Hank.

The boy nodded and she took his hand. He held on tight, seeming perfectly happy to be in her company. Martin couldn't believe how kind and forgiving she was. Some of the Amish women he'd hoped to marry had barely tolerated Hank and his chaotic ways. He was too much work for them. The fact that Hank constantly wanted to be with Martin was a big deterrent for him being able to find a suitable bride. But Julia didn't seem to mind the boy at all. In fact, she welcomed him with humor and grace.

"There is one thing I've learned today," Julia called over her shoulder as she headed down the hallway with Hank in tow.

"And what is that?" Martin asked.

"The attic would make a great hiding place. As long as we don't fall through the rafters, that is." She laughed again.

"*Ja*, now I know where to walk, it'd be a *gut* place for me to hide. I just have to step on the rafters, not on the insulation," Hank said.

"*Ne*, you must not go up there again," Martin said.

"I won't. There are spiders in there." The boy gave a shiver of revulsion.

Again, Julia's laughter rang through the air. Martin stopped for a moment and watched her. She was unlike any woman he'd ever met. In the past, he'd thought all women were the same. One was pretty much just like all the rest. But now, he knew he'd been utterly wrong. Because he'd never met anyone quite like Julia Rose.

Chapter Four

A week later, Julia studied the swatches of colors and cabinet stains laid out in front of her, surprised by the number of choices Martin had provided. For an Amish man, he seemed quite versatile and she felt a tad overwhelmed by her options.

"I wouldn't recommend white for your workroom. It's too light and will show every bit of grime. Over time, your cabinets would start to look dingy. But white might look nice in your store," Martin said.

Standing beside her in the workroom, he pointed at one of the sample strips she held in her hands. Hank was upstairs in the kitchen with Sharon, who was baking cinnamon rolls.

"Oak or maple might be better for your workroom," Martin said.

"Yes, I agree," Julia said. "But there are so many styles to choose from. This beveling would be beautiful, but I don't need fancy cupboards. It's a workroom, after all. Soap making can be a messy job, no matter how tidy I try to keep things."

He nodded and reached out to touch one of the samples. "This one is quite modest and not too expensive. I can put pulls on each drawer and cabinet, to make it easier to open them."

She wholeheartedly agreed. It seemed their tastes were similar. "Yes, let's go with this plain style and the oak finish for the workroom and the white for the retail part of the store."

A smile of approval curved his handsome mouth. "That's exactly what I would choose. I can start building the cabinets today."

She wasn't surprised. Martin worked fast. In spite of the mishaps over the past week, he'd repaired the roof and the hole in the attic from where Hank had fallen through. And just in time, too. As soon as he finished, they had awoken to leaden clouds and a drenching rain. Julia figured Martin and Hank wouldn't show up for work today. After all, they had to drive their horse and buggy three miles into town. But they'd shown up promptly at six o'clock, wearing shiny black water slickers to protect them from the wet drizzle.

"I've been meaning to ask if you know where I might purchase some firewood. My grandfather left me a little money, so I can pay for it. Is there a vendor in town who sells it?" she asked, leaning her hip against the table she'd placed along one wall to set papers on. Martin had provided a rather orderly drawing of blueprints and designs for her workroom and they had discussed a few changes to the layout.

"*Ja*, I can see to it. We're late in the season for gathering firewood but I'll plan an excursion into the mountains to gather dead trees and haul them down to cut up for you within the next week or so," he said.

Hmm. He didn't need another chore to do. But he

never flinched at any of her many requests. Dallin had always shirked her appeals for help. But Martin seemed to understand the needs were real and simply figured out a way to accomplish each task. She couldn't help wondering if that might end once the newness of working for her wore off.

"Do you think you'll have time for that along with everything else I've asked you to do?" she said.

He nodded, rolling up the designs with quick twists of his strong hands. "*Ja*. The day after tomorrow might be a *gut* day to go up on the mountain. Tomorrow is Sunday and the weather should be clear by Monday. I can get the cabinets started today and then bring down a load of firewood next week."

She studied him for a moment, thinking. "And what about the garbage piled out back? How do we get rid of that?"

"On my way into the mountains, I can take all the boxes and junk to the dump. That way, I can kill two ducks with one stone," he said.

She laughed. "I think you mean kill two *birds* with one stone."

He smiled and tilted his head in agreement. "*Ja*, that is what I meant. I'll bring my *vadder*'s large hay wagon and Billy, one of our Belgian draft horses. He's strong and should be able to haul all the garbage as well as bring home a couple of dead trees for firewood."

A draft horse! Although she'd seen some of the giant animals grazing peacefully in the open fields around town, Julia had never dared approach one of them for a closer look. "That would be fine. And I'll put some extra money in your paycheck to cover the rental of your animal and wagon."

"My *vadder* is not using Billy or the wagon right now. There is no need to pay for their use," he said.

"Oh yes, there is." Cutting him off, she bent over to pick up a bucket of murky soap water she'd been using to scrub the grimy floor.

Since she didn't own a car or truck of her own, Julia was grateful for the use of Martin's horse and intended to compensate him fairly. He seemed much too generous. She really liked Martin and didn't want to take advantage of him or his resources.

When she looked up again, she found him watching her, a perplexed expression tugging at his forehead.

"How old are you?" Martin asked her suddenly.

She blinked, as though surprised by his blunt question. "That's kind of personal, don't you think?"

He looked away, thinking he shouldn't have asked. Sometimes he was as bad as Hank. His blunt candor had gotten him into trouble on more than one occasion. His mother had told him not to ask women such personal questions but he really wanted to know.

"I was just wondering," he said.

"I'm twenty-three. Why were you wondering?"

He glanced at her, his gaze moving quickly from her face to her white tennis shoes. "Don't you have a boyfriend? You're kind of old to still be single."

She pressed a hand against her chest and laughed. "Wow! I didn't think so but you obviously do. It's not as if I'm an old maid. Is it?"

He laughed, too, relieved that she wasn't angry with him. "*Ne*, you're definitely not old, but by Amish standards, you would be considered on the edge of becoming a spinster."

Her mouth dropped open and a bit of mischief sparkled in her eyes. "Really? A spinster, huh?"

Actually, by Amish standards, she already was but he couldn't think of her that way. Not this lovely, intelligent woman.

"How old are you?" she asked, turning the tables on him.

"Twenty-five. My *mudder* fears I will become a dried-up old bachelor, useful to no one."

"I doubt that. You have been a lot of use to me. Look at all the good work you've already done."

He turned away and studied the two sawhorses he'd set up on the front porch for cutting boards. "But I have no sons and no daughters to take up my work once I am old. I have no one to pass on my knowledge and my faith to."

She hesitated. "If it makes a difference, I was engaged once, but it…it didn't work out."

He caught an expression of pain in her eyes, but then it was gone so fast that he thought he must have imagined it. He nodded, wishing he'd kept his big mouth shut. It wasn't his business and he couldn't help thinking this was one of those times when his mother would have told him he was too curious and bold for an Amish man.

"I can't imagine you never marrying," she said.

He tilted his head and gazed at her with amazement. "Why do you say that?"

She shrugged one shoulder. "You seem like a family man, that's all. The way you handle yourself. The way you act with Hank. You should be married with an adoring wife and a passel of children around you."

He laughed. "I'm afraid my *mudder* and *vadder* both

agree with you." He agreed, too, but what could he do? He couldn't produce a wife for himself out of thin air.

"So, why haven't you married?" she asked.

He tried to swallow, his throat suddenly dry as sandpaper. "I guess I haven't found the right girl."

"Me either. Or rather, I haven't found the right guy."

He smiled at that.

"Unfortunately, it's not quite that easy to find a suitable spouse, is it?" She glanced down, and her face flushed a pretty shade of pink.

"*Ne*, it certainly hasn't been for me."

"Frankly, I think I'm better off staying single."

He almost gasped out loud but caught himself in time. Not marry? Stay single? He could hardly contemplate such a situation. Not for himself and not for her.

"Why do you say that?" he asked.

She shrugged. "Love hurts too much. If I don't fall in love, I can't be hurt. It's that simple. I'd rather focus on my soap business and build some security for my mom and me. Then I'm in control. I get to say what happens in my life and I'm not at the whim and pleasure of someone who doesn't really care about me."

He nodded his assent. "It is true that if you don't love, you won't be hurt. But you also won't have the joy. And besides, if you marry a man who really loves you, he would never want to hurt you."

"Have you been in love before?" she asked.

"*Ne.*"

"Then how can you know for sure?"

"I sense it in here." He touched his chest, just over his heart. "When I find the right person, I will know. I'll give my whole heart to her and she'll give her whole heart to me. It will be amazing. I know it."

She was quiet for a moment, her face filled with such sadness that he thought she might cry. "I have loved before but he didn't love me in return. He used me. He abandoned me when I needed him most. It hurt more than I can say. Love isn't all it's cracked up to be, Martin. It can be brutal, cruel and destructive."

He realized what she said was true. And yet, he couldn't give up hope. Not for himself. And not for her. He just couldn't. "But it can be *wundervoll*, too."

"For you, perhaps."

"For you, as well. You must have faith. Don't give up on the Lord," he said.

Her lips trembled and he thought she was holding back the tears. "Faith is good for you and other people but it hasn't worked for me. Still, I want to have faith. I want to believe that God really cares for me."

Her words bludgeoned his heart. He hated the thought that this beautiful woman would give up on love. To him, it was the same as giving up on *Gott*.

"He does. You can believe that. You mustn't give up on finding someone to love," he said.

She looked away. "I don't know if I'm willing to try it a second time."

He didn't know what to say. He hated that someone had hurt her so badly.

"Well, I've got some soap to cut into bars," she said, clearly changing the subject.

"You made soap?"

She nodded. "Just a double batch in my kitchen last night. I want to send off some samples to commercial vendors, to see if I can get some more wholesale contracts. I also want to ensure we have enough bars to stock the store for our grand opening the first of December. So, I'd better get back to work."

"*Ja*, me, too."

He picked up a board he had already measured and marked with a pencil. With several quick movements, he cut through the wood with his handsaw. When he turned, she was gone. And just like that, his chest felt empty inside.

To take his mind off their conversation, he focused on his work. With Hank occupied upstairs with Sharon, Martin got one entire set of shelves completed before it was time to go home.

As if on cue, Julia returned and accompanied him outside. Her interest in prayer a few days earlier when he and Hank had been eating lunch had delighted him and he felt compelled to ask a question that had been weighing heavily on his mind all afternoon.

"Would you like to attend church with me tomorrow?" he asked.

Her smile dropped like a stone and she hesitated, hugging herself against the chilly wind. "I, um, I'm not sure."

"We only hold Church Sunday every other week," he hurried on before she could say no. "We hold services in our barns because they're big enough to hold the entire *Gmay*. Each *familye* in the congregation takes turns hosting the meetings. Tomorrow, church will be held at my parents' farm."

"Oh. Where do you live?" she asked.

"Three miles outside of town, along Cherry Creek."

"*Ja*, we live just off the county road," Hank interjected.

Martin whirled around as his brother joined them.

He held a huge cinnamon roll that dripped with white icing. Opening wide, he took a big bite before speaking with a full mouth. "Look what Sharon gave me."

"Mrs. Rose," Martin corrected the boy.

Hank ignored his brother as he swallowed and smiled at Julia. "You want one? Your mom has lots upstairs."

"Maybe later." Julia smiled before turning back to Martin.

"If you're interested in prayer, I figure you could learn more at church," Martin said.

Though she insisted she'd given up on love, Martin wasn't so sure. Her interest in prayer meant there was a glimmer of hope inside her. But then he reconsidered.

Why had he asked? It was presumptuous and rude and much too forward of him. She was an *Englischer*, after all. His parents might not approve of him inviting her to church.

"I... I think I'd like that very much. But how will I get out there? I don't own a car," she said.

She wanted to go!

A feeling of relief and pure panic enveloped Martin at the same time. Relief because he really wanted her to come to church and panic because he knew she was an outsider and he wasn't sure how she would take it all in. It was rare for an *Englischer* to attend their church, which was spoken entirely in Pennsylvania Dutch and German. Julia wouldn't understand what was going on. Everything might seem odd to her and he didn't want to alienate her.

Hank waved a hand in the air before licking icing off his thick fingers. "We can come get you."

Martin nodded. "*Ja*, I'll pick you up in the buggy and bring you home afterward."

"And you can be my girl," Hank said.

Martin gasped, then coughed. "Hank…"

Julia's eyes widened, then she smiled. "I'm definitely your friend, Hank."

"My girlfriend?" the boy asked, looking way too eager.

Julia hesitated, seeming to choose her words carefully. "Well, I'm a girl and I'm your friend. But I'm much too old for you."

The boy's face lit up like a house on fire. "*Ach*, so you're my *maedel*."

Julia looked confused. And little wonder. She didn't speak Deitsch and had no idea that Hank had just called her his girl.

Martin bit his tongue to keep from scolding his brother. At least not now, in front of Julia.

She blinked, turning her attention back to Martin. "Isn't it a rather long distance for you to drive your horse just to pick me up for church?"

"Not at all. That's how I get here to work every day and that's what our horses are for. Your *mudder* is invited, as well," Martin said.

There. That was *gut*. If her mother accompanied them, it wouldn't seem so odd to the members of the *Gmay*. After all, he didn't want his parents or siblings to believe he was interested in Julia romantically, because he wasn't. No, not at all.

A dubious expression covered her face. "I doubt Mom would like to come but I'll invite her just in case. Are you sure you don't mind picking me up?"

"*Ne*, it would be my pleasure. But I would like to make one request."

"And what is that?"

He cleared his throat, which felt suddenly tight. "That you keep an open mind at everything you see and hear and try to feel with your heart. Try not to make any judgments until I can clarify things for you."

As Martin explained about the language barrier and that she might not understand everything that went on at church, Hank continued to stare at Julia with open adoration.

"Don't worry if there is something you can't understand. Things may seem odd at first but we have a reason for everything we do. I promise to expand on it afterward, during the ride when I bring you home. I'll answer all your questions then," Martin said.

She smiled happily. "Of course. We'll have a long chat. Thank you. I'd like to join you very much."

Martin exhaled a slow breath, hoping his invitation wasn't a mistake. It was too late to take back his offer now. Instead, he told her what time he would need to collect her so they wouldn't be late for services.

"I'll be ready," she said.

He nodded, then loaded his toolbox in the back of his wagon. While he herded Hank into the buggy, Julia didn't leave the front porch. She stood watching them with a thoughtful expression tugging at her forehead. As he drove out of the parking lot, she waved and a feeling of absolute dread swept over Martin.

Now he'd done it. He'd only recently met Julia, yet he wanted nothing more than to teach her about his faith. To help her understand his beliefs and perhaps discover her own relationship with *Gott*. Faith was such a huge part of Martin's life. It governed everything he did and he loved it dearly, but his people didn't actively proselytize. They never saw the need to share their religion with outsiders and preferred to show their beliefs in their daily living.

So what would Bishop Yoder say when he discovered Martin had invited an unmarried *Englisch* woman and her mother to church? Worse yet, what would Martin's parents say? As an older unmarried man, he was already fodder for the gossips in his *Gmay*. The last thing he needed was to be associated with an *Englisch* woman.

Yet he couldn't help it. He felt compelled to invite her. And he couldn't take the invitation back. Not now that she had accepted. He'd just have to move forward and hope for the best.

Chapter Five

"You're not serious."

Sharon Rose stared at her daughter with absolute astonishment. Sitting at the dinner table that evening, Julia set her spoon on the table, her stew growing cold in the bowl. She had just told her mom about Martin's invitation to attend church in the morning. But she hated the look of frosty abhorrence in her mother's eyes. Maybe it had been a mistake to tell her. Maybe she should back out.

"I'm very serious, Mom. We've both been invited."

Mom gave a caustic laugh as she reached for a freshly baked roll, squishing it in her grasp. "Well, I sure won't be attending. Not in a million years." She threw a glance at Julia. "I thought you were going to make another batch of soap to cure before our grand opening."

"I've made a number of single batches almost every evening since we arrived in Colorado and they're curing nicely. It won't hurt to take time off to worship God. Don't worry. We'll have enough soap for our grand opening and to mail off to vendors, too."

"You're not really planning to attend the Amish church, are you?" Mom asked.

Julia reached for her glass and took a sip of warm milk before answering slowly. "Yes, I am."

Mom's lips tightened. "It's that young man, isn't it? Martin. You find him attractive."

It was a statement, not a question.

"Martin is just our handyman, nothing more. You didn't mind the two times when I went to Bible study with Debbie. Dallin went with us, too."

She had listened to a couple of people pray at these meetings but had never done so herself.

"That was different," Mom said.

"How so?"

"Debbie wasn't Amish. Neither was Dallin."

Julia placed her elbow on the table and leaned forward, feeling confused. "No, but they were both dishonest. So, is it just the Amish church you object to? Or Martin?"

"Both, I'm afraid. They are one and the same. If you go with that young man, he'll...he'll..."

"He'll what, Mom? Why don't you like him?"

Mom pushed her bowl away, obviously having lost her appetite. "I don't dislike him. But you're too free-thinking to be Amish. You have a mind of your own and shouldn't have to suppress that. And honestly, I'm afraid he'll corrupt your ideas. The Amish aren't like normal people."

Julia laughed. "That's a compliment, Mom. And what are normal people like? I'm not sure I've ever met one."

Mom frowned. "Amish men dominate their women. They rule their homes with an iron fist."

Julia was aghast. Her father had been such a kind, gentle man. She couldn't imagine being married to a dominating brute. "How do you know what Amish men are like?"

"I… I've heard things over the years. I knew some Amish women once, before you were born."

"You like Hank well enough. He comes upstairs and you feed him all the time," Julia said.

"He's no threat to us. He's just a boy with Down syndrome and he deserves a little kindness," Mom said.

"But you don't seem to like Martin at all."

"He's a fully grown man and he doesn't have Down syndrome," Mom said.

Her justification seemed a bit off to Julia and she released a sigh. "I'm just going to church with him. It's not as if I'm going to become Amish. It's just this one time."

Her mother continued to gaze at her and Julia felt compelled to explain.

"I asked him some questions about his faith and he's the first person to give me straight answers that I liked. I don't know why you disapprove so much."

"Because he's Amish, dear. Amish. They don't even use electricity," Mom said.

Julia snorted as she scooted her chair back from the table. "Well, neither do we."

She glanced at the freshly painted ceiling where a light fixture was attached. Because they had no power, the bulbs were dead and they were still using kerosene lamps to light their way.

"That will change once we can pay to have an electrician repair our power problem. When do you think we'll be able to afford that?" Mom asked.

No longer feeling hungry, Julia set her bowl in the

sink and filled it with hot soapy water. "It could be a little while. We'll have to see how the grand opening goes. I want to ensure we have enough money to pay our bills first. Since we've lived without electricity even before we moved to Colorado, I thought we could wait a little longer and save some money."

"Yes, we can wait," Mom conceded.

"And I'm going to church tomorrow. It's just one time and it'll probably come to nothing. But I'd really like to go."

Mom released a deep sigh. "Suit yourself."

What else could Sharon say? Julia was a grown woman. But they didn't speak while Julia washed and Mom dried the dishes. Julia could feel the tension in the air like a living, breathing thing. She hated having friction with her mother. Again, she thought about backing out and not going but had no idea how to get word to Martin so he wouldn't drive all the way into town to pick her up early in the morning. Once he arrived, it wouldn't be fair to tell him he'd come all this way for nothing. Right?

"I'm tired and going to bed now. Remember that I love you more than anything else in the world." Mom leaned close and kissed her cheek.

"I know. I love you, too, Mom." Julia spoke quietly, not knowing what else to say.

She watched as Mom picked up a lamp and carried it to her bedroom. She limped slightly, indicating that her hips were hurting her. The apartment was small but warm and cozy and Julia felt safe and happy here. She didn't want trouble with her mother.

Surely this wasn't worth arguing over. She'd go to church with Martin this one time and that would probably be the end of it. No more questions. No more curiosity about God. That would please her mother. Surely everything would return to normal. She hoped.

The following morning, it was still dark when Martin pulled his horse into the parking lot at Rose Soapworks. A single light gleamed from inside the store. Taking a deep inhale of crisp air, he stepped out of the buggy. As he walked toward the front door, he could see puffs of his breath and knew the first snowfall of the season would hit any day now.

There was no need to knock. Julia must have been watching from inside because she stepped out onto the porch and met him at the bottom step.

"Good morning, Martin," she said softly, her eyes bright, her pale skin glowing in the shadows.

"*Guder mariye*, Julia," he returned.

"*Guder mariye,*" she repeated with perfect pronunciation.

He smiled as she laid a gloved hand on his arm and he accompanied her to the buggy. She wore a long, wool coat, her plain gray scarf tucked high around her neck. Though he could see her ankles and knew she must be wearing a dress, her low-heeled black shoes were quite simple by *Englisch* standards. She'd pulled her long hair back in a tidy bun at the nape of her neck and wore no makeup that he could see. For an *Englisch* woman, she dressed quite plain, but he knew his mother would not approve of the large gold buttons on her coat.

As he helped her into the buggy, he was highly aware of the energy pulsing between them. "Is your *mudder* not coming with us?"

Julia shook her head. "No, she's not happy about me going either."

He glanced at the dark building. "I'm sorry. I don't want to create conflict between you and your *mudder*. It's important to honor your *eldre* in all things."

"Eldre?" she asked.

"Your parents."

She repeated the word several times, as if trying it out on her tongue. "My *mudder* would rather I not go but she knows I'm a grown woman who can make her own choices."

He jerked, pleasantly surprised that she had used a Deitsch word in her vocabulary. But contention was not of *Gott* and honoring parents was highly important to all Amish people.

"Where's Hank?" she asked as she settled herself on the cold front seat.

He reached for a quilt his *familye* kept in the back for traveling during the winter months. "He's at home, helping set up for church." Martin spread the quilt across her legs.

"Danke," she said, sliding her hands beneath the heavy fabric and pulling it up to her waist.

Again, he was surprised. "You're speaking Deitsch now?"

She shrugged, a light smile teasing the corners of her lips. "It seems appropriate. Maybe you can teach me your language."

Ah, he liked that, but he couldn't explain why. She was so different from most *Englischers* he'd met. So humble and eager to learn and try new things. "You don't think your *mudder* would mind?"

"Ne, I can handle my *mudder*," she said.

Again, he smiled, inordinately pleased by her efforts to speak his language. Taking the lead lines into his hands, he slapped them lightly against the horse's back.

"Schritt!" he called.

The horse stepped forward.

"I'll bet Hank wasn't happy to be left behind today," Julia said.

Martin smiled, remembering the temper tantrum his younger brother had thrown when he'd been told he couldn't ride into town to pick up Julia. *"Ne,* he was not happy about it at all."

Neither would his mother be pleased when she found out that Sharon wasn't accompanying them. The only reason his father had agreed to let Martin pick up Julia alone was because he thought they'd be chaperoned by her mother. But there was no help for it now.

"Is Hank your only sibling?" Julia asked.

"Ne, I have three sisters and another brother. I am the eldest."

Her eyes widened and she stared at the road. "Wow! That's six children! Your mother, er, *mudder* must have her hands full."

He chuckled at her comment. "Do you think that's a lot?"

"It sure is. Most people only want one or two kids these days. Or none at all."

"Not us. Children are precious to my people. The average Amish *familye* has six or seven *kinder.* We want all the *gut* Lord will send us. We believe *kinder* are a gift from *Gott."*

"That's a nice way to look at it. But isn't that a lot of extra mouths to feed?" she asked.

He shrugged. *"Ja,* but they also make many hands to

work on the farm. And as they marry, our *familye* expands and we have many people we can call on whenever we need help during times of trouble."

She smiled. "Many hands make light work, or so my *mudder* always says."

He nodded. "Exactly. I have a large *familye* I can depend upon. I'll never be alone no matter what."

She was quiet for several moments, as if thinking this over. "It would have been nice when my *vadder* was ill to have *familye* members to depend on. But I was on my own. It's been difficult being an only *kinder*."

"Kind," he corrected. "Two children are *kinder*, but one child is *kind*."

She smiled at his explanation and doggedly repeated the words. "I always wanted a brother or sister, or both. My *mudder* just wasn't able to have any more after I was born."

"If your parents wanted more, I'm sorry to hear they couldn't."

"My mom told me she almost died giving birth to me."

Martin grunted in acknowledgement. "It happens that way sometimes."

"What is the word for brother and sister?" she asked.

He gave her the words and waited as she repeated them several times.

"Do you really want to learn Deitsch?" he asked.

She hesitated. *"Ja,* I think I'd like that very much. It could be useful when the Amish come into my new store to do business."

He smiled, unable to contain his delight. "Then I'll do my best to teach you."

They rode in silence for several minutes, enjoying

the view of the sun peeking over the tops of the eastern mountains. Fingers of pink, gold and purple painted the valley below. A cluster of black-and-white cows stood grazing in a fallow field, the nubs of dried grass glistening with a layer of early morning frost.

"It's so beautiful here," Julia said.

Martin looked at her, seeing the peaceful contentment on her face. "*Ja*, it sure is."

"Why is marriage so important to your people?" she asked.

He looked away, embarrassed to be caught staring. "*Ach*, because *familye* is so important to us. Without marriage, there is no *familye* and no *kinder* and our way of life would die. Do you…do you want children one day?"

Oh, maybe he shouldn't have asked that. It might sound too presumptuous.

A soft smile curved her lips. "*Ja*, someday if I ever get married."

"Do you…do you want lots of *kinder*, or only one or two?"

"I think I'd like more, but that's a long way off."

He nodded, accepting this. After all, he could never be her husband so it really didn't concern him.

"I may never marry," she said.

He snorted. "Of course you will. Everyone weds. Don't they?"

After all, he still wasn't married. But the thought that he might remain a bachelor all his life had never taken hold in his mind. He hadn't found a suitable wife yet but he knew deep in his heart that he would one day. He'd always had faith that *Gott* hadn't abandoned him. But lately, he wasn't so sure.

"Many people choose not to marry. Or they postpone marriage for a long time. They choose a career instead," she said.

He blinked, staring straight ahead at the black asphalt. "Why can't they have both?"

She shrugged. "I guess they could."

"I want a large *familye*. When I die, I doubt I'll be concerned that I didn't earn enough money. I'll be concerned with how I treated my *familye* and whether I spent enough time with them. That is what really matters. Your *familye* is all you get to take with you in the end."

She looked down at her hands folded primly in her lap. He hoped he hadn't said anything to upset her. After all, he was laying quite a bit of new information on her and it could be rather overwhelming.

"I can't imagine living my life alone either but sometimes we don't get a choice in the matter." She spoke so softly that he almost didn't hear.

Her words sounded so lonely, so hollow, that he felt a rush of empathy for her. And then he knew that neither of them wanted to be alone. Neither of them had chosen not to marry but the opportunity to marry someone who could make them happy had never come their way. Yet.

For the first time in a very long time, Martin wondered if he might remain a solitary bachelor after all.

Chapter Six

The rhythmic clip-clop of the horse's hooves on the pavement seemed so relaxing to Julia. Still, a feeling of anticipation buzzed through her. This was her first buggy ride and her first time attending an Amish church meeting. Everything about Martin seemed new and interesting. It had been a long time since she'd enjoyed a fun outing with friends. But this was so much more. Finally, she could explore the feelings she had for God. Her relationship with God had been pretty lean up to this point and she was hungry to learn more about the Lord.

"Are you nervous?" Martin asked, giving a quick flick of the lead lines to keep the horse going at a steady pace.

"A little," she confessed.

"Don't be. Everything will be fine."

He then described what she should expect. How the church meeting would culminate with lunch afterward. Of course, she had a zillion questions but he answered every one. Their animated discussion brought her a sense of exhilaration. It tantalized her intellect and made her immensely happy. Martin's calm voice sounded so reasonable. It made her feel as if she'd known him all her life. He demystified God and made her feel closer to her Heavenly Father.

Though the day was crisp, the bright sun glimmered in the eastern sky. As they pulled into the yard of his family's farm along Cherry Creek, Julia gazed at the wide pastures surrounding the two-story log house and enormous red barn.

Martin pointed at several black-and-white cows standing in a pasture at the side of the barn. "Those are our milk cows."

Julia blinked, feeling as if she'd stepped back in time to a quaint, bygone era of wholesome living.

Fields of hay lay fallow with brown stubble from the autumn harvest. The barbed wire fences were straight and orderly, the flower beds bordering the house cleared of frozen flowers and weed free. Not surprising. She'd already learned that Martin was hardworking and fastidious. No doubt his parents had taught him well.

The place seemed deserted. No one was there to greet them.

"Schtopp!" Martin called, pulling the buggy to a halt.

They paused next to a long row of black buggies parked along the outer fence. A plethora of horses grazed peacefully in the pasture next to them.

"You have so many horses," she said.

"They aren't ours. Those are the road horses everyone uses to pull their buggies. I'll put our horse in with them and then we can join the meeting," Martin said.

He hopped out and came around to assist her. The feel of his strong hand supporting her arm as she stepped down caused a warm sensation to cascade over her. She quickly straightened her skirt and patted her hair, hoping she looked all right.

"You look fine," he said, as if reading her thoughts.

She realized that was huge praise coming from this man. She'd already learned the Amish weren't given to frivolous compliments and his words pleased her enormously.

She caught the low thrum of voices lifting through the air in song. She turned toward the barn, a feeling of curiosity pulsing over her. The singing continued in long-drawn-out a capella unison. Male voices mingled with female in a solemn hymn that reminded Julia of a medieval movie she'd seen once. The sound was eerie yet beautiful.

"They have started. We must hurry." Martin spoke low.

She caught his urgency as he quickly unhitched the horse from its harness. They must be late.

"Komm." He turned and beckoned gently to her.

Julia followed as he hurried toward the barn. An older man with a full gray beard and no moustache stood at the entrance. He wore a black frock coat and felt hat. His dark, penetrating gaze shifted briefly to her and she felt his curiosity.

Her sense of ease immediately shifted to absolute panic. What was she doing here? These people were strangers. Perhaps her mother had been right and she wouldn't be welcomed. Oh, why had she come?

"It's all right." As if sensing her unease, Martin spoke softly beside her. His soothing voice helped settle her nerves.

"Julia, this is my *vadder*, David Hostetler." Martin

made the introduction in a low whisper that wouldn't disturb the singing.

"Hallo," she greeted the man softly, holding out her hand. He took it and squeezed gently, his gray eyes crinkling with a warm smile.

"Willkomm to our home," he said. Then, he faced Martin. *"Du bischt schpot!"*

Julia caught the mild tone of impatience in David's voice but no anger.

"Ja, I know we're late. I'm sorry," Martin whispered.

"Where is her *mudder*?" David asked, peering behind them.

"Mrs. Rose chose not to *komm* with us today," Martin explained.

With a brief nod, David lifted a hand to indicate they should enter the barn. A matronly woman stood just inside, as if waiting for them.

"Julia, this is my *mudder*, Linda Hostetler." Again Martin spoke low.

Julia met the woman's formal gaze. Her white prayer *kapp* stood out in sharp contrast to her simple black dress, tights and shoes. She wore a crisp, white apron over her dress that Julia found quite lovely.

"Komm and join us," Linda whispered, indicating that Julia should follow her.

The spacious interior of the barn had been swept to an immaculate cleanliness. Looking up, Julia saw rows of hard backless benches lined up where numerous worshippers sat. As she passed, Julia felt the people's eyes on her. A few smiled but some frowned. Whether they disapproved because they were late for the meeting or because she was *Englisch*, Julia wasn't sure.

Rather than sitting with their families, the assembly was seated by gender and age with all the men and boys on one side of the room and all the women and girls on the other. Martin had already explained that this segregation had nothing to do with discrimination but rather symbolized accountability to the authority of the church.

Linda perched on a front bench, indicating that Julia should join her. Julia did so, clasping her hands tightly in her lap. Martin joined his father opposite her. Sitting next to his father, Hank made a sound of exuberance and lifted a hand to wave hello. Martin's father scowled and shook his head and the boy settled down.

David and Martin immediately joined in the song but Julia didn't know the words. Linda handed her a hymnal titled *Ausbund* but it didn't help much since the words were in German. Their voices united in a laborious tempo without musical accompaniment.

Glancing about, Julia noticed many gazes resting on her. Some looks were open and curious but others were downright hostile. When she met their eyes, people looked away, as though embarrassed to be caught gawking. Julia felt suddenly awkward. Even though she wore modest clothes and her long hair was tied back in a bun, the brightly flowered print of her skirt seemed garish and out of place in comparison to the sedate solid colors and prayer *kapps* of the Amish women.

Remembering Martin's request from the day before, she was determined to keep an open mind and try to feel with her heart. She glanced his way, feeling rather anxious. And that's when he did something that immediately put her at ease.

He smiled and winked.

"Ahem!"

Martin's father cleared his throat and Julia looked away, reminding herself to be reverent. This was church, after all. A place to worship God. She hummed along with the song. The slow tempo made it easy enough to follow. It went on and on but seemed rather sweet and she found that she enjoyed the worshipful feeling in the room. For this period of time, she pushed aside all her worldly cares and relaxed, focusing on God.

Hearing her humming, Linda tilted her head slightly and smiled with approval.

Finally, the singing ended and the preaching began. The words were spoken in Deitsch and Julia understood nothing at all. But as she gazed at the minister's intense expression and heard the loving emotion vibrating in his voice, a feeling of peace settled over Julia and she felt the devout message deep in her heart. She was certain Martin would explain the topic on their way home.

The moment church ended, Julia was surrounded by people.

"Julia!"

She whirled around and found herself engulfed in a solid hug by Hank.

"Oof!" She tried to disengage herself. "*Hallo*, Hank."

"*Wie bischt du?*" the boy greeted her rather loudly.

"Hank, that's enough. Remember your manners." Martin tugged his brother's arms free from Julia.

"But Julia's my girl," the boy exclaimed, drawing a number of surprised gasps.

"That's nonsense." Linda's eyes widened with disapproval.

Martin snorted. "She's just your friend. Remember? But you must not hug her. It isn't proper."

Linda breathed a sigh of relief and nodded at her son.

"But I want…" Hank began.

Martin turned away, ignoring the boy. He quickly introduced Julia to Bishop Amos Yoder, Deacon Darrin Albrecht and Minister Jeremiah Beiler, their only minister. The three men gazed at her with cautious smiles that didn't quite meet their eyes. She sensed their hesitation.

"Your *mudder* did not *komm* with you today?" Bishop Yoder asked politely.

Julia blinked, surprised that he'd known her mom might be here. She shook her head. "I'm sorry, but she isn't feeling well and chose to stay at home."

"Martin has told us she has lupus. I hope it isn't serious," the bishop said.

She didn't explain that lupus was very serious. "She'll be fine after she rests awhile."

"Perhaps she'll *komm* with you next time," Linda suggested.

"You must tell her that she is *willkomm* to join us anytime." The bishop lifted his bushy eyebrows in expectation, his bearded face showing nothing but friendship. And in that moment, Julia saw nothing to fear in his kind, intelligent eyes. She decided then that she liked Martin's parents and the church elders.

"*Ja*, perhaps," Julia said.

"I noticed you are speaking some Deitsch." David's voice was filled with approval.

Julia shrugged, feeling a bit shy. "A little bit but I fear I mispronounce most of the words."

"Already, she is learning quite fast," Martin said.

"I'm gonna help teach her, too," Hank blurted, looking mightily pleased with himself.

"*Ach*, that is *gut*. Soon, you will be able to understand what is being said during the preachings," Jeremiah Beiler exclaimed.

"*Ja*, that is very *gut*." Linda smiled, too, her expression one of relief.

They all beamed at her and Julia thought it must be because they thought she was serious about becoming Amish. The fact that Martin was unmarried and had brought her here today must worry them. She was *Englisch*, after all. A woman of the world. No doubt they preferred her to learn Deitsch and join their Amish community rather than pull Martin out of his faith.

But the fact was, she and Martin were just friends. She was here as a one-time guest and had no intention of joining the Amish faith. Especially since her mother didn't approve.

Linda glanced at the door and lifted both her hands in the air. "*Ach*, I'm the hostess today and here I stand around visiting. I should be in the kitchen helping with the meal. Would you like to join me?"

Julia met the woman's gaze, eager for the distraction. "Of course. I'd love to."

As they turned and headed toward the house, Julia changed her mind when Martin didn't move from his place beside his father. She realized he wasn't coming. Perhaps meals were considered a woman's chore and he was expected to remain with the men. Because she wanted to be polite, she followed Linda.

They crossed the green lawn and Julia noticed numerous long tables set up in the backyard. Sitting beneath the branches of a tall elm tree, a rather elderly lady spoke in a loud whisper that wasn't really a whisper at all and carried clear across the yard.

"If you ask me, Martin has become so desperate for a

wife that he's now looking at the *Englisch* girls," the elderly woman said. "You mark my words. Martin will be pulled out of our faith if something isn't done to stop it."

"Marva, what are you saying?" a middle-aged woman asked with incredulous wonder.

"Just that we might lose him," Marva said, lifting her head in an imperious gesture.

Linda came to a halt, staring at the two women as her face contorted with fear and disapproval.

Seeing Linda's expression, the middle-aged woman hurried to alleviate the situation. "*Ach*, Martin would never abandon his faith. He's steadfast. That's why he brought the girl here. Surely she'll convert."

"And what if she doesn't?" Marva asked, her lips pursed like a prune. Looking straight at Linda, she seemed to challenge her, not caring at all that Julia was listening to their words.

"Idle gossip is an unworthy endeavor," Linda said before turning toward the house.

Marva released a pensive "harrumph."

Julia followed after Linda but heard Marva's parting comment.

"The girl seems vaguely familiar to me, though I can't remember how. I feel as if I know her from somewhere," Marva said.

"You probably saw her in town once," the younger woman said.

"*Ne*, I don't think so. I feel certain that I know her from my life back in Ohio, though I don't see how since she's so young and it's been many years since I lived there."

Julia slipped inside behind Linda. As the screen door

clapped closed behind her, she breathed a sigh of relief. Maybe she didn't belong here after all.

Linda paused in the laundry room, resting a hand against her heart, taking deep inhales.

"Are you all right?" Julia asked.

"*Ja*, I'm sorry you had to hear that. Please ignore what they said. Marva Geingerich is a *Swartzentruber* and doesn't approve of anyone," Linda explained.

"A *Swartzentruber*?"

"*Ja*, the *Swartzentrubers* are Old Order Amish and shun any and all change. Marva just turned eighty-nine and thinks she knows everything. I don't happen to share her opinions. Now, *komm* and slice some bread."

Through the open doorway into the kitchen, Julia saw numerous women milling around the counters in organized chaos as they prepared the noon meal. The buzz of their voices mingled together in happy banter. Their dresses were identical with a myriad of solid dark colors, white aprons and *kapps*. She watched in fascination, stunned by the enormous amount of food they had placed on a trestle table.

Without another word, Linda hurried over to the table and handed Julia a loaf of homemade bread and a knife. The women greeted them.

As they worked, Linda made introductions. Naomi Fisher, who looked to be about sixty-five years of age. Lori Geingerich and her four-year-old daughter, Rachel. Lizzie Stoltzfus and Abby Fisher, who were both newlyweds and appeared to be about Julia's age. Sarah Yoder, the bishop's wife. And several other older women. They were all friendly and smiled in welcome.

"I'll try to remember all your names." Julia gave a

little laugh as she slid the sharp knife through the loaf of bread.

"Don't worry. You'll soon know all of us quite well and we'll be *gut* friends." Abby spoke in a buoyant voice.

Lizzie looked up from where she was slicing red apples beside the sink. "Martin tells us that you're opening a soap studio in town."

Everyone turned to look at her and Julia's guard went up like a kite flying high.

"*Ja*, that is why I want to learn Deitsch. So I can speak with all of you when you come in to my new store," Julia replied.

There. That was good, wasn't it? An open invitation to visit and be friends.

Sarah Yoder laughed out loud. Not a sarcastic laugh but simply one of good humor. "That's nice, but I'm afraid we all make our own soap. We really don't have a reason to buy it elsewhere. In fact, Lizzie sells soaps, too."

Oh. Maybe her attempt to find common ground hadn't worked after all. She hadn't expected to be in commercial conflict with any of them.

"Um, perhaps you'd like to sell some of your soaps on consignment in my store," she offered.

Lizzie nodded. "Perhaps."

"May I ask what fragrances you use in your soap making?" Julia asked.

Naomi waved a dismissive hand before returning to the pot of soup she was stirring. "We don't use fragrance. That would be too worldly for our needs."

"But Julia sells her soaps to the *Englisch*, don't you? So I'm sure you use fragrance. That's what appeals to your *Englisch* customers. We do the same when we make things to sell to the *Englisch*, but we don't use it in our own homes." Sarah spoke in a kind tone.

Julia smiled, trying not to show her anxiety. She gazed at the beautiful rag rug beneath her feet, thinking it would take time to get used to these people and their ways. "Yes, that's true. I sell my soaps to anyone who will buy them."

"*Ach*, I don't know any self-respecting Amish woman who would buy soap when she can make it herself," Naomi said. Again, there was no cruelty in her statement but just a simple truth.

A flush of embarrassed heat suffused Julia's face. She was quickly learning how self-sufficient the Amish were. "I... I'm sure all of you are great soap makers. Perhaps you might teach me some of your methods."

"That sounds fun. And maybe you can teach us some of your techniques," Abby said, smiling sweetly.

"Absolutely. And I love the color of your dress. Did you make it?" Julia eyed the lovely dark rose color, thinking all of their dresses were beautiful in their simplicity.

"*Ja*, we make all our clothes," Abby said.

At that moment, Marva Geingerich, the old *Swartzentruber* woman, came into the room. The thud of her cane pounded the bare floor with each step. With her presence, Julia's hands felt trembly.

"If you become Amish, you'll have to learn to sew." Marva spoke the words in a stern, warning voice.

Linda lifted her head. "*Ach*, there's nothing to sewing. I'll teach you. If you can make soap, you can certainly learn to sew."

Julia wasn't sure she wanted to learn. Nor did she

plan to join the Amish but she didn't say so. Instead, she changed the subject.

"This rag rug is beautiful. Did you make it?" she asked Linda.

"*Ja*, I used all the leftover scraps of cloth I've collected over the years."

"Maybe you would like to sell your rugs in my store on consignment, too," Julia suggested.

Linda paused as she filled a teapot full of boiling hot water. Then, she smiled wide. "*Ja*, I would like that. That's very generous of you."

Julia shrugged. "The way I look at it, any kind of business can be good for all of us."

Several women stopped their various chores to look quizzically at her, but Julia just ducked her head and kept slicing. She realized then that making soap was simply part of Amish life. Rather than finding common ground with these women, Julia sensed that she had offended them and she wasn't sure how to make things right. Perhaps it would be best to shut her mouth, get through the meal and hope that Martin took her home soon. Except for sitting on a hard bench all morning, she'd done nothing today. No real physical labor. But it didn't seem to matter. She was absolutely exhausted and ready to leave.

"Martin, I see you've brought an *Englischer* to church with you today."

Martin turned and saw Ezekiel Burkholder gazing at him intently from where he sat at the table waiting for his noon meal. At the age of ninety-five, *Dawdi* Zeke, as they called him, was the eldest member of their *Gmay*. With sparkling gray eyes and shocking white hair and beard, the man was still spry and in complete control of his mental faculties.

Martin walked over to the old patriarch and sat down opposite him. "*Ja*, she is an *Englischer*. Her name is Julia Rose."

Several men, including Martin's father, Bishop Yoder and Deacon Albrecht, sat nearby and Martin realized he was about to get a grilling from them. Before he left this evening, Martin had no doubt they all would know everything they possibly could about Julia and her family. He couldn't help wondering if she was facing the same dilemma inside the kitchen. What was taking her so long? She'd gone inside the house with his mother some time ago and he was anxious to know how she was doing.

"How did you meet this woman?" *Dawdi* Zeke asked.

Martin explained about his job at Rose Soapworks.

"It's *gut* that you are earning money to pay for your barn. But what are your intentions with this woman?"

Here it was. The question Martin had known would come up eventually. A question he wished to avoid.

"I have no intentions at all. She is just a friend and my employer. She expressed an interest in my faith so I brought her to church. I also invited her *mudder* but she didn't want to *komm*," he said.

"He is even teaching Julia to speak Deitsch," David said. His comment was accompanied by a round of *ahhs* and approving nods.

"The best marriages start with a man and woman becoming *gut* friends," *Dawdi* Zeke said.

Several men nodded again, including David, who sat back in his seat, his gaze narrowed on his son. Martin could feel their intensity. Unless Julia converted to their faith, becoming friends with the *Englischer* could only lead to trouble. Especially for an unmarried Amish man in desperate need of a wife.

"When I marry, I will wed an Amish woman or not at all," Martin reassured them, noticing that his father's tensed shoulders relaxed a bit. "But Julia has expressed a great interest in our faith, so I felt it was my duty to lead her to the Lord."

There, that was good. It was the truth, after all. Martin knew that none of the men could argue with this logic. Though they didn't actively proselytize, they still had an obligation to teach the truth when someone asked them for the information.

"That is *gut*, as long as you are vigilant and careful not to be swayed to accept the worldly values the *Englisch* seem to cherish," Bishop Yoder said.

"*Ja*, you must be wary lest this woman tries to entice you to an *Englisch* life," Deacon Albrecht added.

Martin soon found himself receiving all sorts of advice on how to stay strong in his faith while leading Julia to the truth. Having anticipated this beforehand, he took it all in stride.

But as he listened, his thoughts turned to Julia. When they'd first arrived late to the meeting, he could see that she didn't want to be here. He could see the panic written all across her face. Her eyes had widened with amazement, her forehead crinkled in confusion. What seemed normal and mundane to him must seem so strange and eccentric to her.

Then, the minister had started to speak. Julia's attention had been rapt on the man. As she listened, a look of peace had covered her glowing face. She looked so innocent and pure sitting there in his father's barn.

He'd felt highly attracted to her. But just one problem: she wasn't Amish.

To love and marry outside his faith, he would be shunned by his people. They wouldn't speak to him nor take anything from his hand. He couldn't do business with them. He couldn't do anything. For those reasons, he would never do anything to get himself shunned, no matter how much he longed for a wife and *familye* of his own.

At that moment, a stream of women came from the house carrying a variety of bowls and platters of food. The moment he saw the flash of Julia's bright skirt, his senses went on high alert. Not wanting to appear too eager, he forced himself to drag his gaze away as she carried a tea service over to *Dawdi* Zeke and set it on the table. Little four-year-old Rachel Geingerich followed with a plate of cookies for the elderly man. The girl stumbled across the uneven grass, almost dropping her cargo before Julia rescued her.

"Here, let me help you." She spoke kindly to the child as she took her arm while the girl regained her footing.

"Danke," Rachel said, her voice high and sweet as she set the plate on the table next to Zeke.

"I will be going into the mountains in a few days, to collect some firewood," Martin said. Speaking in Deitsch, he'd purposefully changed the subject. If his father wasn't interested in helping gather the wood, he didn't want Julia to know.

David tilted his head. "Why do you need firewood? It's late in the season and we have plenty here for our needs."

"It's for Julia and her *mudder*. They have recently arrived in Riverton and will need fuel for their wood-burning stoves. I thought I could go get some before the snow flies."

"*Ach*, it sounds like it's time for a frolic." Bishop Yoder slapped his hands against his thighs and smiled wide.

"I can help," Jakob Fisher offered.

"And me also," Will Lapp said.

"*Ja*, we can get a work party together and take care of the chore in one trip. We might need an additional day to cut the wood into smaller pieces but that shouldn't be too difficult," the bishop suggested.

Martin nodded, eager for their help. A frolic was usually work-based, with men and women helping to accomplish a specific task. It was a time for catching up on one another's business while they worked to bless someone else's life. And it always included a nice meal at the end. He had wondered how he would have time to bring in enough fuel for Julia's needs before the first snowfall.

Within a few minutes, the frolic was organized and he couldn't help feeling overwhelmed by the willingness of his *Gmay* to pitch in. It was one of the reasons he loved his faith so much. Service was an integral part of the Amish religion and he was overjoyed to be a part of it.

"Rachel! Look out!"

Martin whipped around and saw little Rachel reaching for the teapot filled with scalding hot water. As if in slow motion, he saw the child standing on tiptoe to grasp the handle of the teapot with her tiny hands. Sitting in front of her was a cup and saucer. No doubt she intended to pour a cup of tea for *Dawdi* Zeke. But the pot tilted, the lid slid off and the steam rose from the opening as hot water sloshed over the rim.

Seeing the danger, Martin tried to react, but he wasn't quick enough. Instead, Julia knocked the pot askew. It tipped over but, instead of dousing Rachel's head with boiling water, it washed over Julia's left hand and wrist.

"Ouch!" Julia cried. She shook the hot water off, then held her hand close to her chest to ease the pain.

Before Martin could take another breath, he saw her skin turn a bright, angry red. Tears filled her eyes and he shot out of his seat.

"*Mamm!* We need cold water now," he yelled.

Out of the corner of his eye, he saw his mother turn, see the dilemma and send a boy sprinting to the spring house. Linda grabbed a pitcher of chilled water from off one of the tables and hurried over to Julia.

"Put your hand in here. There, my *liebchen*," she cooed as she thrust Julia's entire hand and wrist into the cooling liquid.

"Eli! We need Eli now!" Martin searched the congregation for the man.

Eli Stoltzfus stood up from his place at the opposite end of the yard and came running. "What is it?"

"She is badly burned," Martin said.

While Martin got Julia a chair to sit on, Eli inspected her injuries. Tears freely ran down her face and she bit her bottom lip. Martin thought she was doing an admirable job of trying not to cry. It took everything within him not to cry, too. How he wished he could take her pain upon himself. He hated to see her injured.

"You have a bad scald," Eli told her.

"Are you a doctor?" Julia asked, her voice vibrating. She looked pale and frightened.

"*Ne*, but I am a certified paramedic."

The boy returned with a bucket of water from the spring house. Eli submerged her hand in the fresh, chilled liquid.

"I… I didn't know the Amish could be paramedics." Surprise flashed in Julia's eyes. She looked so incredulous that several people around her chuckled.

"You'd be surprised what we can be," Eli spoke without looking up.

The paramedic studied her skin. Martin was stunned to see huge blisters forming right before his eyes. They covered the top of her hand and fingers and extended up her wrist.

The commotion had brought the attention of almost the entire congregation. Hank crowded close to see what was amiss.

"Julia! Are you all right?" the boy asked, his eyes wide with anxiety as he pushed his spectacles up the bridge of his nose. Always kind and loving, he rubbed her shoulder in a circular motion.

At that moment, Julia appeared to be gritting her teeth. She nodded and showed a weak smile to the boy. "Don't worry, Hank. I'm all right."

But she wasn't. Martin could tell by looking at her wan face and the angry red burns. The fact that she would offer comfort to Hank when she was in distress caused Martin's respect for her to grow. She wasn't a weak or silly woman. She was strong and compassionate and filled with faith.

If only she were Amish.

"*Ach*, you poor dear," Naomi said.

"She saved my Rachel. Did you see? If she hadn't knocked the pot aside, it would have spilled boiling water all over my little girl." Lori Geingerich spoke with disbelief as she hugged Rachel to her chest.

"*Mamm*, is Julia gonna be okay?" Rachel asked, her voice quivering with tears.

Linda answered instead. "Of course she is. We're going to take *gut* care of her."

She also rested a comforting hand on Julia's back. Seeing his mother's compassion for this *Englisch* woman caused a hard lump to form in Martin's throat. How he loved his *familye*. How he loved his faith. It didn't matter right now that Julia was an outsider. In this moment, they would care for her like they would one of their own.

"We could put butter on the burns," Sarah kindly suggested.

"*Ne*, Eli says that's the worst thing we can do for a burn since it holds the heat into the wound. Cooling compresses are best," Lizzie said.

"*Ach*, I'm glad to know that. I'll remember next time one of my *kinder* gets burned," Sarah said.

"We should take you to the hospital as soon as possible." Eli spoke to Julia, ignoring the comments around him. "I'm afraid you'll experience a bit of pain for a while. Let's keep your hand submerged in the water while we drive you into town."

He glanced at Martin.

"*Ja*, I'll get the buggy." With a sharp nod, Martin sprinted toward the pasture where the road horses were grazing.

"Mar-tin! I wanna come with you. Julia's my girl," Hank called to him.

Martin slowed and glanced over his shoulder, ready to bark an irritated command for his brother to stay behind. He didn't have time to deal with Hank right now and didn't want to argue with the boy.

Thankfully, David clasped Hank's arm and pulled him back. "You'll stay right here with your *mudder* and me, *sohn*. Too many people will slow things down and Eli needs to get Julia to the hospital quickly."

"Ah!" Hank grouched.

Martin hurried on, jumping over the fence surrounding *Mamm*'s vegetable garden. As he passed, his booted heels sank deep into the graveled driveway. He'd get the horse harnessed and ready to go right now.

As he lunged through the gate, the road horses scattered and he forced himself to slow down so he wouldn't spook them. One thought pounded his brain. He had to help Julia. She was hurting badly. He had to get her some relief soon. While he'd watched Eli tending her wounds, he'd felt so helpless. So powerless to do anything for her.

And what would he tell her mother? He was responsible for Julia. It had been his job to keep her safe. He hated the thought of telling Sharon that he had failed.

Now, he had a mission. Something concrete that he could do for her. His horse was well rested and could race him and Eli into town with Julia. They could be at the hospital within twenty-five minutes.

Martin's hands trembled as he harnessed the horse to the buggy. He forced himself to calm down. But he dreaded driving Julia home to her mother afterward. Dreaded the accusing look that would undoubtedly fill

Sharon's eyes. She didn't want Julia to come to church with him and look what had happened.

Julia had to be all right. She just had to be. Because nothing else mattered now except her.

Chapter Seven

"Oww!" Julia dropped the bucket of coconut oil on the floor with a thump and cradled her injured hand close against her abdomen. It was midmorning the day after her accident and she was at home, struggling to accomplish her work.

"I thought you were upstairs resting." Sharon came up behind her, picked up the heavy bucket and set it on one of the new industrial-strength shelves Martin had built for her last week.

A strong gust of wind buffeted the front porch but the overhanging canopy didn't budge an inch. Martin's work was quality and she was grateful for his skills. But the leaden clouds filling the sky were a bad premonition and she feared the weather might change before they were able to go into the mountains for firewood. She hated the thought of parting with more precious funds to buy the wood from a vendor in town but they might not have a choice.

"There's too much work to take it easy. I need to accomplish something productive today." Using her right hand, Julia picked up a birchwood mold and stacked it on a shelf with a variety of other wood and silicone molds.

As Eli Stoltzfus had predicted, the doctor had wrapped the burns on her left hand and wrist in loose gauze until she looked like she wore a white boxer's glove. The thick packing helped cushion the wound while it healed but it was cumbersome and difficult to manage. Because her skin had blistered, the wound could become infected. Thankfully, the scald had been superficial and would heal in time for her to make more soap before her deadline…but not soon enough for her.

At least she still had the use of her right hand. But she was stunned to discover just how much she needed two good hands to do her chores. Simple tasks like washing her face or brushing her hair had become difficult. Also, the copious padding of the compress made it rather difficult to do anything with precision. If nothing else, she was fast acquiring compassion for people who had to deal with such disabilities on a permanent basis.

"The doctor said you should take it easy for a few days." Sharon rested a fist on her hip as she stood next to the doorway.

Martin was outside in the parking lot, cutting pieces of gray Formica to finish the countertops. Soon, he would be ready to install the glass partition to separate the workroom from the retail part of the store.

Julia stepped over to the new glass display case she'd purchased secondhand from the grocery store in town. Using her good hand, she dipped a rag into a bucket of hot soapy water, wrung it out as best she could, then scrubbed one of the shelf inserts.

"I'm not an invalid, Mom," she said. "As long as I don't use my left hand, I should be fine. We have a store to get operational. If I sit upstairs all day, we won't be ready for our grand opening the first of December and I'll go stir-crazy."

"Excuse us, please."

Julia turned. Martin and Hank stood in the open doorway holding a long sheet of Formica. Both he and Sharon stepped back as the men carried the heavy piece over to the framework for the new counter and laid it into place.

"That looks *wundervoll*. It should be easy to clean and won't show the grime and dirt at all." Julia eyed the slate-gray Formica with approval.

Sharon frowned. "You're speaking their language now?"

Julia blinked, then nodded. "It's been fun to learn some of their words and phrases." She'd been studying the Scriptures at night and praying, too. For some reason, she had an insatiable desire to learn more about God.

Sharon cast an accusing glance at Martin, biting her bottom lip as if to keep from telling him off. Her animosity toward the Amish man was palpable.

"Aren't you supposed to be upstairs resting?" Martin asked Julia. He wore leather gloves and laid a hand on top of the new countertop.

Lifting her eyebrows in an *I told you so* expression, Sharon peered at her daughter. "You see? Even Martin agrees with me. You should be upstairs."

"I can clean the cabinet for you," Hank offered. He stepped close and took the wash rag from her hand.

"*Danke*, Hank," she said, though she doubted he would be as thorough as her. To make him happy, she would let him clean most of the grime off the shelves, then return later to make sure the job was pristine.

"Go rest and *beheef dich*." Martin nudged her shoulder, urging her away from the cabinet.

"What does that mean?" Julia asked, determined to stay right where she was.

"It means *behave yourself*. Something which you seem to have a lot of trouble doing," Martin said.

Julia laughed, thinking his choice of words quite funny. She was bored upstairs and her mind was racing with all the work needing to be done. With her damaged hand, she wouldn't be able to help Martin go into the mountains to collect firewood. Snow would soon fly and she wasn't sure what they would do without fuel to heat the building. The electrical heating system was certainly of no use to them now. Not without power. If the store got too cold, their customers wouldn't want to visit. But she didn't want to purchase the wood either. So, what could she do?

"That's right. For once, I agree with Martin," Sharon said.

Martin glowered and Julia thought he was angry with her until she saw a twinkle in his eyes and his lips twitched with a suppressed smile. Again, she laughed and repeated the Deitsch phrase, noticing her mother's frown. Obviously, Mom didn't like her learning the Amish language.

"I'm not going upstairs, so stop badgering me. I'm not in pain and there is too much to be done..." She began the argument but never got the chance to finish. "Hey! What is that?" She pointed out the wide sparkling windows that fronted the store.

Pulling into the parking lot and lining up along Main

Street were six empty hay wagons pulled by the largest draft horses she'd ever seen. Approximately thirty Amish men accompanied the wagons.

"*Ach*, there's *Daed*!" Hank ran outside to greet his father.

Sure enough, David Hostetler sat in the driver's seat of one big wagon.

"It's a frolic," Martin said.

"A frolic?" Confused by this turn of events, Julia and her mother followed Hank and stood on the front porch. The chill wind buffeted them and Julia folded her arms against the bitter cold.

"*Ja*, a work frolic." Without explaining, Martin went to speak with his father and Bishop Yoder. A number of Amish women hopped down off the wagon seats and headed toward the store.

"Harvest season is over with, so what are they doing here with their wagons?" Rubbing her arms briskly with her hands, Sharon whispered the question to her daughter.

Julia shrugged. "I… I think they're here to get firewood for us."

She was fascinated by the sight. How she longed to ride in one of the wagons pulled by two large Percherons or Belgians. Since she knew little about horses, she wasn't sure what breed they were. She could just imagine Martin driving the big animals as he plowed and planted a hayfield. It sounded fun and exciting to her.

"*Hallo*, Julia." Linda Hostetler waved and smiled pleasantly as she stepped up onto the porch.

Sarah, Naomi, Lizzie and Lori waited nearby, each wearing their black mantle coats and white prayer *kapps* and smiling shyly. Even Marva Geingerich had accompanied the women into town. She stood beside the bishop's wife, her black traveling bonnet pulled low across her face as she gazed at Julia with a severe scowl. Julia chose to ignore the elderly woman. After all, she had done nothing wrong and refused to feel shame simply because Marva disapproved of her.

Holding her injured hand close against her abdomen, Julia stepped down off the porch to greet the women. "*Hallo!* What are you all doing here?"

"We are having a frolic. We have come to help with your work," Linda explained with a wide smile.

Abby Fisher stepped up onto the porch. She smiled sweetly as she handed an apple pie to Sharon before speaking in perfect English. "Hello. This is for you."

"Um, thank you." Sharon nodded, looking stunned and skeptical.

Hank ran over to Julia and handed her a yellow tulip bud that had been in a warm spot of the yard and had just started to bloom. "This is for you, because you're my girl."

The tip of his tongue protruded slightly from between his thick lips as he looked at her with those big, innocent eyes and a silly grin.

She gazed at the flower. "*Danke*, Hank. I'll put it in some water."

She reached out and patted his cheek, smiling as sweetly as she could. Then, she looked at the wagons again and blinked. She'd heard the word *frolic* yesterday at church but didn't understand its meaning. "What's going on? What is a frolic?"

By that time, Martin and Bishop Yoder had joined her.

"It's quite simple," the bishop explained. "You were

injured yesterday while protecting little Rachel from the scalding water. Now, you cannot do your own work. Martin has told us that you have an important deadline coming up, so we have come to help you."

"I… I don't know what to say," Julia said.

"There is nothing to say. While the men go into the mountains to retrieve firewood for you, the *weibsleit* will help get your store ready for your grand opening."

"The *weibsleit*?" she asked.

"The womenfolk," Bishop Yoder explained.

She repeated the word twice, a large lump forming in her throat. A sudden rush of tears filled her eyes and she felt dazed by emotion. These were such good people. She'd never known such generosity. All her life, she'd longed for a large family to love. These people weren't her family but they sure had run to her aid.

"I'm overwhelmed by your kindness but I don't want to take you away from your own work," she said.

Martin stepped closer, his expression gentle, his presence comforting.

"Julia, this is what we do," he said. "We help one another. You saved Rachel and now you are in need. It is our way to assist in any way we can. We want to refresh and comfort you in the midst of your stress."

His explanation touched her heart like nothing else could. She looked at each of the Amish men. Gruff men who wouldn't meet her gaze. Some of them sat in the driver's seats of their wagons, holding the lead lines as they held their horses steady. Others stood in the back of the wagons adjusting a variety of saws, axes, mallets, wedges and other tools they used to cut firewood. They laughed and talked together like this was an ordinary day.

She turned and glanced at the women, who stood just in front of the porch, seeming to wait for an invitation to go inside. At the age of twenty-two, Lori was the youngest and shivered in her woolen mantle. With her petite, pretty features, she looked much too young to be Rachel's mother.

In each man and woman's face, Julia saw no guile or resentment. Nothing but expectation and friendship gleamed in their eyes.

Sharon and Marva were the glaring exceptions. Still holding the pie, Julia's mother gaped at the gathering as if they'd all lost their minds. Her eyes were wide with repugnance, her lips pursed tight. In fact, she looked almost as sour as Marva. Sharon didn't want the Amish here but Julia wasn't in much condition to lift, carry and wash right now. With so many people, the work would go fast. She needed their assistance and it wouldn't be kind or prudent to refuse their offer to help.

"Many hands make light work," Linda pointed out in a kind voice, as if reading her mind.

"*Ja*, and we have Ben to help us today," Bishop Yoder said.

"Ben?" Julia queried.

"Ben Yoder, my nephew. He's visiting us from Bloomfield, Iowa." The bishop turned and pointed at a giant man standing in front of the last wagon. He stood at least four inches taller than Martin, had massive shoulders that seemed wider than a broom handle and looked to be bull strong. For all his enormous size, the young man wore a gentle, unassuming expression and Julia couldn't help liking him on the spot.

"Yes, I see you have a secret weapon," Julia said with a laugh.

Bishop Yoder chuckled. "*Ja*, we have a secret weapon named Ben."

Julia exhaled, deciding to swallow her pride and accept their generous offer.

"*Danke!* This is so kind of you all. My *mudder* and I appreciate your help so much," she said.

"*Wunderbaar!*" the bishop exclaimed. "Martin will remain here to build the shelves you need. The rest of us *mannsleit* will be back this evening with enough wood to last you through the winter."

Mannsleit. Julia assumed that meant *menfolk*.

"One of our wagons will go around back and load up all the garbage you have cleared out of your store and haul it to the dump. The rest of us will go into the mountains for the wood," the bishop said.

Ah, Martin must have explained to the bishop that she had piles of debris in her backyard.

"Next Monday, we'll return to cut up the wood we bring down from the mountain. That evening, you both must join us at my home to enjoy a frolic supper." The bishop glanced between Julia and Sharon, his eyes filled with invitation.

"Um, *danke*. That sounds nice," Julia said, not quite sure she or Mom were up to a party right now.

With a polite nod, the bishop walked over to the lead wagon and climbed into the seat. His return signaled the other men that it was time to leave. They scurried into position. With a loud whistle and a slap of the leather lead lines, Bishop Yoder sent his horses into a steady walk down the middle of Main Street.

Watching them go, Julia noticed several people came out of the general store, post office and bank to watch them pass by. It wasn't every day the townsfolk saw six big wagons pulled by giant horses and filled with Amish men wearing black felt hats drive down the middle of their town. It was an amazing site to behold.

The last wagon in the train peeled off and headed down the alley to Julia's backyard. Two teenage boys drove that wagon and she made a mental note to take them hot chocolate as they cleaned up the debris they would haul off to the garbage dump.

Shivering in the wind, Julia held onto her tulip as she faced the women, still feeling overwhelmed by this generosity.

"You look familiar to me. Do I know you from some-where?" Marva Geingerich spoke in her loud, gruff voice as she peered shrewdly at Sharon. Marva took a step toward Julia's mom, who still stood on the front porch.

"No, I'm sure you don't. I'm not Amish." Sharon shook her head emphatically. Her face had blanched white and she wouldn't meet Marva's gaze. Without an-other word, she turned and carried the pie into the store.

"*Ach*, if you'll show us what needs to be done, we'll get to work." Linda sounded all businesslike as she undid her mantle coat and stepped up on the porch.

"Of course." Julia led the women inside, wondering what had gotten into her mother. She was so rude to Martin and his people. She was nowhere in sight and Julia figured she had either returned to their apartment upstairs or gone to work in the back office.

"Hank, will you help me adjust this panel so I can seal it down?" Martin asked.

Out of the corner of her eye, Julia saw him direct-ing Hank to position the length of Formica so it could be secured to the wooden frame of the new counter.

Within minutes, Julia had taken each Amish woman's mantle and stowed them in the office where they wouldn't get sawdust on them. Mom wasn't there so Julia figured she must be upstairs.

Returning to the workroom, Julia directed two women to clean the glass cabinet. She asked another woman to clean an old but charming hutch she had acquired from the secondhand store for showcasing her soaps and lotions.

Linda took up the broom and dustbin and continually swept up sawdust and other debris created by Martin and Hank's work. She fetched and carried, taking some of the burden off Martin.

Marva and Lori sat at a corner table, packaging the lotions and soaps Julia had made for display in the store. Lori used a battery-operated heat gun to shrink a piece of plastic wrap around each bar of soap. Marva peeled off the sticky labels Julia had ordered from an online vendor she'd accessed from a computer at the library and slapped one on each bar of soap. The stickers included the store's rose logo, name and address, and a list of ingredients for each item.

Julia had already mailed off samples of her products to various retail stores in Denver and other major cities throughout the western United States. Hopefully the vendors would place some wholesale orders for her soaps. Always helpful, Carl Nelson had given her a referral to a reputable sales representative out of Denver. Julia had written to them, hoping they could help market her goods.

With everyone occupied with a task, Julia soon found that she had little to do. Martin stepped outside to cut another piece of wood. Hank had gotten distracted and was fiddling with a pair of scissors at the packing table.

"Give those to me, boy. You're going to cut your hand off," Marva snapped at him as she jerked the scissors away.

Ignoring the women, Julia stepped outside to speak with Martin for a moment.

"Did you coordinate all of this?" she asked him.

He glanced up at her before laying a narrow piece of oak across the two sawhorses he'd set up in the parking lot. Using a measuring tape, he calculated the length and drew a tiny line with a pencil he kept tucked behind his ear. Picking up his handsaw, he smiled.

"*Ja*, but it was Lori's idea for the women to help. I told her about your work and she knew you needed to be up and running so you can make soap just after Thanksgiving. Since you'd lost the use of your left hand, she asked Bishop Yoder if she might come and help." He shrugged his broad shoulders. "I also mentioned you needed firewood. One thing led to another. The bishop said we must have a work frolic. So, here we are."

He made a quick cut with the handsaw, then peered at her. "Honestly, I think Bishop Yoder is highly motivated to help you all he can."

"Oh? And why is that?"

"You should know that he hopes you'll become Amish. Since you showed an interest in our faith, they all think that is your intention."

She laughed at that. "I do like your people very much, Martin. But I doubt I'll ever join your faith. My mom doesn't approve and I don't want to do anything to upset her."

He hesitated and licked his bottom lip. The teasing

sparkle left his eyes and he ducked his head over his work. "That is most unfortunate."

Oh, dear. She didn't want to upset him either.

"You should still join us at the Bishop's *heemet* for the frolic supper next Monday," he said. "It'll be a pot-luck with everyone bringing lots of food, and if the weather holds, we will play baseball."

"Baseball? But I can't hold a bat or glove." She held up her bandaged hand. She hadn't played the game since she'd been a child in school. The thought of playing with friends was tantalizing.

"*Ach*, that is no deterrent. I will bat for you and you can run the bases. Since I'll already be working here, I can drive you and your *mudder* to the bishop's farm that afternoon, then bring you home again," he said.

"I'm afraid *Mamm* won't want to go," she said.

"That's all right. She is invited anyway."

She laughed, thinking it might be loads of fun. Martin was just a friend so what could it hurt? "I'm amazed by the kindness of your people. No one has ever been so good, er, *gut* to me and my *mudder*. *Danke*, Martin. Though I don't want to become Amish, I'll be sure to invite all of you to our grand opening on the first of December."

He looked up and flashed that devastating smile of his, but a sad quality had replaced the gaiety she'd seen there moments before. Was he truly disappointed that she didn't want to become Amish? And why should it matter so much to him?

"I'm sure they will like that," he said.

He returned to work and she went inside, her heart and mind full of emotions she couldn't name. She liked these Amish people. She really did. Especially Martin.

Most of them were kind, welcoming and helpful. In fact, Julia was inclined to ask if she could attend church again. She admitted to herself that she wanted to learn more. The Scriptures she'd been reading only gave her more inquiries. And because of her injury, she never got the opportunity to ask Martin all the questions she had acquired at church yesterday.

Just one problem: Sharon. Her mom didn't like the Amish. She didn't want Julia to go to church or learn their language. Maybe Mom feared Julia might fall in love and want to marry Martin. But that didn't make sense. Mom had always told her she could love and wed anyone she chose. So, what was the issue? Why was Mom so against anything to do with the Amish?

Glancing out the window, Julia paused for a few moments to admire the way Martin's blue chambray shirt tightened across the heavy muscles of his back. He was such a tall, strong man. So generous and capable. A man much like Julia's father. Someone to be admired. And for the first time since she'd met him, she wished Martin wasn't Amish.

But it wouldn't matter. Dallin had taught her never to trust another man with her heart. No matter what, she could never be anything more than friends with Martin. And that was that.

"I don't know why you're being so rude to the Amish. It isn't like you to act that way."

Martin stepped to the end of the hallway and paused when he heard the words coming from the back office in a low murmur. Though he couldn't see her, he knew Julia's voice and she sounded upset.

"I don't want you to marry that man, that's why." Sharon's unmistakable voice lifted in a harsh whisper.

Yes, it was Julia and her mother speaking and they were discussing him. Martin took another step and they came into view. Their backs were turned so they didn't notice him.

"I'm not going to marry anyone, Mom. Not after what Dallin did to me. Martin and I are just friends. You have no call to treat him and his people with anything but respect," Julia said.

"Yes, you're friends. Until you fall in love with him."

"Mom, that's not going to happen."

"Maybe not yet but what if your friendship blossoms into something more? That's how it happens when you fall in love. And then, what will you do? If you don't join his faith, he'll be shunned if he marries you. Is that what you want for him? He'd lose everything. His family wouldn't speak to him. He'd be completely ostracized. And you! If you join the Amish, they'll dominate and run your life. They might not even let you visit me because I'm *Englisch*."

"Oh, Mom!" Julia cried in a harsh breath. "Don't be so dramatic. They know you're my mother and that you're ill with lupus. Of course they'd let me visit and take care of you. Besides, I'm not joining the Amish, and Martin isn't leaving his faith. We aren't going to fall in love and we certainly aren't going to get married. So, there's nothing to fret about."

Sharon paused several moments, looking at her daughter. "I still don't want them here. We don't need their help."

"They're a blessing. I don't understand why you're so

against them." Julia shook her head, seeming stunned by how unreasonable her mother was being.

Sharon simply pursed her lips tighter.

The floorboards creaked beneath Martin's booted foot and a gasp followed by dead silence filled the air. He hesitated, ready to go back the way he had come. But too late. The two women turned at the open doorway.

"Martin!" Julia said.

"Ahem! Excuse me, but the *mannsleit* have returned. They have already cut most of the logs and even split some of the wood into smaller pieces of kindling that are perfect for your wood-burning stoves. They'll return on Monday to finish it. They would come back tomorrow but they need a little time to work at their own farms. They're stacking what they've finished neatly in your backyard right now and have piled it far away from your house, so you don't end up with termites." He tried to speak normally but his throat felt like a wad of sandpaper had lodged there. It would be dishonest to pretend he hadn't overheard their conversation. His face flooded with heat and he felt awkward and embarrassed to be caught eavesdropping.

Sharon glared at him with censure. Brushing past him, she went upstairs.

Julia showed a nervous smile. Since she'd been caught talking about him, Martin wasn't surprised.

"I can't believe they got all that work done in one day," Julia said.

He showed an uncertain smile. "They all worked together to get it done."

Julia stepped out into the hallway with him and headed toward the back door. Martin followed, grateful to get away from Sharon.

Standing on the back porch, they observed the Amish men for several minutes. Long logs of aspen and ponderosa pine lay off to the side of the spacious yard, cleaned of all their stubby branches and ready for splitting into smaller chunks. Near the house lay a small pile of split wood, all ready for taking into the house to be consumed by the old black stoves.

As if on cue, the men stopped working, dusted off their shirts and pants and reached for their jackets. Carrying their axes and saws on their shoulders, they headed toward the front of the house, nodding politely as they passed.

Julia waved farewell. "They did so much work. I'm overwhelmed and very relieved to have this done."

"*Ja*, they're going *heemet* now for supper. The aspen burns hotter than the pine and is good for starting fires. The men will return next Monday to finish splitting the wood. Then we'll go to the bishop's house for supper that evening. That's part of a frolic. Lots of fun work and *gut* food."

She lifted her eyebrows in question. "I'm surprised to hear you call hard work fun. Most people don't like work. But the Amish seem to be the exception."

He frowned. "*Ja*, we enjoy what we accomplish with our own two hands. You like hard work, don't you?"

She nodded. "It's how we get what we need to live. And it gives me a sense of accomplishment."

"It's a blessing to serve. By the time the men are finished, you should have enough firewood to last through the winter," Martin said.

She paused, thinking this over. "I just realized something."

"What is that?" he asked.

"The Amish faith isn't an individual, solitary religion. It's a community of members serving one another, looking after each other and seeing to one another's needs. Isn't that right?"

A wide smile split his handsome face. "*Ja*, you do understand after all. We rely on one another for everything. Our *Gmay* is more than just the individual members of our Amish community. It is also the rules we follow, our social structure and how we look after each other."

She nodded, a pensive frown tugging at her forehead. "And you have extended that honor to me simply because I came to your church and protected little Rachel from being burned?"

He shook his head. "*Ne*, you are not a member of our *Gmay*. Not unless you accept our *Ordnung* and are baptized into our faith. Our beliefs permeate every aspect of our life. For my people, *Gott* speaks through our community and we are guided by submitting ourselves to the wisdom of the *Gmay*. But we also believe in serving others in any way we can. And you and your *mudder* were in need."

She nodded. "I see."

"Bishop Yoder is still hoping your *mudder* will join us at the frolic supper next week," Martin said.

She frowned and scuffed the tip of her tennis shoe against the wooden porch. Perhaps he shouldn't have reminded her but the bishop had instructed him to do so. And he wouldn't dream of defying Bishop Yoder.

Sharon was not happy to have her daughter involved with the Amish. And Julia had made it clear she had no intention of joining their faith. But what if Julia changed her mind? What if she just needed a bit more time to get to know the Amish better? Perhaps her heart could be softened and her mind could be changed. It had happened before.

"Even if my *mudder* decides not to go, I definitely want to," she said.

A blaze of joy flashed through his chest. "*Gut.* I'll tell my *vadder* and the bishop that you'll be joining us." He nodded, forcing himself not to laugh out loud with delight. "I had best get *heemet* now. But I'll be back in the morning as usual."

She nodded with understanding. "*Ja*, I'll see you tomorrow."

As he turned away and headed around to the front of the house to find Hank, he felt a bit of doubt. She had said yes and wanted to go to the frolic supper, but her words to her mother still rang in his ears. She had no intention of becoming Amish.

Once he finished his job here, he wouldn't see her anymore. No more teaching her Deitsch. No more working, planning and laughing together. And somehow that made him feel sad and empty inside.

Chapter Eight

On Monday the following week, Julia awoke to the thunk of axes and the burr of saws. Rising from her bed, she slid the curtains open just a bit and gazed out. Shimmering sunlight gleamed against the frost covering the barren trees. A nest of dried orange and yellow leaves carpeted the ground. She really must find time to rake them up before it snowed.

At least two dozen men swarmed her backyard, cutting the long logs into smaller stumps. It had been a week since they had brought the firewood down from the mountains. Tonight, when their chore was done, they would enjoy the frolic supper at Bishop Yoder's farm. And Julia couldn't wait.

She paused beside the dresser in her room, running her fingertips over the pages of her Bible. She'd been reading the Scriptures every spare moment she could find. The passages filled her heart with warmth and gave her a sense of something greater than herself. Accompanied by prayer, her faith and relationship with God was growing more every day.

Hurrying to dress, she dragged a comb through her

long hair, tied it into a jaunty ponytail and raced downstairs. When she stepped to the back door, she found Mom standing there. Dressed in her long pajamas and bathrobe, she was watching the men through the screen door.

"You're up early," Julia said with a smile.

"Not as early as them. Their women woke me up and I let them into the store." Mom nodded at the Amish.

Julia gasped. "The women returned, too?"

"Yes. Three of them. They brought us a fresh loaf of bread and an apple cobbler."

"That was nice of them. Who all is here?"

Sharon shrugged. "I don't know their names."

"Mom! Of course you do. They were each introduced to you last week. You should try to be nicer to them." Julia hated to admonish her own mother but still couldn't fathom her discourtesy.

"How are you feeling?" Julia asked, trying to change the topic. She wrapped an arm around Mom's waist and leaned against her in an affectionate hug. She'd had a bad attack over the past few days and Julia was worried about her.

"I'm fine." Mom squeezed her back.

"Did you remember to take your medication this morning?" With the cooler weather, Mom's joint and muscle pain had increased. Julia knew she hadn't been sleeping well either. Maybe it was time to make another appointment with the doctor in town. He was an older gentleman who had retired here to Riverton but still opened up his office two days per week. A blessing for them.

"Of course."

"Good. Getting the soap store operational isn't as important as you are," Julia said.

Another tight hug and Mom released her. "The Amish certainly are persistent. I didn't think they'd return."

Her voice held an edge of grudging respect and a bit of resentment, too.

"The Amish can be generous as long as you don't cross them. But I can't help wondering at their motives," Mom said.

Julia shrugged one shoulder. "As far as I know, they want nothing from us."

"Hmm," came Mom's skeptical reply.

Julia went very still. She couldn't help thinking the Amish were like the large family she'd always wished for. They were there when she needed them, ready to help in any way possible. And tonight, she would go to the frolic supper and play baseball and have fun with them.

"They haven't asked us for anything, Mom. We don't have much to offer. What could they possibly want?" she asked.

"You," Mom said.

The word was like a slap to her face. It caused Julia to take a quick inhale. She forced herself not to shudder. Her mother's comment seemed a bit sinister. Surely Martin's people weren't that manipulative and conniving.

"I'm not going to become Amish, so you can relax on that point," Julia insisted.

Mom jutted her chin toward the door. "Do they know that? Does Martin know?"

"Yes, I told him. And he tells his parents almost everything, so they all know."

Mom snorted. "The Amish don't take no for an answer."

"Martin is my employee. He's here to do a job. That's all. It won't hurt us to be nice to him."

"I hope you're right," Mom said.

Julia gazed out into the yard. Several men took turns using a two-handled saw to cut the logs into stumps with long, even strokes. Wielding axes, more men rolled the stumps over to a large cutting block where a chisel was used to split the stumps into hand-size chunks of kindling. Each man seemed to know when it was his turn to chop and when to rest. Their happy banter and laughter carried through the air.

"Julia, can I get your opinion on something?"

She turned and found Martin standing at the end of the hallway. His tall silhouette almost blocked the rays of sunshine that glistened at his back.

Without a word, Sharon slipped away and Julia went to greet him. As they walked into the retail part of the store, Julia glanced over and saw Linda and Lori stocking the shelves. Again, she was embarrassed to find them here working while she'd been upstairs sleeping.

Both women knelt on the floor as they slid narrow boxes of homemade lip balms and lotions into the display case. Thankfully, the products had been made long before Julia's hand had been burned.

The low murmur of their voices seemed so comforting to her. Even though it had been such a short time, she felt as though she knew these women well and they were good friends. Surely her mother's fears were unwarranted.

"Guder mariye," she called in a pleasant tone.

"Hallo, Julia." Linda waved.

Lori nodded and showed a shy smile.

"Do you like how we are displaying your notions?" Linda asked.

Julia glanced at the shelves, noticing how the women had lined up each bottle so the labels were front and center. The variety of soaps caused a spicy-sweet scent to fill the air. The light pink and lavender creams looked so appealing that she felt certain the local ranchers' wives wouldn't be able to resist them. At least, that was what she hoped.

"It's perfect. And don't forget to bring in some of your rag rugs. I've got a cute display rack that will be great for showing off your work," Julia said.

"Ja, a number of us women are working on them. We're glad to have the extra income. I'll bring them in time for your grand opening." Linda beamed with pleasure.

Good. Now if only Julia could get the large soap orders made before her deadline. Other than her mother's health, that was her greatest concern right now.

"Take a look at this." Martin gestured toward her workroom. She was surprised to see David Hostetler standing nearby, his work-roughened hands folded beneath his black suspenders. He smiled but didn't speak.

Julia gasped at what she saw. Rising from the Formica countertop, a frameless tempered glass partition reached clear up to the ceiling and separated the retail side of the store from the workroom where she would make her soap. With the glass panel to separate the two rooms, no noxious fumes of lye would bother her customers. Martin's craftsmanship looked perfect and very professional.

"The glass was so large and unwieldy that *Daed* helped me hold it steady while I installed it this morning. I didn't want to take the chance that I might crack the glass while working alone," Martin said.

"I helped, too," Hank chimed in from across the room. As usual, he hurried over to Julia, standing a bit too close as he grinned up at her.

She smiled back.

Martin reached out and ruffled the boy's hair in a loving gesture. "*Ja*, Hank helped a lot. So, what do you think of it, Jules?"

Jules! No one had ever called her that before. With Martin's foreign accent, the name sounded rather exotic. His deep, low voice caused a little shiver of delight to run up her spine. She paused, repeating the name silently in her mind.

"I'm sorry, Julia. I shouldn't have called you that. It just slipped out. I don't know where I even got it from," he said.

She laughed. "It's okay. I kind of like it." Actually, she was glad he felt relaxed enough around her to give her a nickname.

He flashed a smile. "You do?"

She nodded, a hard lump rising in her throat. With the bright sun blazing through the wide windows, he looked so handsome standing there. She didn't have the heart to object. All her life, she'd dreamed of having friends. She'd dreamed of having her own business, too. Seeing all of Martin's hard work and the partition now in place made that dream a reality.

"Ahem! We'll be having the frolic supper this evening. Will your *mudder* be joining us?" David cleared his throat, breaking into her fanciful thoughts.

"*Ne*, she doesn't feel up to going," she said.

Her face flushed with heat and she stepped toward the glass, trying to hide her embarrassment. She couldn't believe she'd actually been flirting with Martin in front of his father, of all people!

"Do you really like it?" Martin asked again from behind.

She nodded quickly, hardly able to speak. "It's perfect. It's just what I always dreamed of."

"I helped clean the glass." Hank followed her, lifting a roll of paper towels and a bottle of glass cleaner that had been sitting on the table.

"I see you did a good job, too. *Danke* for all your work," Julia said.

Hank smiled so brightly that she thought a zillion sunbeams must have exploded inside his head.

Julia turned toward David. "And *danke* to you, as well."

"It's my pleasure." The older man smiled politely and ducked his head.

"I'll get the stove and fridge installed later this afternoon. *Daed* will help the men outside, then go *heemet* to do his work before the frolic supper tonight," Martin said.

She glanced at David, noticing his calm, friendly gaze. If only she knew what he was thinking. He was Martin's father and for some crazy reason, she desperately wanted his approval.

"I can't tell you how grateful I am for all your help. I feel so bad that you've left your own chores at home in order to come to my aid," she told him.

"It's no problem. You saved our little Rachel, so it's the least we can do to help you." David spoke in an even tone, yet he seemed a bit guarded. After all, she was *Englisch* whether she was interested in his faith or not.

"*Kumme helfe* cut the firewood, Hank." Picking up a bucket of rags, David glanced at his younger son.

"But I want to stay here with Julia," Hank whined.

"*Ne*, you will *komm* with me now." As if expecting the boy to obey, the man walked outside.

With a backward glance at her, Hank followed begrudgingly. Through the wide windows fronting the store, Julia watched the two of them walk around the house to the backyard. She figured they would help the other men stack wood. From the looks of things, they'd be finished soon.

"I've almost completed my work here," Martin spoke softly.

Julia jerked, surprised to find him standing right next to her. A feeling of sadness pulsed over her. Once he was finished, she wouldn't see him anymore.

"May I attend your church services again?" The moment she asked, she wondered if she would regret it. She didn't want to give him the impression she was going to join his faith, nor did she want any more contention with her mother. But she couldn't seem to help herself. She really wanted to go.

"*Abselutt*," he said with a smile.

She tilted her head in question and he explained.

"Absolutely. I will pick you up and drive you this coming Sunday. This time, it will be held at the Fishers' farm."

"I'll bring a casserole to help with the lunch," she said.

"I'm sure they will appreciate that."

She nodded, then looked at the partition again, trying to ignore the feeling of butterflies swarming her stomach. "I hope the appliances work okay."

She had taken Martin's advice and her appliances would not be powered by electricity.

"They will work fine. You're using gas appliances upstairs in your apartment now. Propane and compressed air can drive your fridge and stove top just as well as electricity," he said.

Out of necessity, she would have to trust Martin's judgment. After what Dallin had put her through, it was a big leap of faith for her. But Martin hadn't let her down yet. And even if the electricity went out again, she'd still be able to power her appliances. That was a big plus.

She stepped through the open doorway to her workroom, running her fingertips over the smooth Formica counters. The oak cabinets and drawers were lovely. There wasn't a bit of dust or grime anywhere to be seen. The white paint she'd applied to the walls gave the room a clinical, sterile appearance, which was perfect in case she had an unannounced FDA inspection to ensure her business was compliant with the law.

She admired the gleaming stainless steel sink and new water faucet Martin had installed. It was a tall, swan's neck spout that loomed high over the sink with plenty of room for her large stockpots to rest inside the basin below. The arch of the faucet would make cleanup much easier.

She turned and smiled at Martin. He stood in the threshold, his strong arms braced over his head against the doorjamb, his right ankle crossed over the left. It was a completely male stance that reminded her what a strong, capable man he was.

And attractive, too.

Shaking her head, she tried to focus on her work. A slight frown tugged at his forehead. He looked worried. No doubt he was concerned she might not like his work.

"It's beautiful. Exactly what I envisioned," she said.

His facial features softened. "I should have everything completed by Thanksgiving. That will give you plenty of time to meet your soap making deadline."

A laugh of relief broke from her throat and she held up her left hand. "*Ja*, I'm cutting it kind of close. I'll get the bandages removed the day after Thanksgiving and plan to make soap right afterward."

Lowering his arms, he stepped nearer and gently touched the thick gauze on her hand. Though she could barely feel his touch, she felt mesmerized by his closeness as she looked up at him.

"Even though the bandages will be removed soon, your hand may be weak from lack of use," he said. "I will be here that afternoon to help you make soap. I can lift the pans off the stove and pour the batter into the molds. I don't want you or your *mudder* to have to lift those heavy pans."

She nodded, realizing he was right. And frankly, she'd gotten used to him being around. She would miss him when he was gone. "*Danke*. I would appreciate it. You've been so great, Martin. I couldn't have done all of this without you and Hank and your people."

"As my *vadder* said, it's our pleasure." With a dip of his head, he reached for his toolbox and busied himself with tidying things up.

Feeling odd and out of place in her own store, she

left him to his work. Stepping back into the sales room, she caught the low murmur of the women's voices. One of them laughed and she drew near. Their camaraderie and friendship had become dear to her and she couldn't wait to attend the frolic supper with Martin later that afternoon.

"It'll be nice to have a new member join our *Gmay*," Abby said.

With her back turned toward Julia, Abby sat with Lori and Linda at the worktable. They were cutting lengths of thin grosgrain ribbon to tie around the lip balms and didn't notice she was there.

"*Ja*, once Julia converts, she will make a good *fraa* for Martin. You must be excited to have a new *schwardochder*." Lori smiled at Linda.

Fraa? Schwardochder? Julia's ears perked up at the two unknown words. Hmm, she'd have to ask Martin what they meant, but she feared she already knew.

Like a bolt of lightning, Mom's words rushed through her head. Was it possible Martin's people were only being kind because they hoped to nab her as a new convert to their faith? And what if they found out she had no intention of joining them?

A sick feeling settled in her stomach. Julia hated to disappoint Martin and his family. And once again, those old feelings of hurt and betrayal came crashing in on her. Dallin and Debbie had lied and used her. They'd taught her to distrust people.

She wasn't going to convert to the Amish faith simply because they had chopped her wood and helped in her store. She had to know deep within her heart that the Amish faith was true. She would only convert if she believed in their religion with all her heart. For whatever reasons, Mom didn't approve of the Amish and didn't want them here. Though she'd always longed for siblings and a family of her own, Julia loved her mother most of all. She would never do something to defy or alienate her mom. No, not ever.

Besides, Martin hadn't spoken of marriage to her. They weren't even romantically involved. They were just good friends. Weren't they? That was all they could ever be. Because she was *Englisch* and he was Amish.

But what if his family and the rest of his congregation had made incorrect assumptions about her relationship with Martin? What if they thought she was going to marry him?

She'd have to broach the subject with Martin. But if he thought she was going to join his Amish faith and abandon her mother, he was dead wrong.

"Have you invited Julia to church on Sunday?"

Martin whirled around and found his mother standing nearby, leaning against a sturdy broom. She spoke in Deitsch.

He had just set the giant mixer into place in the workroom and was wiping off a splotch of grease from the large stainless steel bowl. Julia was in the retail part of the store, painting the trim on an old chest of drawers. The chore was perfect for her since it didn't require the use of her injured hand. It was early afternoon—almost time to leave for the frolic supper.

"I… I didn't have to. She asked if she could *komm*." Even though he was a grown man, he felt tongue-tied on this subject.

"*Ach*, that's *gut*," Linda said.

Something hardened inside of Martin. He didn't want to get his hopes up that Julia would join his faith.

"*Mamm*, you mustn't expect too much," he said. "I don't want to push Julia. She's told me her *mudder* doesn't approve and she has no intention of joining our faith."

Linda nodded wisely, her cheeks plumping with her smile. "And yet, she asked if she can *komm* to church again. That means she is interested. So, we shall see. The *gut* Lord works in mysterious ways. Julia may receive a conviction of the truth without intending to. Only time will tell."

Linda turned and reached for her black traveling bonnet and heavy shawl. "We're going *heemet* now, to pick up the other *kinder* and my casserole dish. I'll see you at the bishop's farm for supper."

He nodded but didn't speak as she called to the other women. They came at once, bidding Julia a cheery farewell. Setting her paintbrush aside, she hugged each one in turn. It seemed odd that they were all such good friends, yet Julia insisted she didn't want to become one of them.

Stepping outside, he saw the men had gathered most of their tools and were climbing into their buggies to go home. Their laughter mingled with the mild breeze. Hank was with his father, though the boy was arguing just now. Martin could hear him complaining that he wanted to stay with Julia.

"You'll see her at the frolic supper later on. Now *komm*," David said.

Thankfully, the boy went willingly. Martin suspected his father had purposefully taken Hank with him, to give Martin time alone with Julia. His parents hadn't said so but he knew they hoped Julia would be baptized and Martin would marry her. Funny how they accepted Julia now that they thought she would join their faith. He just hated to disappoint them.

Waving goodbye, Martin rounded the house to the backyard. For some reason, he wanted to be alone for a while. Several tidy piles of firewood had been set back away from the house. All the wood had been cut except for one cord of tree stumps. The men had left that work for Martin to finish.

Lifting the chisel and ax, he placed them on a stump and brought the ax down hard. The crack of the wood sounded in the air as he split it into hand-size pieces. The physical labor felt good and before long, he had to remove his warm coat.

"It's hard work, huh?"

Martin jerked around and found Julia behind him, a safe distance away from the ax. Sitting on a tree stump, she gestured to the scattered wood he'd tossed aside until he was finished and ready to stack it in a pile.

He smiled, not minding the work at all. "*Ja*, but very worth the effort."

"My father told me once that firewood warms you twice. When you cut it and when you use it to heat the house."

Embedding the steel of his ax into the stump, he rested his forearm on the wooden handle. He chuckled, the sound coming deep from within his chest. "*Ja*, your *vadder* was a wise man."

"What does *fraa* mean?" she asked suddenly.

He tilted his head, wondering where she'd heard the word. Probably from one of the women inside. "It means wife."

"And what does *schwardochder* mean?"

"Daughter-in-law," he said.

"Oh, I was afraid of that." She frowned, looking down at the ground.

"Is something wrong?" he asked.

She shook her head but wouldn't meet his eyes. "*Ne*, nothing is wrong. Nothing at all. It's just that I overheard the women talking today and…and… Martin, do your people think you and I are a couple? That we're more than friends?"

She spoke in a rush, her face flushing red. Martin stared, taken aback by her blunt question.

"I'm not sure what they think." He spoke truthfully, feeling suddenly at a loss for something intelligent to say.

"What about your parents? What does your *mudder* think?"

Here it was, the topic he'd been avoiding. It was an odd situation, really. Julia was his employer. She had hired him to do a job. And because she had saved little Rachel from being scalded, his people had come to her aid at the soap store. But they were just friends. They couldn't be anything more.

Could they?

"My *mudder* wishes I would marry but she knows you are *Englisch*," he said.

"And my mom wants me to remain *Englisch*," she said.

"*Ja*, it seems both our *midder* are at cross purposes. But they only want what they believe is best for each of us."

"*Midder?*" she asked.

"One *mudder*, two *midder*," he explained.

She nodded, repeating the new word. Each time he gave her a new Deitsch word, she seemed to remember it easily. And over the past couple of weeks, they had been adding more and more complicated words and phrases to her dialogue. She was now able to piece together simple sentences.

"My *mudder* believes that women are treated like chattel by your men. She thinks Amish women are no more than servants to their husbands and that their entire life is filled with drudgery." Her eyes were filled with sadness, as if she hoped this wasn't true.

He snorted and reached for his coat, sliding his arms into the sleeves before shrugging it up around his shoulders.

"I can't speak for what goes on in other Amish homes, but my *mamm* is definitely not a servant to my *vadder*. He calls her his queen and treats her well. He counsels with her and they make plans together. He seeks her opinion on all matters. *Mamm* and my sisters help in the barn, shop and field. Likewise, my *daed*, brothers and I help in the garden and around the house. I have even hung laundry. Once I marry, I plan to treat my *fraa* the same way."

She nodded. "Okay. Thank you for that explanation."

"Honestly, I think my *vadder* is more afraid of *Mamm* than he is of the bishop. And that is saying a lot," he said.

She laughed, the sound high and sweet. It seemed to melt the frigid ice of their conversation. But in his heart of hearts, Martin couldn't imagine ever abusing Julia or any woman. In fact, the thought of someone hurting her made his chest tighten and his hands tremble. He was a pacifist and had been taught to turn the other cheek but he truly didn't know what he would do if he ever caught someone abusing Julia.

A door slammed somewhere inside the house and she jerked her head in that direction. "It's getting late."

He flashed a smile. "*Ja*, we should leave for the supper."

She stood and turned toward the house. "If you'll give me a few minutes, I'd like to change out of my dirty work clothes."

He nodded. "When you're ready."

Watching her go, his thoughts were a jumble of turmoil. She was curious about his faith but had no intention of converting. *Mamm* thought she might be convinced otherwise. But Martin would not force her. She would have to come to his faith of her own free will. Otherwise, she could change her mind later on down the road. Years could pass and then they'd have disastrous consequences. It must be her choice alone.

Tugging the ax free of the tree stump, he put it away in the shed so the damp weather wouldn't cause it to rust. His father had taught him to be fastidious and careful in everything he did. It was who he was. And in choosing the woman who would one day be his wife, he could be no different.

He walked to the front of the house and leaned against the porch railing as he waited for Julia. She was so different from the Amish girls he knew. So independent. He wasn't sure he could get along with such a woman. In the Amish faith, wives were partners with their husbands but the man had the final word on important issues.

But something had changed between him and Julia today. Something he couldn't quite put his finger on.

They had actually discussed having a deeper relationship. But that wasn't possible. They were only friends and nothing more.

Chapter Nine

❧

"They're here! They're here!"

Julia heard Hank's cry from clear across the yard as Martin turned his horse into the pasture. As they walked toward Bishop Yoder's farmhouse, she saw the boy running toward them, his short stocky legs moving as fast as they could go.

Since her left hand was still bandaged, she had let Martin carry her ham-and-potato-cheese casserole for her. Though they only had another hour or so of sunlight left before it got dark, the November day was crisp yet pleasant. The perfect evening for a fall frolic.

"Mar-tin and Julia!"

Hank cried their names over and over until he reached them. Though he didn't touch her, he immediately sidled up next to Julia.

"You're finally here," he said, panting and sweating from his exertions.

"*Hallo*, Hank. *Wie bischt du?*" She smiled at the boy.

"I am *gut*! But we've been waiting for you and I'm about half starved." He skipped along like a little child rather than a fifteen-year-old boy.

Julia laughed at his melodramatic statement. "I'm sorry we're late."

"*Ach*, it's *allrecht*. We can eat now you're here." Hank flashed a good-natured grin in spite of the loud rumblings of his stomach.

Children raced across the yard in a game of chase while the teenage youths bunched together to discuss their day. The gathering was just like that on Church Sunday, except that everyone still wore their work clothes. But no one was eating. They were obviously waiting for her and Martin.

"Is the entire *Gmay* here?" Julia spoke low to Martin.

"*Ja*, and they're happy to see you," he said.

Julia wasn't so sure. The men sat at the tables or stood talking in clusters while the women bustled about setting out food. Since she'd attended one of their church gatherings and had worked with many of them at her soap studio, Julia knew most of them by name.

"I hope they're not irritated to be kept waiting," she said.

"*Ne*, of course not. You are their guest of honor. They only wish your *mudder* could be here, too," he said.

She stumbled over the uneven ground. Holding the casserole with one hand, Martin shot out his free hand to steady her. He just as quickly released her but not before she felt his firm, strong fingers around her arm.

Realizing his people were watching, Julia felt a flush of embarrassment. "Many of them have been working at my place all day. I would think they'd be sick of me by now."

Martin shook his head. "*Ne*, that isn't our way. *Gott* expects us to care for and serve one another."

His words touched her deeply. Was he for real? His

attitude seemed so different from Dallin's. Whenever she'd asked her ex-fiancé for help, he'd done so begrudgingly. Not with a willing heart and a smile. "I don't know how to ever repay them."

"No payment is necessary."

His words reminded her of a scripture she'd read last night about when Jesus gave His apostles a new commandment to love one another as they loved themselves. "Then you will just have to let me know when you have another work frolic and I will be there to help."

He smiled at that. "*Gut!* I am glad to see you understand how hard work can bless everyone."

As they reached the group, Julia saw that they all looked tired from their day's labors but they didn't complain and they all wore happy smiles on their faces. Yes, Julia understood what they were feeling. It was the fatigue and the joy of accomplishing wonderful things that day. She decided then that she loved the Amish work ethic.

"*Hallo!*" several of them called to her.

Julia smiled and waved, then immediately went to help the women lay out the meal. They welcomed her like a long-lost friend. Since it was a potluck, everyone had brought food items to contribute to the feast. A variety of casseroles, pickled beets, breads and pies were arrayed on the long tables. Julia pointed to where Martin should set her casserole, happy that she had contributed to the meal.

"That looks delicious." Linda nodded at the dish and hugged Julia.

Feeling happy inside, Julia smiled and returned the woman's embrace. "*Danke*, but I can't take credit. My *mudder* made it. She wanted me to pass on my thanks to all of you."

Linda drew back in surprise, her eyes wide, her mouth curving in a smile. "*Ach*, your *mudder* made the casserole? That was nice of her."

"*Ja*, very nice." Several other women stood nearby, nodding in approval.

"But she didn't want to join us?" Lori asked.

"*Ne*, I'm afraid she isn't feeling well."

"I'm sorry to hear she is sick," Abby said.

"She has *gut* days and bad days. I'll let her know you asked about her," Julia said.

"How is your hand?" Eli Stoltzfus stood up from the table to greet her and nodded at the bandages.

"*Gut*. I get the bandages off the day after Thanksgiving. Thanks to you, the doctor believes I will have very little scarring," she said.

"The thanks should be to *Gott*," Eli said, his gaze direct yet humble.

Julia nodded in understanding. She was gradually learning that the Amish were a meek people who didn't seek praise. It was their way to give all the credit to God, which was just one more thing she liked about them. More and more, she was coming to realize the Lord wanted them to serve one another.

"Let us pray," Bishop Yoder called in a loud voice to get everyone's attention.

They each went very quiet and bowed their heads, even the small children. After the prayer, they ate their meal. Martin came to sit next to Julia and she felt instantly relieved. Somehow his presence eased her fears. She was worried about upsetting her mother, yet she also wanted to please herself.

"Vie gehts?" he asked low.

"I am fine. Don't worry so much," she responded.

He smiled at that. She was trying to reassure him, yet she still felt a little uncertain.

"Do you have plans for Thanksgiving dinner?" he asked.

She nodded. *"Ja*, my *mudder* always roasts a turkey."

"Just the two of you?" Linda asked from behind as she reached past them to fill their glasses with water.

"Yes, just us two," Julia said, wishing her father was still here.

"You could join us, if you like. We have plenty of room," Linda said.

"Oh, thank you. But my mother looks forward to cooking every year." Knowing her mother would never agree to having dinner with Martin's family, Julia forgot to speak Deitsch. She was grateful when Linda didn't push the issue.

As Julia ate, she met Martin's gaze. The two of them didn't need to speak for her to know exactly what he was thinking. He was worried about her. He wanted her to feel happy and comfortable among his people. And she did, for the most part.

"Where did you say you were from, girl?"

Julia looked up and saw Marva Geingerich sitting across the table from her. "I'm from Kansas."

Marva narrowed her eyes, her forehead crinkled in a deep frown. "And who are your people?"

Julia forced herself not to stutter as she responded to the old matriarch. She always got the feeling that this woman didn't like her and that made her feel uncomfortable. "My parents are Walter and Sharon Rose. You met my mother last week."

"Hmm. And what was your *mudder*'s maiden name?" Marva asked.

"Miller," Julia said, trying not to bristle at this interrogation.

"Miller?" Marva's lips thinned with disapproval. "I knew a lot of Millers among the Amish when I lived in Ohio."

"Miller is a fairly common name. My *mudder* isn't Amish and I don't think she ever lived in Ohio," Julia said, trying not to feel a bit defensive.

"Julia! Hurry and eat. I want you to play baseball with me." Hank sat nearby, his cheeks bulging with food as he wolfed down his meal.

Whew! Julia was thankful for the interruption.

"Henry David Hostetler! *Sei net so rilpsich,*" his mother reprimanded him in a stern voice. "You should swallow your food before speaking."

Looking ashamed, Hank instantly swallowed with a big gulp. He then leaned one elbow on the table and looked dejectedly at his plate, no longer interested in eating. Julia had never seen the boy look so forlorn.

"What did your *mudder* say to him?" Julia whispered to Martin.

He chuckled softly. "She told him not to be rude."

Julia's heart wrenched. "But he looks so sad now."

"Then hurry with your meal and we won't disappoint him," Martin said.

Avoiding Marva's steady gaze, she ate quickly. Soon, she laid her fork down and took a last swallow of water. "I'm done. Shall we play baseball?"

Hank popped out of his chair like a jack-in-the-box and came to take her good hand.

"*Ja! Komm* on," he cried.

As she turned, she saw that a game had already started in the fallow hayfield. They didn't wait for Martin to untangle his long legs from beneath the table as they hurried toward the baseball diamond. Julia tossed him a glance over her shoulder, knowing he was following behind, laughing and shaking his head.

Right then, she decided that she loved work frolics with the Amish. In fact, there were a lot of things she loved about these people.

"Run, Julia! Run!" thirteen-year-old Alice Schwartz yelled.

"*Ja*, run, Julia," Hank chimed in.

Martin had hit the ball for her and she sprinted toward first base. Even with the extra encouragement, she wasn't fast enough. James Yoder, one of the bishop's teenage sons, tagged her out.

Martin frowned, thinking he should have assigned himself to first base and had someone else hit for Julia. He would have ensured that she made it in safe. For some reason, he felt protective of her.

Like always, she took the out good-naturedly. He was impressed by what a good sport she was.

"You're too fast for me, James," she said with a breathless laugh. "Next time, I'll ask Martin to knock it to the other side of the field."

James just smiled shyly. Julia returned to the dusty area on the outskirts of Bishop Yoder's hayfield that had been designated as the "out" area.

"That's okay, Julia. I get tagged out all the time. I'm never fast enough either," Hank said.

Martin watched the two as they laughed and chatted together. Hank was like a younger brother to her.

Too bad her mother hadn't joined them today. Martin was sure that, if Sharon would simply soften her heart, she would enjoy being with them, too. Over the past few weeks since he'd known them, he'd observed that Sharon had no friends. She didn't do anything but work and rest when she got too tired. That wasn't much of a life. And even though he'd been as kind to the woman as possible, he didn't know how to get through to her. Julia was all light, fun and joy. But Sharon seemed the complete opposite—dark, morose and sad. He knew something was holding her back from becoming friends with the Amish. Something big. Why did she dislike his people so much?

The next batter got another out, so they changed sides. Now Julia became the first baseman.

Little Hannah Yoder, the bishop's six-year-old daughter, came up to bat. The child looked tiny standing there, her legs and arms so thin as she lifted the heavy bat.

"Pitch softly," Martin called to Jakob Fisher, who was the pitcher.

Jakob nodded and tossed the ball ever so gently, ensuring the girl got a hit. Pressing her tongue to her upper lip, Hannah swung hard, knocking the ball just a few yards away.

"Run, Hannah! Run!" the other children yelled. Martin noticed that Julia screamed encouragement, in spite of being on the opposing team.

Hannah took off at a sprint, running as fast as she could go. As she approached first base, her long skirts tangled around her legs. She fell, reaching her arms toward the base and skidding in the dirt.

"Oh, Hannah!" Julia cringed.

"Safe!" one of the boys called, waving his arms over top of the sprawled girl.

Hannah promptly pulled one knee up against her chest and burst into tears. Martin watched as Julia scooped the child into her arms to comfort her. She held her injured hand away, using the strength of her forearm to cuddle the child.

"There, there, sweetums. Let me see. Where are you hurt?" Julia spoke in a sympathetic voice.

Martin hurried to the base, accompanied by the other players. As they crowded around, Hannah continued to cry.

Julia drew back enough to see the injury. The child's black tights had been shredded across the knee, her skin bloodied by the small abrasion. Thankfully, it didn't look too serious.

"I got hurt," Hannah cried as giant tears rolled down her cheeks.

"I know, *boppli*," Julia cooed. "But I think you'll be okay. We need to clean this up and put a bandage on it. You're so brave." Julia looked up, searching the crowd of faces until she saw Martin. "Can you carry her to the house?"

He nodded, his heart swelling with joy that she had sought him out.

"Of course. *Komm* to me, Hannah." Copying Julia's sympathetic voice, he reached for the child. Still crying, Hannah thrust out her arms and clung tightly to his neck as he carried her across the field.

A trail of children followed.

"Is she all right?" Hank asked, trotting along beside him.

"*Ja*, she'll be fine." Julia looked into Hannah's eyes and smiled. "Won't you, *boppli*?"

Hannah nodded, her little chin quivering as she tucked her face against Martin's chest.

The moment Sarah Yoder saw her daughter was hurt, she came running.

"What happened?" she cried.

Julia quickly explained, trying to lighten the moment. "But she made it safe to first base."

"She did, huh? That's *gut*!" Sarah seemed surprised as she examined the wound.

"*Ja*, she ran really hard," Hank said.

"*Ach*, that's my girl. Now, let's get you inside." Sarah took the girl into her own arms and headed toward the back door to the kitchen.

Julia went with them but Martin blocked the way so the other kids wouldn't follow.

"Hannah is going to be okay. Go on back to your game now," he told them.

They did as asked and Martin entered the house. He found Julia seated at the table. Hannah was perched on the kitchen table with Julia rubbing her back in a circular motion. Sarah was searching the cupboards and soon pulled out some antiseptic and little bandages.

Within moments, the ruined tights had been removed and the wound cleansed. When Sarah reached for the bandage, Hannah hugged tight against Julia.

"I want Julia to do it," Hannah said.

"That would be fine," Sarah said, handing over the bandage.

Smiling as if she had been awarded a great honor, Julia pulled the sticky strips off and put the bandage on the wound, pressing it down with a gentle touch.

"There! That didn't hurt too much, did it? You're almost good as new," she said.

Hannah looked at her knee and smiled, showing a tooth missing in front. "*Danke*, Julia."

"*Gaern gscheh, boppli.*" With one last hug, Julia set the girl on her own two feet.

Once again, Martin couldn't believe how good Julia's Deitsch was getting or how sweet she was with children. Without a doubt, he knew Julia would make a wonderful mother.

"Would you like some ice cream? Your *vadder* churned it especially for the frolic," Sarah told Hannah.

The girl nodded and took her mother's hand. The two walked outside together.

"That was nice," Martin said.

Julia nodded. She didn't speak for a few moments. Her eyes shimmered with moisture as she stared after the child.

"You know, I was so sad when Mom and I first moved here to Colorado," she finally said. "I felt lost and afraid. But now, I feel so happy inside. So calm and peaceful. And I know it has to do with all that I've been learning about God. I feel closer to Him than ever before. It also has to do with you and the new Amish friends I've made. Because of you, I don't feel alone anymore."

He stared at her, fascinated by the way her hair glimmered in the fading sunlight. "That's nice. I'm glad you feel that way. I liked how you cared for little Hannah."

"She's a sweet girl. I felt so bad that she fell down."

He grunted. "You're very nurturing."

She laughed. "That's not a characteristic I would use to describe myself. I always thought I was a bit rough, not nurturing at all. But with both my parents' illnesses, I've learned a lot."

He shrugged. "We are always changing, growing and learning. Certain situations bring out different sides to our personalities that sometimes surprise us. My *grossmammi* used to say the older we become, the more we become the person we really are inside."

"Grossmammi?"

"Grandmother," he supplied.

"That's a nice saying. I like it," she said. "It's probably true. I used to think I was weak and dependent upon my parents. Maybe that's why I clung to Dallin so much."

"Dallin?"

"My ex-fiancé. He dumped me so he could marry my best friend, Debbie. He lied and stole from me, too."

"Ah, that wasn't very kind," he said.

"No, it wasn't. I was afraid of being alone. But after my father died, I learned to be strong and independent. My mother depends on me and I can't let her down. I promised him I'd always take care of her," she said.

"One of the Ten Commandments is to honor your father and mother. Sharon is blessed to have a dutiful daughter like you," he said.

She laughed off his words. "Well, I don't know about that."

He stepped closer and she looked up at him. For several moments, he felt mesmerized as he gazed into her beautiful eyes.

"Julia, would you *komm* with me, please? There's something I want to show you before the daylight is gone."

He held out his hand. Without speaking, she reached

over and enfolded his fingers with hers. The warmth of her touch sent currents of energy pulsing up his arm. He led her out the back way, skirting around the house so they wouldn't be seen. In silence, he harnessed his horse to the buggy and they drove away.

"Will we be missed?" she asked as the horse settled into a quick trot.

"My *vadder* will know not to worry about us," he said.

She chuckled. "I doubt that will provide any solace for Hank when he discovers we're gone."

"*Ja*, he is crazy about you. He tells everyone that you are his girl," Martin said.

She smiled at that and they rode for a time in silence.

"Where are you taking me?" she asked once they were a mile down the road.

"You will see."

Within minutes, they arrived at their destination and Martin pulled the buggy off the side of the road. The dusky sky allowed just enough light for them to see before the sun faded behind the Wet Mountains to the west. With the Sangre de Cristo Mountains in the east as a backdrop, the vast fields before them showed nothing but drab brown.

"In the summer, this will all be green with growth," he said.

"Where are we?" she asked, huddling within her coat and shivering.

He reached into the back and grabbed the warm quilt he kept there before spreading it over her legs. "This is my place. My farm."

He tried to prevent a note of *hochmut* from entering

his voice. *Hochmut* was the arrogant pride of the world and something he should shun.

She nodded, gazing at the barren land with curiosity. Without looking, he knew it was dotted by a few boulders and scrubby trees that he would remove once he set the plow to the fields. But just now, he could hardly take his eyes off Julia, eager to see her response.

"It's lovely. I can see why you bought this land. It's close to town and filled with promise," she said.

He exhaled, realizing he'd been holding his breath. For some reason, he wanted her approval more than anything. "I'm glad you like it. I've got sixty-five acres with good water rights. I'm going to grow barley, oats and hay. It may not look like much right now, but one day, this land will all be fenced off. The rocks and boulders will be removed and the fields will be full of life."

"It'll take a lot of hard work but I know you're up to the task," she said.

He nodded and pointed to the east. "Over there, I'll build a fine barn like my *vadder*'s. And over there, I'll plow the ground for a vegetable garden." He pointed to the west. "Over here, I'll build a fine house for my *fraa*. I'll put up a clothes line for the laundry and build flower beds and a nice lawn for my *kinder* to play on."

She stared, her eyes unblinking as she took in his every word. "I imagine you'll want a chicken coop, too."

He laughed and nodded. She seemed so intuitive. "*Ja*, my *familye* will need plenty of eggs and chickens to eat."

"Have you ever killed a chicken?" she asked, her eyes crinkled with repulsion.

"*Ja*, many times. Does that upset you?" Oh, how he hoped she wasn't squeamish about such things. After all, the Amish raised what they ate. It was the way things were on a farm.

"*Ne*, I've cooked meat many times. It doesn't bother me as long as I don't have to kill it myself."

"Then I would do it for you," he promised.

She frowned and looked away. It was then he realized what he'd just said. He hoped she didn't assume he was proposing marriage. Because he wasn't. She was *Englisch*. They could never wed.

"Jules, I... I didn't mean that you and I would, that we would—"

She held up a hand to stop him. "I know what you meant. It's all right."

She was quiet then, as if absorbed in her own thoughts. He gave her some space, letting her think. Then, he decided to confess something to her.

"I've almost given up hope of ever marrying but I have faith *Gott* has a plan for me. It's just that you're so easy to talk to, Jules. And sometimes, I feel as if I can confide anything to you. It's like I've known you all my life. But in my heart of hearts, I know we can never be anything more than friends," he said.

There. He'd spoken what was in his heart. The next step would have to come from her. She would need to decide what she wanted in life and whether she would convert or remain *Englisch*.

"If I were to convert and marry an Amish man, would my husband let me keep my soap store and continue selling my products?" she asked.

Hmm. He blinked. Interesting how she'd asked that question. "I cannot speak for all Amish men, but I certainly would allow it. I wouldn't tell my wife what she could and could not do."

"I'm glad you're not like that," she said.

He heaved a deep sigh. "I've heard that some Amish men are cruel and domineering, though I know Bishop Yoder would never tolerate such abuse within our *Gmay*. He'd put a stop to it quick."

She smiled. "Yes, knowing the bishop as well as I do, I don't believe he would allow such things to go on. And I can't imagine him dominating Sarah."

Martin laughed at the thought. "Many of our *weib-sleit*, including my own *mamm*, make crafts to sell in town. Baked goods, cheese, rag rugs, furniture, you name it. It helps supplement their *familye* incomes."

She nodded, deep in thought.

"I believe both spouses should be in their marriage by choice and not because they are forced," he said. "I would rather lead my *familye* to do what is right with love and kind persuasion, not with an iron fist."

"That is *gut*. I'm happy to hear that," she said.

They didn't speak again for several moments and he hoped he'd said the right things. But deep inside, he meant every word. He didn't know what to expect. For Julia to fall into his arms and ask to be baptized immediately? No, of course not. Her life wasn't that simple. After all, she had her mother to think about. Converting to the Amish faith was a huge and complicated commitment. Her first obligation was to her mother.

As night closed in on them, he drove her home in silence. And when they arrived, they found her mother standing on the front porch, waiting for them. She had a heavy shawl wrapped around her shoulders, her face creased with concern.

Martin helped Julia out of the buggy. "*Danke* for going with me tonight."

"And *danke* for a *wundervoll* evening." Her voice sounded whisper soft.

He nodded, hardly able to speak. As she turned and hurried to her mother, his throat felt tight and he couldn't swallow.

"Hi, Mom. Oh, how I missed you. I wish you could have gone with us." She embraced Sharon in a tight hug.

"It's late and I was worried," Sharon said, her voice trembling.

Martin wondered if she'd been crying. He hoped not.

Together, the two women went inside and Martin couldn't hear the rest of their conversation. As she closed the door, Julia glanced back at him and waved.

Martin climbed into the buggy and headed home. As he drove through the cold night air, his chest ached. He would never ask Julia to go against her mother. He could see that they loved each other and it wouldn't be right. His faith taught him that a child must honor their parents. And because he would never leave his faith, that meant he and Julia could never marry.

They would never be anything more than friends and that hurt most of all.

Chapter Ten

The electrician came the following Wednesday. It was the morning before Thanksgiving and he worked all day installing a new fuse box on the outside of the house and running new wires to the attic. He brought the entire system up to code. Other than that, Julia had no idea what he was doing. When he finished, he smiled wide as he flipped on the kitchen light switch and they had power.

Mom was elated but Julia felt a heaviness inside that she couldn't explain. Not only did the repair bill cost a lot of money but it was as if she were betraying all that Martin had taught her about being humble. As if she had just let the world inside her home.

Thankfully, Martin wasn't here to see what was going on. Because she was *Englisch*, Julia knew he wouldn't say a word about her having electricity in her home but she knew he wouldn't approve. And no matter how hard Mom encouraged her to do so, Julia couldn't bring herself to use the electrical switches or appliances such as hand mixers, toasters and can openers.

She'd attended church with Martin again. During

the many times they'd been alone together, she'd asked him lots of questions about his faith and he'd patiently answered every one. Coupled with her personal prayer and study of the Scriptures, his responses seemed so logical and she liked what she heard. In spite of her mother's resistance, Julia felt a sense of calm as she listened to Martin's explanations and it only made her hunger for more.

Thanksgiving was a lonely affair. More than ever, Julia missed the warm camaraderie of a loving family and friends. But most of all, she missed Martin.

Mom made a roast turkey breast with mashed potatoes, gravy and rolls. Julia made pumpkin pie with whipped cream. Sitting alone together in their quiet apartment, they didn't talk much and Julia picked at her food.

"You're not hungry?" Sharon asked.

"Not much but everything is delicious," Julia said.

She couldn't help wishing they had accepted Linda Hostetler's invitation to join Martin's family for their feast. But Mom wouldn't hear of it.

"Mom?"

"Hmm?" Sharon didn't look up as she scooped a spoonful of cranberry sauce onto her plate.

"What would you think if I decided to become Amish?"

Mom's fork clattered to her plate and her mouth dropped open with shock. "You're not serious."

Julia swallowed hard. "I've been thinking about it."

Mom stood and scooted back her chair so hard that it toppled to the floor. With stiff, angry movements, she set it back up, then grabbed up her plate and stormed over to the kitchen sink.

"I can't believe you would even consider such a thing. The Amish? Really, Julia!"

She watched her mother for several moments, trying to gather her courage. After all, she was a fully grown woman who worked hard and paid the bills. She should be able to make choices for herself.

"I don't know why you're so against them," she said. "They're kind, hardworking and devout. I love their faith. It's come to mean a great deal to me."

Mom turned to look at her, holding the dish cloth in one hand. "Yes, and if you choose such a life, you'll forfeit all your freedoms. You'll be controlled by whatever whim your husband and the church elders might force upon you."

Julia just stared. Dallin had been so manipulative and domineering that freedom of choice was extremely important to her. But she and Martin had discussed this issue and she didn't believe he would treat his wife that way. She longed for a family of her own. Loved ones she could care about and shower her love upon. She'd thought she was going to have that with Dallin. But Mom's accusations sounded so authentic. What if Julia was wrong? What if Martin wasn't as he seemed?

"I've never seen any of the Amish men treat their wives like that. Why do you think that's the way they act?" she asked.

"When I was a girl, I saw Amish men treating their wives and daughters quite poorly. They're careful and quiet about it but it's still there, hidden behind the walls of their homes where outsiders can't see in," Mom said.

"Martin isn't like that. He would never treat me that way," Julia said.

Or would he? She didn't think so, but she hadn't known him very long.

"Has he…has he asked you to marry him?" Mom asked, her voice filled with fear.

"No, he wouldn't do that. Not as long as I'm *Englisch*. We're just friends." And yet, she wished they could take their relationship to a more romantic level. But that couldn't happen as long as she wasn't Amish. And she couldn't convert as long as her mother disapproved. So they were at a standstill.

Mom nodded, her eyes shimmering with tears. "Has he asked you to convert?"

Julia shook her head. "He wouldn't ask me to do that either. Not as long as he thinks I'd be going against your wishes. He wants me to decide for myself. You see? You're wrong about him. He only wants my happiness and what is best for me."

Though she said the words, Julia wasn't sure they were true. Was Martin really as wonderful as he seemed? How could she ever know for sure?

Mom turned and made a pretense of washing dishes but Julia could see she was upset. She stood and went to her mother, touching her shoulder.

"Mom, what is it? What's wrong?" she asked.

Mom whirled around and hugged her fiercely. "I… I'm just so afraid I'm going to lose you to those people."

"Those people? You talk about them as if they're monsters. And they're not."

"But they don't like the *Englisch*. They won't let you come see me very often, if at all."

"No, Mama," Julia soothed. "You'll never lose me as long as I live. Put your fears at ease. I won't let anyone or anything come between us. I promise you that."

And Julia meant it. As long as she had breath in her body, she would look after her mother. She'd given her word to her father. She would never become Amish if it meant turning her back on her mother.

They stood there for some time, until Julia felt her mother's body stop trembling. Then they washed the dishes together and retired to the living room where they took turns reading out loud from an Agatha Christie novel. Later that afternoon, they napped and relaxed and spoke no more about the Amish. That evening, Julia found some solace in the Scriptures. But in her heart, she felt no peace. She missed Martin more than she could say and longed to be with him. And she realized that, whether she liked it or not, her feelings for him had grown.

The next day, they received their first snowfall. As Julia stared out the chilled windowpane in her bedroom, she felt mesmerized by the gently drifting flakes that soon increased and blanketed the ground in pristine white. Kansas had snow but not like this. In the night, the temperature took a dive and she was more than grateful Martin had repaired their roof and secured the firewood they needed.

She couldn't help thinking about the night of the frolic when Martin had taken her to see his farmland. As she'd listened to him describe his plans to build a barn and a fine house to live in, she'd caught his excitement and longed to be a part of his dreams. Though he hadn't proposed to her, she'd caught the gist of the moment. If she were to convert to the Amish faith, he would pursue her.

When she'd moved to Colorado, she hadn't planned to fall in love but she had. With Martin and with his

Amish people. To all appearances, they were just friends. But in Julia's heart, he meant much more to her. The love she felt for him was different from what she'd felt for Dallin. It was sweet and pure and made her realize they could never wed.

As Julia got ready for the day, a feeling of dread and anticipation thrummed through her veins. Today, she would have the bandages on her hand removed and make her first batch of soap. Martin had promised to come into town that afternoon to help. And the thought of seeing him again made her fizzy with happiness.

Though she tried to fight off the feeling, she couldn't wait to see him. But being near him only prolonged the torture. His work for her was almost finished. Her relationship with God had grown and her belief in the Amish faith was strong.

But she couldn't defy her mother by converting. Which meant she had to put a stop to their interaction. After today, she might bump into him or one of his people on the street, but nothing more. And that thought made her want to cry.

"Have you asked her to convert?" Bishop Yoder asked.

It was midmorning and Martin sat in the bishop's home, having come to seek his advice. It was the day after Thanksgiving and Martin was on his way into town, to help Julia make soap.

"Maybe she just needs a little incentive," the bishop said.

Martin leaned back on the old sofa and crossed his arms. The black woodstove nearby provided plenty of warmth. Even so, he still felt a chill run up his spine. He would love nothing more than to ask Julia to be baptized but he couldn't do that. She had to make this decision on her own.

"Honestly, I fear her answer," Martin said. "Her *mudder* is ailing and doesn't approve of the Amish. I'm afraid Julia would choose her *mamm* over conversion to our faith."

The bishop's eyes were filled with compassion and wisdom. "*Ja*, she is hardworking and devoted to her *mudder*. That is *gut*. You wouldn't want her if she were the type of woman who would desert her *mamm*. If she would convert, she would make a good *fraa* for you."

Martin stared, thunderstruck by his feelings. He cared deeply for Julia. He loved her. It was that simple. But because she wasn't Amish, he could never think of her as anything but a friend. So, what could he do?

"She doesn't need to abandon her *mudder* in order to convert to our faith. She can still visit and care for her *mamm*. Perhaps she doesn't know that. You might want to tell her," the bishop said.

Martin tilted his head. "I appreciate you saying so but I think she knows. The problem is bigger than that. She was engaged to be married once before and her fiancé treated her rather badly. Also, I don't think Julia will convert without her *mamm*'s blessing. Sharon is so against the Amish faith and I don't believe Julia will defy her *mudder* even if she has the conviction that it's right."

"*Ach*, I see. She seeks to honor her *mudder* just as you would honor your *eldre*. This is a difficult dilemma. I don't know what you want me to tell you, *sohn*," the bishop said.

"I'm not sure either," Martin said.

Bishop Yoder leaned forward in his chair and rested

his elbows on his knees. His gaze drilled into Martin's with a steely edge. "If she will convert and agree to live by the *Ordnung*, I would be happy to baptize her. Perhaps after that, the two of you might wish to marry. We shall see."

Yes, they would have to wait and see.

"But I must warn you, Martin. Don't let your feelings for Julia draw you over to the *Englisch* world. A lot is at stake here. But you already know what you must do if she won't convert."

Yes, Martin knew only too well. He must turn and walk away and never look back. If she wouldn't join his faith, it would be too dangerous to remain friends. It might give the wrong impression to his people and it could lead to other dangerous things. To abandon his Amish faith was tantamount to turning his back on his eternal salvation. He'd be shunned by his people. He'd lose everything that meant anything to him. His *familye* and friends. His home. His sense of belonging.

His *Gott*.

And he couldn't do that no matter how much he cared for Julia.

The bishop sat back, having said his piece. Martin nodded and came to his feet. He knew what he must do. Knew that he must be strong. If Julia chose not to join his Amish faith, he must let her go.

Chapter Eleven

By early afternoon, Julia was in her workroom, ready to make soap. She lifted a heavy stainless steel stockpot off the shelf and carried it to the work counter. Using the strength of her arms to support the pan, she avoided straining her left hand. The doctor had just removed the bandages and pronounced her wounds completely healed, though her muscles had atrophied from lack of use and would take time to build up their strength again.

After measuring out some of the oils, she picked up the pan to move it over to the stovetop. She lost her grip on one handle and felt the pot falling. But suddenly, a pair of large hands reached to take the brunt of its weight.

She whirled around in surprise. "Martin!"

He must have just arrived. He'd promised to come help her make her first batch of soap today and she admitted silently to herself that she was delighted to see him.

"*Ach*, you shouldn't be lifting heavy things yet. What did the doctor say about your hand?" He showed a dubious frown as he set the pan on the stove. He then removed his winter coat and black felt hat and set them aside on a chair.

"It's fine with minimal scarring." She almost flinched when he reached for her left hand and took it softly into his.

The pads of his fingertips felt rough as he caressed her fingers. He turned her hand as he eyed the new skin. His touch was infinitely gentle and she felt currents of excitement pulsing up her arm.

"Look! My left hand is smaller than my right." Giving a jittery laugh, she pulled free of his grasp and held up both hands, which showed a slight disparity in the size of the two.

Martin nodded. "*Ja*, I saw this happen when Jeremiah Beiler broke his leg. But don't fear. Within a couple of weeks, you won't even notice that your left hand was ever injured."

His reassurance gave her the courage to maintain a positive attitude. She peered behind him for some sign of his brother. "Hank isn't with you today?"

"*Ne*, he has a bad head cold. *Mamm* made him stay at home. She didn't want him out in the chilled air."

She frowned, feeling doubtful. "I'll bet he wasn't happy about that."

Martin flashed a smile that didn't quite reach his eyes. "You are right. He wasn't happy at all when I left this morning."

"Well, be sure to tell him I missed him," she said.

Not wanting him to see her sad expression, she turned to face the stockpot. After all, today was their last day to work together in the soap studio. Though she would never admit it out loud, it was a melancholy time for Julia. There'd be no more detailed discussions about the Amish beliefs. No more frolics or tulips from Hank or thrilling buggy rides.

And no more Martin.

He glanced around the tidy workroom. "Where is Sharon today?"

Julia shrugged. "Like Hank, she isn't feeling well. She's upstairs resting."

"Then it's just us two?" he asked.

She nodded, not trusting her clogged voice.

"Then we can practice your Deitsch. *Weller daag iss heit?*" he asked suddenly.

She blinked, surprised that she understood most of his question. He had asked her what day it was.

"It is *Freidawk*, the day after Thanksgiving," she said, indicating it was Friday.

To distract herself, she reached for a jug of olive oil and slowly measured it into the pot. She jerked when he reached to help her, taking the bulk of the weight in his two strong hands.

"*Gut.* Now, can you repeat my question back to me?" he asked, setting the empty bottle aside.

"Sure! *Weller dog iss heit?*"

He promptly burst into laughter.

Without thinking, she buffeted his shoulder in a playful gesture. "What? Did I say it wrong?"

"You did. You just asked me what dog is it."

She laughed, too, wondering why she was trying so hard to learn his language. After all, she wouldn't see him anymore and speaking Deitsch wouldn't be fun without him. But then she reminded herself that she still wanted to be able to talk to his people when they came into her store. For a few brief moments, she thought about asking him to continue giving her lessons a couple evenings each week. But no. That would only invite trouble.

He went suddenly very still, his gaze trained toward the hallway. Julia caught a movement out of her peripheral vision and turned to find her mom standing in the threshold leading to the back rooms. She must have heard their laughter because her scowl looked dark and deep.

"Are you almost finished?" Sharon asked, her voice stern.

"No, Mom. We've only just started the first batch," Julia said.

"Well, I'll be upstairs if you need me." Sharon's eyes narrowed on Martin and Julia knew the comment was for him, to let him know she was nearby.

Before Julia could say anything else, Mom turned on her heels and climbed the stairs to their apartment above.

Julia faced Martin again, feeling a tad embarrassed by her mother's actions. "I… I'm sorry about that. She really is feeling under the weather today."

He nodded. "*Ach*, there's no harm done. Now, what do you need me to do?"

She stepped over to the work counter. Except for the heavy buckets, she'd already set out the various ingredients they would need.

Seeing Martin's curious glance, she pointed at a bowl of grayish powder. "This is colloidal oatmeal. Today, we'll be making two super batches of oatmeal, milk and honey soap."

He tilted his head to one side. "Super batches?"

"*Ja*, super batching is when you make four or more batches of soap at one time. I'll need to make dozens of super batches in order to fill all my orders by the end of January."

He grunted. "That's a lot of soap."

"*Ja*, and it will take time to make it and then four to five weeks for it to dry and cure. My oatmeal soap smells delicious and should sell well during the month of February."

He blinked. "It sounds good enough to eat."

She nodded and rested her fingertips against a stainless steel pitcher of goat milk, which she'd acquired from Martin's mother. "Except for the lye, you could definitely eat my soap. It's made of all-natural ingredients that most people cook with on a daily basis. Olive oil, coconut oil, palm oil... It lathers beautifully and is nourishing to the skin. And it doesn't dry you out like manufactured soap does."

"Why is that?"

"The manufactured soap is filled with chemicals I can't even pronounce," she said.

He chuckled. "All right, you're the expert. What should I do?"

He rolled up the long sleeves of his shirt, ready to work. For a moment, she gazed at his muscular arms, wishing things could be different between them. Wishing they could...

She shook her head and walked over to the heavy-duty shelves he'd built for her and reached for a large bottle of canola oil. Before she could lift it, he picked it up with very little effort.

She pointed and he set it on the counter beside the stove. After popping off the lid, she measured out what she needed, turned the stove burner onto low and pointed to the next ingredient. Working together, Martin lifted the heavy containers while she measured everything out. Soon, she had the oils melting inside the stockpot and turned her attention to the distilled water and lye.

Handing Martin a face mask, a pair of goggles and some rubber gloves, she indicated that he should put them on. She did likewise, laughing at how funny they both looked. She wished she had a camera but knew the Amish didn't take pictures because they didn't believe in making graven images of themselves. But she didn't need a picture. As long as she lived, she would hold this memory in her mind.

With careful precision, she poured the lye into the distilled water. Martin reached for a plastic spoon to stir the mixture with.

"It's nice that you and my *mudder* have so much in common," he said.

She agreed. In many ways, she felt closer to Linda than she did her own mother. Linda was so accepting of Julia, while Sharon insisted on rejecting Martin and anything to do with the Amish. Under the circumstances, it would be difficult to stay friends with Linda but Julia hoped they could.

He watched earnestly as she stirred the lye water. It immediately turned cloudy, then went crystal clear after a few minutes.

Using a battery-operated thermometer gun, she measured the temperature of the lye and the oils. She rested the palm of her hand against the outside of the metal pitcher.

"Touch here," she said. "You can feel the heat of the lye. The moment you add it to the water, it can race up to a temperature of two hundred degrees."

He felt the container and his eyes widened. "*Ja*, it is very hot."

"While we make soap, we must remember that we have become scientists and we're working with some volatile chemicals. We always want to be careful not to make mistakes." She stepped over to the stove and gave the oils a quick stir, checking to ensure it didn't scorch.

"I always loved science when I was in school," he said.

"Well, even though you only go to the eighth grade, you can still learn things just by working and living life," she said.

He nodded. "You do understand us, don't you? I've never really felt like I quit school. On the farm, I learn something new every day."

His expression was filled with curiosity as she measured out the fragrance oils and micas to color the soap.

His nose twitched. "That smells *gut*."

Thinking the same thing, she reached for the goat milk and poured it into the oil mixture. After blending, she added the ground oatmeal and honey. He stood near, leaning over her to watch. She felt his warm breath touch her cheek. He smelled of horses and peppermint. His presence so close beside her made her highly aware of him as an attractive man and her hands shook slightly.

"Do you need me to stir that for you?" he asked quietly.

She shook her head, embarrassed that he had noticed her nervousness.

Working fast, she poured the lye mixture into the oils and used a battery-powered stick blender and long, oversize plastic spoon to mix it to a thin trace. Then she divided the batter into other containers and added the colored micas. Martin watched with wide eyes as she then did an in-the-pot swirl of white, light shimmery gold and a darker gold color. The brilliance of the micas seemed perfect for this creamy soap as they swirled together.

"Those colors are beautiful. *Mamm* always makes our soap plain white," he said.

"The secret is to not overmix or you'll lose the design. It's now ready to pour into the block molds." She nodded at the huge molds she had already set on a wooden rolling dolly and prepped with freezer paper and Mylar liners.

"Can you lift and pour it for me?" she asked.

He nodded, clasped the handles of the stockpot and poured the mixture evenly into the two big molds. What was normally a heavy, challenging chore for Julia seemed like a simple task to a man of his strength.

"Someday, I'd like to buy a pot tipper. You just use a lever to pour the batter into the molds," she said.

She used a flat spatula to scrape down the sides of the pot, getting every drop of soap into the molds. Then, she lifted one mold and tamped it to get all the air bubbles out of the soap. With her weak hand, her actions weren't very effective.

"Here, let me do that." He brushed her aside so he could lift each mold onto the solid floor where he smacked them gently several times.

"How much soap does each mold hold?" he asked as he set the soap back on the cart.

"Twenty-five pounds. I'll get 172 squares of nice, fat bars that fit well in a person's hand and don't dissolve as quickly as a thin bar."

He took a little inhale, his face mask sucking inward.

"That's a lot of soap. I don't think *Mamm* has ever made that much for our *familye*."

"*Ja*, but your *mamm* doesn't sell her soap. She just makes it for your own use."

He removed his face mask and took another deep inhale. "Mmm, the soap sure smells *gut*."

"Yes, it does." She couldn't help feeling pleased that he liked the fragrance. She had invented this soap on her own and was rather pleased with the results.

Sliding the dolly over to the far wall where it wouldn't be disturbed, she covered the molds with a sheet of cardboard she'd saved and then wrapped it all with an old, tattered quilt.

"Why do you wrap it up like that? Are you afraid the hot soap might get cold?" He chuckled at his own humor.

She laughed, too. "I know it seems odd but I want the soap to go through a gel phase where it will get very hot. The result is that the colors brighten and look beautiful after we cut it into squares tomorrow."

"Ahh, I see. Do you need me to *komm* help you cut the soap?"

She hesitated. Seeing him again in the morning would be wonderful but she couldn't. She'd already told Mom that this was his last day of work. For her own sanity, she didn't dare see him again either.

"*Ne*, I think Mom and I can manage all right. I will also make a super batch of lavender soap and one of orange calendula. On Monday, I'll make a super batch of apple sage and one of black raspberry."

He frowned. "Are you coming to church with me on the next Church Sunday?"

She froze. For a few moments, she'd forgotten that

she planned to stay away from the Amish. She thought about going to church with him again but knew it was foolhardy. It would only confuse their families and his *Gmay*. It would be better if she went to the Christian church here in town, though she knew it wouldn't be the same. Something about the Amish doctrine really spoke to her heart. Something she couldn't deny. Yet, it also brought her mother's disapproval. Julia's relationship with God had become so strong and she wasn't willing to give that up.

"We'll see. Can I let you know when we get closer to Sunday?" she asked.

He nodded but didn't meet her eyes. "Of course. Whatever you like. I'll check with you again next week."

Julia turned away, trying not to be afraid that she was losing him.

Martin didn't try to persuade Julia to join him at church. He was struggling to remember that it was her choice. But he'd be sure to stop by her store next Saturday to invite her again and see if he could give her a ride.

They worked in companionable silence, making another super batch. At lunchtime, they shared some sandwiches and fruit. The afternoon passed quickly and it was soon time for him to leave.

Julia stepped over to the chair and picked up his hat and coat, handing them to him. As she walked with him to the front door, she whisked an envelope from off the counter beside the cash register and held it out to him.

"This is for you," she said, not looking at him.

He took it but didn't open it. He already knew what was inside. His final paycheck.

"Is there nothing else I can do for you? I... I don't need to get paid. I can help you just because we're friends," he said.

How he wished she could come up with a long list of chores for him to do. How he wished he could stay here with her forever.

"There's nothing else left to do except work my soap store. You've done wonders and I'm so grateful." She turned and looked around the room. Everything was tidy and in its place. Cheery and inviting. A delightful store for customers to shop in.

She walked to the door and opened it. She even stepped outside with him onto the front porch. He gazed out at the skiff of snow that was just starting to fall. It was dark already and he wondered where the day had gone. He should be getting home.

She shivered against the frigid air and folded her arms. He didn't think before he swung his warm coat around her shoulders. As he held it closed just beneath her chin, he stepped nearer. Their gazes clashed, then locked. He felt lost, drowning in the beauty of her face. Before he thought to stop himself, he ducked his head down and kissed her gently, so softly that it felt like the brush of a butterfly against his lips. She gave a little sigh, telling him she felt the connection between them, too.

"Jules, I wish things could be different. I wish—"

The rattle of the door caused them to jerk apart. Julia gasped in dismay.

Looking up, Martin saw Sharon standing in the threshold, a prudish look on her face.

"The snow is getting worse and the roads will be icy.

It's time for you to leave, Martin." Sharon spoke in a stern voice as she folded her arms.

"Um, *ja*, you are right. *Gut nacht*, Jules," he said.

"Goodbye, Martin." Julia held out his coat to him.

Their fingers touched briefly as he took it from her and quickly put it on. He nodded to her, trying to offer his silent support, yet feeling confused and mortified and even a little angry at the situation. Why did Sharon have to be so hard-hearted? Why couldn't she see that Julia belonged with the Amish?

He stepped back, closing his coat. As he did so, he caught Julia's light scent and couldn't help taking a deep breath.

Snowflakes stuck to his eyelashes and he blinked. Soon, the wet flakes would soak him clear through and he'd be cold on the ride home. If he didn't leave now, he never would.

He hurried over to his horse and buggy. As he climbed inside and closed the door, his thoughts were filled with turmoil. He gathered up the leather lead lines, forcing himself to go home.

The snow continued to fall as he pulled out of the parking lot. He gazed into his rearview mirror and stared back at the soapworks. Sharon went back inside but Julia stood right where he'd left her. He watched her until she faded from view.

Chapter Twelve

On December 1, Julia was up early. Though it was brisk outside, the morning blazed with sunlight. Perfect weather for the grand opening of Rose Soapworks and just in time for holiday shopping. She'd had some flyers and posters made and spread them around town several weeks earlier to advertise the event. She'd even put an ad in the local newspaper. Even so, she couldn't help feeling jittery inside. What if no one came? What if she was stuck with all this soap, lotions and other products she and Mom had worked so hard to make?

What if her new business flopped?

No! She mustn't think that way. Martin had taught her to have faith in God. She'd worked and prayed so hard, asking for help to make the store a success. Asking to know how to handle Mom's resistance to the Amish faith. She'd even attended the Christian church here in town but it wasn't the same as the Amish church. The message of Christ's atonement didn't sink as deeply into her heart as it did when she attended with the Amish. She'd only attended their church a couple of times but it had been enough. She'd felt the spirit of God in her heart and knew it was what she wanted in her life. And she missed the people she'd grown to love. Martin's *familye*, Bishop Yoder and even waspish old Marva Geingerich. She missed them all. And she realized that Martin had deepened the experience for her into a solid love of God and the Amish faith.

Determined to trust in the Lord, Julia pulled on her warm winter coat and carried the ladder outside. She had a large Grand Opening sign she wanted to hang across the front of the store before she opened the front door in twenty minutes.

"Martin!"

Bundled with a scarf and gloves, he stood leaning against the outer wall. Since she hadn't seen him for days, the shock of finding him here was even worse. A rush of joy, relief and dread washed over her all at once.

"What are you doing here?" she asked, dropping the unwieldy sign on the porch.

Pushing off the wall, he walked to her, a gentle smile curving his lips. That was how Martin was. Always calm, nonjudgmental and soothing.

"You mentioned last week you had a large sign you wanted to hang across your storefront. I figured you might need some help," he said.

His consideration touched her like nothing else could. "*Ja*, I do need help. Mom's back is in so much pain that she can hardly walk. The cold weather makes it worse."

He picked up the heavy sign. "Then let me help you."

He placed the sign in her hands, his touch so gentle, his gaze so inviting that she felt mesmerized. Without speaking, he showed her a heavy-duty staple gun he must have brought with him. Then he slid the ladder into position in front of the porch canopy. Stepping up on the rungs, he turned and reached toward her.

For a moment, Julia just stared. Then she moved into action and handed him one edge of the sign. He lifted it high, holding it in place with one hand. The crack of the staple gun filled the air as he affixed the sign to the canopy overhead. He then stepped down and moved the ladder over a bit. Julia held the weight of the sign up so it wouldn't sag and rip through the staples. Within minutes, Martin had the whole thing secured above the wooden porch and stepped down off the ladder.

The sign waved gently in the crisp morning breeze. The bright red lettering was so large that a person could see it way down at the other end of Main Street. Hopefully the townsfolk and ranchers' wives in the area would be curious and come check out her shop. But regardless of how her retail store did, she still had her soap contracts with KostSmart to depend upon.

Seeing the banner hanging across her storefront brought a welling of tears to her eyes. This moment meant so much to her. If Martin weren't here, she'd cry with happiness. Today, she would officially open her soapworks for business. Today was the culmination of so much effort. It was the outcome of a dream she'd had for years. And Martin had helped make it a reality.

"Oh, *danke*, Martin. *Danke* so much. I'm so glad you're here to share this moment with me," she exclaimed. Before she thought to stop herself, she gave him a quick hug.

He stepped back, blinking in surprise. "I… I… You're *willkomm*. I know how much this means to you."

"Can you stay for the opening of the store?" she asked.

"*Ne*, my *vadder* expects my help on the farm today. I have to leave now or he'll be worried."

Something about his manner made her believe his father didn't know he was here.

Carrying the staple gun, he stepped down off the porch. She stared after him, not wanting to let him go.

He gazed at her for several moments, as if he didn't want to leave either. "It was *gut* to see you, Jules."

She took a quick step toward him, wishing he could stay. "But when will I see you again?"

Oh, she shouldn't have said that. She'd been the one to push him away and now she was asking to see him again. She felt so confused. Her common sense told her that he must go, yet her heart wanted him to stay.

He hesitated. "My work is finished here. The bishop doesn't want me to *komm* into town unless I have business here."

"So, we can't be friends anymore," she said.

He looked reticent. "I... I'll *komm* again tomorrow morning. Now I must hurry. I hope you sell everything in your store. I know it will be a great success. Just have a little faith."

Watching him go, a fresh burst of tears filled her eyes. She nodded, biting her bottom lip. His encouragement meant everything to her.

Tomorrow! He'd come see her again in the morning.

Without another word, he turned and climbed into his buggy. As he directed the horse out of the parking lot, he lifted a hand in farewell. She waved, too, longing to run after him but knowing she must not.

Tomorrow! She'd see him again. The fears Dallin had instilled within her seemed to fade away. Martin would never hurt her the way Dallin had done. She could trust

Martin. She knew that now. But seeing him again was futile. It would only prolong the pain. Because nothing would change between them. Not as long as her mother disapproved of him and his religion.

Julia stood there until his buggy moved out of sight. Then she carried the ladder around to the back shed to put it away. Inside the store, she unlocked the front door. It wasn't opening time but she was ready for business. She gazed about the room. Everything looked so bright and cheery, like a Christmas wonderland filled with amazing secrets to explore. In each windowsill, battery-operated candles sat atop a bed of spun angel-hair glass. Hanging above them on green, shimmery ribbons was an assortment of red ornaments and white sparkly snowflakes. A pine cone wreath with red holly berries had been hung on the front door along with a little tinkling bell to alert her when someone came inside.

Quilted Christmas runners with cheery designs lined each tabletop where she showcased her hand-made soaps, creams and lip balms. Garlands of tinsel hung from each display case. The air smelled sweet, a mixture of the fragrant soaps she'd made and the cinnamon and spice incense she'd set near the old mechanical cash register. Everything looked so jolly, yet Julia felt a leaden weight in her heart. If only Martin were still here, it would be a perfect day.

She'd see him tomorrow.

Clinging to that thought, Julia arranged a pile of dainty paper napkins beside the punch bowl. She and her mom had pulled out all the stops in decorating the store. With one exception: Julia had refused to put up a Christmas tree. Rather than tell her mom the Amish didn't have trees, she simply explained that she needed the room to display her soaps. Thankfully, Mom hadn't argued.

"I heard the front door. Was someone here?"

Sharon came into the room at that moment, carrying a platter of frosted Christmas cookies she'd baked the night before. She set them on a special table with a red cloth and the glass punch bowl. It wasn't every day that a new store opened in this sleepy town and they wanted to welcome their customers with refreshments. Because of the novelty of the store, Julia was certain every rancher and farmer's wife from miles around would step inside her door just to take a look. And since it was Christmastime, they'd be searching for just the right gift.

"Um, I just unlocked the front door. But Martin was here. He stopped by to help me hang the Grand Opening sign. He just left." Julia wouldn't lie to her mom but turned away and fussed with a display of Christmas soaps, hoping to avoid another argument.

Mom didn't say a word as she poured red punch into the large bowl. Julia helped her, eager to hear the tinkling sound above their door ringing again and again.

She didn't have long to wait. They had just set out throwaway cups when the tinkling was followed by a group of Amish women wearing black traveling bonnets, heavy capes and black ankle boots.

"Linda! Lori! *Willkomm!* It's so *gut* to see you." Julia rushed over to hug each woman. How fitting that Martin's mother was her first official customer. But Julia would never tell the woman that her son had just left.

"And it's *gut* to see you, as well." Linda smiled.

"*Ja*, we have missed you," Lori said.

Out of the windows, Julia saw little Rachel, Sarah

and Abby stepping up onto the porch. They came inside, their cheeks and noses bright red from the cold.

"Oh, it's so *gut* to see all of you," Julia exclaimed. "I'll bet you would like one of these."

Leaning down at eye level, she held out the tray of cookies to little Rachel and smiled as the child chose a frosted snowman.

The doorbell tinkled again. Before Julia knew it, the store was filled with happy chatter and laughter as several ranchers' wives and people from town came inside to inspect her wares. Julia soon found herself embroiled in explaining the various scents and ingredients of her products. Between keeping the cookie tray and punch bowl filled, Mom also ran the cash register. As she tended to her customers, Julia lost track of the many sales they made.

"Do you have anything without scent?" Sarah Yoder asked.

Ah! Thankfully, Julia had thought about her Amish customers and their desire to live a simple life.

"*Ja*, I've got a lovely plain soap with no added fragrance or colors." Julia lifted a creamy-looking white bar to show the woman. "It lathers beautifully—"

A harsh gasp caused her to turn. Marva Geingerich stood just in front of the open door, clutching her gray woolen gloves in her hands. White snowflakes dotted her black traveling bonnet, melting into little droplets of water. She must have just arrived and was staring across the room at Sharon.

"I knew I recognized you." Marva's loud voice carried across the room.

Mom stood at the cash register, speaking to Essie Walkins, the owner of Tigger the cat. As Mom reached for a bar of lavender soap, she looked up and saw Marva. An expression of surprise drained Mom's face of color.

Marva lifted a bony finger and pointed at Sharon. "Now I remember where I know you from. Your *vadder* was Michael Miller and you abandoned your faith when you were eighteen years old to marry an *Englischer*. When you left, you broke your poor *mudder*'s heart. She died a year later, followed by your *vadder* only months after that. It's no wonder you ran away and were never heard from again."

A hush fell over the entire store. Everyone stopped and stared, their eyes filled with shock. Even the townsfolk, who had no idea what Marva was talking about, looked shocked and uncomfortable.

Sharon's spine stiffened and she lifted her chin higher. "I don't know what you're talking about. I am not Amish."

Without another word, Mom turned and walked out of the room. Julia stared after her, her mind racing. Marva's words played over and over again in her brain. She didn't know what to think. She couldn't breathe. Couldn't move. A myriad of thoughts scrambled inside her mind. A sick feeling settled in the pit of her stomach. She didn't know what was going on but she intended to find out.

"Linda, would you mind tending to the store for a few minutes, please? I'll be right back," Julia said.

Linda nodded with understanding and Julia handed her the bar of soap she'd been holding. She hurried across the room and down the hallway.

She found Mom upstairs in their apartment, the door closed and locked firmly.

Julia rapped on the wooden panel. "Mama, it's me. Will you open the door, please?"

"No, not now. Go away!" came Sharon's reply.

Julia knocked again. "I'm worried about you. I'm not leaving, so you'd better open the door now."

A long pause and then she heard the lock click. Turning the knob, she stepped inside and found her mother sitting on the sofa, her face buried in her hands.

"Mom, what is going on?" Julia sat beside her mother and rested a hand on her back.

Mom sniffed and sat up straight, staring across the room. Her eyes were red with tears. "I... I hoped you would never find out."

"Find out what?"

"That...that I was raised Amish."

Julia gasped. "Oh, Mom. What are you saying?"

"It's true. I... I was raised Amish. I left the faith in order to marry your father over twenty-six years ago."

Julia's mind went blank. This was news to her. All her life, neither of her parents had given her a clue that her mother had been raised Amish. They'd told her that Mom's parents had died. Apparently, that was true but why hadn't they told her the full truth?

"I was treated very harshly by my family and church elders," Mom continued. "Oh, please, Julia. Please don't join their faith. I beg you. It isn't just a commitment of faith but would require a change to your entire way of life."

"I've already told you I'm not planning to join their church," Julia said.

"That's good. If you join them and marry Martin, their church elders won't let you visit me anymore because I was raised Amish and abandoned the faith. They'd shun me."

Julia covered her mouth with her hand to keep from crying out. "No, Mom. Tell me this isn't true."

Mom met her gaze and Julia saw the tears streaming down her cheeks. "I'm afraid it is. Now you know why I've fought so hard against you spending time with Martin. Neither my Amish family nor your Grandpa Walt approved of your father and I marrying. They all tried to break us apart. So we left Ohio and moved to Kansas, seeking a fresh start. In his anger, your father refused to speak to your Grandpa Walt again. We thought it best that I keep my past life a secret from everyone, including you."

"But why tell me now?" Julia cried.

"Because Marva Geingerich recognized me and I can't lie to you any longer. Marva never was a nice woman. Always so harsh and judgmental. That's how I was treated by everyone when I left to marry your father."

Julia cringed. She figured there were good and bad people in all faiths and nationalities. She shook her head, hardly able to believe what her mother had told her. Now, everything made sense. The secretiveness, the disapproval.

"I think your Grandpa Walt regretted the fight he had with your father," Mom said. "That's why he left you this store. It was his way of making amends for past hurts. But I don't want to see you go through the same pain I was forced to endure in order to marry the man I loved."

Julia nodded in understanding and shock. "It's not an issue anymore, so don't worry about it."

Regardless of what her mother had told her, she could never marry Martin. She'd promised her father she'd look after her ailing mother. There was no way for her to join the Amish faith and still be a part of her mother's life. Not as long as her mother felt the way she did toward the Amish.

During the church meetings and other gatherings Julia had attended, she'd heard a few whisperings about shunning. The only reason the Amish had welcomed her was because she'd expressed a deep interest in their faith and they thought she'd be baptized. But Julia would never turn her back on her mother. Crying about it wouldn't change a thing.

"I understand." Julia stood and reached for a tissue before wiping her eyes and nose. She couldn't sit here in the doldrums. She had people downstairs and a store to run. It was their grand opening and she intended to make the best of the day. Their livelihood depended on it.

"Where are you going?" Mom asked as Julia crossed the room.

Julia turned, her hand on the doorknob. Looking at her mother's pale face, she shrugged. "Downstairs. I have a store to run. Life must go on. But I love you, Mom, no matter what. Nothing will tear us apart. I promise you that."

Mom didn't try to stop her as she closed the door quietly behind her. Standing alone on the landing, Julia felt her heart breaking all over again. Except this time, she didn't feel angry. She just felt numb and empty inside. No doubt Linda would tell Martin what had happened and that Marva had recognized Sharon. The news would soon spread among the entire *Gmay*. Since Sarah was in the store when it happened, Julia figured Bishop Yoder would hear about it before lunchtime. There was no way around it.

Julia couldn't see Martin tomorrow. No, nor any other day after that. After what had happened with Dallin, maybe it was best if she never loved again. Her path was set. She could never convert to the Amish faith. She couldn't attend church with Martin again and they could never be together. It was that simple.

Chapter Thirteen

It had been three torturous weeks since Martin had seen Julia. Three weeks since the grand opening of her soap store. With just two days before Christmas, he felt like a caged animal. Pacing inside his father's barn, he sought to relieve some pent-up energy. It was early afternoon and the snow had fallen deep, covering everything in a blanket of white. Otherwise, he'd go outside for a long, brisk walk.

Now, even the contented lowing of the milk cows couldn't soothe his jangled nerves.

He loved her. He knew that now. He couldn't get her off his mind. He loved her but he couldn't have her. And the pain was almost more than he could bear.

He stared outside the open door. When he exhaled, he could see his breath on the air. The pristine glow of new-fallen snow seemed surreal and lovely. It was a good day to stay indoors. He had no reason to go into town.

As promised, he'd gone to Julia's home early the day after the grand opening of her store. His mother had told him of its success. She'd also told him that Marva Geingerich had recognized Sharon from when they both lived in Ohio.

She'd told him Sharon was raised Amish.

Suddenly, everything made sense. Sharon's protests when Julia had accompanied him to church. Her refusal to join them at any Amish events. Her look of disgust whenever she saw him.

Sharon didn't want an Amish life for her daughter. In order to abandon her family so she could marry an *Englischer*, Sharon must have hated her faith. And yet, it couldn't have been easy, turning her back on everything in her life to be with the man she loved. Martin didn't want that to happen to him and Julia.

He'd been beyond disappointed when Julia didn't greet him at the door that morning. Instead, Sharon had presented him with a letter. He'd never forget the chill that swept over his body as Sharon handed him the envelope, then closed the door in his face.

He'd sat inside his buggy and ripped open the letter to read the pages. The message was simple and to the point. Julia didn't want to convert to his Amish faith. She expressed her joy and gratitude for him teaching her so much about Jesus Christ but asked that he not see her anymore.

He'd crumpled the pages in his fist, filled with such frustration and grief that he could hardly stand the pain. All his life, he'd been taught four key precepts: be slow to anger, slow to take offense, quick to repent and quick to forgive. These principles had governed his entire life. But now, he longed to cast them aside. To yell and scream and cry.

He loved Julia and wanted to make her his wife. He couldn't stand to lose her, yet that's exactly what had happened. The news of what her mother had done didn't diminish that love. Nor did it mean he didn't miss Julia like crazy. After all, it wasn't her fault that her mother had abandoned her faith. But he was a strong man. A man who loved God. And now, he must honor Julia's wishes even if it wasn't what he wanted.

"*Sohn*, it's too cold out here in the barn."

He jerked around and found his parents standing in the doorway. It was his mother who spoke. She wore her warm, woolen shawl draped over her shoulders, a fretful expression on her face.

"Why don't you *komm* into the house where it's warm?" David asked.

Martin turned away. His parents were the last people he wanted to see right now. "I'd rather stay here."

"You're pining for Julia, aren't you?" David asked.

A rustling came from the hayloft overhead but Martin paid it little heed. His thoughts were in turmoil. All he could think about was Julia.

"*Ja*, I miss her very much," he said.

"That's understandable. You love her," Linda said.

He couldn't deny it but he didn't acknowledge what his parents already knew. Surely the love he felt for Julia and the pain of losing her showed on his face.

"Even so, you must not see her again." David's tone was soft and sympathetic.

Hearing these words spoken out loud caused a panic like he'd never felt before to rush over Martin. His throat felt tight, his ears clogged. It was as if he were under water and couldn't breathe. He was drowning and couldn't save himself.

"But if she has an earnest heart and truly wants to

know more about our faith, we have an obligation to teach her," Martin argued.

"That time has passed, *sohn*. She has told you she doesn't want to convert so you must let her go. The Lord has something better in mind for you," David said.

Like what? What could be better than Julia? Nothing!

Martin looked to his mother for support. Surely she understood what he was going through. Her eyes were filled with tears, her face creased with sorrow but she didn't say a word. From her past examples, he knew she would never go against her husband's word. Not on something as important as this. And not if it meant she would lose her eldest son.

"You fear I might leave my faith in order to marry Julia," he said.

It was a statement, not a question.

"*Ja*, we know how strong love is. It can pull you in the wrong direction. But you must fight it, *sohn*. You must remain solid in your faith. Nothing can be stronger than your relationship with *Gott*." David spoke passionately, with all the love and conviction of a good parent trying to save his eldest child.

Strands of hay fell from above, wafting through the air. A low murmur of timbers hinted of movement in the hayloft and Martin thought a barn cat must be up there, nesting in the warm straw.

"I promise if you will hold firm, all things will be made right again. The Lord will bless you," David said.

His mother nodded in agreement.

Martin slashed his hand through the air. "Spare me your promises. I love Julia. She is the choice of my heart. And now you're telling me I can't have her."

Martin was a grown man. He should be able to

choose whom he would wed. But he also knew he must not challenge his church elders or his parents. To do so could put him in the position of being shunned by his people. Something he would rather avoid at all costs. But in his heart, the thought of never seeing Julia again left him feeling sad and empty inside. He couldn't stand to live without her. He couldn't!

David stepped over to him and rested a hand on his shoulder. "*Sohn*, we know you care for her. We all do. But she is *Englisch* and has made it clear she won't be baptized into our faith. You must not see her again. Do you understand?"

It took a long time for Martin to respond. And even as he said the words, it didn't ease his burden. "*Ja*, I understand."

"*Ne! Ne!*"

The cry came from above. Hank appeared suddenly, poking his head over the edge of the hayloft. As they stared in shock, he scrambled down the ladder. He stood before them, strands of hay sticking to his hair, gloves and coat. He must have been up there listening all this time.

"Julia is my girl. She's not gonna marry Mar-tin. She's gonna marry me," the boy yelled as he jerked his thumb toward his chest.

"*Ach*, Hank. Julia isn't going to marry you. She isn't going to marry Martin either. Don't be *dumm*," David said, shaking his head with impatience.

"*Ja*, she is. You're trying to steal my girl," Hank insisted as he glared angrily at Martin.

Before Martin could respond, the boy turned and raced out of the barn. He plowed through the depths of snow, running toward the brightly lit house.

"Hank! *Komm* back," David called, but Hank kept going.

Linda stepped over to the door, her features crinkled with concern. From her expression, Martin could tell she didn't like this contention in her family.

"David! Martin! Go after him," she cried.

"He's just blowing off steam. He'll go to his room and think about it for a while. It's best to let him be alone for now. I'll speak to him later," David said.

But that wasn't the case. When they finally went inside, Hank was nowhere to be found. The other children hadn't seen him either. And when Martin looked outside, he saw a trail of footprints in the new-fallen snow leading up to the main road.

"Do you think he ran away? It's too cold to be outside for very long and night is coming on," Linda said, wringing her hands in worry.

Martin took a deep breath and blew it out in a quick exhale. He had a bad feeling about this. Hank had run off once before after a bad fight with one of his sisters. It had taken the entire *Gmay* to find him the next day down by the creek. But that had been during the warm summertime.

Mamm was right. The winter coat, boots, scarf, hat and gloves Hank was wearing were warm but not if he got wet and not if he was outside for any great length of time.

"David! Martin! Please go find him," Linda pleaded, looking worried.

Martin hesitated, thinking fast. His father was a good, pious man but he had never taken Hank's tantrums seriously. Frankly, the man didn't know quite how to deal with Hank's Down syndrome. David loved Hank dearly but he didn't understand the boy and thought he should buck up and cope. He didn't realize how much Hank adored Julia.

Hank wanted to be a normal kid like everyone else in the *Gmay*. He didn't understand that his Down syndrome made it impossible for him to wed one of their Amish girls and manage a farm and family on his own. Martin hated to be the one to explain it to Hank.

Martin reached for his warm leather gloves and jerked them on. He hadn't had time to remove his scarf, coat and boots, so he was ready to go.

"I'll hitch up the horse to the buggy," he said.

"Where are you going? Just wait a while and he'll *komm* home on his own," David demanded.

"*Ne*, I don't think so. Not this time. I've got to find him and bring him home." Jerking open the back door, Martin stepped outside and headed toward the barn without a backward glance.

He was standing in the horse stall prepping the animal for a winter ride when his father found him.

"*Ach*, perhaps you're right, *sohn*. I'll go with you," David said.

Martin nodded, putting aside his own grief for the time being. Though he longed to resolve his problem with Julia, he must think of his brother now. Hank was mourning the loss of Julia, too. Martin should have been more understanding of his brother's feelings. He should have realized Hank was hurting. No matter what, Martin had to find the boy. He just had to. Grief and anger could cause Hank to do something very foolish and dangerous.

Martin had already lost the love of his life. He couldn't lose his little brother, too.

Chapter Fourteen

For the third time that morning, Julia counted the stack of small cardboard boxes she used to fulfill her online mail orders. Sitting in the packaging room next to her office, she felt a draft of cold air and shivered. It was Christmas Eve and she had just opened the store. From where she sat, she could hear the bell if someone entered the store and go wait on them. But since it had snowed nonstop all night and the plows were just now clearing Main Street, she didn't expect much business today. Thankfully, the storm had finally ceased. The local farmers were pleased by the moisture. So was she. It would ensure Martin had plenty of water for his crops next summer.

She counted the boxes again, trying to take her mind off him. How she missed him. For three weeks, she'd longed to get up the nerve to go and see him. But what would she say? He was Amish and she was *Englisch*. They were as different as night and day. But she loved him. She knew that now without a single doubt in her mind. He wasn't like Dallin at all. The fact that Martin had stayed away told her that he respected her and her decisions. She loved him and she couldn't be with him. Not as long as her mother disapproved.

She shivered again. Maybe the woodstove needed more fuel.

Scooting back her chair, she stood and poked her head into the hallway leading to the apartment upstairs. The back door stood wide open, a frigid breeze rushing into the building along with a spray of morning sunlight. She had shoveled the walk earlier. Though the skies were clear, it was still freezing.

Brr! Julia walked to the door and leaned outside. "Mom? Are you out here?"

"I'm in the store." Mom's voice came from the front of the building and she soon appeared in the hallway. "Did you need me?"

Sharon held a stick of kindling and must have been feeding the stove in the store.

Shaking her head, Julia closed the back door securely and locked it. "No, I was just wondering where you were."

Hmm. Maybe Mom had opened the back door to retrieve some firewood and then not latched it tight. It had happened before. She thought of asking Martin to repair the latch, but no. He'd do it in a heartbeat but it would only cause her more anguish to bring him back.

Julia turned away, still hurting from what Mom had told her three weeks ago about being raised Amish. Since that time, they had only briefly discussed the topic. Their relationship had changed somehow. All her life, Mom had kept this giant secret from her and Julia felt betrayed. It would take some time to rebuild the trust between them. And in the meantime, Julia was aching for Martin.

"Do you still want to close the store early today?" Mom asked.

Julia nodded. "Yes, we'll close at noon. After that, I suspect most people will be home with their families celebrating Christmas Eve."

Funny how Mom deferred to her on business issues. Julia was tired from all their hard work and they'd sold a lot of their products to local customers. No doubt Mom was fatigued, too. As far as Julia was concerned, their grand opening had been a huge success. She would close early and share a quiet dinner with her mom and celebrate the birth of the Christ child. Whatever else, Sharon was her mother and Julia had to forgive her. No matter what, she could never turn her back on her mom.

"I thought I'd make lasagna for dinner tonight. It's kind of a festive dish. Does that sound all right?" Mom asked.

Julia barely heard her mother's words. She was still lost in her own thoughts but nodded vaguely as she walked into the office.

The bell over the store door tinkled gaily and she turned. Mom followed as she walked down the hall and entered the cheery store.

"Martin!" Julia exclaimed.

He stood in front of the door with his father and Bishop Yoder. The three men looked imposing, wearing their black felt hats, gloves and warm frock coats. Their boots dripped water onto the large rug she'd laid in front of the door for this exact purpose.

Removing his hat, the bishop stepped forward. "Julia, we are sorry to intrude."

Each of their faces seemed drawn with worry, their eyes filled with anxiousness. Something was wrong.

"What is it?" She walked to them, conscious of Mom standing in the hallway but able to see and hear their conversation.

"Have you seen Hank?" David asked.

She shook her head. "No, I haven't." She glanced at Mom, who also shook her head. "Why? What's going on?" Julia asked.

"He's run away. He's been missing since early last night," David said.

"Run away? But why?" she asked.

"He...he had an argument and ran way," was all David would reveal. "We were able to track his footprints in the snow up to the county road leading into town but then they disappeared. We are worried about him."

A lance of fear pierced her heart. She was worried, too. It was fiercely cold and snowy outside. "He's been missing since last night?"

"*Ja*, and we thought he might have *komm* here," David said.

Martin didn't speak but Julia saw from his expression that he was beyond worried. She longed to speak to him. To ask how he was. To tell him how sorry she was for hurting him. But now wasn't the time. Not with both of their parents and the bishop standing near.

"No, I'm sorry. He hasn't come here," she assured them.

"If you see or hear from him, will you contact us immediately?" the bishop asked.

"Of course. I can even shut down the store and come help you look for him," she said.

David held out a hand. "*Ne*, that isn't necessary. The

entire *Gmay* is out looking for him. Just let us know if you hear from him."

"We absolutely will." She folded her arms and watched as the three men turned and left her store.

Martin looked back at her from over his shoulder, his gaze meeting hers. In that one glance, she knew he was worried.

Through the window pane, she caught a glimpse of several other members of the *Gmay* walking down the street. No doubt they were out searching for Hank. Under the circumstances, she didn't feel like she could join them. She'd quickly learned how the Amish grapevine worked and they wouldn't feel comfortable being around her now that she'd said she wouldn't convert to their faith.

Instead, she busied herself with tidying the store while Mom went up to their apartment to prepare supper. Frequently, Julia paused in her work to step outside onto the front porch and search the abandoned street for some sign of Hank. But she didn't see a thing.

Right at noon, she was restocking the lip balms and creams when Mom came into the store carrying her warm coat and purse.

"Where are you going?" Julia asked.

"I need more mozzarella for the lasagna. I'm just going to dash down to the general store. They're closing at one o'clock today, so I'd better hurry. I won't be gone long."

Julia stood and set the box of lip balms aside. "Why don't I go get it for you, Mom? I don't want you to slip and fall. Or I can go with you and hold your arm. It'll give us a chance to look for Hank while we're out."

"No, no!" Sharon waved her off. "I want to go alone. And they've probably found the boy by now."

"I hope so but there's no way for us to know since they don't have a phone."

"I'll ask Berta when I get to the store. She'll have heard if they've found him." Berta Maupin was the owner of the only grocery store in town and knew all the local news.

"Are you sure you want to go alone?" Julia asked again.

"Yes, I've been cooped up in this house far too long and need a good, brisk walk by myself. The doctor said exercise would help relieve my pain. The plows have been out and I'm sure the shop owners have shoveled their sidewalks. The afternoon sun has melted off a lot of the ice, too. I'll be fine."

Hmm. Mom acted like she really didn't want Julia to go with her.

"Okay, just be careful."

With a nod, Mom slipped out the door and hurried down the porch steps. After watching her go, Julia locked up the store and went upstairs. Spreading a warm afghan over herself, she reclined on the sofa, trying to read a book. Her eyes drooped wearily and she felt herself relaxing. Sometime later, she awoke with a start. How long had she been asleep?

Glancing at the clock, she realized it had been almost two hours since Mom left.

Something had roused her. Some small noise but she couldn't be sure.

"Mom?" she called.

No response. Julia sat up and folded the afghan, setting it aside. The fire in the woodstove had burned low and she stoked it up with fresh kindling. But where was Mom? What was taking her so long? And had they found Hank yet?

She turned, intending to go downstairs, put on her coat and boots and go look for her mother. A scuffling sound came from overhead, followed by the moaning of timbers. This old drafty building. It seemed she would never get used to all its creaks and groans.

Reaching for the doorknob to go downstairs, she hesitated. Hank was missing. Was it possible that he'd sneaked inside and gone up to the attic? It was dangerous up there and he knew it. Martin had told him not to go there again. Surely he wouldn't have disobeyed. Or would he?

Turning, she retrieved a flashlight from a kitchen drawer, then walked down the hall to her bedroom. Kneeling on the floor of her closet, she pulled the attic door open and peered inside. A whoosh of frigid air rushed over her. She really must have more insulation spread across the rafters. But that chore would have to wait until spring.

Stepping onto the narrow stairway, she flashed the beam of light along the rickety steps. Thick shadows gathered around her. A narrow ribbon of light came from the vent set high in the outer wall. It was so dark and cold up here that she was tempted to go back. But a low whimper came from across the room and she shined light in that direction.

A bulky shape lay huddled near the far wall. It moved, then stood up.

"Hank!" A flood of relief washed over her. The boy was here. He was safe! "Oh, Hank! What are you doing up here?" she called.

"Julia," he cried.

She took another step, beckoning to him. "Come here. It's all right. Come to me."

Stepping on the strong beams, he followed Martin's instructions not to walk on the drywall. She took his hand as she pulled him into her arms for a tight hug.

"Oh, you're frozen clear through. Let's get you into the apartment where it's warm."

Taking his hand, she urged him to go first down the rickety stairs. In her exuberance, she moved too fast and the rotted stairs gave way beneath her feet. She screamed, feeling herself falling. Suddenly, she found herself caught by two strong arms. They lifted her safely to the landing.

"Martin!" she cried, gazing into his eyes.

He held her close against his chest. She was so grateful to see him that she clung to his neck, unable to hold back tears of relief.

Within moments, Martin had pulled her and Hank into the safety of her bedroom. As he secured the little doorway to the attic, she looked up and saw her mother, Bishop Yoder and David all crowded in the small room.

"What…what are you doing here?" she asked, beyond confused.

"There's plenty of time to explain. But first, let's get everyone warmed up. Come into the kitchen." Mom waved to them all and they followed her, crowding around the small table and sitting on the sofa.

Within minutes, Mom had poured each of them a cup of hot chocolate and set out a plate of frosted sugar cookies decorated like candy canes for them to enjoy. Hank gulped down the liquid and asked for more. As he gobbled down cookies, Julia noticed he tossed hateful glares at Martin. The boy was obviously hungry but still angry.

Finally, Martin shifted nervously beside Julia, his gaze constantly returning to her.

"Are you all right?" he whispered.

She nodded, so happy to see him that she didn't even pretend to hide the love that must be shining in her eyes. She couldn't hide it anymore. Nor did she want to.

"How long have you been in the attic?" the bishop asked Hank.

The boy looked down and brushed some crumbs off his lap, an expression of shame covering his face. "All night. And it's really cold up there."

"All night? But when did you arrive in town?" David asked.

"Just a while after I left you last night. When I reached the main road leading into town, someone stopped and picked me up. They gave me a ride to town in their car."

"*Ach*, you could have been kidnapped," David said.

Within a few moments, he explained to Julia and her mother what had happened the night before when Hank ran away. Julia was touched by the boy's loyalty but wasn't sure how to handle his infatuation with her.

"Who gave you a ride?" Martin asked.

Hank simply shrugged. "I don't know. They were a *familye* with little kids. They were nice to me." He picked up another cookie to munch on, looking completely unconcerned by what he'd done.

It was a relief to know that Hank wasn't outside in the cold for very long. They were all outraged yet happy with this news. Outraged because they had no idea who had given him a ride but happy he was all right.

"But what brought you back here to the soap store? How did you know Hank was here?" Julia asked the three men.

Mom shifted nervously. "I think it's now my turn to explain a few things."

Julia nodded, listening quietly to her mother.

"When I read your letter to Martin several weeks ago, telling him not to come see you again, I realized how much you truly loved him," she said.

"You…you read my letter to Martin? But that was private," Julia exclaimed, hardly able to believe her mother had violated her privacy in such a manner.

Sharon nodded. "I'm sorry, dear, but I had to know what you said to him. Then, I watched you over the past few weeks and saw how utterly miserable you are without him."

Julia just blinked, not knowing what to say.

"You don't laugh anymore," Mom continued. "You rarely even smile. You haven't made any new soap in two weeks. It's like the life has gone right out of you."

Yes, that was exactly how Julia felt. Losing Martin had drained her of all joy.

"Martin has been acting the same way. He's not himself anymore," David said.

Sharon nodded in understanding. "So, when I went to the grocery store today, I asked Berta if she would deliver another message to Martin. She agreed and drove to his farm for me. She spoke to his mother and asked her to send him here as soon as possible."

"*Ja*, my *mamm* brought me a letter from your *mudder*, explaining you were in trouble and needed me and asking if I would *komm* immediately," Martin explained.

"My mom did that?" Julia asked.

He nodded.

"And you came?" Julia said.

Another nod. "As quickly as possible. Of course, we didn't know yet that Hank was here, hiding in the attic. But we hoped you had found him."

Julia gave a quivering laugh. "I guess that was an added bonus for your trip into town. Thankfully, he's safe."

Martin laughed, too, gazing at her with adoration.

Mom lifted her head and glanced at the bishop. "I'm sure you've already heard that I was raised Amish. I hope the good things that have happened today will impact your decision to let Julia be a part of my life after she's baptized."

Julia inhaled a subtle gasp. Everyone in the room stared at Sharon.

"What are you saying?" David asked.

"Just this…" Sharon looked at Martin. "I want you to marry my daughter. She has my approval and my blessing to become Amish. But I don't want to be baptized. I made my choices years ago when I married my husband. I will love him to my dying day. But I want you and Julia to be happy and I know she won't be unless she's with you."

A shallow laugh escaped Julia's throat as Martin took her hand in his. Out of her peripheral vision, she saw Hank's angry glare. The boy obviously didn't like Martin paying her any romantic attention.

"Julia's my *maedel*," Hank said.

The bishop stood and opened his mouth to speak but Sharon cut him off with a slight wave of her hand.

Looking at Hank, Sharon smiled sweetly and leaned

forward to cup the boy's face with her palm. "My dear boy, Julia is going to be baptized into the Amish faith and will marry Martin. Because she'll be your new sister-in-law, it won't be possible for her to be your best girl anymore. Instead, Julia will be your new sister. Doesn't that sound nice?"

Hank hesitated, thinking this over. Then, his eyes widened with delight and he nodded. "Julia will be my sister?"

Mom nodded, still smiling. "Yes, she will be your sister forever but not your girlfriend. Not anymore. Is that okay?"

Hank looked down, his forehead crinkled. Then, he nodded and grinned wide.

"*Ja*, I think I'll like having another sister very well. She'll make me cookies and soap," he said.

They all laughed.

"*Gut*," Mom said. She then spoke in perfect Deitsch to Martin, expressing her love for Julia and pleading with him to look after her little girl.

"Ahem! There's just one problem," Julia said. "I won't be baptized. Not if it means I'll have to shun my mother. I need to be a part of her life and I need her to be a part of my life, too."

A long pause followed this declaration.

"I believe that, since Sharon was never baptized into the Amish faith, she will not be shunned," Bishop Yoder said. "I see no reason why Julia cannot be baptized and marry Martin. Nor do I see any reason why she cannot be a part of her *mudder*'s life."

A startled gasp escaped Julia's throat. "Really? But I thought you would shun my *mudder*."

Martin squeezed her hand and she felt the surprised happiness emanating from him, as well.

"*Ne*, she was never officially a member of the Amish faith so how can she be shunned?" the bishop said.

"Oh, Martin!" Julia turned into his arms and he hugged her tight.

Julia hugged her mother, too. She was speechless as tears freely washed her face. "Oh, Mom, *danke. Danke*, my dear *mudder*."

They stood motionless for several moments, overcome by emotion. Then...

Martin leaned close and whispered something in his father's ear. David nodded, then cleared his throat.

"Ahem! I think we should leave these two young people alone for a while, so they can decide what they want to do." He lifted an arm, directing Hank to leave the apartment with him.

Taking his cup of hot chocolate, Hank went along willingly. Mom and the bishop followed, leaving Julia and Martin completely alone.

Tears flooded Julia's eyes as she looked up at the man she loved. "I don't know what to say."

He nodded, his eyes crinkled with compassion. "I do. I love you, Julia Rose. I love you more than anything. Please, will you marry me and make me the happiest man alive?"

"Oh, Martin! Of course I will. I love you so much. I was sick with grief when I thought I'd never see you again. I can't tell you how happy I am right at this moment."

Lowering his head, he kissed her. She clung to the folds of his coat, so happy that she could hardly contain the joy.

When he released her, he looked down at her, his eyes sparkling with mischief. "I guess this means I won't be building a barn in the spring."

She tilted her head in curiosity. "Why not?"

"Because we're going to need to build us a house first. The barn will have to wait another year. I need to provide a home for my new bride to live in."

She laughed. "Do you think the bishop will coordinate another work frolic for us to build a house?"

He nodded. "*Ja*, I know he will. Once we're married, we'll need a place to live."

"We can stay here with my *mudder* until the work is completed on our own home," she suggested.

He frowned. "Do you think Sharon will mind? After all, you'll be Amish then and can't use electricity."

She pulled him close, snuggling against his solid chest. "*Ne*, she won't mind at all. She's given us her blessing."

He smiled and kissed her again. And after that, no more words were spoken. She had all that she needed and wanted right here in her arms. And her love and faith were the best Christmas gifts of all.

Epilogue

One year later

Julia stepped out onto the back porch of her new home and set the large wicker basket she was carrying onto the wooden bench. Like the spacious house itself, Martin had made the seat and most of the furniture inside with his own two hands.

A chilling breeze whipped past and she tightened her warm winter coat up high to her chin. Her sensible black tights and shoes weren't fashionable but they were warm and sturdy. She patted her white organdy prayer *kapp*, making sure her hair was pulled back into place.

The clothes of an Amish woman were quite plain but she loved her burgundy dress and its simple beauty. In fact, she found it comfortable and easier to move. As promised, Linda had kindly taught her to sew and Julia had made her dress and white apron herself. Though she was learning that *hochmut* was not of the Lord, she was secretly proud of her efforts. Between making soap, cooking meals and sewing clothes for her and Martin, she was learning something new every day. And loving every bit of it.

It wasn't easy juggling her work here at home with making and selling her soap products at Rose Soapworks, but she found that she enjoyed the challenge and would never begrudge her new life. The Lord had truly blessed her.

With some of the funds Grandpa Walt had left her, Julia had paid her new sales rep in Denver to schedule some ads on local TV. While Julia did the heavy lifting and soap making, Sharon did a lot of the desk work and was becoming quite computer savvy. She had reported that they'd received lots of raves from fans on social media. While Julia didn't own a TV or maintain her own website or social media accounts, she'd received several more wholesale contracts with some commercial vendors. Additionally, numerous online orders were constantly pouring in. Even with Mom's office help, Julia could barely keep up with the workload. And with the latest development in her life, she knew something would have to change in the coming months. And soon!

Taking a deep breath of cool, clear air, she gazed at the fallow fields glistening with a sheen of white. This past summer, Martin had fenced off a portion of his land and grown hay and oats. He hoped to save enough money to buy some Percheron mares and a stallion next summer. It had snowed two days earlier but the rainfall last night had cleared most of the white stuff off the county road. They should have no problem driving over to Martin's parents' house to celebrate Christmas dinner with them. Speaking of which...

"Martin! We're late! We've got to leave, my *lieb-*

chen," she called toward the large shed in their back-yard. Martin had built it to house their milk cow, horse and buggy until they could construct a giant barn in the spring.

At that moment, Martin came out of the shed, leading the horse. The animal was already harnessed to the buggy. Martin secured the shed door, then drove the buggy across the graveled driveway to park beside the house.

As he hopped out, Julia thought he looked more than handsome in his fine black frock coat and white shirt. Grasping her basket, Julia walked out to meet him. He took the basket from her hand and set it on the ground, then clasped her arm and pulled her close against his chest.

"*Guder mariye*, Mrs. Hostetler," he breathed against her lips before kissing her.

She swatted playfully at his shoulder and pretended to pull away. "*Guder mariye*, Martin. You know, some-one might see us. It isn't seemly for you to kiss me out in the open like this."

She spoke entirely in Deitsch, having learned the language quite well over the past year.

He glanced around, as if looking for someone hiding nearby. "Who will see us on our own place? There's no one out here and we are most certainly alone."

To prove his point, he kissed her again and she didn't fight him at all. Not when she loved him so much. When he finally released her, she rested the palms of her hands against his chest and gazed lovingly into his eyes.

"Do you regret not being able to build your barn first?" she asked.

"*Ne*, of course not. We couldn't live with your *mudder* forever."

She arched her eyebrows in a playful glance. "Oh, I don't know. She didn't mind. Not really."

He snorted. "I don't think Sharon would like living with me the rest of her life. Besides, we will build the barn this next spring. I'll always choose you over worldly possessions. As long as I have you, I don't care about an old barn."

"But we won't always be alone, you know," she said.

He arched one of his eyebrows. "*Ach*, why not? Do you fear your *mudder* will need to come live with us soon?"

Lowering one hand, she rested it over her abdomen. "*Ne*, but our *boppli* will be here and you won't be able to take such liberties with me anymore. Nor will we ever be alone again."

He tilted his head to one side, his eyes crinkled in confusion. "Our *boppli*? Jules, are you…are you telling me that…?"

She nodded. "Uh-huh. We're going to have a new little one to join our *familye* soon."

Dawning flooded his eyes and a look of absolute joy covered his face. "A *boppli*? Truly?"

"*Ja*, we're going to have a *boppli* of our very own." She could hardly contain her own happiness as she shared this special news with him.

"Woo-hoo!" He picked her up and swung her around.

She laughed with abandonment, letting the dizzying joy fill her up. All her life, she'd longed for a home and family of her own. People to love and care for. And somehow, the Lord had blessed her with her heart's desire.

"You *bensel*. Now we are well and truly late for dinner at your *mudder*'s house," she teased him, trying to sound stern but unable to contain the laughter fizzing inside of her.

"*Ach*, so now I am a silly child, am I?" He opened the door to the buggy as she picked up her basket. He waggled his eyebrows and reached to lift a corner of the white cloth she had laid over top of the basket.

"What is inside?" he asked with a wicked smile.

Again, she gently swatted his hand. "Some pumpkin muffins, a fruit salad and an apple pie. Your *mudder* is preparing most of the meal, although I'm sure my *mamm* will bring something, too. Perhaps next year, we can hold the *familye* dinner here at our home."

He smiled with approval and held her arm as she lifted her foot onto the step and climbed inside. "You are becoming a very *gut* cook. At this rate, I'll become quite fat very soon."

He patted his lean abdomen for emphasis. Since he worked such long, hard hours, she doubted he would ever gain much weight but didn't say so.

"I'm afraid I'm the one who is about to gain some weight." Sitting in the buggy, she rested both her hands on her lower stomach and lovingly caressed the slight swelling there.

Glancing down, he flashed a wide smile. "I can't wait. The bishop has told me he will schedule another work frolic for us to have a barn raising in April or May. We'll have a new *boppli* to love and I'll get another field cleared and fenced off."

"*Ja*, it'll be a busy summer," she said. "We're getting so many orders at the soapworks that I'll need to hire some employees. I can ask the *Gmay*. I'll bet a couple of the girls or boys who are graduating from school might like a part-time job."

He tugged lightly on one of the ribbons on her prayer *kapp* before kissing the tip of her nose. "*Ja*, I'm sure they would. Is your *mamm* meeting us at my folks' house today?"

She nodded. "Now that she has bought a car, she is getting around the community quite well on her own. Lately, my mother is so happy that I can hardly tell she is ill. In fact, I think she's getting better every day."

Once she gave her blessing for Julia and Martin to wed, Sharon no longer took issue with the Amish people. Though she still missed her husband and adamantly did not wish to convert to the Amish faith, she attended many of their frolics and joined them for every family dinner.

"I can't believe the difference in her. It's like *nacht* and day," Martin said.

"I know what you mean. I think it's because she's so happy," Julia replied.

"*Ja*, contentment can change who we are inside. It can make us a totally different person," he said.

He closed the door and Julia sat quietly as she waited for him to hurry around the buggy and climb into the driver's seat. Though she was bursting with energy today, she also felt calm and tranquil inside. It was an amazing contradiction but she felt joyful and completely at peace.

Martin took the leather lead lines into his hand but paused, looking at her with a soft expression creasing his expressive eyes. "Tell me, when is our *boppli* due to arrive?"

Our baby! Oh, how Julia loved the sound of that.

"I'll need to visit the doctor in town, but I believe it will be the end of July," she said, unable to contain a smile.

He nodded, his eyes gleaming with delight. "In the summer. Just in time for all the other new beginnings here on our farm."

Our farm! Again, Julia felt a flood of happiness flowing through her veins. This was her home. Their home! They had the soap studio in town, as well, but her mom was living there. Their farm was only two miles away and Julia went to work in town during the weekdays, to make soap and other merchandise and to package and ship her products all over the nation. But this farm and Martin were her home now. Forevermore.

"*Ja*, it seems like we're celebrating many firsts," she said.

He slapped the leads lightly against the horse's back. The buggy lurched forward. "Won't our *eldre* be pleased when we announce that we're expecting our first child this summer? Our *midder* will be so happy. It'll be their first grandchild."

"*Ja*, I know it will mean a great deal to my *mamm*," she said. "You know, one day she may be too ill to live at Rose Soapworks by herself. She is doing well right now but that could change."

Martin pulled the buggy onto the main road and the horse settled into a steady trot. Though it was cold outside, the sky was a clear azure blue with not a single cloud to mar this lovely Christmas Day.

"And when that time comes, she will move here to the farm so we can look after her," he said. "We will deal with it together, one day at a time. But I promise she will be cared for and you will always have Rose Soapworks for as long as you like."

Pleased by his words, she scooted over and hugged his arm. "*Danke*, Martin. You are so *gut* to me. I couldn't ask for a better Christmas gift."

He lowered his head and kissed her forehead ever so gently. "Nor could I. You have gifted me with so many treasures. The Lord has blessed us with so much abundance. This truly is the best Christmas ever."

As they sped along toward his parents' home, Julia could think of no better words to speak. She had her heart's desire. A large *familye* and friends to love and a husband who doted upon her. She breathed a happy sigh and enjoyed the ride. Her heart was so full and she couldn't ask for more.

* * * * *

"You don't ever complain. You take care of someone else's *kinder* without hesitation, and you're giving them a home they haven't had in who knows how long."

"Trust me. There was plenty of hesitation on my part."

"I do trust you."

Beth Ann's breath caught at the undercurrent of emotion in his simple answer. "I'm glad to hear that. I got a message from their social worker this afternoon. She was supposed to come tomorrow, which is why I stayed home today to make sure everything was as perfect as possible before her visit."

"I wondered why you didn't come to the project house today."

"That's why, but now her visit is going to be the day after tomorrow. What if she decides to take the children and place them in other homes? What if they can't be together?"

Robert paused and faced her. "Why are you looking for trouble? God brought you to the *kinder*. He knows what lies before them and before you. Trust *Him*."

"I try to." She gave him a wry grin. "It's just…just…"

"They've become important to you?"

She nodded, not trusting her voice to speak. The idea of the three youngsters being separated in the foster care system frightened her, because she wasn't sure what they might do to get back together.

"Don't forget," Robert murmured, "as important as they are to you, they're even more important to God." His smile returned. "How about getting some Christmas pie before we have to fish three *kinder* out of the brook?"

With a yelp, she rushed forward to keep Crystal from hoisting Tommy to see over the rail. Robert was right. She needed to enjoy the children while she could.

Don't miss
An Amish Holiday Family *by Jo Ann Brown,*
available November 2020 wherever
Love Inspired books and ebooks are sold.

LoveInspired.com